Also by the author:

Land O' Goshen

PICKETT'S CHARGE

a novel

CHARLES MCNAIR

LIVINGSTON PRESS

THE UNIVERSITY OF WEST ALABAMA

Printed on acid-free paper.
Printed in the United States of America by
United Graphics
Hardcover binding by: Heckman Bindery
Typesetting and page layout: Joe Taylor
Proofreading: Joe Taylor, Emma Kay McClung, Verdie Coleman III, Alison Law
Cover design and layout: Emily Mills Burkett

Livingston Press is part of The University of West Alabama,
and thereby has non-profit status.
Donations are tax-deductible.

first edition
6 5 4 3 2 1

PICKETT'S CHARGE

Dedication

I dedicate this novel to my father, Charles Cunningham McNair, and my mother, Nora Joyce McCrory McNair … and to all storytellers.

Chapter 1, A Visitor

Summer 1964 – Room 13, Mobile Sunset Home, Mobile, Alabama

In the yellow dark of an Alabama nursing home, an old, old man opened two remarkable eyes.

"Brother! Wake up! You burnin' daylight!"

It had been a difficult night.

After curfew, a great booming Gulf Coast thunderstorm rattled the world. Threadgill Pickett's long colorful dream stopped cold when the lightning flashed. It felt like the moment when the attendants at Mobile Sunset Home tweaked a little knob on the TV set and all the 1960s picnic people and white houses and happy dogs funneled down into one small bright white light, and – *pfft!* – passed away.

For an instant, dreamy voices and memories spun around the room, a gossamer gunsmoke. Morning leaked in under cheap Venetian blinds.

Ah, me, the old man thought bitterly, staring at the ceiling. *To live and die in Dixie.*

Out of weary habit, Threadgill stretched a sere hand toward his bedpost. A floppy gray hat hung there, mostly invisible, a permanent part of the shadows.

He fit the hat securely onto his head, snugged it down. A faded yellowhammer feather jutted from the crown.

Threadgill relaxed. His hat hid his head. The only important task of the day was now accomplished.

He settled back into a sour pillow, counting his heartbeats under musty bedcovers.

For all the pyrotechnics and rolling thunder, it hadn't rained much in the night. Easy to tell. After a really big downpour, the brown watermark in the plaster ceiling spread and darkened. This morning, the splotch looked about the same as the last few weeks, vaguely like a map of the eastern United States.

A stagnant-water puddle browned Maine. Spiders webbed New Jersey, and Indiana crumbled piecemeal, chunk by little chunk, onto the linoleum floor at the foot of Threadgill's bed. Down south, Florida drooped like an old sad penis into a yellow ocean.

No, the map hadn't grown. Threadgill was sure. Alert. After ten watchful years in the rest home, he could instantly spy new territory.

The stain started at about South Carolina, the year Threadgill turned 104 and first arrived at Mobile Sunset Home after his long refuge on Goat Island. Year after lonely year, discoloration spread slowly through the plaster, annexing new frontiers. Texas and Minnesota most recently joined. The old man secretly wondered if he'd live long enough to see California a part of the map.

He would be right here, waiting.

Waiting for his moment.

"Pitiful," sighed a voice in the gloom. "Pitiful, pitiful. Threadgill, it's terrible what all y'all have to go through down here."

Threadgill Pickett twisted on his creaky bed. He felt a kind of sudden terror.

He hadn't dreamed it.

Who else was in his room?

A lanky young man, barely more than a boy, sat before the window. He was nicely backlit by the strip of dawn beneath the shade. Threadgill could make out a mass of tousled hair, a cotton blouse, homespun trousers.

"Don't go all flippity, brother," the visitor grinned. "I got good tidings."

"Land O' Goshen!" Threadgill breathed weakly. "Ben?"

An unearthly blue light glowed in the visitor's face. But something seemed far from brotherly in that aspect. Threadgill never imagined an angel would look so … well, rough. What angel had a black eye, a scab on the chin, a swollen lip?

"Brother?"

"It's really me, Gill. It is."

Threadgill began to tremble. Something nearly broke inside him. A cry, sheer and elemental, welled from his heart and scalded a path up his throat, out his mouth.

"Oh!" Threadgill wailed. "Help! Help me, nurses!" The old man shouted and thrashed on the squeaky bed, sheets and pillow flying. No one seemed to hear.

As Threadgill convulsed, Ben nonchalantly produced a fresh lemon from his blouse. In the morning sunlight, it seemed to Threadgill like the yellowest thing on earth.

Ben's sharp fingernail knifed a circle through the bright citrus peel. The youngster brought the lemon to his lips, hesitated.

"Go on and yell, Threadgill. You always were hard-headed. Just yell till you're ready to hear me." Ben took a suck of the lemon. His face twisted. "Aw, shoot! At's *good*!"

Threadgill did yell. Bloody, holy murder. He screeched till he went hoarse. He kicked the bedcovers into the air. He toppled a bedside stack of Dixie cups, and his bedpan clanged across the room.

Ben worked the lemon. *Suck, suck, suck.*

Threadgill carried on. He threw a vase at the door. He tipped over a metal IV tree. He raged. He roared.

At last, Threadgill fell still, shuddering. His heart kicked at its bony stall, a frightened horse in a burning barn. He wanted to panic and run – right through the window and out splashing into Mobile Bay. He could do it! He was still a strong man! He'd kept himself hard and fit for all these years, counting down the hours, the years, to a day of final reckoning.

Threadgill's heartbeat shook the entire bed.

"Ahhh!" sighed Ben. He tossed the empty lemon – *bong*! – into a metal trash can. He gritted his teeth in satisfaction. "At's *mighty* fine!"

Threadgill's twin brother, long gone from the world but here this morning by some miracle or hallucination, wiped the back of long fingers across his wet mouth.

"I ain't going!" Threadgill croaked. "I still got a mite of business, Ben! I ain't ready to leave this vale! Don't take me!"

The visitor tut-tutted.

"Threadgill, listen. I ain't here to haul you off to glory. Pay attention, hard-head."

So Threadgill did. Finally. Not one toe twitched. He closed his eyes. The country music on the Philco down the hall – Buck Owens, *Together Again* – grew dim and distant.

The young man in the chair leaned forward and spoke in a conspiratorial whisper.

"Threadgill Pickett, it's time."

The old man sharply drew in his breath.

"Ain't but one Yankee left now, Gill. Just one. He's up in Bangor, Maine, and he lives in the biggest house you ever saw. He's a millionaire … and he lives all by himself. You hearing me? Hear what I'm sayin'?"

Oh yes.

Threadgill heard.

He listened fiercely to his visitor now, and did not move a muscle.

A new light gleamed in Threadgill Pickett's eyes.

A cold sun.

Chapter 2, Yellowhammer

Summer 1864 – Near Atlanta, Georgia

Threadgill Pickett rose to his feet, confused, his heart hammering.

No mistake. An uproar – *who? what?* – surged over the hill.

What was *it*? Last night had been the stillest Threadgill could ever remember, silent and motionless and already black dark when he and his twin, Benjamin, wearily slumped down to rest. For hours, they'd seen no other man or work of man – no frightened fugitive travelers, no rain-blackened cabin, no campfire or rail fence. In such isolation, the two footsore brothers for once felt safe to bed down out of the wildly foreboding woods, to lie under open stars.

No stars twinkled now. The sky soared toward eternity – a blue eternity, where a black wagon wheel of vultures turned slowly around and around.

A cheer rose, voices yelling raucously over the hill.

Did a Yankee attack sound that way?

Fourteen-year-old Threadgill gaped blindly into the blazing Georgia dawn. He grabbed for his floppy yellowhammer hat, slapped it on his head, stared anxiously left and right.

He could make a run for it. But where in God's name was Ben?

At the foot of the hill, a shining creek glinted through a torn hem of trees. The slow water disappeared in a tangle of poplar tulips and cypress. Good cover lay a hundred yards in that direction – any one-eyed Yankee who stepped over the crest of this hill could shoot Threadgill down like a dog before he made it halfway.

The boy frantically scanned the hillside, the front of his clothes dark with the morning dew. Lord! How stupid to sleep a country mile from a hiding place! What was Ben thinking?

God knows, thought Threadgill Pickett, *we deserved it – a good night's sleep*. It was quite a walk from Eufaula, most of a long, hard month. The young men had worn home-made shoes the first two weeks, till the Georgia roads beat them ragged.

Wish I had those shoes now, Threadgill lamented. He looked down the long hillside. Knots of blackberry grew in green spots, prickly spines everywhere. Wild red roses frothed up in another place, near a white rock.

The catcalls and whistles over the hill grew more rambunctious. Many men – maybe dozens – joined the hooting.

Whose foolish army made so much noise?

And where in the Lord's name had Ben gotten off to?

A shadow whipped past, fast over the ground, crossing Threadgill's bare feet. A buzzard. Truth be known, the skyfull of vultures spooked Threadgill. He hadn't expected two-hundred flesh-eating birds to be circling when he opened his eyes this morning. What kind of sign was that?

Threadgill could see the pink bird heads clearly outlined against the blue sky. The pulpy skin looked something like the human insides he'd seen just two days before, blown out of a Confederate soldier. Threadgill had thought of almost nothing else since he and his brother made that fly-blown discovery along the northbound road. The corpse had been lying long enough for the maggots to get well along in their work. The death odor filled Threadgill's head for hours.

War didn't seem so noble and gallant all of a sudden. Yankee bullets could do that to me, Threadgill realized, seeing the corpse over and over again in his mind. Or Ben.

He ought to get off this windswept hill. He ought to skeddadle. Now. But would Ben leave him?

Dumbstruck, Threadgill had a thought.

Maybe he already did.

Maybe Ben left *me*. Am I alone now?

Fear dug in sharp claws.

Threadgill made a hasty salvage. He pitched together the belongings of twin lives: Two bedrolls stuffed with matched bundles of filthy clothes. A leather Bible. A big skinning knife. Some minie balls (both boys hoped they'd be lucky enough to get a gun when they found the Confederate army). They carried a tinder box, a small skillet, a leather bag for dried beans, completely empty now, a strip of rawhide.

As he stuffed the dusty haversack, Threadgill's knees boned their way through holes in his tattered pants. The weeds felt soggy, oozing morning dew onto his kneecaps.

Finished! Now run, Threadgill!

The boy jumped up, shouldered his equipment. He could still make it to the woods. Surely his big brother was down there, safe and sound, gorged on fresh-picked blackberries, washing the sticky purple stains off his paws in the creek like a big raccoon ...

Threadgill turned to flee. But he then heard something so odd and unexpected – so completely strange – it stopped him dead in his tracks.

A fiddle.

A familiar melody floated over the brow of that green Georgia hill. An unpracticed hand skirled the tune, but the fiddler played with workmanlike determination, sawing out the notes. His familiar song mingled with cheers and shouts that rose in volume on the gusting breeze.

The song was "Dixie."

A big grin broke over Threadgill's sunburned face.

Boy, you needn't have spooked after all! No sir! Them soldiers are playing "Dixie"!

Threadgill thought of throwing his newly feathered hat into the bright air and doing a barefoot dance, briars be damned. Surely "Dixie" was the finest, happiest piece of music ever written!

Threadgill Pickett now stood up against the skyline, tall as a grown man, and noticed how the eastern side of the hill glowed in honey-colored sunlight. A soft, downy look blessed the landscape. Threadgill impulsively rubbed his own chin. It itched with very thin reddish whiskers.

The smile on Threadgill's face spread to a satisfied heart. No person in the world felt prouder that moment, that morning in Georgia, August 1864.

Two boys set out alone, Threadgill age fourteen and his brother Ben five minutes older, to walk a hundred and eighty-odd miles, to join up and fight for the Confederate army. Thirty yards farther up this hill and the greatest goal of their lives so far would be fulfilled.

The Confederate army!

Threadgill felt a pounding pride in his heart, the elation of a boy who just proved himself a man. Now, at last, he and his brother would be Confederates!

The fiddle tune wafted upward on the fine morning, bearing along the shouts and calls of men. Ben must surely be part of that huzzah.

Humming, Threadgill swaggered to the hilltop.

The music stopped abruptly. The last note froze forever, mid-air.

It took Threadgill a moment to comprehend. Then he felt his bowels turn to ice, and his feet freeze solid to the earth.

The soldiers wore blue.

Twenty or so stood in a circle on the red dirt road, bayonets fixed and glittering in the morning sun. Their flag popped in the northerly breeze.

Yankees!

A heavy cavalry trooper with a pink face held the fiddle. He sat on a restless mount just outside the circle of men. The trooper played the musical instrument wedged beneath one of his sweating chins. Like a raised saber, the fiddle bow hovered. Billy Yank had ended his blaspheming version of "Dixie" righteously, with a flourish, piggish eyes closed.

Threadgill spied Ben. His brother stood in the center of the blue web of Yankees. Caught. Ben looked like one more ragged, pitiful Confederate. A runaway scarecrow. He had danced his bare feet bloody to the fiddler's tune.

Threadgill grasped the situation. Plunging Yankee bayonets, aimed at heels and toes, kept his poor brother leaping frantically, ridiculously. With jeers and taunts, the blue soldiers shoved Ben, sprawling, back into the circle each time he jumped too far from their wicked game of mumblety-peg.

"Please! Please – y'all!" Ben screamed, out of breath, his feet bright with new blood. "Don't do – this – to me!"

"Please, y'all," mocked one of the Yankees, to whistles of derision. "Y'all do-o-on't. Y'all sto-o-p. Y'all all go back to Jaw-ja and aall faall dow-wnnn ..."

Up the road, beyond the cruelty in the vale, Threadgill saw many more Yankees on the march, their long, snakelike blue column raising a red cloud that gusted into roadside pines.

The shabby gray figure below all at once stopped his marionette leaping. Weakly, Ben struck out at one Yankee who had mocked him, a young soldier with a trim waist like a blue wasp. He looked no older than Ben.

The men in blue jeered. "Whoo! Johnny Reb's mad now! Look out, Sanders!"

Ben's exhausted blow was little more than a slap. It barely turned the Yankee soldier's cheek.

But it raised blind rage.

Sanders leaped forward, clawing at a heavy black revolver on his hip.

"Don't! Lord, help me!" Ben begged. "Threadgill! THREADGILL!"

Ben fell roughly to his knees, bleeding feet beneath him.

My brother's last prayer, Threadgill thought. *Does Ben see me?*

"Give it to him, Sandy!" a Yankee shouted.

Sanders jerked out his revolver. He stepped directly in back of the kneeling prisoner. The Yankee's crisp blue uniform seemed to never have been dirty, except for a coat of red Georgia dust over his good black boots.

Billy Yank aimed the revolver at the back of Ben's head. Even at age fourteen, Threadgill's brother's hair thinned at the crown, and the balding spot made a kind of bulls-eye.

"Johnny Reb!" Sanders screamed. "Go to hell!"

The pistol hammer snapped. The dry sound made Threadgill think of a small bone breaking.

"Ohoooo!" The Yankee soldiers howled with laughter. Some doubled over, slapping their shanks, their bayonets scraping furrows in the hard dirt road. "Ohoooo! Sanders forgot to load his pistol!"

His young face violet, the furious Yankee swung the heavy gun barrel like a club and knocked Ben forward. The stunned boy, on his all fours, bled from the nose. Sanders maniacally attempted to load his revolver, dropping two bullets onto the road before he jammed one into the firing chamber.

"Now!" he screamed, leaping back over the slumped figure. "Now laugh, sonofabitch!"

The gun jerked in the blue soldier's hand – *boom*! – and he turned his back abruptly, the way a man does after he throws the latch to a pen holding a vicious dog.

Threadgill watched his twin brother topple forward, one foot jerking.

The road beneath the executed rebel turned dark instantly, and a pearly gob of smoke floated up and away, like a soul.

Threadgill would never forget what a man looked like as he died, how spastic and foolish.

Threadgill's mind reeled, and he closed his eyes to shut out the sight. He felt something crack and pour out inside him. A gorge rose from his stomach, hot and hard and violently sour, and he fought it down.

Threadgill would go home now.

He had seen enough. Now he knew. His brother was dead.

He had seen the great Civil War.

Chapter 3, The Unmentionable

Summer 1964 – Mobile Sunset Home

Bruce and Threadgill faced The Unmentionable twice a week, just after lunch.

The colored attendant got right to work. He took off Threadgill's shirt and began mopping his lean body with a sopping orange sponge.

"Whoo! You sho musta been a fightin' rooster in yo' day, Mustah Gill," Bruce whistled. "I swear, you got 'nuff holes an' cut-up places to sell 'em in packages."

Threadgill didn't bother to check the mirror. He knew the man in the glass. And Bruce could only see the scars on the *outside* ...

Threadgill Pickett haunted a 114-year-old carcass that resembled some eerie, lonesome badland out West. Father Time had transformed the green hills and valleys of Threadgill's youth into an arid landscape of pale, battered gullies and purple buttes. Rows of white scars and ridges of weird growths, scaled over with permanent white-and-purple crusts, rose like rocky monuments from his old hide. Age spots the color and size of leeches clung everywhere. A big scar glistened in the center of his chest like raw biscuit, and Threadgill supposed he carried a smaller one in the middle of his back where the bullet entered long ago.

The worst sight – The Unmentionable – came last, under the hat. Bruce, inevitably, with great and deliberate ceremony, lifted Threadgill's feathered headgear and took a deep breath.

There It waited.

Imagine a sculpted globe of raw, discolored chicken meat. Imagine it dipped in yellow egg yolk, scorched in a skillet, then left in a damp cellar to grow purple-black mold spots. The tops of both ears a little melted.

Fate spared Threadgill's face, at least. Not a bad one, either. The bonnie-blue eyes still twinkled, set defiantly into a head as round and hard as a hickory nut. Threadgill liked his eyebrows, at least – a pair of patient, outstretched wings, snow-white hawks, hovering over blue waterholes.

His nose stood out – remarkable, aquiline, aristocratic. It might have been even prouder than that prow of brother Ben's. Sensitive too. Even now,

Threadgill could filter out smells like a bloodhound.

A drop of Indian blood, the family shame, gave each cheek prominence, tugging the wide mouth up at its corners. A wisp of snow-white hair fluttered from his chin, a goat's beard on a windy day. It partly hid the saggy stalactites of skin clustering Threadgill's neck.

Vengeance turned out to be a pure Fountain of Youth. It kept Threadgill tough and vigilant and focused. It kept him fully and manfully alive years after he should have been cold bones under cold stones.

"You keep on wigglin', we'll have to wash you all over again, Mustah Gill. Old folks gets dirty just wigglin'." Bruce, bless his heart, kept up a cheerful, animated conversation, even with the pulsating raw horror right under his nose. "Besides, this soap water might drip all on yo' mattress."

Threadgill sighed, made a joke. "Sure better not wet the mattress, Bruce. I don't want Miz Lantern coming around with her big old adult diapers."

"I keep her out, Mustah Threadgill. But you got to hold still. It ain't easy to get you wrinklesome folks clean. We got to get you ready for Shangri-La."

"Shangri-La!" Threadgill made a sour face. "I'd rather sit here in my room and hit my toes with a hammer! Bruce, you tell 'em."

"Aww, now, Mustah Gill, it ain't nothing but singin' some songs. Everybody s'posed to come to Shangri-La and be real happy."

The door eased shut. Threadgill felt . . . alone. Something puzzled him too. Why did Bruce talk the way he did to Threadgill? More than once, Threadgill heard the attendant out with other colored folk on smoking break, and Bruce sounded like an announcer on the TV news. Bruce used a whole separate language when he bathed Threadgill and shuffled around the home on his chores. Curious.

Threadgill hitched up his nerve and glared into the mirror one more time. His own bubble-cap of a head glistened, throbbed, eerie under the fluorescent light. Held just the right way, it looked something like a fly head.

Threadgill jerked at his hat in fury and yanked it all the way down to those warlike eyebrows.

Shangri-La.

Hell on the half-shell. Shangri-La can kiss my leathery ass.

This would be a *perfect* night to march to Maine.

Chapter 4, Shangri-La

Summer 1964 – Mobile Sunset Home

Young Guy Young hosted Shangri-La every Sunday night, rain or shine, hell or high water.

Old Guy Young – Young Guy Young's daddy – was a Somebody in Mobile. He served on the board of directors of the biggest bank in town. He owned a shipyard, ran the Rotary Club, deaconed at a Baptist church, declaimed against the evils of Mardi Gras. He had supper with his wife and son one night a week, no matter what.

Somewhere along the line, Young Guy Young threw over family plans for a similar career in bank ledgers and shipping manifests. He took up lounge singing instead.

His lucky pedigree earned Young Guy Young countless invitations to society events around the bay, and he quickly became *de facto* entertainer of choice for socials in Mobile – cotillions and teas and weddings and debutante parties. He held a monopoly on the nursing and funeral home circuits.

The ladies clubs especially loved him, the pudgy cheeks, the blond froth of curls. Young Guy Young's twin little chins trembled irresistibly when he sang "What Do The Simple Folks Do?" He reminded a certain kind of woman of the son she either had or never had.

The Bridge Dames and the Cotillion Cotillionettes and the Garden District Lady Lancers and a mystic society called the Polka Dots fattened Young Guy Young through several pants sizes on casseroles, congealed salads and fine layer cakes. The sequined white vest Young Guy Young wore to wedding rehearsal-party performances showed off a paunch made ever-more dramatic by their good works.

Young Guy Young sat this Sunday night at Mobile Sunset Home's single musical instrument – a sour-keyed old Baldwin upright. The piano shed its black skin on one side. The performer adjusted a mic, leaned over his sheet music, fiddled a bit. He came carefully coifed in white curls and flounces. Threadgill hated Young Guy Young's hair even worse than he hated that prehensile snake braid of Miz Lantern's. The hairdos of both seemed to symbolize everything he despised at Mobile Sunset Home.

The moment Young Guy Young opened his mouth, Threadgill pictured a poodle loudly pinned under the claws of a starved wildcat.

> *Michael ... row your boat ashore! Yeah!*
> *Hallelujah! Go Mikey!*
> *Row Mikey!*
> *Row for shore, boy!*
> *Row for show!*
> *Yes, Jesus!*
> *Go row your boat ashore, Mikey baby!*

The squeaky piano pedals received a merciless workout. To hit the high notes, Young Guy Young rose inches above the piano stool on flexed buttocks. It looked to Threadgill as if his large behind extruded a short, rigid stem.

Ah, Shangri-La! Threadgill thought longingly of the soft beans left uneaten on his plate at supper. He only wanted two now…one to plug each ear.

The old man thought back to all those years ago in Eufaula. Once upon a time, churches didn't have pianos. People accompanied hymns with the shuffling of feet, the strong rhythms of boot heels, straw fans. Voices wandered heroically, note to note, like Hebrew children in the wilderness. Music was pungent, ancient, fearless.

A melancholy filled Threadgill Pickett.

Folks he knew as a boy in Alabama scratched out a living from red dirt. They lay down with their necks sunburned and their muscles sore at the end of every single day. All those generations lived and died and chopped cotton and had children and defended a few acres, and all their sacrifice and toil had come down to this – a tubby, grub-white sissy banging away on a helpless piano.

What had happened to the world after the Yankees took over?

The entertainer now slid into something that actually startled Threadgill – an oleaginous version of "Dixie."

Young Guy Young played the anthem of the old Confederacy in a way that made Threadgill think of the music that spewed from Eufaula's one old riverfront hotel on a hot summer night.

"Dixie." Whorehouse-style.

Well sir, that did it.

Threadgill rose up from his chair. The staff of the home loitered behind him smoking cigarettes – nobody paid much attention to the residents during Shangri-La here in the Jungle Room. Even the geriatrics went to sleep when Young Guy Young played.

Not Threadgill. He slipped up close beside the piano.

Young Guy Young finished off "Dixie" with a theatrical touch, his pudgy hands suspended dramatically over the keys, eyes squenched tight, the picture of righteous sincerity.

Threadgill waited a respectful moment. He cleared his throat.

"That was just something special," he declared. "It made me want to cry."

Young Guy Young's eyes popped open and swiveled towards the praise like lighthouse beams. His face sparkled.

"There is *so much love* in this room tonight!" gushed the performer. He flashed his gemmy teeth and waved a hand to indicate the old folks. From this vantage point in front of the room, the residents looked to Threadgill like what might lay scattered along the roadside after a truck filled with mannequins overturned.

"Yes sir, brother Young, it's truly true," Threadgill agreed. "There is so much love in this room."

Young Guy Young's eyes shone like silver dimes.

"I just wanted to say ... the way you played 'Dixie' was just ..." Threadgill paused to dab at his nose with the back of his shirtsleeve, "... just so very, very special."

"Oh no problem!" Young Guy Young's white vest swelled. "I arranged that one special for all my fans here at Mobile Sunset Home."

"Did you?"

"Oh yes. I do my own arrangements."

"Well, that is ... magical."

Threadgill leaned forward now, and spoke more confidentially.

"Son ... would it be possible for me ... to give you a little something in return for this gift you've shared with all of us tonight?"

"Bless your little heart, yes," Young Guy Young said, happily. "I actually plan to pass the hat later, but you can certainly be generous right this moment if you feel a calling."

"Wonderful. Yes, I'm going to give you something right now," Threadgill whispered. He leaned very close. "I'm going to pass the hat … right now!"

Threadgill lifted off his yellowhammer hat.

He thrust his mutilated head forward, and it actually nudged Young Guy Young's mouth. The head flesh pulsed moistly in the Jungle Room's fluorescent lighting.

Young Guy Young couldn't have leaped back any faster if a live monkey had leaped onto his face.

"Shithell!" he screamed. "Hellshit!"

A doughy flailing hand knocked sheet music off the piano in all directions. The young singer's elbow crashed dissonant thunder from the bass keys. His stool splintered loudly and collapsed.

The raucous commotion roused Sunset Home residents from swoon and stupor.

Threadgill never expected what happened next.

"Get him!" cried someone from the audience. "Get the piano player!"

One of the invalids surprised everyone. Old Cletus Cline, more or less a vegetable for years, amazingly rose like Lazarus, fully to his bare feet, and hurled a Dixie cup of water clear across the room. It wetly smacked the Baldwin. Water drops freckled the piano's black varnish.

"Cut off his pecker!" screamed 93-year-old Victoria Brown.

"Bite his fingers!" yelled Dawn Eagle.

"You'd make my cat puke!" yelled Mr. Napoli, the feisty Italian retired from up north, his fists raised. "Get your patootie outta here!"

Like rotten fruit, laughter and jeers flew thick.

"Stick that sheet music where the sun don't shine, boy!"

"No good piano would let you touch it!"

"I'd rather listen to my colostomy!"

Threadgill now advanced on his prey, brain-matter-gray scalp glistening like bubbles on a swamp pond.

Young Guy Young made a shameless retreat. The pianist clutched a few precious sheets of music to his sequined vest. He ducked out the Jungle Room's emergency exit, ripping his white jacket on a nail in his panicked haste. The entertainer's face appeared red and swollen, a devil with mumps, as he fled into the blue evening.

A mighty cheer rose, and Threadgill turned to see old hands triumphantly raised high in the air, old feet dancing again. Was it his imagination, or did he suddenly hear lively music playing somewhere? *Happy Days Are Here Again?*

Threadgill felt a strong grip on his arm.

"Mustah Gill, what a mess o' trouble you done cause."

Threadgill turned to Bruce defiantly. Without a word, he slapped his floppy yellowhammer hat back onto his head.

Bruce was big and gentle, the kind of country boy who looked as though he'd eaten a whole pot of black-eyed peas every week of his life. Threadgill's eye fell on Bruce's shirt pocket. He noticed the hand-lettered ID tag— B-R-U-C-E – its final "E" written backwards.

He felt his anger soften.

"I simply had to take my hat off, Bruce," Threadgill explained, "to that young man's exceptional talent."

"You scairt the doo-doo out him, is what. Ain't right to do such, Mustah Gill."

Threadgill wasn't about to apologize. He couldn't, anyway. Bruce suddenly spotted bigger problems.

"You done got this room in such a state. Look yonder. Miz Monk done thowed up beans and weenies all over herself. She gone to choke on that mess. I be back."

That put-on talk again. Threadgill watched Bruce hurry to help with Mrs. Monk's ventilation.

After a while, the staff restored order. They used folded newspapers and parlor fans to round up the chickens – *Shoo! Shoo! Go on now*! Rickety, giddy old folks tottered down the corridors toward their rooms. Two attendants remained, stalking here and there, angrily jerking up and folding metal chairs, throwing them onto stacks with ear-splitting racket. No one made eye contact with Threadgill.

Someone tossed a whole package of cocktail napkins into the Jungle Room's aquarium, and one or two of the angelfish wore wilted shrouds. Afraid to swim, they simply floated like ghosts until they bumped glass walls.

Angels. Ghosts. Threadgill felt tingling.

With a shock, his proud old nose knew why.

"Fire!"

Threadgill waved his arms at the two attendants.

"I smell smoke! There's a fire! Get everybody out of here!"

His warning failed to draw even a glance.

"Fire! You've got to believe me! Sunset Home – it's on fire."

Out of nowhere, a twisted, angry face popped into Threadgill's. Its breath smelled of Lucky Strikes and deviled eggs. Red hair fringed it, and thin liver-colored lips curled back from its long yellow teeth.

If she were Buddhist, Tommie Lantern, CEO of Mobile Sunset Home, might well come back in her next life as a wharf rat.

"Stop crying wolf and get back to your room immediately, Mr. Pickens!" Miz Lantern waved her hands at him, karate style. "Look at the trouble you caused here! You ruined Shangri-La! You deliberately ruined Shangri-La!"

Threadgill would not be calmed.

"There's a fire in here, Miz Lantern! I smell smoke strong ..."

The administrator, her face purple with rage, snatched Threadgill completely around now. A little bubble of snot ballooned from one of her nostrils, quickly popped.

"Go to your room Mr. Pickens," she snapped. "For you, lights out – NOW!"

Threadgill stalked to his room … but with head-wheeling worry.

Each step down the corridor, a thickening acrid smell grew stronger in his fantastic nose. He barely felt Miz Lantern's steel talons hooked into his upper arm. He really didn't notice the final shove she gave him into his room. He was equally oblivious to the violent crash as the door slammed behind him.

It closed so hard that the door's brass numeral – 13 – pinged loose and danced musically, madly, down the corridor.

Threadgill walked straight to the closet.

He prepared, on the spot, for a long journey.

Chapter 5, A Fire in the Woods

Summer 1864 – Near Atlanta, Georgia

From the Georgia hilltop, the circle of Yankees around murdered Ben Pickett looked like the blue iris of an eye ... with a bloodshot gray pupil.

One of the Yankees dragged Ben's corpse out of the road by his bare ankles.

The body left a long dark streak.

Fate turned its gory head then, and fixed an eye on Threadgill.

"Godamighty! A rebel! On the hill!"

Men in blue ran pell-mell, a shellburst of flying hats and stumbling legs and lost equipment. Yankee soldiers rolled away over the ground, arms covering heads.

The big horse spooked and reared beneath the fiddle player. Forelegs pedaled the air, and its blue-coated rider pitched heavily backward, fiddle flying. The trooper hit the ground hard. He didn't get up.

For a moment, Threadgill might have been Gideon at the vanguard of his avenging army, bearing down with brass trumpets and blazing torches on the stunned Amonites, launching one of Yahweh's memorable slaughters.

But Threadgill understood the truth. The spreading blue panic gave him one chance to live. He unrooted himself from the horror of his brother's death and bolted off the crest of the hill.

Threadgill sprinted like a deer down the open slope, past last night's campsite, fearful eyes locked on the faraway creek in the woods. Huge black grasshoppers zinged up from the grass before him. The sun bounced around the sky. Buzzards swerved and flew off at crazy angles.

One hundred yards! One hundred yards and he just might live forever!

But Threadgill stumbled and fell – *thump! bump! roll*! He sprawled and slid in the dew, tumbling headlong, grabbing at tussocks of goldenrod, pokeberry, anything. His bedroll and haversack bounced wildly, under and over, crashing his hips, his back. His floppy hat flew away and rolled into briars.

Dizzy, Threadgill found his feet. He spit out leaves, then tore off again, shirt ripped open, blackberry spines all in his hair.

Bruises or scrapes would not stop him. Only the shining creek at the bottom of the hill mattered now.

I'll die, Threadgill thought, *if I don't make it to the trees.*

I don't want to die. I don't want to die. I don't want to go with Ben ...

The first rifle shot tore the ground ahead. The Yankees had climbed the hill with their repeaters, and thirty yards of open field still yawned between Threadgill and the cover of woods. Threadgill's legs moved faster than they ever had, than they ever would again in his long life.

A bullet whined past his right ear. It sounded for all the world like a hornet whizzing past on any hot morning of a summer day.

Then a hornet stung him.

What a surprise!

The blow knocked Threadgill down. He couldn't get to his feet for a moment. He tasted hot bitter metal in his mouth. The sky changed color, to dazzling white, in one frightening instant. Everything around him seemed to speed up, going faster than it should have.

Threadgill focused his eyes. He saw, just ahead, the shining creek.

The beautiful creek.

The boy dragged himself to his shaky feet. He staggered forward again. More angry hornets buzzed by and, as Threadgill reached the woods, bark popped off hickory and sweetgum trunks, and twigs showered down on him.

Threadgill vanished into the shadows.

***

The air felt cool here.

Threadgill stepped slowly, hands clutched to his breast like a monk in prayer. Gradually, he grew dizzy. He leaned his cheek against a huge beech, its bark smooth and cool as river stone.

After a few moments, Threadgill worked up the courage to look at his wound. The hornet had flown all the way through him, back to front. He touched the injured spot in amazement. Dark blood covered fingertips.

His own blood. His own fingers.

If Threadgill took his hand away, the wound welled and began to bleed in earnest. Sticky redness spilled into his shot-torn breast pocket, then slowly overflowed it, spattering the dry leaves, the tops of his sunburned feet.

Oddly, Threadgill felt nothing. If it hurt, it hurt so badly it went past any

kind of pain he knew how to feel. He would always remember the oddness —
this hole in his own chest where no hole had ever been. A hole, but no feeling.

He now heard desultory shots, more voices, the Yankees moving in no
particular hurry into the woods, coming for the kill. The blue soldiers had
seen Threadgill fall, and now they would track his blood trail just as they
would a wounded buck until he fell and fell again and, finally, didn't get up.

Threadgill felt very tired.

There's nothing to do, he thought. *Nothing but to wait under this green tree.*

He pulled the skinning knife from his haversack and laid it across his lap.
The sun burned down.

In a while, Threadgill heard men speaking back and forth in their odd
Yankee voices. Not a bird sang in any tree.

Once, a careful, shuffly tread of boots on dry leaves passed, then grew
faint.

Threadgill used his knife to cut away a piece of shirt. He wadded it with
leaves, stuffed it into his wound. It slowed the bleeding. But he felt more tired
now, weary enough to lie down and go to sleep forever.

How odd he wasn't scared any more.

Did it hurt, Ben? Did it hurt when the big door opened and let you through?

Threadgill squared his back against the beech trunk and took a deep,
painful breath, bloodstained feet spread wide apart, a stray shaft of canopy
sunlight bright on one set of pale toes. The little creek chattered among dark
tree roots.

Water.

Threadgill cleared his throat, suddenly so thirsty.

The woods throbbed in strange, heavy silence.

A cloud passed over the sun.

The Yankee stepped clumsily, warily, around one side of Threadgill's
beech tree.

The soldier had lost his cap — his ivory face fully caught the sunlight. His
blue back was turned to Threadgill.

The Yankee's uniform was sopping, black with sweat underneath the
armpits, the small of his back a soggy indigo. Wet hair, blond as hay, wore a
faint imprint left from the band of his lost cap. Threadgill saw the soldier's
pale-lashed eyes — overlarge, frightened. His mouth hung open; he breathed

hard and loud. The Yankee's finger fidgeted on the trigger of a pretty new Springfield.

Elsewhere in the woods Threadgill heard metal clink on metal, a faraway hoot, someone clearing a throat. The stillness of the forest seemed to amplify sound – in fact, for Threadgill a kind of hollow, supernatural silence had taken hold, and he could hear the same way a wild animal hears, every tiny stirring and twitch, every heartbeat.

He heard, or imagined, a distant cry from Ben, but it came from overhead, above the sunny forest canopy.

A stick broke sharply beneath a boot.

The blond Yankee boy crouched, tense. His eyes swept the green point-blank confusion of trees across the creek. Who's there?

Unsure, the trooper took a wary step backward, closer to Threadgill.

Threadgill's fingers tightened on the bone handle of his skinning knife. He felt a blinding sudden pain now in his breast – *oh, so here you are* – at the moment he quietly shifted forward from the beech trunk to his knees.

Hurt then, dammit.

Threadgill raised the blade of his knife. He picked a spot on the back of the Yankee's sopping shirt. In a moment, the dark fabric would turn even darker.

In his mind's eye, Threadgill saw Ben's leg jerk, helpless. Then Ben's body stared face-down in the road. Murdered.

Threadgill raised the knife blade, sticky with his own blood. Sharp and deadly.

A roaring fury filled him. This knife would slip through skin and flesh like new butter – dressing out white-tailed deer back in Alabama had taught Threadgill that.

He would kill his enemy.

He would.

A big black ant crawled, desperate, across the Yankee's back.

Threadgill screamed. He slashed the knife blade in a wild bright arc … but instead of into Yankee flesh, he plunged it with every ounce of ebbing strength into the cool topsoil of the Georgia woods.

The startled Yankee wheeled. Every scared animal Threadgill ever saw stared from his wide eyes.

The Springfield jerked to a blue shoulder, its barrel wobbling.

Threadgill saw the unsteady hand that held the rifle. In its fingers, the Yankee clutched a dirty broad-brimmed gray hat … with a yellowhammer feather. Billy Yank had lost his own kepi, but found Threadgill's hat on the hillside and picked it up. A Confederate souvenir.

Threadgill pointed a bloody finger.

You got my hat, he meant to say, like a friend. But blood dribbled from his mouth instead of words.

The Yankee recoiled, now frightened even more. He was such a young man. Threadgill could see it now. The Yankee had tried to grow a moustache, but it came in pale and thin. The cheeks glowed baby pink.

His eyes met Threadgill's.

A flicker passed, some hopeless communication.

The Yankee breathed in violently and shouldered the rifle and sighted down its shaky barrel.

Threadgill wanted so badly to speak. He opened his mouth to try again. Something about Ben.

Then the blue soldier's hair gave a little twitch in back, and something wet flew from his forehead.

What happened?

Eyes staring wide in wonder, the Yankee lowered his rifle. A little dark rosebud in his forehead put out red vines.

He dropped to his knees.

He toppled across Threadgill's legs, already dead.

***

A dream of the damned appeared from thin air.

Swarms of Confederate soldiers, gray as wraiths, flew past Threadgill, resolving out of tangled woodland shadows across the creek.

The rebels seemed to rise up yelling from under dry leaves. They emerged from tree trunks, appeared solid out of rotted logs, popped up from burrows in the ground. The woods suddenly boiled with Confederates. Squirrel rifles shot pink fire from their muzzles. Swords and bayonets flashed, and rebel yells split the air.

Threadgill flopped back heavily against the beech trunk, the dead Yankee over his knees. Out of nowhere, a panicked white-tailed buck leaped clean across them both. The animal frantically bounded away into a wailing, confused wilderness.

A field piece detonated with a heart-stopping jolt, off in the woods to Threadgill's right. He saw the smoking barrel now; the carriage and caisson were previously invisible under their camouflage tent of leaves. A second battery discharged farther out in the woods – BOOM! – and Threadgill saw this cannon kick backward on oversized spoked wheels. Soldiers who looked gray even without their shirts swabbed the Parrots, reloading.

Threadgill, in a revelation, understood the world would be different from now on for him if he lived.

Oddly he felt embarrassment for the Yankee corpse across his legs. He wished he could move the dead man, but Threadgill hurt very badly now. He wrenched his eyes away instead and stared up into peaceful trees.

A shaft of sunlight, white as a column on a big porch, soared down through the overhead canopy. Hornets flew in and out of that light now, and green leaves twitched, trembled, let go.

Threadgill suddenly wanted to be home. Back in Alabama, back on Aunt Annie's place again, to never, ever leave. He'd plow, and plant corn or cotton, and maybe make enough money one day to buy a hog or a mule – why not? He would marry and show children how to carve a whistle and trap a rabbit. He would smoke a pipe and sit on the plank porch in the summer nights and watch the lightning bugs flash in the woods.

Only yards away, a spark from one of the cannon blasts settled in dry leaves. Threadgill watched a little flag of fire flicker to life.

With a slow-dawning horror, Threadgill saw how quickly flames could climb the dry tinder of an old pine trunk and claw their way into its crown of dry needles. An instant storm of white heat, violently popping and snapping, sent soldiers hustling away in all directions.

A burning tree.

It seemed dreamlike at first, a lovely thing, a fire from some other world, dancing and dervishing, without harm or consequence.

But Threadgill heard a wounded soldier scream. And at once a surge of panic tore a new kind of hole in his own chest.

Jesus oh Jesus, Threadgill prayed. *Not fire. Not this way. Please dear God.*

He closed his eyes, moved his bloody lips with fervent words.

Please let it stop. Please make the creek stop the fire, dear God.

The creek did not stop it.

Flame leaped the water in two places at once, sparks flying, blazing birds ahead of a summer breeze.

Chunks of hot red began to fall everywhere along the dry floor of the wilderness. These emissary blazes leaped up fiercely. They gobbled out charred circles on the ground. They swallowed saplings whole, raced fallen tree trunks from end to end.

All around Threadgill, the fierce pop and crackle of the conflagration smothered even the roar of battle.

Before the crashing wave of yellow fire, the Confederate artillerymen abandoned their cannon, fleeing in terror as the holocaust rolled down. Wounded soldiers in blue and gray alike dragged themselves desperately through forest leaves trying to reach the thin creek.

The flames closed fast, burned up their screams.

Threadgill, frightened back to his senses, attempted once more to heave the burly Yankee corpse from his legs. If he could somehow get free, he could crawl to the creek too. He could lie in the cool water and be saved …

But Threadgill couldn't move the corpse. Billy Yank was heavy as stone. And now Threadgill's body would not obey. His arms swung like wagon tongues, unable to grasp and hold. His legs simply slept. Something in his chest gurgled when he breathed.

Threadgill felt blood drip from his nose.

Oh, dear God! Oh Ben! Lord God Almighty, help me!

A flag of fire fell near his leg, out of thin air. Threadgill watched it catch the leaves, flutter to life.

He spit blood at it. He desperately willed his hands to fling dirt in that direction and, at last, he made the fingers work a little. But the leaves and old humus he spattered only fed the fire, made the flame more eager.

Threadgill jerked his yellowhammer hat from the stiffened fingers of the dead Yankee, and flapped clumsily at the flames.

They grew hotter, larger.

So Threadgill surrendered. He sank back against the beech. He felt too tired to even pray.

Threadgill smelled burning leather – one of the young Yankee soldier's fine new boots had caught fire, a flame rising from the heel.

Threadgill shut his eyes.

He saw Aunt Annie's house back in Eufaula, the paltry brave rows of corn and beans lined up like prisoners in the hard red dirt of the field.

He imagined a fire-red fox, on its hind legs, eating hard pears off the scraggly tree in the side yard.

He recalled a white shirt – empty forever – draped over a limb, one sleeve blowing.

He remembered Ben. Mischievous, daredevil Ben.

A magazine for the Confederate artillery went off, a terrific blast that blew the wheels of one cannon clean out of sight into the trees and tumbled the steel barrel end over end, plowing ground, humming like a church bell. Threadgill saw men, blue and tattered gray, fighting hand-to-hand in the smoky pall where the barrel heavily clanged to rest.

The morning turned dark as night, smoke and fire close now.

Threadgill placed his yellowhammer hat over the hole near his heart.

Now he prayed.

Don't let it hurt, the boy whispered. *Lord Jesus, Ben, just please don't let it hurt..*

Chapter 6, The Great Escape
Summer 1964 – Mobile Sunset Home

Investigators would determine the historic blaze at Mobile Sunset Home originated just outside the 8' x 10' first-floor room where Elba Mayhaw had lived the past seventeen years. There had never been another fire at the home – not from lightning, electricity, residents playing with matches, spontaneous combustion, or any other cause. Yet somehow, on this summer night in 1964, an azalea plant under the window of Room 19 mysteriously transformed into a burning bush.

The fire ate through Mrs. Mayhaw's cheap screen and immediately ignited her paper pull-shade. That flaming roll of cardboard sent hot sparks over Mrs. Mayhaw's bedsheets, setting them afire.

The rest of the rest home quickly followed.

Old Mrs. Mayhaw later told state authorities of the moment she woke. She observed out the window, framed in flames, a chubby, curly-haired, demonically leering apparition in a glittering vest. It looked, she declared, much like Young Guy Young. He stood among safety matches spilled into the azaleas all around him. The mystery figure receded, laughing in the smoke, his jowly head thrown back.

Through Mrs. Mayhaw's story and many others, fire officials outlined the entire disaster – a riveting story remembered and retold for years by eager journalists and coffee shop regulars. Twelve horrified jurors sent Young Guy Young away to another kind of home – the mental institute in Tuscaloosa – where he lived out his days playing piano for audiences not so very different from Mobile's.

The fire gobbled a hole through Mrs. Mayhaw's ceiling. Hot flames raced over and under the pine joists and rafters of the attic, spreading fast as heat lightning through sixty years of bird nests and spider webs and old boxes packed with medical charts and accounting ledgers. The resin-rich timbers of the nursing home simply exploded in one big fireball, and emissary blazes flew in all directions.

Below, in the living quarters, blazing squirrels – squirrels made of fire – skittered up window jambs and stuck flaming faces through keyholes, under shower curtains, over transoms. Long, flailing octopus tentacles of flame waved from the roof, grabbing and shaking and singeing 300-year-old live oak trees. Fearless, brainless roosters of combustion wandered the facility and attacked anything in sight – stairways, refrigerators, bedpans, one another.

It took just fifteen minutes for the west wing to merrily blaze from end to end.

Forty miles east across Mobile Bay, folks at night-time softball games or on front porches in Fairhope, Foley, Summerdale – even distant Magnolia Springs – marveled at orange dragons mounting the western sky. The strange happenings over on the Mobile shore never ceased to amaze.

Fire alarms sounded all over Mobile – only in empty firehouses. That evening, as fate would have it, marked the 50th Annual Firemen's Summer Ball in the Azalea City. Only a few firefighters, those with the lowest seniority and the most miserable luck, pulled firehouse duty that night. All had gotten drunk fast and early.

A police reporter later wrote of four firefighters – good Catholic boys, all – discovered in the cab of one fire engine, naked as worms, singing songs from the ever-popular musical, *Oklahoma*.

Other citizens, of course, bravely performed their duty that fateful evening. The administrators of Mobile Sunset Home, including Mrs. Tommie Lantern, galloped up and down the smoky corridors in moon-eyed panic, pounding on doors, their voices shrill as clowns on helium.

"Lord God wake up! Fire! Wake up and run for your lives!" they warned. "Get out! FIRE!"

It worked.

Miraculously, the Great Fire claimed no lives.

***

Threadgill ran for his own.

His dislodged door numerals – 1 and 3 – lay glowing orange in the corridor, like the hot eyes on a stove. The brass doorknob singed his hand.

Mrs. Mayhaw wandered past in the hall, smoking holes in her nightgown.

"Hold on, Elba!" Threadgill shouted. "I'll save you!"

He led the dazed denizen into his room. A freight train roared overhead. The cushion in the chair where Ben's angel sat just this morning now sported bright flames. The ceiling map of the USA gushed smoke in a dozen spots. Gnawing, sawtoothed creatures of fire poked snouts out of South Carolina.

Threadgill yanked up his travel gear – a stuffed laundry sack and a hastily improvised duffel of hospital blankets and canned foods. He guided Elba Mayhaw straight to the window … or at least where he remembered the window to be. The smoke blinded now.

Threadgill's scalp tingled under his hat. He remembered breathing smoke another time – gun smoke and acrid wildfire. That didn't seem so very long ago.

Threadgill lifted child-sized Elba Mayhaw, completely wrapped in her smoldering pink blanket, and pitched the old lady headlong through window glass and rotted screen.

Craaaaash!

Elba made a spectacular landing, completely dousing a flaming azalea. And Threadgill followed the old trailblazer, poising first on the windowsill with his gear to make sure he didn't squash the little lady. He made a catlike spring – if the cat were deep into its nine precious lives. Then Threadgill dragged Ms. Mayhaw to safety by one wrinkled foot.

The outside air felt cool, cool, cool.

***

A mother-of-pearl mist hung over Mobile Bay. The smoky grounds of Mobile Sunset Home twinkled with flares and flashing lights. Figures frantically sprinted to and fro.

One look at the conflagration, at the furious hurricane of fire, said all.

Fire left nothing but charred scars.

People in street clothes attended Elba Mayhaw and dozens of others now. Threadgill limped away from their grunting, cursing labor, farther out onto the rest home grounds. He didn't realize the heels of his own boots sported little mercurial flames.

A grimy attendant dressed in nursing-home white hustled up to Threadgill, aimed a fire extinguisher at his feet and blasted so hard that he knocked the old man flat. Threadgill's hat flew off.

Another attendant galloped up to help, an oxygen mask and a candy bar in one hand, a flashlight in the other.

His flashlight beam caught Threadgill's bare head.

The Unmentionable.

A screaming split the sky.

"Oh, my God! Sweet Jesus in Heaven!" the voice wailed. "This one burned so *bad*!"

The horrified attendant dropped his gear and ran away so fast one of his shoes flew off and hung in a low branch of a gnarled live oak.

Threadgill Pickett picked himself up. He brushed off his clothes, fetched his soggy hat and returned it to his head, shook out his dignity. He also took the abandoned candy bar and flashlight.

He shot one last look back at the burning Mobile Sunset Home.

Threadgill would remember this place.

A spark stung his cheek like a hornet, and Threadgill swatted it.

Serves me right, he thought, *for standing still too long.*

***

Yet, he dallied.

Threadgill watched the nursing home, all its beds and starched sheets and pillows and mops and all the filing cabinets and Social Security numbers and IV bags and rectal thermometers and hot water bottles and cotton balls and packets of Jello and everything else, all of it, go up in famous smoke that summer night in 1964.

Safe at a distance, Threadgill and the other lucky residents formed a mob under a scorched live oak tree near the bayside. Most residents shivered and wept as their only home in this world boiled away in black smoke.

Threadgill now spotted one of the pretty nurses urgently directing attendants and staff. She wore her nightclothes, only a thin bathrobe over her soft girlie places.

Desire welled in Threadgill.

But that exact moment, as the evening's wild climax, the entire south end of the home sprouted fiery wings. They flapped wearily one time, slinging off hot feathers, then the structure tumbled – *whump! whoosh!* – to the earth. A blast of hot air almost blew Threadgill's hat off a second time.

The old man fixed his headgear back in place. He smoothed his chin beard. Then he turned resolutely, walked away from the home, headed toward the bay waters.

Mobile Sunset Home gradually steamed to death under twin parabolas of spray from two puny garden hoses – the local volunteer fire department turned out to be ill prepared for a blaze of this scale. An hour and a half later, five backup fire crews from Mobile and Pensacola howled onto the scene ... in time to stir melancholy ashes.

Threadgill Pickett wasn't there to see.

The old soldier eased unnoticed to the bayside, his yellow roll of blankets and his bag of provisions scorched and spotted as leopard hide. He wondered if the odor of smoke would ever wash from his clothes. His scalp tingled; his sensitive nose ran like a tap.

But here by the water, he felt free, clear-minded, broken loose.

Floating, hissing timbers jostled on the patient bay tides. Already, charred nursing home flotsam sloshed ashore. Thousands of scorched adult diapers, blown loose from strewn and splintered crates, floated on the dark water like jellyfish.

Out there, in the confused wreckage, Threadgill spotted a little wooden oyster boat with one dangling oar. While every other eye goggled at the conflagration, Threadgill waded out waist deep and caught a broken length of rope that dangled from the boat's bow.

Finders, keepers.

Immersed in Mobile Bay for the first time in years – the first time since Goat Island – Threadgill made his way along the shoreline. He guided the boat like an obedient pet. He reached a spot where bull rushes grew taller than a man's head.

Threadgill Pickett heaved his gear into the vessel, then bellied over its pitching side.

The single oar fit his hands.

Threadgill turned the nose of the tiny craft east and north, and he put his back into a few strokes. The vessel lurched forward, an outsized canoe.

The old man spent a good number of solitary minutes concentrating on his strokes. Gradually, under rowing's hypnosis, Threadgill found himself thinking again of the nursing home fire. Then of his own fire. Of Ben. Of all he ever lost.

Revenge would be sweet.

Sweet.

All these years, all this waiting kept him strong for this day and hour. Strong and ready.

Vengeance added adrenaline to every stroke.

Little by little, the western shore faded behind Threadgill until every trace disappeared in muffling fog.

Pickett's Charge had begun.

Chapter 7, The Hospital Wagon

Summer 1864 – Georgia

Black rain.

They jolted to a stop in a chorus of groans.

Men climbed into the dark under the soaked wagon canvas and began to haul out the dead. A voice complained bitterly.

"Son of a bitch is *heavy*."

"Dead and dead weight," growled another voice. "Just get 'im off."

Threadgill did not want to be taken out with the dead. He did his best to move a finger, a foot. But he couldn't sort out the parts. Terror filled him, and pain now, terrible pain. His chest felt as if an arrow protruded from it, back and front. His burned head, covered in a makeshift bandage torn from his shirt, dropped charred hair and flesh into his blinking eyes. A different kind of rain.

A rough hand lifted his head in the dark, quickly dropped it.

"Damn! This one's scalped!"

The second voice neared. A lamp swam over Threadgill, bright as heaven even through the bandage.

"Here. Move on. He's alive."

Bright, warm light. And against his blistered lips, wonderfully, Threadgill suddenly tasted the wooden wet mouth of a canteen, a splash of cool water. He sucked the spout, gulped and gulped, chugging so loud that it momentarily drowned out the suffering around him.

Clumsy hands wound a fresher bandage around Threadgill's head. The torn strips of shirt reeked with sweat and, more faintly, urine.

The light moved on.

After a moment, the wagon bed rose, men jumping out its back. Threadgill imagined the lamp floating away through the downpour to another covered wagon. Behind this hospital wagon waited another and another, pulled by bony horses, maybe, instead of mules. More wagons trailed into wet, dark woods. One after another, white as ghosts, ambulance wagons stretching out of sight.

Now a new load of men clambered into Threadgill's wagon, jostling for space. These arrivals hunkered into cramped openings where dead men lay only minutes before, the spaces still cold. From the way these men groaned and sighed, Threadgill knew they must be injured too. Walking wounded.

Outside, a skinner cluck-clucked. A whip popped and chains rattled, and the wagon jerked abruptly forward, slow in the mud. The new men in the wagon lurched and caught themselves as they could, though one fell, raising a volley of oaths and cries of pain.

Threadgill hurt, but not so badly he lost consciousness. He felt the wagon clatter and creak, drivers cursing the braying mules. A chill surged his raw burned skin now and again, flooding him top to bottom, convulsing his legs.

Hours may have passed. Threadgill considered things. He grew alarmed, his heart beating fast, then still faster.

Something did not feel right. Something about this wagon didn't square. Who were these people? Who drove? Where would he be taken?

I do not want to be on a wagon bound for a graveyard! I do not want to be buried alive!

Was poor Ben in here? Was Ben one of the corpses they pulled off at the last stop? *Where was Ben?*

Threadgill's hearing seemed muffled, damaged somehow by battle and fire. His scorched skin felt a rain of pain – each time a muscle twitched, he heard a crackling sound inside his head. His mouth tasted of ashes. In blind darkness, even his keenest remaining sense abandoned him – the guts-and-blood stench inside the wagon proved so overpowering that Threadgill could smell nothing else. The improvised bandage on his head felt stiff, dirty.

Time to time, Threadgill could feel hot wind gust up through splintery cracks in the wooden bed of the wagon. Once, a puff followed the bullet hole in his chest all the way through him.

Time passed. Rain passed too.

Morning light paled the wagon canvas. Threadgill could now make out at least a dozen men rocking along in bloody silence. More lay flat and still, swathed like mummies. He saw arms bandaged, or heads. Blood oozed from a bare foot near Threadgill's face.

"Lord God I wisht I had a plug of terbacco," someone gruffed, the first words Threadgill had heard in hours.

"You'd mos' likely just put it in your mouth and chaw it."

The wagon rocked along.

"Aw hell. Here go, Bert."

A squatting man turned his face in surprise to a second soldier, shot through both legs. The speaker had an accent Threadgill didn't recognize. Was he Confederate or Yankee? Why couldn't Threadgill tell? Everyone looked the same here.

Threadgill watched the squatting man extend one arm – his other splinted – and take, yes, a plug of tobacco.

"Last I got. Won't need it where I'm goin'."

"Obliged."

Some time later, Threadgill drifted into a dream. A ball of fire rolled around and around a field, burning cotton rows and pea patches and farm animals, scorching black the earth.

That ball of fire kept on across the South, burning everything it touched, candling humans, black and white and young and old, igniting antebellum houses and log cabins and plank shacks, blasting the crowns of trees, scalding rivers dry right down to black fish and charred stones.

***

The wagon creaked to a stop.

Threadgill came back to wakefulness in the new round of groans and pained cries. His own scorched skin kept up a steady hissing, a skillet of bacon sizzling in his head.

He heard a new sound, a dragon chuff, pierced by squeals, and some kind of ringing bell.

These noises would have frightened Threadgill if he'd never heard a train. But the boy Threadgill once left flints on railroad tracks near Eufaula and watched sparks flare from the iron wheels that rushed past, crushed past.

He now heard fretful horses blend with the locomotive sounds. Voices approached the ambulances.

Strange voices.

Terror gripped Threadgill in a merciless black claw again. *Is it happening all over?* Had Threadgill gone through hope and agony and fought back a rolling sun of pure fire all these days to be cruelly taken by men in Yankee blue after all?

He thought of Ben, convulsing in the middle of a Georgia road, a dark spot spreading beneath his head.

Yankees did that.

Now men climbed into the hospital wagon and stood over him.

"This one. This one too. This one later – just move him out of the way. Get ours out first, boys. Easy now."

Hard boots on the wagon bed. Threadgill felt an excruciating nudge, the point of a black boot. A polished boot, new.

This can't be happening, Threadgill's soul cried out. *Only Yankees wear new boots.* His mind ran as fast as a galloping horse down a long corridor with a bright open window at one end …

"Able to walk, son?"

Threadgill wanted to answer, even had the right word in the right place in his mouth. Before he gave a sound, though, rough hands jerked him by his upper arms and lifted. Sheer pain struck him dumb. An incredible lightning strike flashed through the constant dreary pounding rain of misery. Threadgill's tongue cleaved to the roof of his mouth – he fought to keep from swallowing it. He couldn't breathe for pain.

A fourteen-year-old soul rose momentarily toward heaven.

He floated, feet-first, through white space. The air grew lighter, cooler.

Boots shuffled awkwardly, and men made the grunting sounds men make under a heavy load.

Threadgill floated down from the wagon, gentled onto the ground.

Soft grass kissed his wounded back.

Firewood crackled. Outside the stifling wagon, Threadgill could smell once more. He turned his head as far as he was able, peeked beneath the crusted bandage.

He lay in a clearing filled with wounded soldiers. A doctor toiled at a makeshift plank table. The doctor's sleeves were rolled, arms red to the elbows. Amputated arms and legs made a curious pale jumble on the ground at one end of the table. Threadgill saw a bonfire, a black pot of water at full boil. A colored man assisted the surgeon, stuffing bloody sheets into the kettle, pushing them down with a broken oak limb.

Footsteps.

A shadow fell over Threadgill.

He squenched his eyes.

"Son, let's see what we got here. You'll feel my hand. Be as still as you can."

Threadgill could barely understand the words. What language? What kind of place? Was he a prisoner? What would Yankees do to him? What they did to Ben?

The man snipped with scissors at the crusted cloth that covered the top and back of Threadgill's head.

The boy took a deep breath and flinched his whole body. He already knew how bad this would be.

The cloth lifted. The whole top of his head peeled away, adhering to bloody cotton strips.

Threadgill could see his own suffering, just as plain, held up and examined with shock by the stranger. For a wild moment, the marvelous green circles in the sky looked like lily pads, layers of them, floating over him in bright blue water.

They resolved as leaves on a huge tulip poplar tree. They moved ever so slightly in the wind, and a white bird burst out of them and flew away.

Now the man's face, wearing no expression at all, replaced this view.

A neatly trimmed little beard. A big nose. Little gold-frame glasses. Eyes like black buttons. A battered leather bag. Those new boots.

"God in heaven help you, son."

He wore a filthy uniform, full of holes.

Confederate gray.

Chapter 8, Lash LaRue

Baldwin County, Alabama – Summer 1964

Threadgill slung the bedroll to his shoulder, winced a little. Sore muscles. He straightened his hat and crossed a tattered, sandspurred, bayside park. His head bobbed like a pack mule's.

He flopped his gear down smack between the wheel ruts in the middle of a sand road. No shrinking violet here.

I got a war to finish, Threadgill said.

He squinted at the morning while he stuffed in his shirt tail. An angry, purulent sun fumed back of a few clouds – the seed of a blazing hot day in Alabama.

Threadgill hadn't ridden in many cars. He wasn't really fond of the experience. He always felt like something packed in a can.

Still, a man with a war to settle couldn't wait stuck by the road. Not in this Alabama heat. Not at 114 years old. A car might be awful, but it went places fast.

With luck, he might even reach Montgomery in a single day.

The sandy road fronted a long row of wind-twisted live oaks. Gray Spanish moss licked the breezes.

Down the dirt road a mystery car appeared, then disappeared behind a curve.

White dust rose over weeds, marking the car's approach.

The black Cadillac exploded into view in a cloud of dragonflies, ruptured cattail tufts, terrified nutria. Vines trailed like green guts from the car's bumper.

Threadgill Pickett felt a shiver of apprehension.

The careening Cadillac braked. It warily sniffed the ground in front of Threadgill. And it must have liked him – unexpectedly, the windshield wipers leaped energetically to life.

S*pit! spat! spit! spat*!

Threadgill heard a gruff curse, a loud thump. The merry wipers stopped mid-windshield.

An electric window purred down.

The utterly bald head was already talking when it thrust out into the sunshine. Threadgill wondered if the owner of such a voice gargled with buckshot every morning.

"Just imagine, Hoss! You're fifty-five years old, no spring chicken now, but you got a roomy little car, a might old, but still a little crackerjap – wait! Hold on!"

The wipers, apparently on their own, swept the windshield again, swatting aside fallen leaves and wild grapes. The stranger pulled his head into the car and brought a fist down so hard on the dash that a piece of bright metal pinged out the window and landed in the weeds. The wipers surrendered a second time, hands straight up in the air.

The driver leaned into the sun again. He hawked up a loogey and loudly spat. The sticky yellow gob hung glistening on a dead log. Fire ants capered toward it, delighted.

Threadgill caught a whiff of something foul from the car.

The driver yawped. "See, Hoss, you got you a Cadillac. You got you a full tank of gas with a tiger in it. You got a sewing machine under the hood. Best thing, you got a head fulla ideas just waiting to turn into crisp new dollar bills. You savvy?"

Threadgill stared. His old ears howled, suddenly full of confused wolves. Was this driver drunk? Out of his mind?

"I'm trying to get to Maine," Threadgill interrupted. "I'm going up there to kill the last Yankee."

The driver, wordless now, whistled softly. Respect showed in his eyes.

"Sir, you just got yourself a ride to just this side of Montgomery. Me and my friends in back will be honored to share your company."

"Much obliged."

The man grinned, extended a big dirty hand.

"Laaaa-RUE!" he yelled. "Larry LaRue! They call me Lash!"

"Threadgill Pickett."

Threadgill stepped around to the passenger side, threw his gear on the front floorboard. Threadgill now saw that LaRue's right arm ended in a sort of weird crab pincer – an artificial limb, gold or brass, with a hook attachment. The prosthesis gleamed in sunlight.

The left arm was nearly as fantastic as the artificial one. An elaborate blue tattoo entwined the limb, choking out the flesh in a thicket of vines, anchors, ribbons, Chinese dragons, women with swords, pierced hearts, bare-breasted mermaids, Celtic knots, stylized names of ladies, heraldic shields, and copulating snakes.

Threadgill climbed in on the passenger side. To his surprise, LaRue turned out to be a smallish man, enlarged greatly by bluster and his gargantuan black car. He did boast a giant's voice though, deep and crackly, a baby bullhorn.

"Did you know?" LaRue squinted at Threadgill over his pair of blue pilot shades. "If you drink enough whiskey, it will purify you from the inside?"

***

Twenty miles inland, the Cadillac moved like ebony lightning through south Alabama's potato and corn fields.

"So, Hoss, that's my genius idea," LaRue announced. "Remind you of any other genius?"

"Can't rightly say." Threadgill was forced to shout over the wind that hurricaned out of the car's mighty air conditioner.

LaRue winked and tapped the tip of his hook against his cranium. A tiny jewel of blood appeared there.

"Old Bert Einstein!" he declared. "This genius idea of mine is big as any Old Bert Einstein ever come up with! You heard of him? Well, it don't matter. Old Bert Einstein knows who he is."

Without warning, the incorrigible windshield wipers leapt to life again. They scrubbed halfway across the glass but stopped cold with a grinding noise after LaRue clouted the dashboard once again with a clenched left fist.

"Hammer of God!" LaRue muttered hotly. "Anyway, my point is this, Hoss. Every soul that stops by the Snow White Motel in Hope Hull, Alabama, from now on till Doomsday is gonna want to own one of Uncle Lash LaRue's little Unky Monkeys! Man, woman and child!"

Threadgill glanced over his shoulder with a sort of vague dread.

A single large chicken-wire cage took up the back seat. It held at least three dozen squirrel monkeys.

Tiny furious assassins glared at Threadgill.

Sullen and silent, their faces swollen like bad drunks, the animals appeared to want nothing in this world more than to crawl down Threadgill's throat and bring his ripped kidneys back up, dripping, in their sharp white teeth.

"I reckon that's a strong cage," Threadgill said.

LaRue's crazy grin nearly hit the dashboard.

"Chrome steel! Strong as a goddamn bank vault!"

Threadgill Pickett took a deep breath – one he fervently wished he could hold all the way to Montgomery. His gear teetered in the front floorboard between his knees. He looked down on the sly, to make sure nothing wet trickled under the seat.

LaRue flourished his artificial hand. "Genius ideas just strike me like durned lightning bugs out of the blue. Ever had that happen?"

"Never cared much for the blue."

The air conditioner made a little popping sound, then a hiss. A few drops of water spewed onto the floorboard.

LaRue grinned dreamily.

"See, Hoss," he breezed. "I'm watching a Tarzan movie on TV when a little voice comes on in my head and says, 'Larry LaRUE! – just like that – Larry LaRUE!' You go buy up a bunch of them adorable squirrel monkeys with little babydoll hands and feet, little enough to sit in a man's palm of his hand, just that size, and bring 'em back home to sell to travelers for pets. Hey! Unky Monkeys! That's what 1964 people want in this country! That's happening!"

LaRue hitched up his pants with his hook.

"Now, honest to Pete, ask yourself one little question here, Mister Pickett. Just look back there – wouldn't anybody want one of these cute little animals in that back seat? One to carry on a silver chain and dress up in a red velvet vest or maybe a gold-lamé jacket like Liberace? One to hold a parasol over your old lady while she cuts okry out in the hot sun? Sure they want one, Hoss! Folks gonna pay good money!"

LaRue crowed like a rooster.

"They'll put up a marble statue to Lash LaRue one day!"

More than a little, LaRue reminded Threadgill of a big weird bird. The beak, a nose broken more than once to judge from its crooks, could open a can of Spam. His right arm was a brass talon. The bald vulture head sported lonely black hairs, flagpoles on pink moles the size of pencil erasers. He even wore a black shirt; its short sleeves fluttered like feathers in the car's powerful air-conditioning.

Threadgill liked the AC. The air in the car felt cool, if canned and unnatural.

"You wanna know what else?" LaRue sniffed.

The driver jerked the car around a farmer's green tractor, chugging down the road, its tail raised threateningly toward the Cadillac like a scorpion.

"Anybody out there coulda had this idea. *Anybody*. All they had to do was to take out the back seat of the car, put in an extra big cage, drive to the monkey smugglers down on Mobile Bay, and shell out enough cashola to buy forty-two cute little squirrelly boogers. But you know what?"

"No," Threadgill confessed. "I don't."

"Nobody actually up and did it but one man, and one man alone – and that was Larry LaRue. And you know why?"

LaRue, with enormous significance, tapped his forehead again with the sharp shiny point of his hook. Another spot of blood.

"Old Bert?" Threadgill guessed.

"Durn tootin'."

Threadgill heard the moist sound of bowels loosening.

He turned to the cage. The monkeys panted and drooled, rolling their eyes like bad silent movie actors doing death scenes. One foamed at the mouth. Only a few appeared able to lift shaggy heads off a flyblown mound of dog food, banana peels and feces clotting the bottom of their ramshackle cage.

"You know," LaRue continued," I wouldn't have waited so long if I'd known there were monkey smugglers that put in right there at Mobile Bay. Hey, turns out there's *every kind* of smuggler comes in here. Monkeys, parrots, Mexican babies, stuff to keep your pecker hard, dope – you want it, they got it chuggin' right up the bay, twenty-four-seven.

"The way I see it," he went on, "a man will smoke dope and his money's just gone up in smoke. He can suck that powder up his nose, and nothing's left sooner or later but one big white nostril. But give a man a monkey, and he's got a friend. For *life*. A clean, hygenic little pal that's gonna live by his side for thirty, forty years. I looked it up. Hell, that's a better sidekick than Gabby Hays."

Threadgill watched one of the monkeys roll backward in a swoon, fall stiffly against the wire. Wet fur slathered its dried-apple face. A grotesque red dart of tongue flickered in and out. All at once, white vomit brimmed over the animal's cracked black lips. It spilled like boiled milk over a half-dozen other monkeys.

"These fellers are bad sick," Threadgill offered.

"Naw!" LaRue turned and stretched his prosthesis over the seat. Through the chicken wire, he nudged one of the monkeys that appeared surely to be dead. It lay stiff as a mummy on the floor of the cage. But it made a soft sound like a kitty in its sleep. Then it spit up too.

"Seasick!" LaRue said happily. "That's all. This old car sloshes them around just like that shrimper boat did. They ain't got their land legs. But they bounce back pretty fast. Little boogers got right lively parked back in those reeds where we loaded 'em up."

LaRue bounded the big Cadillac onto an improved four-lane and gunned the engine.

"Awooooooo!" he howled.

The G-forces slid the monkeys in a solid lump across the slick floor of their cage.

Acceleration! Threadgill felt the thrill too. He suddenly understood why all those chase scenes forever happened on TV shows.

"I got one everlasting bulldog of a car!" LaRue exulted. "Four-hundred and fifty horses! My future and my fortune in my own back seat. Awwwoooo!"

The driver crammed a soft stick of Juicy Fruit into his mouth. He turned to check the cage; eighty-four glowering, contemptible, furious eyes glared back. LaRue widened the stares with a wild laugh, his hook hand rattling the cage.

"Y'all perk up!" he barked cheerfully. "Pretty soon we'll all be drinking Bubble Up and eating that Rainbow Pie. Whoo-ee!"

Threadgill slipped toward weary sleep.

As he drifted off, an old memory came unstoppably marching, with the foul car odors, right up his sensitive nose.

A three-day dead Confederate soldier leered up, wreathed in flies, from a hot roadside in Georgia.

The carcass smelled so bad the buzzards staggered away weeping, shaking their heads like mourners, shabby hands in their pockets.

Threadgill dreamed.

Chapter 9, Yellowhammer

Johnny Yellowhammer. Up it hops, limb to trembling limb. Dreamy, springwhite dogwoods.

Blossoms shake free, miracle snowflakes.

A hot sun sets. Yellowhammer lifts its beak to purple clouds, flutes a lilting spill.

Four notes. Four more notes. Four higher notes. It never repeats. Music like moonlit water, stone over stone.

White flicker. Yellowhammer flutters over the dogwoods and into cathedral heights of poplar, gum, hickory. The air cools, limbs wonderously fanned by late breeze.

Stars glint. Moon rises.

Yellowhammer peers down, telescopically. Keen eyes see sugar ants trickle the trunk of the poplar, a glistening serpent of flowing black particles. Beetles on the ground ram heads in combat. Earthworms slide like sighs in, out of moist black soil.

Down there, an old man lies asleep, stiff as a Golem.

A memory causes him to stir. He raises a hand quietly to his face, settles again. He does not wake.

Yellowhammer sees the signal … and takes flight.

Yellowhammer fixes the bright crumb of Polaris with an anthracite eye.

It climbs. The poplar tree falls away, and pale dogwoods shrink to whitecaps on a wide black sea.

Yellowhammer swings north.

Over troubled Montgomery. On to troubled Birmingham.

Jones Valley seems a strewn fire, the steel mills sprawled, breathing dragons. Gas flares flutter. Scorched people hurry in and out of molten underworlds. The workers might be sugar ants too, rivering along paths. Instead of eggs or morsels, they haul tools, paper sacks, loads of steel pipe, buckets, boxes. They speed in tiny vehicles, bright as shellac when they pass under a light. Their faces shine with soot.

A massive statue of Vulcan, god of the forge, raises a victory torch, ignites one low star after another.

Yellowhammer remembers the songs passed down by generations. Once upon a time, birds sing it, the world rose out of earth and seed, the world started green. Every blade of grass. Every forest.

Green as the eyes of God.

God's eyes grow sooty now.

Yellowhammer crosses the humped hard spine of Red Mountain. It shadows gravestone-white row houses. Tricycles rust in deep weeds, in caustic dew. Old ladies sit on porches and gasp asthmatically into handkerchiefs. Parts fall off cars. Slag spills off roadways, charred, white as ash. Sunbleached plastic flamingoes, one-legged, lie fallen on bitterbrown lawns.

Things fall apart.

Yellowhammer remembers the songs of men in blue and gray, the songs of blacks, stripped to the waist. Did all of them really fight and struggle and die to end up with a world so bleak?

Yellowhammer feels fresher over open countryside.

Tincture of moonlight.

Gigantic monsters creep far below highways. Each holds a cargo of coal and a single lonesome driver, face lit eerie, ghostblue, in dashboard light. Steaming coffee rises, bitter as hemlock, to pinched mouths. Yellowhammer can hear, far away, human songs squawling from radios that keep the drivers awake, country songs surrogate for missing homes and hopes and happiness.

Gray wings lap the miles over miles, endless miles.

Wood.

Field.

River.

Cropland.

Burning animal eyes glare at sky. Their cries rise like prayers.

Yellowhammer skips one ridge to the next ridge, soars over arched dorsal fins of mountain.

Sand Mountain. Cahaba Mountain. Double Oak Mountain. Lookout Mountain.

Peace in their valleys.

New bright lights, clustered urban campfires. Chattanooga clouds, strangely like the smoke of battle, hug a ridge.

Yellowhammer recalls the tale: Audacious bad-ass Yankees scrambled straight up the wooded face of this promontory to seize the clouds.

Damn the torpedoes. Damn the mouths of cannon, the sharp rebel bayonets. Damn the Yankees. They climb hard.

They put a business on top of every mountain.

Chapter 10, LaRue's Last Stand

Alabama – Summer 1964

In the first hours, LaRue slowed only once.

A gaggle of hysterically laughing cracker children stood, sunburned, in the middle of the highway north of Stockton. As they fanned away gnats and blue smoke, the kids took turns puffing a huge cigar, then putting it to the stubby tail of a miserable, doomed snapping turtle caught halfway across US 31.

The Cadillac's deceleration and the delighted shrieks of the children briefly stirred the monkeys and old Threadgill back to wakefulness. But LaRue sped up again, Threadgill sank into the buttery softness of the Cadillac's black upholstery, and the monkeys fainted back to silence.

Time passed. Miles passed.

The travelers rocketed through little picture-perfect towns set under arcades of ancient, elephant-gray oaks. Sunlight draped the heavy limbs, and resurrection fern glowed gold and green in the high places.

Between catnaps, Threadgill briefly studied the luxuries of the Cadillac. The dashboard boasted ranks of electric switches and dials, complicated as a pipe organ. LaRue simply touched a button here, a button there. A window slid up. A door locked. The air conditioner gushed. White magic.

Especially the AC.

On any given summer day in the tropical South, temperatures melted candles inside houses, and tiny dragons hatched in bags of rice in kitchen cupboards.

But here in Lash LaRue's car all was well with the world.

It was coooooooooooooooool.

So what made LaRue switch off the air every few minutes and roll down his windows?

He read Threadgill's thoughts.

"Gremlins. All in the wires. I run the air too long, red lights pop up on my dashboard. Looks like Christmas," LaRue explained. He buzzed down all four windows and the thundering heat of Alabama engorged the car for a moment. "Get it fixed here directly with my monkey money!"

Threadgill felt eyes on him, and glanced back. The monkeys now lay together in one corner of the cage, a miserable, foul-smelling, overheated, bemerded mound of fur, feet, prehensile tails.

"Looka here, Hoss! Tourists! Hooo!"

The target of LaRue's high spirits now was a sunburned family huddled under a concrete awning at a roadside picnic area. They blinked like stunned refugees, their mouths working corners of pimento cheese sandwiches. The daddy of the family sucked at the mouth of a tea jug. Three scruffy redheads, all boys, sat at a separate table, throwing sandspur sandwiches to the seagulls. One child crushed a boiled egg in his hand like a soft little head. The mother, uselessly protesting, held a red-hot, screaming infant against her shoulder.

"Honey bunny!" LaRue hollered at her. "Nice titties!"

The Cadillac tore past a bait shack and a beer store. These appeared to be the last signs of human habitation before the highway entered the tangled everglades of the Mobile River Delta.

Here, if possible, the heat grew even worse. Threadgill decided they might as well be driving through the middle of the sun. No breezy roadside zephyrs cooled the car. No chilly breaths exhaled from the swamp. Even the visual aids failed; there were no Annette Funicellos wandering the sidewalks in cute shorts, no carefree Frankies in funny bermuda shorts. All the roadside distractions lay behind: Bait Land, Alabama Snake Farm, The Boobie Trap Exotic Dance Barn, Holy Land Amusement Park. Threadgill felt heat and heat alone: alligator-breeding, fruit-fouling heat.

LaRue appeared heedless. Windows still down, he whooped sporadically to spook a great blue heron into flight or scare a snake off some low cypress limb. One big cottonmouth hung close enough to snag with a crowbar.

"I've seen my fifty-fifth summer!" howled LaRue. "I've held the hottest job in the Navy, working down in the boiler room in the steel guts of a Hell-cat carrier! I've stoked the engines when kamikazes swarmed over the whole goddamn ship like yellow jackets! I gnawed off my own arm, durn it, to get away from that ugly Filipino gal without waking her up. Yessirree, old timer, if there's one thing I know, it's HEAT! And heat ain't killed Larry LaRue yet. Hear?"

He yelled right up at the sun, squinting.

"Not yet, you goddamn summer pus bump!"

LaRue flipped on the radio. It spit out a big spark at him – *Zzzzrrp*! Then Roy Orbison got in the car. Mooning, moaning, all out of sorts.

LaRue yelled at the singer too.

"Bad luck, Roy Boy? Phooey! You got to fight it, Orby! Fight it, pussy boy! You got to haul out the big dream, get tough, get going …"

Threadgill flinched at a plaintive monkey cry in falsetto. LaRue eyed the rearview mirror in surprise. The creature trembled in a spasm, rolled over, shook violently against the cage door, a little dried leaf in a hurricane.

"Heat stroke!" LaRue barked at him. "Seen it a hundred times. It don't kill hardly nobody."

Another monkey had a seizure. The tiny hand opened and closed once on the wire of the cage.

The radio babbled at full boil. *Dangerously hot*, it singsonged, the deejay with a voice like spoonsful of ice cream on chilled strawberries somewhere. *One hundred four degrees – Saturday's got a fever, folks!*

The monkey convulsions seemed to bring LaRue closer to earth.

"Hmm. One hundred and four. Might be too hot after all for little things in fur coats today," he suggested to Threadgill. "I better chill 'em down!"

LaRue flicked on the air conditioner. Instantly, Siberian winter howled in. Threadgill felt delicious chills over his scorched body. A little whining moan rose from the dashboard.

LaRue winked at Threadgill.

"Man versus heat! Man WINS!" he yelled.

One window glided up.

"Man wins again!" he yelled. Windows two and three closed.

"Man — "

Now came a terrific soul-rending brain-splitting screech of pain from the back seat. It rose in a wobbly crescendo, louder, LOUDER, finally big and fierce enough to chatter the very windows of the Cadillac.

It was the end of time.

It was the Scream of the Universe.

Jesus! What WAS it?

LaRue twisted to look, then immediately recoiled so violently that he banged his shocked head on the rear view mirror.

A frantic, doll-sized monkey flopped and flipped against the glass directly in back of Threadgill. The power window had pinned its head. In agony, the monkey thrashed and wiggled like a fur snake with its head trapped under a stick. Its scream hurt even the back of Threadgill's eyes.

If that sight didn't shake LaRue, the next one surely did.

Forty-one furious fellow monkeys slowly, sickly, oozed in one moist brown mass out the gaping open door of the chicken wire cage.

The lock on the cage had failed.

LaRue lost the car in his dismay.

The black Cadillac bounded onto the rutted, cat-tailed shoulder, flattened a PERDIDO 17 MILES sign and came sideways around in a fishtail of mud, rubber and ripped vegetation. The engine coughed. The car shivered a moment. Then all went perfectly still.

It came to Threadgill at once. *This will be very, very bad.*

Without motion, the monkeys felt no motion sickness.

Threadgill quickly opened his duffel bag, put his feet inside, yanked the heavy laundry canvas completely over him like a cocoon. He wrapped the blankets of the bedroll over his head and shoulders. Then, deep in padding, Threadgill's hand pinched shut the lone opening at his face, and he disappeared from view.

Larry LaRue only had time to gulp once before a slick brown wave crashed over him from the back seat.

***

Threadgill found his thoughts drifting, little white heedless balloons floating up through the quiet eye of a cyclone.

He recalled frying bacon, in boyhood years ago, the smoking skillet, the grease popping – *ouch!* – onto his arm.

He thought of the time he saw a wild fox tear the heads off Aunt Annie's chickens.

He remembered a dream. A poor fellow stood in the door of a burning house, all on fire, waving both arms in slow motion like a flaming snowman.

The Cadillac rocked on its axles.

Threadgill distantly heard LaRue's cries over the chilly gale of banshees. He imagined LaRue as a giant covered with very fast, very fierce, fantastically agile biting gnomes with serrated teeth and forty-two unholy grudges.

Threadgill envisioned the breakout. In one corner of his suspecting mind, he saw a clever little monkey hand reach through the chicken wire with a rusted six-penny nail, pulled from some loose joint in the cage. The creature poked nail into keyhole – *voila!* A fateful click, a lock opened, snatched free.

LaRue must have been too busy yelling out window to notice.

He'll listen next time, Threadgill thought. *If he still has his ears.*

He dared a peek.

Monkeys covered LaRue like a fur disease.

Rebel yells had turned to painful screams now. Threadgill wondered how LaRue even made those.

Monkeys savaged his lips. They put their heads into his mouth and bit his tongue. They chewed his cheeks. They ripped out his nose hair and loosened their bowels down the neck of his black silk shirt. Assailants attacked from every side. They even went after his hook – Threadgill got a snapshot view of dozens of small, toothlike indentations over a saliva-slick brass surface.

The escaped prisoners vented their rage on the Cadillac too. Monkeys tore foam rubber padding from the seats. They emptied their bladders over the dashboard and spurted feces down the AC vents. They flew through the air in acrobatic leaps, ripped open a carton of Camels and hurled broken cigarettes in all directions. They brutally shredded road maps, pulled monkey wrenches – monkey wrenches! – and empty Suncrest orange bottles from under the seat and beat LaRue with them. The driver's expensive sunglasses covered the seat in blue chips.

Something electrical went wrong too, once and for all.

The car's air conditioning coughed, newly gummed up with monkey excrement. The dash panel issued a piercing sound like a dental drill, then a white spark leaped from the control console. A mushroom puff of black smoke followed, billowing out of the dashboard, rising to destruction against the roof.

Frantically, LaRue flipped open vents to clear the air. The act brought new and even blacker clouds of smoke roiling from the AC, followed by a sudden jet of frothy burned-pimento-cheese liquid that dribbled over his shoes.

The car became unbelievably hot at once. Threadgill's blankets were now his sweat lodge. Huge black pansies bloomed in his field of vision.

There came a pattering, and Threadgill knew the monkeys attacked his own blankets. A tiny wicked face actually popped into his peephole. Bubbles of raging snot shot from the creature's nose. Threadgill quickly pinched off that view.

He felt the whirlpool of monkeys close, linger, leave abruptly for LaRue again like a migrating flock of birds.

He peeked again.

LaRue wore a toupee of biting monkeys. Toothmarks cratered his scalp, and his ear hung like it was stapled on. His cranium looked like a freshly skinned possum.

The driver's good hand fumbled in the floorboard, desperately groping for car keys, these wickedly snatched away by his tormentors.

No keys.

Finally, LaRue grabbed the door handle. Threadgill was surprised his surrender took so long.

The door stayed shut.

It was welded, the power locks electrically overruled.

Smoke poured from the dashboard.

Black acrid midnight gathered inside the Cadillac.

Then – a plain stroke of Providence – LaRue's flailing hand somehow found car keys.

His scream of triumph momentarily froze the monkeys. Just for a second. Just long enough.

LaRue jammed the keys into the ignition. The engine roared. The car lurched ahead, woozy but mobile.

The instant the Cadillac moved, the monkeys immediately melted away into docility, motion sickness taking the fight from them. Wherever they were in the car, they swooned feebly back against the seats, doors or windows.

As hot as it was, Threadgill refused to come out of his teepee.

***

The speeding Cadillac traveled north.

Crickets and cicadas yelled with all their might outside. *Let 'em yell*, Threadgill thought. *They could yell for all eternity and never fill up a thimble.*

Threadgill *drove* the black Cadillac now. He'd never been at the wheel of an automobile before. He'd only ridden in a few – once a police car, once an ambulance, once a trip to a doctor for geriatrics who wanted to study him, simply amazed at his robust health.

Now Threadgill drove.

It was effortless for him at 120 mph.

The white stripes on the highway hypnotically danced under his humming wheels. Threadgill thought of swimming sea snakes in a gray ocean. Telephone poles flickered past. Every time Threadgill crossed a rickety bridge over some nameless slough, the racket of roadside insects in the woods briefly ceased. A gust of silence.

The road was very lonely. Not much traffic in these parts. The grumbling 18-wheel Macks and Peterbilts traveled faster routes, leaving the godforsaken lonely back roads to black Cadillacs with old men at the wheel.

Ahead in the road, the glowing eyes of some creature blinked red semaphore. Threadgill watched a cloudy shape on four legs gallump into the weeds.

Live to fight another day, possum. Threadgill cast the thought, like a prayer, into the dark where the animal disappeared, where overgrowth lay down on either side of the road to worship as the Cadillac passed.

The dashboard clock said 3 a.m. Who knew if that was right? Who cared?

The Cadillac passed a mobile home. A husky red-haired boy chunked rocks at bull bats dive-bombing a streetlight. The boy threw a rock at the Cadillac too.

Crack!

Threadgill lost the road. A wheel dropped off the pavement and dragged a thousand feet of goldenrod and dog fennel down a muddy shoulder. Threadgill wrestled the steering wheel, and slammed the brakes in a panic.

A large shape filled the windshield.

The Cadillac's tires screamed and smoked.

Then everything stopped.

Chapter 11, Oak House

January 1850 – Near Eufaula, Alabama

Her belly was swollen. Her back hurt. Still, seventeen-year-old Katherine Pickett did her best to keep cheerful.

It wasn't easy. Endless unbroken overcast days came and went. No letter arrived from Mexico. Something stood on her bladder, and morning sickness hung on.

Worst of all turned out to be her sister's house.

Something felt dreadfully wrong here.

On occasion, the newest and largest mansion in southeast Alabama seemed quite fine to the young mother-to-be. Its wrought-iron balconies swarmed with ornate classical scenes, masterfully forged by craftsmen from Paris. Its plaster faces displayed fantastically wrought botanical designs, these by New Orleans artisans. Its woodworked banisters and balustrades and cabinets carried charm and spoke of class.

Outside, pewter-gray gardens stretched away in the rain, misty and silent, the fruit trees leafless. Superb oil paintings of these same fields, happily flooded with sunlight, hung over a dozen blazing fireplaces. Beveled-glass windows, imported all the way from Murano in Italy, let through a jeweled church-light in fleeting moments when the sun briefly glinted through midwinter clouds.

Most hours, though, the eighteen high-ceilinged rooms stood in gloom. It felt as quiet here as a house beneath water.

Kate read novels and imagined herself among supernatural characters in the elegantly drowned cabins of some enormous wrecked galleon at the bottom of a cold sea.

***

Kate Pickett never really grew up close to her big sister Sealy, not in emotions or age – sixteen years separated the siblings. But Kate's move during her pregnancy to Oak House from the wild country at Baker Hill had made practical sense.

Old Sparks-family wealth built Oak House – Kate would always be comfortable in Sealy's care, now that her big sister had married Sparks money. In fact, Dr. Deed Sparks had earned himself a good reputation above and beyond his planter family's. Excellent medical care would be close at hand in Oak House. It proved a comfort to Kate, who feared childbirth and had vivid and terrible premonitions about it.

Twins, Dr. Sparks told her. Due in January, a month after Jesus.

Kate's husband, Lieutenant Randoll Pickett, served with the United States Cavalry in Mexico. He wrote now and again, letters filled with plans and encouragement and misspelled words, all hastily scratched onto stiff parchment with what might have been a cactus spine, to judge by the faintness of the ink.

Last of nine Pickett children, Rand inherited a hind-tit forty acres a few years earlier when his father passed away. The teenager attempted for several seasons to make small cotton crops as his father had done, and his father before him. But after years of overwork, the gummy clay of the old Pickett place produced blackberry vines and pine trees and honeysuckle faster than any cash crop.

Rand had one way out – an older brother in the army. And Rand could read and write. Every few months, his letter from Mexico brimmed with a yarn of adventure and derring-do. *We are finding desperate outlaws hidden with their long knives in the mountains. I ride this morning to a stone temple in the jungle taller than the tallest house in Alabama.* Kate wondered how everything her husband wrote could possibly be true.

Rand Pickett had shipped out in midsummer, 1850. Coming from Clio after he cleared up a few business accounts, he rode up to their marriage cabin in the woods near Baker Hill on a handsome black horse, just at dark, a skyful of stars over one shoulder. Dressed in his blue uniform, he stepped down and bowed to Kate, who stood with one trembling hand in the tangle of honeysuckle climbing the rough porch post.

She had dreaded the departure day for weeks.

That evening, Kate lit tallow candles and placed them in the bedroom windows of the cabin. The flames danced and trembled all night with their lovemaking.

The next morning, two children grew inside Kate. And Rand Pickett rode away to serve in the U.S. Army along the border with lawless Mexico.

Rain fell on every window the day Ben and Threadgill were born. It fell over the steeples of Eufaula, over the briar-scraggled fields, over the black-limbed hardwoods on the bluffs along the Chattahoochee River.

The young girl with the swollen belly sat awkwardly on the cold floor of her room in Oak House, thinking how much she despised days like this, and winters so dark and hours so lonely.

At age six, when still a Flannery, Kate had seen enough bad weather, in a single dose, to last a lifetime. She remembered, with a chilly shudder, the misery of her family's transatlantic passage from Cork – endless wet days, with nights so cold that icicles broke from the ship's rigging and daggered down onto her sleeping brothers and sisters. All thirteen Flanneries huddled under a tattered canopy on the ship's deck for five long weeks. The family stayed seasick, and Kate remembered how big-sister Sealy's hands chapped so badly in the raw winds that she couldn't hold onto a crust of bread.

Kate's father, Seamus Flannery, had dreamed all his life of moving from the south of Ireland to the American West. The burly, white-locked farmer scrimped and scraped, bewitched by the notion of wide open skies and free land. When Sam Houston's fighters opened Texas, he secretly began to hoard coins from his three-cow dairy business. He hid his treasure in a crock under a flat stone in the high field.

Famine came, of course. Potato blight ruined farm after farm. Granite bones showed through the skin of Flannery fields, and one day after a close neighbor walked away from his cottage and closed the door behind him forever, bound for America, Seamus Flannery made his own decision.

One sodden dusk, Kate Pickett's father stamped through the door and dropped his secret crock on the hearth – *crash!* – before the amazed eyes of his wife and children. They couldn't have been more surprised if he'd dragged in a squirming leprechaun with a pot of gold.

The coins bought ship passage from Skibbereen, with enough left over to purchase in the port of Charleston a rattletrap wagon and a tired horse.

Things went badly. The Flanneries tried to live off the land as they traveled, but feeding a family of thirteen with a single muzzle-loader had its challenges. Kate would never forget exactly how a skunk tasted ... or the look on the faces of her starved, hollow-eyed brothers and sisters as they cracked little gray bones to suck the marrow.

Wretched weather didn't help. The elements continued to curse their journey across the southern pinelands. Everyone kept a cold for weeks.

Mairee, Kate's little sister, passed with fever. She was gone in just two days. Seamus Flannery fell to his knees weeping as they lowered his youngest child to rest in the sticky red soil of this strange country.

Within days of that sadness, Mr. Flannery's horse dropped its leg unexpectedly into a gopher tortoise burrow. The steed had to be put down.

The 50-year-old patriarch and his seven sons then, heroically, dragged the covered wagon for twenty-two days with their own hands. They might have hauled it all the way to Texas too, but for the rain-swollen Chattahoochee.

For a miserable week, the Flanneries waited by the rising water, nearing starvation. *How is starving here better than starving in Cork?* fussed Mrs. Flannery, her patience finally eaten clean through by hunger.

Desperate, the boys at last lashed together a log raft, dragged their wagon aboard, then precariously made to cross the muddy flood from Georgia to the Alabama side. They ended up fifty miles downriver, but safely over, after a dizzying, rudderless journey.

The Flanneries set off toward the sunset once more, men and boys rolling the muddy wagon wheels, lifting the tongue clear of bushes and stumps, bellowing like oxen under the load. Mrs. Flannery and the older daughters shepherded children along the trail behind this ruckus.

Finally, the wagon played its own cruel prank. Pushed beyond its rickety endurance, it collapsed for good less than twenty miles from the Chattahoochee crossing.

Seamus Flannery decided these piney woods looked enough like Texas.

His wolf pack of boys took axes and mauls and hewed out a respectable cabin and clearing in just six days. Under shelter again, their luck seemed to change. Spring arrived, and the woods swarmed with deer and wild turkey. Fresh water ran everywhere. The family put in a crop of potatoes, the seed crop brought all the way from Ireland in a sack.

They were saved.

On this homestead, Kate Pickett grew up. Both her mother and father rested in the earth there now. At the start of every spring, Kate pulled the weeds on their plots and raked away the long pine needles.

A tall, skinny boy from the next farm over helped gather the Flannery crop one year.

Later, Rand told his young bride, "The first time I saw you, you were running from a rooster in the yard. That very second, I knew."

Kate was 14 then; Rand was 17. He later told her it nearly killed him to wait a year to come courting.

***

Both Kate's parents passed away that next summer – diphtheria – and Rand Pickett saw his future. He promptly moved out of his family's cabin and built a separate one-room structure with his own hands on the piece of Pickett land nearest Kate Flannery.

He came courting. Dressed in his Sunday best, every hair wet down and perfectly in place, he broke in a pair of new shoes walking back and forth once a week through the woods to the Flannery cabin. Kate had a rough-hewn brother or two still living on the place, and they glared at the stranger. But big sister Sealy, already married to her doctor Sparks and his family money, approved the match. Sealy actually made carriage trips from Eufaula to sit in the Flannery cabin as Kate and Rand got acquainted.

Sealy kept quite busy as a chaperone that year. All three remaining Flannery girls married in eight months, to young men making their pledges. No girl wanted to live on their hardscrabble farm alone, scratching a living out of stingy topsoil and tending rough brothers.

So the circuit-riding preacher came to the woods three times that winter and spring. Redbirds flew through the branches, and the land flushed green. As the sisters went, so did the brothers, most simply disappearing into the woods on a sunny morning, off to join the world.

Rand kissed Kate for the first time on their wedding night. Her life would be complete now, he declared. He promised all the love a young man could shout down from the sky.

And he told her one other thing – he'd joined the U.S. Cavalry, signed the papers a week before their vows. He wanted to build a life she would be proud of. He would serve three years. He would come back with money. Here was their chance to get a start in this world.

***

Now nine months later, Kate fretted, filled with aches and pains, and she thought how her body seemed oddly like this new house, enormous and strange to her. She spent hours before the full-length mirror – the first she'd ever seen – examining her pregnant image.

"What is happening to me?" she wondered. "I have never been this person. I have never *seen* this person."

One rainy morning at the end of January, Kate settled onto the bedroom floor to paint a wooden rocking chair. She set out a bowl of leftover Christmas sweets and a cup of English tea. She unwrapped the imported chocolates, one by one, and ate them – a dozen in all. She stacked all the pretty papers.

Ben and Threadgill stirred.

Kate put her palm on her stomach. She felt lucky, a surge of happiness, all at once.

Deed Sparks made a good living, he had family money. He took care of the world's aches and pains. He provided, and Sealy was a good sister to let her baby sister stay here, in this safe, warm place, till her boys came. Her boys. Somehow Katie knew. She'd even picked out their names and secretly – daringly – signed them already onto the onion-skin pages in the front of Sealy's family Bible.

Benjamin and Threadgill would be her companions forever. Nothing would separate them and Kate – no power in this world.

If she could only stand the pain of it. Childbirth.

Rand Pickett would be so proud of her when he came home. Proud too of the names she'd chosen – Ben, Threadgill. She'd found them scratched onto the pages of his own family's Bible, two of those spidery blue etchings scrawled by a hand so old that no living person could now describe the writer's face.

Kate imagined her husband. He wore his spangled blue uniform. He rode high in the saddle on a handsome black stallion, with the blazing sun overhead. His tender thoughts traveled to her on the Mexican wind, arrived like caresses.

Rand Pickett was a strong, true man. Kate and he would have a wonderful life together, with bouncing babies on the cabin floor. Why, the day he came home with a hero's medals and a pouch of coins ...

The front door burst open, flew wide, slammed hard against a bookcase.

"Sealy!"

Gruff. A man's voice.

Kate nearly leaped out of her skin. Her startled babies kicked sharply.

A smallish figure in a soaked black greatcoat gusted in with a flurry of wet leaves. Mud caked the man's fine boots, and he did a little dance from the cold, spattering raindrops.

"Good God Almighty!" he exclaimed, flapping. "Cold as a priest's pod out there!"

That moment, Deed Sparks spotted Kate. His cold cheeks grew even redder, if that was possible. With embarrassment.

Or something.

"Why, Miss Kate," he recovered smoothly, making his way down the short hall and into her room. "I thought that was Sealy seated there. I mean … I didn't expect *you*."

His little gold pince-nez glasses fogged in the warm house. He self-consciously brought out a white cotton handkerchief from some hidden pocket.

He looked up, polishing, and stared straight at Kate. His eyes burned with a strange light. He spoke in a conspiratorial whisper.

"I didn't expect you, Katie Pickett," he said, "but how anyone could mistake you for Sealy is completely unforgivable. Because you, my dear, are completely beautiful. Especially beautiful. With child. Or without."

Katie dropped her head, distantly angry, and resumed her brushwork on the rocker.

"Yoo-hoo!" The call rose from a distant room. "Deed? Is it you?"

"Me, Sealy! It's me! Who did you think? One of the field hands?" He gave a nasty little sniggering laugh.

Sealy's heavy tread approached.

The doctor, still snorting, set his tiny glasses back to his nose. Little rain beads played chase around the brim of his hat, and his brown beard looked sodden.

"How do you feel, darling?" Doctor Sparks turned back to Kate, his voice overfilled with caring warmth.

She brushed red paint, a little roughly. "Very well, Deed Sparks. Like usual – like I swallowed two pumpkins."

Deed Sparks showed his fine white teeth. *A-hah-hah-ha!*

"Well, I do expect we'll be seeing our little jack o' lanterns soon now. It's still Deed and Sealy, is it?" The doctor swept off his hat and hung it soggily from a carved-cherry rack by the door.

Katie glanced then, knowing Deed's back was turned. Something seemed unsteady about him. He wore the heavy outer coat, partly unbuttoned now, a finely made white silk shirt and a woolen vest. He pulled off Kidd gloves and dropped them onto a froth of French lace on a parlor table. Then, from somewhere in the wet folds of his coat, he produced a package, large, wrapped in brown paper, tearstained with raindrops.

Sealy made it to the foyer. The room immediately grew smaller.

"Oh, Deed," she said, without a hello. "You're soaked. Let's get the help to take you out of those wet things. Nobody here is smart enough to doctor you, if you get sick."

"I'm sure I'll be fine, dear," Deed said. Looking up at the plaster ceiling, he snapped open the clasp of the wet topcoat and swept it off.

He gave Sealy a slight bow and handed her first the coat, then the brown package.

"Now before you even ask, dear," he began, "allow me to report the big news today from the Alabama medical world."

Sealy and Kate both lifted their heads.

"Eufaula," he said, "as of ten o'clock this morning, lays claim to Alabama's one and only seven-toed blacksmith."

"Jack?" Sealy asked.

"Jack McRae. The very same. Thick as a plank. Jack dropped an anvil on his foot and smashed three toes. This was the middle of last week. Of course, he didn't come to see me then, when it wasn't raining cats and dogs. When a doctor might have done some good. Oh no. He waited till the foot went septic and his toes turned black as little rat turds – *excusez-moi*, young Mrs. Pickett, for my graphic medical descriptions. Anyway at ten o'clock this morning, Jack McRae hurt so bad he'd have given me his firstborn child to get relief."

"You've been drinking, Deed."

Sealy delivered the words like a verdict.

"Why, yes, my dear. Yes I have. Very keen of you. But before you become too critical, have you ever seen what a drunk surgeon can do with a scalpel? One-handed, too – I used the other hand to pinch my nose so I wouldn't have to smell that bastard's rotting phalanges. And, my dear ... I brought you something ... a surprise ..."

Sealy turned pale.

Deed slipped his hand into his vest pocket. He brought out a carefully folded white handkerchief. A smile spread across his flushed face.

Kate stopped painting, or even pretending to.

"Deed!" Sealy warned. "Don't!"

"Voila! Les petit doigts, mesdames!"

The doctor brought forth from the cloth three small black objects the size of wild grapes. He squeezed one, and a shocking white-and-red flash of gristle showed where it once connected to the blacksmith's foot.

"You know," Deed remarked, "I could smell these putrid little turds all the way out on old McRae's front porch. I mean, right through the walls of his house and out in the pouring rain."

Sealy's horror rooted her to the floor. When she spoke, her voice broke.

"You get that – those things – out of my house! Now! "

Deed, with a shrug, did exactly as she asked. He turned, cracked the front door slightly – the wind snapped his breeches legs – and he flipped each of the toes, like a boy shooting marbles, across the wooden porch and out into the stormy front yard.

"Done!" Deed cried. He seemed all good cheer as he slammed the door and cut the two women off from the outside world. "What's for lunch?"

He rubbed his hands together like a fly.

"No, wait!" he announced suddenly. "Seal, first let's see what else the good doctor brought you – your other surprise!"

Kate couldn't even look now.

"Go ahead. This present came all the way from Gay Paree. Happy Birth-day!"

Kate's outsized sister had dwindled somehow, holding the big package to her breast. The doctor stood on his drunken tiptoes, and he was the one who filled the room now, blustering, loud. His face glowed like a stove.

"Aw, for godsakes, open it, Sealy. It's not going to bite you. It's something to help that poor old aching back you're always groaning about. Your god-damned aching back."

Unsure, Sealy began to tear the paper away. A striped, gaily printed box emerged. Brown paper drifted to the floor in shivering strips.

Was today really Sealy's birthday? Kate wondered. Oh dear! Another thing she'd forgotten …

"Now." Deed almost snarled at his wife. "Go on. Take the lid off …"

Sealy did. She let the top fall, and from the box she lifted an enormous woman's undergarment. Her eyes went wide, sad and astonished.

Kate had seen corsets before, but never one this size. It stretched wide like an accordion.

"Genuine whalebone!" Deed crowed. "From a genuine whale! It's just what the doctor ordered for you, darling!"

Sealy burst into tears. "Oh me," she said, covering her face with one hand. "Oh Deed ..."

"Now don't cry. We're just getting started," Deed said. "Put it on. And dry up those tears. Your backache days are over!"

The clock ticked loudly over the mantel, and Sealy's sobs filled the intervals.

"Put the damn thing on!" Deed snapped. "You'll feel so much better about yourself."

It might have gotten even worse. Things always could get worse at Oak House.

But that very moment, Kate saved her sister further humiliation.

Kate's water broke.

Things could always get worse at Oak House.

Chapter 12, The Snow White

Summer 1964 – Near Greenville, Alabama

Threadgill awoke at the very best part of his dream … or vision … or hallucination.

He found himself wrapped in swaddling clothes, mummy-deep in a torn blanket on the passenger's side of the front seat of Larry LaRue's Cadillac.

A dream.

No Threadgill in the driver seat. No wild ride with an old man at the wheel.

Larry LaRue? Gone too, like the dream. And all his bad monkeys. Every one.

Litter covered a wide area around the twisted, hissing Cadillac. Twigs. Chinaberries. Monkey fur. Broken glass.

There seemed to have been some kind of accident. The car's crumpled hood and front grille hugged a badly skinned chinaberry tree. Hot radiator steam geysered into the dripping leaves. A flock of blackbirds, knocked from their roosts, flopped shabbily around the car in the dark, confused but afraid to fly.

Threadgill gingerly rubbed a big and painful bruise on his bare head under the broad-brimmed hat. His eyes stung when he touched the swelling, and his fingers brought down a little fresh blood. The front windshield of the wrecked automobile held a bloom the exact size and shape of an old man's head.

Threadgill peered cautiously out the window of the Cadillac, but kept a nervous grip on the blanket. Who knew what moment savage monkeys might leap back onto him? Ripped and torn, stained with spoor and urine, the bedroll had saved his life.

Seven little saltbox cottages roosted in the woods around the wrecked Cadillac. The cottages reminded Threadgill of fat dirty hens. Porch awnings spread like protecting wings, one front, one back. The awnings sported bug lights, little yellow enchanted pears. Weathered doors and jalousied windows showed less unappetizing color, something like mustard smeared on old socks.

Where in the world *was* this place?

Threadgill studied a cyclone of dust-brown moths attacking the yellow lights.

Right now, the old man thought, *the inside of my head feels just like that.*

He smacked his lips. Some water would taste good – Threadgill felt he could purely breathe water right now, just inhale it like air. It would also be very nice to wash the monkey funk off his skin and clothes.

He gingerly touched a raw scab on his knee.

One of the little squirrel monkeys had gotten to him – just one, among all those working so furiously to murder him. This tirelessly focused creature chewed and chewed and chewed and chewed and chewed and finally got through the tough canvas laundry sack just above Threadgill's patella, only moments before the irresistible car met the immovable tree and ended its journey, grille-first, in a shower of chinaberries and grackles.

Threadgill HAD felt the monkey bite. He peeked out the viewing hole in his blanket to see that small enraged simian gape up with a mouth full of pants and something like pomegranate in its teeth, juicy and red. Threadgill popped a fist from the blanket, grabbed the little monster by its head, and hurled it onto LaRue.

One more monkey on Lash LaRue hardly mattered.

Then the chinaberry tree came very fast toward the car – remembrance came rushing back to Threadgill now.

Things went black for a while.

***

Now a weird cry rose from the woods that dwarfed the cinder block cottages. What was it? Threadgill couldn't see far into the black puzzle of trunks and branches.

Maybe it's best to move on ... fast, Threadgill told himself.

The old man scratched together his goods, strewn everywhere now in the car's nasty floorboards. Threadgill's own door didn't open, of course, so he pitched his canned items and other stuff through LaRue's shattered driver-side window. A moment later, Threadgill wedged himself through the opening, headfirst, protected once more in his bedroll from the jagged glass at the window edges. Broken glass could open a man up just like a jack knife.

Threadgill spilled to the ground. His provisions – cans of rest-home beans and Vienna sausages and sardines and even a few dollar bills – clattered around his feet as he stood. His bruised head throbbed under the yellowhammer hat as he reached full height, and his ears gave a little toot like a tea kettle.

Threadgill slumped back down for a moment in the summer night.

Fresh air! He might have been inhaling sweet candy. His keen nose thrilled as it came back to life in the open woods.

Threadgill expected a crowd with all the commotion. It was a car wreck! A man crawling free of a Cadillac, spilling tins of food!

Not one light burned in the cottages.

Threadgill pondered this peculiar stillness.

Where in the world was everyone? Did a Cadillac full of mad monkeys crash into a tree every night around here? Were the guests in those cottages stone deaf? WERE there guests?

Maybe it was best not to know some things.

He refilled his canvas bag, re-rolled the grue-spattered blanket. As he yanked and tied shoestring thongs, Threadgill's fine nose really began to enjoy itself. Somewhere close by, bacon fried in a skillet. Miles off bubbled a pot of chicken and dumplings. Threadgill sniffed honeysuckle from the woods, the first really fresh breath of the world he'd savored since early that morning on Mobile Bay when he rowed ashore.

The night smelled like some kind of salvation.

A blackbird tiptoed past, croaking. Others cowered under the automobile, oily black rags dropped from some careless mechanic's pocket.

"Go on," Threadgill mumbled, slapping his gear together. "Go on and curse the dark. You can't ever tell what awful thing might happen in life, can you?"

***

Surely the ride with LaRue had been a trial, a first test of Threadgill's commitment to his quest.

Here was the question. Was Threadgill true and tough and determined enough to continue his quest? After all those hours in the hurtling Cadillac, hotter than forty hells, ravaged by tiny apes, the funk of forty sphincters – after such tribulations, did Threadgill yet remain true, tough and determined enough to march on to Maine? To make things right by Ben and by his own soul?

Hunkered in his canvas cocoon, deep in his blankets and cooked like a corn dog, Threadgill *had* wavered. That was the truth. He *had*, for a moment, weighed unconditional surrender. He considered an escape at the next rest stop, a wave ta-ta to Larry LaRue and his smuggled goods, a trip back to the old comforts and familiarities of Mobile Sunset Home.

But the Sunset Home was burned. Gone with the Gulf Coast wind.

In that moment of crisis, Threadgill ventured a peek out the Cadillac window, brushing a stiff monkey from the glass to see out.

Dusk.

The sun set, red as a boil, above the flood plain of the Alabama River. Vast cotton fields flowed down the river banks. Torn-open bales of cumulus topped the sky over the fields. Water oaks crowded the river's edge, green, thirsty sinners praying to God, stretching and keening, imploring heaven for rain.

Alabama. The South. His sweet home.

Threadgill's resolve found footing. *This is what the Yankees tried to take from me. They took it from Ben. Why? Why did they hurt me? Why did they kill Ben? What did Ben and I do to them?*

He squared his shoulders in the cocoon.

Bangor.

True north.

***

A flickering, moth-mad, blue neon sign haunted the roadside in front of the seven cottages:

Snow White Motel
$4 per night. $.75 per hour

That neon sign seemed blaringly bright to a man whose head hurt so bad. The Cadillac's grille had stopped steaming now, but a powerful burned-rubber smell fouled the summer night. And then there remained that smell inside the car.

Threadgill had to sit down on the ground again. He squenched his eyes to wish his headache away.

When he opened them, the moon glowed much closer – bright red, ugly with knots and moles.

Surprise!

It wasn't a moon after all.

It was the face of a long-lost cousin, Otis, gored by a bull in a green pasture and killed dead when Threadgill was just ten. Otis had been a tiny tow-headed four-year-old child, fey and disobedient.

Threadgill always thought his cousin lay in a grave in the red clay of Barbour County. Threadgill was *sure*. He'd often seen the child-sized tombstone, broken by vandals. Under it, Cousin Otis was a pile of chalk.

But this instant Otis stared down at Threadgill through an intensely blue pair of eyes, blue as the neon on the motel sign. He was older now, middle-aged. Otis wore the garb of a car mechanic, a dark green pair of coveralls, a pink rag wagging from a hip pocket.

This sawed-off little mechanic clicked his flashlight and glowed it into Threadgill's face. The eyes behind the beam shone cool as two blue quarters.

"Evenin,' Otis," Threadgill said painfully.

The flashlight beam clicked off.

***

A gravelly voice woke Threadgill.

"You been asleep on and off for ten days, mister. I was beginning to wonder if you'd ever come back."

The greeting rose from green darkness.

"Jabberin' in your sleep like a drunk auctioneer. I never heard anything to beat it."

Threadgill elbowed up. He reached to make sure his hat still covered his head. Yes, by damn.

Ten days? Threadgill's head still pounded even now.

The light hurt his eyes, but he could dimly make out cement-block walls, a rickety chair, a wooden crate, a pile-up of race-car magazines. Some of the magazines had nearly naked women on their covers. Threadgill's mattress leaked dirty cotton, the blue ticking blotched with dark stains and the petroglyphic whorls of rusty bedsprings.

"Naturally, if you're really on your way to kill that last Yankee, you can rest here 'til you're good and ready." The anonymous voice sounded kindly now. "Ten days ain't so long. Anyway, today is Sunday. Good book says to rest on Sunday."

The only door to the tiny room stood wide. Through it, Threadgill caught sight of a cluster of faint stars holding on for dear life in the coming dawn.

A heavy figure, smoking, moved against the door frame.

"Ben?" Threadgill husked.

A measured answer. "Hmmph. I reckon we'll need to find you some eyeglasses."

Threadgill elbowed up. "Who then? Where am I?"

The tip of a tiny Dutch Masters cigar glowed orange, and Threadgill could vaguely make out dumpling cheeks and smart black eyes riveted on him, unblinking.

"Name's Johnnie. Watch your cup now."

Through his stupor, Threadgill made out a white Styrofoam cup with a gnawed lip. It balanced shakily on the mattress. It held a smoking liquid dark as motor oil.

Coffee.

Threadgill got his nose into the stuff. Ahh. Yes. Pure 40-weight. Mighty damn good.

"Bet you're hungry. I imagine sawing logs a week and a half works up an appetite."

Threadgill issued a tremendous fart that actually rattled the single window of the little cottage.

"Woo! Listen at that! Life in you yet, old man!"

"Excuse me, mister. I know that ain't polite. I couldn't help it."

Threadgill heard a dry laugh.

"Like I say – mister – we gotta get you some eyewear. But not till after we eat. How 'bout you get dressed? Your clothes are all clean, washed and folded. Right over yonder. I'll go crank up Nadine, and we'll run down the road and visit Jerry's place. Jerry makes pretty good breakfast."

Threadgill squinted at his benefactor. Nerves and muscles and blood started to purr inside him now – the cup held a strong brew. Threadgill had a flash in his head of someone lifting a steaming cup to the lips of an old stone Confederate statue in some town square, and it coming to life, skipping about, dancing a jig in the day lilies.

The cottage's door frame stood empty now, the stars all gone, Sunday coloring the treetops.

Threadgill flipped back his sheet, swung his gaunt feet to the floor. He heard a chorus of laments from his body as he first sat up, straightening his floppy hat. He accidentally touched the bruise the car wreck left on his noggin. The room briefly spun, a green green green green green green merry-go-round of leaves and lizards.

The heavy-set figure returned to his doorway.

"I took a peek, playing doctor," Johnnie said, nodding at Threadgill's naked self. "That knot on your noggin sure as hell must of hurt."

The speaker flicked away the cigarillo butt and stepped inside. Threadgill, still dizzy, did not glance up at first.

When he did, naked as the day he was born, the shock nearly knocked him cold again.

"Whoa!" Threadgill hollered. "Whoa now!"

Johnnie was a she.

Threadgill first grabbed at his yellowhammer hat, to clap it over his privates. It was half lifted before the dilemma struck – which naked head would be more embarrassing to show?

"Don't look!" he yelled. "This ain't for you to see!"

He rose out of bed confused, cringing, hands over his gray pubis. He skipped, in reverse, across the cluttered room. He looked like a man on a miniature invisible stick horse, riding backward …

"Watch my magazines!"

Threadgill's mount spooked and reared. He fell ass over Styrofoam coffee cup, avalanching down a slick heap of automotive and girlie magazines. One hairy bare leg waved to the ceiling. Hot coffee puddled under his naked hips.

"Aw shit!" Johnnie said.

The old man struggled for a weak moment. Then he realized he could not get up without help in this compromised condition.

The stout woman with chopped iron-gray hair cracked a smile.

"Shenanigans! And that's enough of that. Mister, you ain't got to go ape-shit around me ever again. I done had my little look, Rip Van Winkle. Believe you me, I clapped that old hat back down on your head like the lid on a boiling pot."

Threadgill felt his cheeks get hot.

"What in the world happened to you, anyway?" Johnnie asked. She drew another Dutch Masters out of the pocket of the man's shirt she wore. "You scalped by red Indians?"

"Lady, you didn't have no right –"

"You ain't got to worry about your chastity, or whatever," Johnnie snorted, twin plumes of cigar smoke boiling from her lungs. "You ain't my flavor, honey. You might as well know it right now."

They stared at one another.

"I'll let you get dressed, old man. But then you come on quick as you can now. Miz Johnnie's got an appetite."

***

Johnnie had, indeed, laundered the whole kit and caboodle of his gear. Threadgill admiringly lifted a pair of clean pants and roundabout, his freshly laundered shirt, folded socks. A spotless canvas laundry bag, dried stiff as a giant sock in the sun, hung from the window sash. His blanket, scorched and holey now but also spotless and good-smelling, aired over an ancient cast iron radiator. Johnnie had even wiped Threadgill's boots clean. The smoke and soot and bay-bottom mud and monkey mess were long gone.

Threadgill smelled pretty much like a lemon tree.

Johnny had given Threadgill other attentions. His mixed bankroll of Confederate paper money and Yankee dollars sat in the open windowsill, the bills carefully spread to dry, weighted down by loose hex nuts and a small paper sack of six-penny nails. His knife, some coins, a ball of string, band-aids, the rest of his pocket paraphernalia – all present and accounted for.

"Decent now, old man? Mind if I come back inside my own place for a second?" Orange morning glowed over Johnnie's wide shoulder now.

"Yes'm. I'm decent." Threadgill cleared his throat. "Just now – I didn't mean you any disrespect, you understand."

"Sugar, I've seen it all, and I've heard most of it I ain't seen. You ain't got to apologize."

Johnnie took to rearranging the mattress, restacking her magazines and whatnot, toweling up the spilled coffee.

"I've seen worse'n you in my time. Some of it hard as the devil to live with too. You got that ugly spot – it don't bother me. I ain't the kind that cares about mess like that."

"I got it from Yankees," Threadgill said.

She waved a hand dismissively. Threadgill noticed grease under her nails.

"You been telling me that for ten days. You can pay 'em back real soon, darlin'. But not before we eat breakfast. Get your shoes. You can put 'em on in the car. Miz Johnnie's *really* hungry now. And …"

Johnnie stubbed out her thin cigar in her palm.

"… Miz Johnnie don't like to be hungry."

Chapter 13, Yellowhammer up the Blue Ridge

Chattanooga felt unhappy in the end.

Night sloshed over shining lights like motor oil over marbles. Railways centipeded through shambled warehouses. Stray dogs staggered empty streets. From the center of the earth, lonesome train whistles rose.

Yellowhammer flies on, straight across Tennessee.

Yellowhammer reaches the Blue Ridge.

Below stretches rocky Tennessee, North Carolina, a puzzle-piece corner of Kentucky. The shaggy hills soften. Cedar trees march straight and soldier-green behind stone fences. Horses stand still as statues. Holes freckle limestone landscape. Some of the depressions look like shell craters. They slosh molasses-colored water.

Soft fires glow in the hills. Yellowhammer can see whiskey being born out there.

Green River curls among the hills, a snake in wet black leaves.

Yellowhammer bears slightly east. It can feel the air change over Virginia. Every state exhales its own unique breath. Naturally, a creature as sensitive as Yellowhammer senses every difference.

Virginia gentles the Appalachians away into nothing much – lined fields lipped by moonlit streams, small pastures stobbed down at corners by tobacco barns. Forests show here, there, bushy as bird nests. Tiny towns, asleep and dreaming, comfortably snuggle among the nests.

There's Charlottesville.

Yellowhammer sees two humans. They peer through a telescope from a patio deck on top of a big house.

Yellowhammer passes. For the briefest moment, a flickering shadow divides telescope lens and heaven. The man pulls back, surprised, from the eyepiece. He removes his glasses, rubs them clean on the woman's long black sleeve. She laughs and kisses him. He peeks into the lens again.

A second Venus shimmers. The couple's pale faces glow in the moonlight.

The man on the deck can see a trillion miles into space.

Yellowhammer sees a thousand miles ahead.

Chapter 14, Jerry's Cafe

Summer 1964 – Near Greenville, Alabama

Jerry's Café sat by the Greenville Highway. A red chicken and a blue catfish danced together on a big sign out front, and a pig in a tuxedo jacket played a banjo.

Threadgill and Johnnie hunched into a small red booth with a pink-and-white Formica table top. Neither said much. Threadgill's head still hurt, in fact, and he kept glimpsing small furry things in the corners of his eyes.

Johnnie shoveled down a half-dozen cat-head biscuits and about that many fried eggs, dusted black with pepper. She ate grits too, and bacon and link sausages and a thick pile of pancakes with cane syrup. Johnnie was obviously a regular – the waitress, Doe, brought her a free plate of fried tomatoes plus a big bowl of fresh sliced peaches for dessert. Doe balanced the order up and down long freckled arms to get it all to the table.

Threadgill first tried a ham biscuit and coffee. He waited for a while, until his stomach had time to remember how to be a stomach. Then he ordered again, and tucked into a pile of pancakes and Daddy Bucks syrup. He had one more biscuit then, with homemade dewberry jelly.

They started to talk. Between bites, Johnnie filled in a ten-day gap in history.

Johnnie lived at the Snow White and made her living driving Nadine – her faithful white taxi cab. A week and one-half ago, Johnnie got home late after hauling a full-bull Army colonel and his two girlfriends from the Snow White back to Gunter Field. Those three, Johnnie said, had shacked up in Happy (the seven cottages at Snow White carried the names of all seven dwarves in that Disney movie). Happy, she remarked, was the cottage most often requested by fornicators.

When Johnnie returned from that ride, LaRue's newly wrecked Cadillac sat smoking in the lot, wrapped around the chinaberry tree.

"In fifteen years living out here, I never saw the beat of it," she told Threadgill. "I thought we'd been bombed. Somebody mistook us for the Viet Nams or some such."

Johnnie took action that night. She pounded on the door of the motel owner, Ralph Weed. She first thought Ralph might be dead from the blast, but it turned out he'd just gone off for a week to bet on the greyhounds at Ebro.

"Never thought much of that sumbitch," Johnnie confided through a big bite of jelly biscuit. "But I ain't got to like Ralph to live at his cottage."

Johnnie discovered Threadgill propped against the car "like a tarbaby," she said, with his scattered stuff all around him. She picked him up all by herself, blanket and clothes-sack too, and hauled him to her cottage – the one named Grumpy.

"I ain't no good Samaritan," Johnnie said. "But I ain't no bad one neither."

"I'm much obliged," Threadgill said, with a twinkle in his eye at last. "I might of caught a bad cold."

Johnnie forked a link sausage off Threadgill's plate.

"Worse'n that," she chewed. "Been a mess of rattlesnakes out this summer. One coulda crawled up under you to keep warm. I figured you'd be better off sleepin' on my bed than on a poison snake."

Johnnie chewed thoughtfully.

"But now I will tell you this – you smelled so durned bad I just propped you up on a cement block and turned the hose on you before I tucked you in. You never did even wake up. That knot on your head was swole up like a football. You came here one messed up man, Mr. Pickett."

At some point along here in the conversation, no doubt convoyed by just the right combination of caffeine, sugar, and biscuit, Threadgill felt his memory flicker timidly back to life.

Ahh, there it was. It ignited in stages, like the neon sign coming on in front of the Snow White. Threadgill now recalled the blaze at Mobile Sunset Home. The long night paddle across Mobile Bay. LaRue's wild ride north. Threadgill enjoyed a surge of caffeinated warmth in his long limbs now too, and energy from nutrition seeped through him.

"I put a poultice on your noggin," Johnnie explained, pointing her fork at Threadgill's hat. "And, durned if I didn't accidentally mash your TALK button. You just started goin' and goin', tellin' me somebody's whole life like I needed to write it down every detail. It was durned interestin', but who in the world can listen to a feller talk without stopping, night and day, for ten solid days? Wore me plum out. Stuff all about fires and hurricanes and giant critters on some durn island, and I don't know what all. A time or two there I thought about breakin' out a roll of duct tape ..."

Threadgill dipped a whole hot biscuit in a jar of purple jelly. He saw a light pulsing behind one of his eyes, and while it flashed he nodded, chewing thoughtfully, crumbs in his goat's beard.

"So," Johnnie exhaled, almost scornfully, "I reckon this morning, the first time in a blue moon you can make your mouth work on your own, you *ain't gonna talk?* That would be about like a feller."

Threadgill swallowed. "Sorry, Miz Johnnie. I'm mighty grateful. Some of the words for talkin' just ain't lined up right in my head yet."

Threadgill heard a skillet sizzling again. He felt a sudden wave of relief when he saw there really *was* a skillet, frying bacon, on the grill.

Even with his headache, happiness filled Threadgill for a moment. Did anything in the world smell better than bacon in a skillet?

Threadgill wiped his mouth. On the spot, he made a vow.

If the good Lord was willing and brought him marching home again, he would return to sit at this same table, by this same window, and tell Miz Johnnie the end of the Threadgill story. Since she already knew the first part, he'd fill in the last.

Johnnie reached for the sugar dispenser, one of those that look like a little glass silo, and poured her coffee stiff.

"Well, if you ain't much for words right yet, then here's MY story." Johnnie's spoon made brisk music as she stirred. "It's a short one. And sweet."

She paused to taste her spoon.

"When I was thirteen years old, I felt a calling to drive a taxi. Started right then, that month, without no driver's license. Been driving folks ever since. Lived right here close to Hope Hull and Greenville and Montgomery every day of my whole life. I've owned two taxis, and Nadine is the second one, and the best. That's about all there is to tell. That's the story of Johnnie Johnston."

Over his coffee cup, Threadgill studied this odd woman who nursed him. Johnnie had heard him fight his demons in his sleep. She saw him in his feathered glory. She doctored the terrible goose egg on his noggin down to barely a pecan. She'd been kind to Threadgill.

But who WAS she?

Johnnie was not fat. She lived in a huge solid frame, though, broad in her shoulders like a man. Her soft brown eyes were hard set in rounded high cheeks. Chicken and dumplings, Threadgill thought.

Johnnie's nose, red and gin-blossomed, could have belonged to any old drunk's. She had a faint moustache under her nose, a few of the hairs extraordinary, long and spidery. Threadgill put her at about age fifty – a mere girl. She wore no jewelry at all, not even a ring. Her clothes didn't deserve a description. Man clothes. And every word she said crackled like a radio, years of tobacco smoke in it.

"My taxi," she explained, "is the one true love in this world old Johnnie Johnston was ever meant to have, I reckon. Nadine's got 390,000 on her now. Oh, don't look like that. Mostly highway miles. She runs just fine."

Nadine did look like a well-loved vehicle. Threadgill watched the white Studebaker bask just outside the café window in the hot morning. She did have one red scab of Bondo over a dent near the back tail light. The grille grinned like a traveling salesman.

"Three hundred ninety thousand miles," Threadgill marveled. "How many trips to Maine and back'd that make?"

"Well sir, I don't know rightly know how far it is to Maine. But I *can* tell you it's something like fifty trips around the world." Johnnie lit up an after-breakfast Dutch Masters, waved her match out. "But, hey now, you listen to Johnnie. If you're angling for a taxi ride to Maine … you can just get that fool notion out of your head. I ain't never leaving Alabama again. I did it once, and I paid the price. People are way too strange out yonder."

She sounded funny, sad. Threadgill changed the subject.

"Ain't taxi driving a ton of work?"

"It is. Especially due to the fact I keep Nadine up myself." Johnnie looked vain for an instant. "Oh yeah – I do for myself, mister. Fixed cars since I could tote a wrench. Could be makin' a livin' under the hood of a race car, I reckon. But, see – I prefer taxi drivin'. Like I said – it's my callin'."

She wiped up a drip of syrup with a broad finger.

"It's some weird shit happens, though."

Threadgill now distinctly heard that plangent note in her voice again. What? Why?

"One reason I like it is there ain't a lot of women in taxis. I think it's special to those of us who got the callin'."

The waitress popped up, that sweet young Doe. She smelled like red lipstick and Juicy Fruit.

"Johnnie," Doe smacked, batting her lashes at Threadgill, "who IS this handsome feller?"

Doe wore a red-and-white apron. Her red fingernails were perfect, a necessary complement to the gold and silver rings on every finger. She came with a stub of pencil back of one ear. She was well endowed.

"Tell the truth, Doe, I don't even know this feller's first name. Ain't that a kick? Been stayin' at my place for ten days, and ain't learned his full name yet?"

The waitress winked lewdly at Threadgill.

"Ten days? Sugar, I reckon you two been *busy*!"

Threadgill felt himself redden – the blush made his head hurt.

"No, now. It ain't like that, Miss. My name ain't no secret. I'm a Pickett – Threadgill Pickett. Come from Barbour County years back, but I been down around Mobile some time now." He thought a moment. "A hundred years."

"Oh, listen!" Doe gushed. "I got Picketts on my mama's side!"

Threadgill sat up. "Well, we sure might be kinfolk …" Did Threadgill actually have relatives still running around Alabama? How had this possibility eluded him all these years?

"Might be!" Doe announced. "But not on my Daddy's side. You know why?"

She flashed her name tag: Dorine Leech.

"Cause there's Leeches on my daddy's side!" she shrieked.

Johnnie cackled so hard it brought on a ripping smoker's cough, and she had to raise her arms.

"Doe, honey, you a mess."

Doe triumphantly smacked Juicy Fruit.

"Well, Johnnie, I might be a mess. But now I ain't the one brought in some big old love interest for breakfast. How long did you say? Two weeks? Two *weeks* locked up together at the Snow White Motel! Mmm. Mmm. Mmm. What got into you, Johnnie girl?"

Johnnie made a sour face. "Nothing's got into me. Not a thing. Won't, neither."

"Well, you messin' up, girl. He's a cute one." Dorine Leech bathed in Threadgill's blushing discomfort. "Even that tore-up hat can't hide a plain fact."

Johnnie tapped yet another little cigar out of its box.

"He's more trouble than he looks, Dorine. Eats in his sleep, talks in his sleep, goes to the potty in his sleep. Bet you most ladies would swap me a green banana for him."

Threadgill tried to smile but came up empty. His head still hurt.

"Seriously, Dorine. This here's the feller that come in on the Cadillac with that Lash LaRue feller that night."

Now Doe Leech's eyebrows made two triangles of surprise.

"Well," she exclaimed. "He don't *look* like a squirrel monkey!"

Johnnie laughed again till she coughed. Threadgill even rasped up something like a laugh. That completely surprised him. He couldn't remember making such a sound in …well … in a long time.

Doe got tickled too. She laughed so hard she had to reach up and catch the little waitress hat she wore. It was white cardboard with *Jerry's* on it in red script.

"Mr. Pickett – you really did come to town with Larry LaRue?"

"Yes ma'am. You know that man?"

"Know him?" Dorine Leech suddenly blazed. "The man ought to be tied to a creosote post and horsewhipped an' then hosed with Clorox! I'll be happy to do the whuppin' too, if you want to know." Doe Leech raised her hand in the air and brought it down like she held a little cat-o'-nine tails. "Plus I'd like to squash his damned balls with pliers."

Johnnie couldn't stop coughing and laughing now, and pure tears of mirth spilled onto her round cheeks.

"It's a pure crime, what Larry done to them poor little monkeys! They all out in the woods now, and Sheriff Tedder says they got to be rounded up and put to sleep. Every last one. Says some of 'em had the rabies, or some such."

"Doe!" Johnnie exclaimed, no longer laughing. "You are *not* serious? They ain't really gonna kill those little monkeys?"

Johnnie's dark eyes suddenly grew serious again. "Lord, I'll take one. Wouldn't that be a sight? A cute little monkey critter to ride shotgun up on

Nadine's dash?"

A man's voice yodeled now, all the way in back of the café.

"They GOT to exterminate 'em, Johnnie. Monkeys with the rabies, that's a health crisis. It ain't no foolin' when it's rabies."

The scab on Threadgill's right kneecap tingled.

A man with a long, foxy face and densely freckled forearms came around from behind the grill. He wore a red-and-white apron like Doe Leech's, only stained with egg and ketchup and bacon grease. He wagged a wiping rag.

"Mornin', Miss Johnnie. You doin' good?"

"Mornin', Jerry. Meet Mr. Prichard –"

"Pickett," Threadgill corrected.

"Pickett?" Jerry wondered. "Like the Charge at Gettysburg?"

Threadgill nodded.

"He's passing through, up from Mobile," Johnnie explained. "Says he's on his way to kill the very last Yankee soldier, somewhere up yonder in Maine."

Jerry shook Threadgill's hand. The cook's grip was too-warm, a bit greasy.

"Jerry Coe," the man said. "And don't even ask – yes, my mama and daddy did name me for that Bible story where the walls come a' tumblin' down."

Doe smacked gum and interrupted.

"Jerry, what did Sheriff Tedder sit right yonder at the counter and tell us yesterday morning?"

The cafe owner plainly loved to deliver community news.

"Well he told us every last one of those monkeys was gonna be caught and put down. He was gonna deputize the whole Butler County Coon Hunters Association, and get out the blueticks to track down the little boogers. Ought to be easy to track a monkey, if they smell as bad as that car did."

Johnnie snorted violently across the table. The coffee sloshed in Threadgill's cup.

"Doe, you know what?" Johnnie growled. "I don't think even an all-day horsewhippin' would be good enough for Larry LaRue. I'd like to chain his feet up to my trailer hitch and let Nadine drag him up to Montgomery and back. Just to start with."

Doe's eyes and nostrils fiercely dilated, and her mouth set a firm line.

"Next time he steps in here to eat – if he ever gets out of the jail, I mean – I'm gonna personally put rat poison in his biscuit."

Jerry raised his freckled hand. Threadgill saw cold grits on the backs of the owner's fingers. He cleared his throat dramatically.

"Now, ladies, let me go on and tell Mr. Pickett here the rest of what the Sheriff said."

Jerry waited, a pregnant pause, all eyes settled on him.

"Sheriff Tedder told me he found three of the things dead at the car crash out at Snow White. One of 'em was a big old rascal – might go thirty pounds, he said. Some kind of a howlin' monkey, mixed in with them others by mistake, I reckon. And then Tedder told how some niggers killed this other monkey up at Barry Hannah's – them rascals plum had Barry cornered in his outhouse, scared to open the door. And over at Pintlala Bea Fennelly's fyce dog got in a fight with one, and they pure killed each other. Sheriff said Miz Bea is all tore up about losin' her puppy, and she's put in to sue Larry LaRue."

Doe interrupted. "That's just six monkeys! And I'm hearin' folks say Larry LaRue drove in here with more than a hundred!"

Jerry just went right on, wagging a finger like a band conductor.

"Anyway, Sheriff said that 'un they killed on Barry's outhouse was foamin' at the mouth and just about ready to jump on anything that moved. A Montgomery health officer come over and chopped off its head. Oh, he had right smart of cut-off heads that night – skunks and raccoons and a bat, I seen 'em myself – and he sent all them heads in a croker sack to the state lab for those tests they do and the monkey one come back positive for the rabies.

"Sheriff Tedder said he already knowed it was the rabies. He's seen plenty of rabies. Even arrested two or three fellers had it. Plus, Sheriff says a rabid animal ain't got fleas … and wasn't a flea to find on a single one of them monkeys. Now ain't that somethin'? You ever hear of an animal without a single flea on its whole body? But that's exactly what Sheriff Tedder said. Ain't that right, Doe?"

Doe nodded vigorously.

All of a sudden, Threadgill felt a twinge on his kneecap, and sweat popped out everywhere his clothes touched his body.

"So," Jerry finished, flapping his rag in the air. "It ain't really no telling what kinds of *other* disease they carry neither, a carload of squirrel monkeys right off the boat from Nigeria or China or wherever the hell they come from. I reckon they got scarlet fevers and yellow fevers and blue fevers and every other color fevers. Monkey fevers. So, ladies, don't go to wah-wahing about saving a bunch of smuggled-in squirrel monkeys. You GOT to put 'em down. We ain't no choice."

Johnnie looked more than a little alarmed.

"Well … has Larry LaRue come down with anything? Or maybe …" She nervously cut her eyes over at Threadgill, her sentence unfinished. Doe backed away from Threadgill ever so slightly.

Jerry Coe pulled a serious face.

"Truth to tell, old Larry LaRue got chewed up pretty bad. They can't honestly say if he's doin' so poor due to the three hundred and fifty-something monkey bites on him, or if it's one of them monkey diseases. Something weird too – they found a couple of bullet holes in him. Ratshot from some kind of pistol."

Jerry swiveled to face Threadgill.

"You pack heat to face down that Yankee in Maine, Mr. Pickett?"

Threadgill looked at Johnnie and shrugged.

"He ain't got a gun, Jerry." Johnnie scoffed as she spoke. "I went through every particle to his name. I would have found a pistol … unless he threw it away on the trip somewhere."

That hung in the air a moment.

"Well," resumed Jerry, "I DO know one thing."

Nobody at the table had taken a bite in five minutes.

"I DO know Larry LaRue is gonna spend at least six months in jail and get fourteen rabies shots in his gut. And who knows how long he'll stay in the quarantine."

Johnnie piped up. "Hey, I seen a rabies shot needle one time. Looked like a durned railroad spike."

Doe again, with a baffled look. "What's a quarterine?"

"Quar-an-TEEN!" Jerry scolded. "That's how Sheriff Tedder said it."

"Well, what IS one?" Doe persisted.

"Hell, I don't know," Jerry shrugged. "Somethin' like a iron lung, maybe."

"Lord, lord," Johnnie sighed, now avoiding Threadgill's eyes.

"If you ask me, Larry LaRue would be a big *improvement* with the rabies," Doe announced. "Probably be a lot nicer feller, and he would *definitely* have better manners on a date ..."

Jerry grew distracted at this point by something out the window. He raised slightly on his toes, craning for a better view through the window blinds. He gave a low whistle.

"Uh-oh, Miz Johnnie. I hate to be the one to tell, but Larry LaRue ain't the only one's got a problem this morning. Look a yonder."

Johnnie pinched open the blinds and squinted at Nadine.

"Well shitfire. Must of been that piece of plywood we hit on the way here. Picked up a nail. Dang it. Y'all let me out."

Threadgill spoke up. "I'll help you, Miz Johnnie."

"No hell you won't," Johnnie answered. She spoke so forcefully it sat Threadgill right back down. That was that.

Johnnie's big bosoms nearly dragged two plates off the table as she cleared the booth. Apparently, Doe *was* allowed outside to help Johnnie change Nadine's flat. The little bell on the door jingled as the women passed through.

Jerry started to clear the breakfast dishes.

"I reckon us red-blooded men could have changed that tire pretty quick," Threadgill suggested to Jerry, looking out at the women beginning their hot work.

"That would be the right thing to do for any other lady in the world, Mr. Pickett," Jerry agreed, sweeping his rag. "But that's a hard-headed woman yonder, that Johnnie, and she likes to do for herself. We'd just get dog-cussed for our trouble."

"Great big pair of dinners," Threadgill observed.

"Smother a feller," Jerry whistled. "Even more of a waste the Lord made her the way He did. It beats me – I can't hardly believe any woman would want to do romance things with another woman."

Threadgill let this sink in for a moment.

"I'll tell you this," Jerry Coe declared. "I bet you Johnnie Johnston gets more poontang than me and you put together. It's cause of the taxi business. She does real good with these young college girls, just back home from some fancy this or that la-de-da university. They ship off to college and go plum wild."

The two men watched as Johnnie expertly handled the tire change. She assembled the tire jack – *what a contraption*, Threadgill thought – then muscled the car's back end high into the air. She located the puncture on Nadine's tire with expert probing fingers, a doctor checking vital signs. It was a nail, all right – a roofing tack. She left it in the treads so she could later plug the leak and reuse the tire.

Next she effortlessly lifted the spare, bounced it once like a basketball, spanked it ahead to the wheel hub. She pulled the tire tool free of the jack assembly, spun lug nuts free. The tool twirled like a silver propeller in dazzling Alabama sunlight.

A professional at work.

"So Mister Pickett, you're on your way to kill the last Yankee," Jerry said idly, studying Johnnie too. "I'd be mighty proud to buy breakfast for a man like that."

Jerry's voice next grew manly and confidential. He nodded toward the parking lot, a strange light shining in his eyes.

"If you don't already know, you might ask Johnnie there what it's like to kill a man. I mean, just in case you never had that particular pleasure."

Threadgill blinked up in surprise.

"Oh, yes sir," Jerry whispered. "Happened about a year back. This feller took a taxi ride in from the airport, wanted to go all the way to Columbus, Georgia, slam outside of the whole durned state. Now there's a big famous whorehouse in Columbus, if you never heard of it, and it's a pretty rough destination. You know, everybody talks about how bad Phenix City is. Columbus ain't no better, really. It's all them soldiers.

"About the time Johnnie pulled up front of the whorehouse, she looked around and that passenger had a pistol pointed at her. Bad mistake. They say Johnnie snatched it off him, and she put all six bullets up the poor sumbitch's ass. Right there in the back seat of the taxi, I mean. Bunch of people saw it, too, and testified in the trial it was self-defense. Course Johnnie got off, or she wouldn't be out there huffin' and puffin' with that flat this morning."

The cafe door jingled, and Jerry hushed.

Threadgill smelled the Juicy Fruit before Doe skipped past with a tall iced tea in a double Dixie cup. She fetched that outside to Johnnie, then waved toodles with long fingers and red nails through the window at the two men.

Threadgill wiped his mouth.

"You mind if get some more coffee?" he asked. "I ain't had a cup so good in years."

Jerry smiled. "How 'bout I bring you the whole danged pot, Mr. Pickett?"

While Jerry was gone, Threadgill watched a fly in the cafe window, butting at the two women changing the tire.

Jerry returned with a steaming fresh pot of brew. He slid in across the table from Threadgill, accidentally spilling a little. He grabbed paper napkins from one of those little dispensers that look like a mailbox.

"You know," Jerry Coe said, "I still got my great granddaddy's Civil War sword. He took if off a dead Yankee up at Pine Mountain. Course he got killed too. That was in all that sorry mess with Sherman there toward the very end."

Threadgill felt his scalp throb.

"Ain't none of us in this family ever forgot that Gram fought and died for what he believed in," Jerry said. "We never *will* forget."

Threadgill answered softly.

"I ain't making this trip for him. I'm makin' this trip for *me*."

"Well, naturally you are. I'm just sayin' … Hey, Mr. Pickett, I wish you'd take along some extra biscuits and ham for the road, compliments of Jerry Coe and Doe Leech and Miz Johnnie and other good folks in these parts?"

The bell jingled over the cafe door. In came the two women, job done, Nadine back in working order. Johnnie smiled and waved a black glove of grime. She headed off to the washroom.

The smell of Juicy Fruit returned.

"Doe," Jerry said, "how's about you fix Mr. Pickett a take-along sack? Make it deluxe. Would that suit you, Mr. Pickett?"

Threadgill marveled. Good country people. Why couldn't everybody in the world be as decent as this?

He only wished his knee didn't hurt. And his head didn't hurt. And these flashes of light and streaks of color would stop.

Chapter 15, Lt. Randoll Pickett

September 1856 — Barbour County, Alabama

Naked as a salamander, six-year-old Threadgill staggered out of the swimming hole. The icy water had shrunk his organs to nubs, and even in the dazzling early-afternoon sunshine he hugged himself tightly, trembling, blue with cold. He clambered barefoot up the slippery bank, gasping, pulling himself toward the crest with the rope swing. His teeth chattered – he couldn't make them stop.

"AwwwwRIGHT! Big splash, boy! Go again!"

Atop the grassy bank, trees shaded the man who barked out the orders – Lt. Randoll Pickett. Threadgill's father.

Lt. Pickett wore a perfectly white dress blouse, sleeves rolled to the elbow, and a pair of blue uniform pants tucked into gleaming black cavalry boots. His hair and eyes gleamed as black as the boots, like a Creek Indian's. He lay propped on his elbow, half in the shade, slicing an apple. A sharp military knife flashed as he worked, and a perfect unbroken spiral of red peel uncoiled from the apple onto the grass.

"It's c-c-cold!" Threadgill chattered.

His father, though only in his twenties, seemed older. Something in his eyes. The man popped a crisp, moon-shaped slice of apple into his mouth and chewed without expression or satisfaction. He motioned his knife at the rope swing.

"Cold?"

He swallowed before he spoke again.

"You GO, little girl! Water ain't *that* cold."

Threadgill stung under the words, but they didn't hurt as badly as his last awkward bellyflop and the cold, throbbing shock of the spring-fed Alabama pond. Threadgill wanted to tell his daddy how the water came out of the ground so cold the cows wouldn't even wade in it.

Little Threadgill made it to the top of the bank and plopped down wetly, first clearing a place with one hand for his bare bottom in a litter of oak leaves and old acorns.

"I ain't no little g-g-girl, Daddy," Threadgill protested, after a hard minute. "It's real cold water."

"Brother Ben would do it. That one's a pistol. Your Aunt Rose Nell down in Mobile says that one ain't afraid of a durned thing. I believe he's some taller'n you too."

The rope swing creaked in a breeze. A few late grasshoppers and a distant V of birds in the sky told a story of deep September. A yellow tinge had lately moved in under the hard greens in the woods.

Threadgill closed his eyes, bit his lip in pain. His whole side and back were scalded pink from hitting the water so hard. Something hurt in his side too, under his ribs. But he didn't dare mention that. Not now.

His father crunched the whole apple this time, made loud chewing sounds like a horse. Threadgill waited respectfully, a buzzing fly of anxiety inside.

Any moment he expected it – the next order from headquarters.

Instead, Randoll Pickett lazily pointed the knife again, toward Aunt Annie's house. She'd just come out to the well, a dipper gourd in hand for a drink of cool water. Aunt Annie was Lt. Pickett's oldest sister. She was raising Threadgill now. Rand Pickett chased banditos in Texas and old Mexico with the U.S. Cavalry. Annie raised one of his boys.

The twins were fated to go separate ways after Kate Pickett died in childbirth on that dark, cold day at Oak House.

***

Threadgill loved Aunt Annie.

She took him in at three months old. A stubborn case of colic in both twins completely discouraged their poor Aunt Sealy and her husband Dr. Deed Sparks from any further thoughts of having children – or even raising any. Three months with two screaming, gut-tortured newborns changed their minds forever.

Threadgill would later realize how much more than colic played into that decision. Aunt Sealy could hardly bear responsibility for her own life, much less two others – especially her dead sister's wailing brats. For his part, the good doctor Sparks felt a black crow of guilt flutter down and perch on his shoulder and croak into his alcoholic ear every time he laid eyes on the two motherless boys.

Annie was the oldest of all the Pickett siblings, the only Pickett girl who never married. After Katie died in childbirth, she felt an urgent, probably psychic, call to visit Oak House. She arrived without invitation, but with a welcome, and she quickly saw – and loudly heard – the Sparks' unhappy predicament.

Doctor Sparks and Sealy did not raise a single word of protest when Annie offered to take the miserable babies away, to be raised near Clio, some fifteen miles off. Annie got the impression that fifteen or so miles might be just far enough – out of crying range, beyond the constant guilt.

In a few months, Annie gave over the raising of the older and healthier twin, Ben. Her little sister Rose Nell had married well and now lived in good circumstances, in Mobile. Rose Nell had come down with rheumatic fever at age nine, and the doctors told her she would never be blessed with children. Well, now she would. Annie Pickett grieved to split the boys, but she worried even more that she wouldn't be able to keep both of them safe and healthy in this wild land. Two boys might prove too much for a single woman running a farm.

Now, years later, Ben grew smart and strong, the letters said. He kept asking when he could one day meet his "baby brother."

Threadgill had outgrown his colic too and become this bounding, happy young goat of a boy. His father occasionally sent lieutenant's money from Mexico to help with expenses, but he really could have saved it. Annie Pickett had a talent in life – running a farm.

With good luck and hard work, Annie single-handedly transformed the Pickett family place. When drought or flood or bugs wiped out the plantings on farms all around her, Annie somehow brought in crops of corn and sweet potatoes and, yes, cotton. Always cotton. She built a barn and a chicken coop and stacked firewood and threw up fences with her own two hands. Her plantings grew, from one acre to three, then five, then all forty. Annie, first alone, then with an old horse named Dinah, and finally with a thin, worried-looking African – Amos's face made Threadgill think of a mask of dark leather – every year they cleared away more Alabama woodland, opening the red ground to sunlight and seed.

The Pickett log cabin grew too, into a clapboard house. Next, it became a house with real glass windows, then a house with a room for guests. Life got better. Some silver pieces showed up on the sideboard. Household goods like oil lamps and oak furniture graced the place.

Amos, the slave, lived more or less unseen when he wasn't opening the field with an iron plow or hunting game on endless acres of forest around the Pickett place. The strange little man actually carried a spear into the woods, a weapon he fashioned himself from some hard black tree he found deep in the shadowy wilds.

Though greatly curious, Threadgill was not encouraged to visit Amos … and Annie absolutely *forbade* him to hunt. Annie gave only vague reasons why, but Threadgill once overheard the owner of the hardware store in Eufaula call Amos "that cannibal."

When Threadgill learned what the word meant, he kept his distance from Amos until the fear passed.

Along with her farm, Annie Pickett built Threadgill's childhood. How many times had he run in the woods or trip-trapped through overhead rafters, or clambered the cool dirt under pine-plank floors to peer up through knotholes into Annie's musty, mysterious rooms? How many happy hours had he meddled a trail through dusty and quiet rooms, sometimes bouncing on cobwebbed furniture, sometimes opening boxes filled with mysteries – buttons, old coins, scraps of colored cloth?

The original thirteen members of the old Pickett homestead had distilled to three now – just Aunt Annie, Threadgill and Amos. But the whispery ghosts and shadowy spirits of all the family came and went with Threadgill on happy childhood excursions.

The youngster had no way of knowing he would love this home more than any other place in his life.

***

Looking down at the cold pond, Randoll Pickett spoke suddenly, and hard.

"I got to get some more niggers to help y'all up here. It don't do to have just an old woman and a boy and one skinny old darky living out at the edge of the world this way."

Threadgill felt his feelings pinch again. "Aunt Annie ain't old," he protested. "She just looks like that."

His father snorted. "It's a dangerous business to live without a man around the house. You two need somebody can take care of you. Anything might happen."

Scalding tears squenched up in Threadgill's eyes. *But I'm the man around here*, he wanted to yell. *Where are* you *all the time, Daddy?* He could defend the place, he reckoned. He would do it for Aunt Annie, he knew. He would fight hard.

He wished with all his heart that his father would leave today – right now – and go back to Mexico, back to soldiering. Maybe it was a sin, but he didn't like this man. He wasn't kind. He wasn't like Aunt Annie. He wasn't like anybody nice.

Pickett must have read his son's mind. He stared at the boy, still naked, crouched like a frog.

"You learn to shoot that gun I left?"

Threadgill dropped his head to hide the tears. He swiped leaves from his wet foot. "No sir. Aunt Annie give it away."

His father frowned, then wiped his knife on oak leaves and slipped it back into its scabbard. "Well, I've got my service pistol. We'll have some shooting lessons this afternoon. It won't hurt a thing for the man of the house to learn how to handle a gun. You're old enough, Gill. No matter what Annie thinks."

Then the lieutenant jumped to his feet. He grabbed the rope swing with one hand and began to haul off a boot, hopping on one leg. "I'm gonna show you how to splash this pond without cryin' salty baby tears."

Threadgill, grinning, took his father's boots one at a time.

Now he'll see, Threadgill thought. *That water's cold. He'll be sorry.*

***

His father had been in Clio two weeks now. He arrived unannounced. He'd traveled by sailing ship from Vera Cruz to Mobile, where he first dropped in on his sister Rose Nell and met Ben. He came most of the way to Eufaula by locomotive. He actually beat the arrival of his "I'm heading your way for a visit" letter by days.

He rode a roan government horse up the Clio road and into the front yard, surprising the boy and his aunt late one Sunday afternoon. They sat over a reading primer at the pine table in the kitchen.

Threadgill had just puzzled out a brand new word in the day's lesson, a hard one – "surprise."

A horse nickered at the gate, and Threadgill remembered how his aunt pinched the curtain aside to stare out, then stood up straight with her knuckles to her mouth.

No hugs, only polite hellos, passed between her and the tall soldier. This was the Pickett way. Annie let the man come in from the porch, and she introduced Threadgill and he said hello and the man said hello back to him, with hardly any expression on his face at all.

The three of them sat in the parlor. Annie made tea, and served it on her special silver tray. Lt. Randoll Pickett still wore his uniform, bright with ribbons and brass buttons, and told amazing tales about Mexico.

It was the first time Threadgill Pickett had ever seen his father. At least in memory. Aunt Annie sometimes reminded Threadgill how his father came home briefly after his young wife died – Threadgill and Ben howled his whole visit with their colic, though theirs was hardly the only misery in that family.

No photographs of Lt. Pickett existed, and Threadgill's entire impression of his father had been based on stories told by grown-ups about long-ago and far-away things he did.

That first afternoon, Annie fluttered in and out with her tray. Little pieces of homemade fruitcake covered one. Fresh figs, the last of the season, and cups of hot tea filled another. Between moments of hostessing, Threadgill's aunt perched on a straight-back chair. Annie and Amos had been working the forty acres out back earlier that day, and she wore homespun breeches and sat with her legs spread apart like a man.

"Let me know if that tea suits you, Rand," she said. "I remember you like it sweet."

"It's sweet enough," he answered. His nose whistled a flat note, like a kettle.

Threadgill sat terrified at the far end of the small couch shared with his father. The man's bedezined uniform, all blue and white, struck the boy dumb. He felt vaguely the way an auctioned slave might feel, he reckoned, at the moment when a new master suddenly appeared in his life.

"You doing right?" Lt. Pickett finally turned and asked his boy, his first direct question.

The youngster fought back panic. He wanted to run out of the room, or jump through a window. What did his daddy mean by "right?" What could he say?

"Yessir," Threadgill stammered. His tongue stupidly fluttered the word, then tumbled to the floor of his mouth like a shot bird.

His father nodded sagely, nose up, nose down – the Pickett nose. Somewhere in the house, a clock stroked slowly.

Threadgill's father stared intently out the parlor window, tea steam curling from his cup. He squinted down the long road back toward Eufaula.

Threadgill could stand it no longer.

He wet his pants.

In horror, the boy watched helplessly as his breeches darkened in front, then down the sides. A little wet puddle formed on the couch around him.

The man chose that moment to turn toward his son. He pressed his big knobby grown-man fingers down on the couch seat. He leaned nearer.

"Annie tells me you're a good student."

"Mighty smart!" chirped Aunt Annie from her chair. "You would be proud. His mother would be proud."

"I'm sure she would," Randoll Pickett nodded. His face seemed as big as the moon, if the moon had a huge fleshy nose filled with shining brown hairs.

The stream of urine began to slowly meander down the sofa.

Threadgill trembled, flinched, closed his eyes in horror. The man beside him cleared his throat, started to speak, stopped.

Lt. Pickett reached for his cup. He sipped tea again, pouring it into his huge, unknowable face.

The pee stream puddled at a seam in the cushion, overflowed it, then glided straight toward Randoll Pickett like a deadly snake.

That exact instant, a miracle happened.

Some sort of fit seized Threadgill's father, a shuddering paroxysm that threw the man back onto the sofa and snapped his eyes up, spooky white, into his head. His tea spilled, splattering up and down the sofa, thank god. The china cup flew from his hand and clattered, spinning round and round, on the plank floor. Miraculously, it didn't break.

"Oh Lord!" exclaimed Aunt Annie. She rushed to her brother and flung her arms awkwardly around him. "Now, now, Randy. You just go on now. We all miss her. Threadgill looks so much like her. Poor brother!"

Threadgill could stand it no more. He bolted from the room, streaked out the parlor door, shot across the yard. He leaped completely over the front rail fence and tore across the road and fled into the endless woods.

He couldn't see the house at all when he finally threw himself down in the fallen leaves, crying his heart out, confused, scared.

Would this man kidnap him to Mexico? Wouldn't Aunt Annie try to stop him? She already gave his big brother away. He didn't want to go away from Annie. He loved her more than anyone.

After a long time, Threadgill's sobbing stopped. Gradually, his heart pounded more softly, and he could hear the wind and the mourning doves and the settling noises of the woods. He lay on his back in the leaves out there, watching treetops sift the golden late-summer light.

What will my life turn out to be like? he wondered *What in the world will happen to Threadgill Pickett?*

At last, after a very long time, the boy got to his feet again.

He threw a dead stick, tomahawk-style, at a big sourwood tree. A hidden deer, just a few steps away, chuffed and bolted.

Dark minted a few early stars and a big coppery moon before Threadgill decided his pants were finally dry.

"I ain't going to Mexico!" he yelled, leaves in his hair. "They can't MAKE me go!"

He tricked his way back out of the woods to the rough road. There, he discovered the day's *surprises* weren't yet finished.

Threadgill heard the hooves first. *Clop-clop-clop-clop.*

Out of the twilight, his father trotted up on his huge black horse.

Lt. Randoll Pickett reined in. He seemed five times as tall to Threadgill now, a giant on a giant steed, stars over his shoulders.

Threadgill couldn't decide if he should turn and run again. He wasn't brave, he decided. But he stood there, trembling like a snared rabbit, half hidden in spears of dog fennel along the roadside.

The man on the horse stared down at him solemnly. He could have been a centaur or some other unreal creature from one of Aunt Annie's story-books. A cavalry saber gleamed at his side in the moonlight.

His father said nothing for so long Threadgill thought he might pee in his pants all over again.

Finally, Randoll Pickett cleared his throat.

"Boy, I ain't blaming you for what happened to Kate. To your mama," he said. "I know it weren't your fault. Nor your brother's."

Threadgill dared a glance upward at his father's face then. He saw something in the eyes that he'd never seen before in his life.

What? What was it?

Lieutenant Pickett looked away. He jerked the reins, yanked his horse clean around in the road.

"*Yaaahh!*"

The big stallion shot away, eyes wide, startled, spurs put sharply to his flanks. The soldier stood high in the stirrups, wind whipping back his long black hair, his hat raised atop his sword.

"Yeeeehaaaawww!" he screamed. "Run, horse! Goddammit, you *run*!"

Threadgill's father thundered off, a blurry silhouette that shrank smaller and smaller. Leaves swirled in the road.

Threadgill never forgot that moment.

***

Now Threadgill watched his father shrink and shrink and shrink away into distance once more – this time flying out over the mill pond on the end of the long rope swing.

"Yeeeehaawwww!"

Away, away, out over the sparkling water soared the bare-chested giant. His black hair flew behind him.

One foot accidentally brushed the pond, and bright spray fanned to either side of it. Immediately, Randoll Pickett began a dizzy spin in the air, around and around, out of control. Still, he held on, arm and chest muscles taut – out to the very end of the rope's exhilarating arc.

At that perfect, suspended moment, his father let go. He dropped, legs pedaling the air in the blue woolen uniform pants.

The instant before Lt. Randoll Pickett splashed into the pond, he wore the happiest face Threadgill ever saw on a grown-up.

His father's eyes shone. The knife-thin body arched downward now, tense but letting go, like a nervous man settling onto a bed for a long sleep.

Aunt Annie watched too, from the yard, the dipper gourd in her hand.

A tremendous slap – soft flesh on hard water – launched a white geyser of spray into the sky. A deeper follow-up splash, percussive as thunder, sent up a second shower of water drops, sparkling, spattering.

Magnificent!

Huge ripples spread from the dive, and the cattails at the edges of the pond shook crazily.

Threadgill waited.

Any moment a sleek, otter-like figure would burst head-first from the green water, gasping air, a triumphant smile on his face.

His father.

The ripples began to fade.

A black crow flapped over, a sudden blade of shadow on the water.

Now Threadgill could see Aunt Annie stumbling down the far hill, the gourd flung away, rolling over and over behind her, the spooked cows clumsily loping out of her path.

Threadgill heard her cry from the far hillside. His aunt sloshed into the water to her ankles, to her knees. She stumbled there, flopped forward, struggled back up, her apron washed away, hair streaming.

"Randoll!" A reflection in the pond opened its mouth and screamed at the same time Aunt Annie screamed. "Randoll! Oh, sweet Jesus!"

Threadgill remained motionless, hugging his naked knees, high up the bank. If he didn't move – if he sat perfectly still – he felt sure the bad luck coiled around this pond, rattling its tail in the air, wouldn't strike anyone else. Him or Aunt Annie. *Just be still*, Threadgill. *Let the bad go past.*

The swing creaked overhead now like a gallows rope.

Behind Threadgill, Lt. Randoll Pickett's white shirt hung from a limb. The man's boots and his knife and the apple peel lay perfectly still on the ground under the shirt's thin, swaying shadow.

"Randoll! Please dear God!" pleaded Annie's voice, far below, her cries mixed with helpless frantic splashes.

Surely, his father would surprise him this way, appearing out of thin air with a wet grin atop the bank. A devilish prankster. Like his brother Ben.

Then Threadgill began to roll down the hill, helpless to stop. A blackberry vine tore his naked white skin, and leaves tumbled into his eyes, his mouth. He felt he was a small piece of landslide, just beginning.

Crash! Bang! Tumble! World and sky, confused.

He came to a jarring stop. Threadgill clutched a double-handful of soggy, uprooted reeds, his bare legs in icy water, his naked torso smeared with mud and grass in the bitter sunlight.

He looked up.

Randoll Pickett's empty white blouse hung on an oak.

It waved an empty arm in the wind.

Chapter 16, Two Montgomerys

Summer 1964 — Montgomery, Alabama

From the windows of Johnnie's flying taxi, Threadgill watched the first capital city of the old Confederacy resolve from the morning mist, house by house, mysterious as images on photographic paper.

The images emerged in black and white.

White Montgomery mostly gleamed, a place of new and handsome red-brick suburban ranch houses with strewn-emerald lawns. Closer to the city center, the white folk lived in finer two-stories, with broad porches on the upper floors. A colossal columned mansion rose every so often, as lordly as those back in Eufaula. These houses boasted swimming pools and separate guest cottages and long green caterpillars of azaleas. Broadleaf trees shaded cobbled driveways, shiny cars. Chandeliers blazed in early-morning windows, and through one of these Threadgill spotted a pale, frowzy-haired family in pajamas transfixed before the pale blue light of a TV. The father and mother and children all looked as if they had mysteriously died.

Threadgill saw the black Montgomery too, Negro, a town of largely unpainted shacks with dirt yards or shabby tarpaper row houses trimmed in gaudy colors. Crepe myrtle and kudzu grew wild. Older folks, sullen as bears, sat on beaten couches on their front porches, waving paper funeral-parlor fans to keep cool. One lady lifted a pink-palmed hand to wave at Johnnie. White chickens dashed away from a barefoot man.

In both kinds of neighborhoods, things felt … strange.

This was summer, children out of school. But where were they? Threadgill did see adults moving pell-mell, but few children. The adults seemed frantic, mouths open and arms waving. Grown men and women leaped over clipped boxwood fences between neighborhood houses or ducked their heads under fluttering clotheslines as they scooted here and there carrying out some urgent, undetectable business.

What in the world was going on?

Threadgill remembered once on Goat Island when a hurricane bore down on his little piece of creation. A first hint something bad lay ahead came from the little anxious insects – fire ants and sweat gnats and termites

– all rousted from their nests with some early-warning instinct. They crawled everywhere – on logs, on beaches, on tree trunks, making for the heights, stagger-crazy from summer heat and apprehension.

Johnnie answered Threadgill's perplexion.

"Mr. Pickett, look at this tomfoolery! You'd purely think this second colored army marching from Selma was the end of the world!" She snorted. "Who knows if it's even true? Just look at all this mess!"

Johnnie rolled down her window, so Threadgill did so too. A pleasantly cool Alabama morning gusted back the front brim of his hat.

The noise!

Montgomery sounded like hard rain on a million tin roofs. Threadgill winced at shouts from white workers carrying barricades, pushing overloaded wheelbarrows, clanging crowbars against stubborn planks, backing up cement trucks. Commercial delivery vehicles offloaded bags of Portland, roofing tacks, rolls of barbed wire, sheets of corrugated metal, pop rivets, rebars, extension cords, boxes of nails, lumber, sheet metal. Threadgill saw one big-bellied white man with an electric drill holstered in his belt like a cavalry pistol. He directed traffic around a doggy white street crew that sweated and cursed with pick-axes, ripping up pavement in front of a drug store.

Yes, folks prepared here for something big and bad. Some kind of cataclysm.

Downtown, white people screeched saws through plywood, banged 2"x 4"s over doorways, hammered windows shut and jerked down the shades. Suburban home owners lugged sandbags off the yawning tailgates of their pick-up trucks, hobbled cursing over their groomed lawns, heaved the bags atop other stacked bags. Barricades rose around doors and windows. Threadgill thought of the sandbag walls around anti-aircraft guns in World War II movies he'd seen at Mobile Sunset Home.

An Oldsmobile raced through a red light, horn blaring at Nadine. The lumber lashed to its roof slap-whapped like bamboo fishing poles on the way to a good bluegill hole.

The madness equally unhinged the citizens of black Montgomery.

Colored men in overalls nailed pine planks over the door of a barbeque shack, then embellished the barrier with spray-paint – "BAD DOG!!!" The artist of the crew added a very fierce dog head with fangs, plainly for the benefit of potential looters who couldn't read. Threadgill saw a frail old woman the color of river water wrestle paper bags of wax candles and Colonial bread and Octagon soap up the warped board steps to her front door. Two black men filled milk bottles from a hose in her perfectly raked dirt front yard.

"Look out! Clear a way!"

Shouts, hard as gravel, flew from a megaphone. A fleet of big rumbling vehicles – the telephone company, the power company and the gas company, all in brawny mechanized convoy – tore past Nadine. The vehicle drivers whipped around the next street corner, leaving pandemonium, swirling dust.

Threadgill and Johnnie, coughing, rolled their windows back up.

Threadgill had heard tell of this same thing happening in another scared-white city, long ago. Most likely, they acted this way one summer afternoon in good old Atlanta. People tried just this hard to pull that town back into its mansioned white shell before Sherman's avenging army closed blue claws to pinch it to death.

A century ago, General Sherman and 60,000 hard-eyed Irish boys toughened on three years of war approached Atlanta. Killers and a killing machine. Threadgill could swear without a Bible that those boys had been looking all their lives for any excuse to shoot or strangle or bayonet or blow up or scald or gut or boil or drag or grapeshot or roast some other human being. *Any* excuse. Burning Georgia, to them, was a birthday party with a million candles.

Burning Threadgill too.

But how could some ragtag passel of coloreds, five or six hundred foot-weary souls toting a few misspelled signs down the highway from Selma, put the fear of God into *this* modern city?

These Montgomery folks behaved as if magnolia blooms were about to close up forever.

Nadine stopped for a red light.

"It just beats all," Johnnie said. "The nigger army already come through here before, back in March. That Martian Lucifer Coon, an' all them. Now there's a rumor they're marchin' here again just to get back on TV some more. Folks have gone pure crazy this time."

***

Pickett's Charge

A milk cow, escaped from some nearby neighborhood, lumbered into Nadine's path. Its hooves slipped on the old street brick under a missing section of pavement, and the cow went down, sprawling. Nadine eased around the beast's frantic twisting efforts to regain a footing. The cow's terrified bawling mouth slung a sticky white trapeze of saliva onto Nadine's windshield.

"Cow spit," Threadgill announced.

Johnnie didn't even answer.

Nadine finally threaded a path through the mayhem and accelerated up a short, steep hill and turned onto Dexter Avenue. The chaos of the commercial district fell behind. Businesses and stores gave way to Alabama government buildings, vast and white, gleaming marble with tobacco-stained sidewalks. Not a soul in sight up there.

"Right yonder," Johnnie indicated, "is why I brought you here through all that mess."

Threadgill leaned forward in the seat and squinted into the sun.

"What is it?"

"The whole durned reason you takin' this trip, Mr. Pickett. You go up there and you'll see. This is the end of the line for me and Nadine. I'm droppin' you at the Capitol."

Threadgill now saw, floating like a dream among gray pigeons and green trees, Alabama's historic Capitol building – cool, monumental, a white-columned Taj Mahal. Here stood the first Capitol building of the Confederacy. Slave muscle and sweat made the brick of the foundations, the plaster walls, even its gorgeous dome.

Over his shoulder, Threadgill could see back down Dexter Avenue clear to the Alabama River, a gray sash in the distance.

From this prospect, Threadgill could envision how in a day, maybe two, the new Selma marchers might arrive, streaming up this broad street in a black river, a roaring, surging collection of tributaries flowing in from hot fields and scorched highways, more climbing off buses, unpacking from cramped cars.

Maybe I've got it wrong, Threadgill considered. But if the clamor in town gave any honest clue – *and who could tell the future?* – the new invading colored army might number in the millions.

What would happen to Montgomery if a million coloreds crossed the river and just went hog wild?

What would happen all over the South?

Was that what scared all these folks to death?

Chapter 17, Flashback

Summer 1964

That instant, as Threadgill considered Montgomery's madness through the windows of the Studebaker Nadine, a ringing noise different from other ringing noises hurt his head. Threadgill felt the view change before his eyes. The world transformed woozily from cement city to sultry swamp.

Threadgill realized with a disoriented shock that he had somehow already lived through this scene summoned to his eyes. This memory. A memory he did not remember at all until this instant.

Threadgill watched the memory in the same way a bystander watches a scene between strangers. He saw everything. Heard everything. Knew everything.

He now recalled something that happened along the road with Lash LaRue and his terrible crew.

***

In the swampland of the delta, the noon sun blazed. Sunlight danced in oily mirages up and down the highway.

A long-haul trucker, his rig overweighted with dying Leghorn chickens in cheap crates, sweated over a flat tire at a small dirt pull-off. The long causeway through the swamp, thank God, had one or two emergency stops like this.

The truck driver's cheeks and neck burned madly from the brief ten minutes of hot sunlight he'd endured. Up north, the weather felt cool. But here, in this godforsaken Alabama hell ...

Around the trucker spread a half-moon-shaped, auto-flattened clearing littered with tossed oil cans, hubcaps, baby diapers, filthy magazines. Torn, abandoned tires lay all through the overgrown green fringe of dollarweed and sawgrass. Knobby and black, the tires reminded the trucker of alligators.

A paranoia about gators, in fact, kept him glancing nervously over his shoulder, eyeing the weeds to make sure nothing crawled close.

He came by the case of jitters honestly. As a youngster on vacation in the Florida panhandle, an alligator ate the family dog, a friendly dachshund leashed for the night outside a riverside hotel called Sopchoppy Inn. His parents actually made the discovery next morning, stepping out the door to find an empty collar and two praying pup feet. A long sandy trail, red with strange dew, led from the porch to a nearby pond.

Now the trucker had been two days and two nights on the road without sleep, popping pills. His face looked clobbered. He was a winter-whitened family man on a route out of Lima, Ohio, assigned to bring a load of Leghorns back alive, unseasonal heat or no heat, and his tire was blown out and he was surrounded by alligators, maybe, a long, long way from home.

The trucker spotted, far down the highway, a black Cadillac. It weaved precariously, lane to lane, and growled like a badly wounded animal.

Something about the vehicle alarmed the trucker. In the last fifteen months, the teamster had been robbed twice, once in broad daylight. The second time, a hitchhiking thief, a little dwarf of a man, clouted him in back of his head with a screwdriver, a blow so hard it knocked his false teeth clean through the front windshield.

The trucker took no chances now. He felt in his belt for the small pistol loaded with ratshot he bought specifically to protect him on this new southern route.

The Cadillac, sure enough, slid onto the pull-off and stopped, idling, its wipers flapping happily as a friendly child waving its hands.

Wipers? In this hellish sunny weather?

The trucker stood up, hands black with axle grease. The crack of his butt felt sunburned when he hiked his pants.

Flap, flap, flap went the merry wipers.

The trucker squinted for a closer look. It was hard to see inside – the windows appeared to be painted jet black. The car stunk too – *Good God, what a smell!* – something like those awful things the southern truckers called chitlins. When that crap got on a good boiling roll, you couldn't stay in the room.

Behind the smoke in the car there seemed to be a disturbance of some sort.

What in the devil was going on?

Carefully, his hand on the gun in his pocket, the trucker stepped around the big frowning grille of the black car and closer to the driver's window.

He would never forget what confronted him at the end of that short walk.

Some say the face of Christ can sometimes be revealed in a tortilla, a rock formation, a patch of kudzu silhouetted by the late sky.

What the Ohio trucker saw, summer 1964, was surely the Devil.

Old Nick wore a nasty fur suit. He sat shrouded in brimstone smoke at the wheel of a black car. He waved in the air a meat hook – or was it a soul hook? – and attempted to butt his way out the door.

Thanks to the angels eternal, it didn't open.

Then he heard a growling voice.

"Hell! Hell meat!"

The frightened trucker turned white. He was a sinner, sure. And just like the Bible promised, he had finally heard the Devil calling for his soul from inside this Cadillac.

"Hell Meat!"

The trucker's hair stood on end.

Goddamit! I ain't Hell Meat yet!

He jerked the gun. He shot blindly at the window. The blast sent a thumb-sized dazzle of glass over the beast inside. Roaring, crying demon noises now escaped the car, awful animal sounds bubbling up from the deepest holes on earth.

"Not yet! I ain't Hell Meat yet!"

Another pistol shot knocked off a big chunk of the thing. There was more screaming, louder, more souls in torment. And, Sweet Holy Christ, Son of God, what happened next was horrible to behold.

The furry, shot-away part of the thing *got back up and leaped again onto the whole awful seething unholy inhuman mound*! It joined other parts that started to crawl over the ugly body again, all together, long viney maggoty whips and tentacles flailing on an odious something vaguely shaped like a man!

Foul smoke boiled from the Cadillac's bullet holes. Yelling began again, a demogorgon's cries.

"Flee! Flee, Mister! Hell Meat! Oh flee!"

Bright flakes of glass burst from around the bullet hole in the window. A pointed metallic claw appeared, wicked as a snake tooth, pulling madly, shaking the whole window.

"Nooo!" yelled the horrified trucker. "Satan, get *behind* me ..."

He fired again.

Bulls eye!

The hook disappeared. The screaming stopped.

Now the Cadillac roared away again, onto the tarmac, slinging shell and gravel behind it. It sped off on a wobbly path, blood-red taillights flashing on and off at random.

The trucker took aim and fired. He fired again, and he continued to fire the little pistol until he couldn't see a black car any more, or that hate-soaked creature, or those ominous windshield wipers scrubbing away.

The Devil's Cadillac was on its way back home ... to Hell!

The trucker sank to his knees in the scrubby roadside grass. His legs went weak after the crisis. A bird sang in the glades.

The trucker looked up, spread his arms to the wondering, heat-stunned chickens in their hundreds of crates. *Do you brainless, soulless, suffering chickens hear that*, the trucker shouted. *A singing bird! Dear Sweet Jesus, what a beautiful sound!*

The long-haul trucker thanked the god of birdsong, sunshine and blue skies for his humble life on this magnificent morning.

He looked at the pistol in his hand, brought it to his heavy lips, kissed the hot little barrel.

Thank Jesus he owned a gun.

He got to his feet, walked around the truck, checking his windblown chickens, all of them suffering, glucking and clucking in the heat. *Be glad for suffering*, he wanted to tell them. *Suffering means you're alive.*

Almost as an afterthought he whirled, quick as Billy the Kid, pistol raised. He stared back at the roadside weeds and scattered chunks of tire.

"Run! Run, ya friggin' gators!" he whooped. "I'll make suitcases out of ya!"

Thank God some more.

Nothing moved out there.

But he'd better hurry.

Chapter 18, The Capitol

Montgomery, Alabama – Summer 1964

"Mr. Pickett? Are you … alright?"

Brilliant sunlight glared off the white Capitol dome.

"Mr. Threadgill Pickett?"

Johnnie used a mild voice now, worried words.

Threadgill came to. The ringing ceased.

"Miz Johnnie," he stammered. "Take this money, please. Your meter's been running – I see it, right there. And I piled up on your mattress all them days. You bought my food and washed my clothes. I don't *like* to be beholden."

He surprised Johnnie, coming back into phase that way. Then Johnnie surprised him.

A little red-eyed, she waved his words away. Threadgill saw short black shiny bristles, like those on a shoat, covering her arm.

"Businesses don't take Confederate money any more, Mr. Pickett. And *I* don't take the other kind – not from you. Plus, if you don't hurry up and get your skinny butt out of Nadine," she forced a joke, "me and her might just haul you all the way back down to Mobile and make you start this trip slam over."

Nadine chuckled at the curb.

After a long quiet moment, Threadgill reached across the seat and patted the back of Johnnie's hand.

He hopped out, dragging along his newly organized gear, the foodstuffs from Jerry Coe. For this parting moment, Threadgill stood on the sidewalk as tall and straight as he could. The big woman blinked out the window at him.

She didn't have to say a thing. But she did. "Old man," Johnnie half-whispered, "I lived a good life and tried hard and prayed every night. You know?" Tears filled her eyes suddenly, and her nose glistened.

"Yes'm."

Johnnie stopped, bit her lip. "Ever night I lay down to sleep, I wonder if Satan the Devil is stabbing a burnin' pitchfork in the eyes of a pore bastard I shot dead in this very taxi one time. Sonofabitch tried to rob me, and I shot him a lot more times than I had too. Now I get scared wonderin' if he's suf-ferin' in Hell because of me."

"Yes'm."

"Maybe he coulda been saved. You know?"

"Yes'm."

"And I sometimes get to wondering if maybe there's a pitchfork waitin' on me Down There too," she sobbed. "Since I took his life, and the Bible says it's a sin. I really do get scared … because … oh, me …" Johnnie broke down, head on her arm, arm on her steering wheel. Huge tears dripped onto her broad lap.

Threadgill reached for words. He found hardly any.

"Now then," he finally clucked. "Don't, Miz Johnnie …"

Johnnie raised a hand – enough. Her fingers still wore faint black grime from the tire change. Her nose glistened when she looked up again, her little moustache visible in the mucus.

Nadine's engine revved.

"You be careful, Mr. Pickett." Johnnie sniffed. "You tell me you're bound and determined to kill some man you never even met. I been thinkin.' You brought that soul of yours a long way and a lot of years. It would be a shame to lose it down this highway. Even if the whole world thinks you're doin' the best thing you ever done. The Lord's gonna let you know what's right."

"An eye for a eye," Threadgill said, fiercely. "That's what the Book says."

"Jesus didn't kill a single soul. And don't none of us know how God's gonna judge revenge and killin'," Johnnie answered, her face breaking again. "It ain't a thing to do lightly, is all."

Nadine barked her tires, and Johnnie the taxi driver disappeared down the long hill home. Threadgill watched her hairy arm wave once out the window.

Threadgill turned and looked up at the Confederate flag on top of the Capitol.

Old hurt, Threadgill thought all at once. *A man ain't got nothing else in the end. That's what they teach us, anyway.*

***

Compared with the town in turmoil below, Capitol Hill seemed a little piece of Eden.

Mockingbirds sang in the trees. Threadgill even heard bees humming. A yardman waltzed through one of the flower beds, dragging a rake, the only other human in sight.

Scratch, scratch, scratch.

The big trees lifted Threadgill's spirits.

Threadgill blinked and, shockingly, everything turned red for a moment, and a hot nail of pain pierced his head. The scab on his knee throbbed. Then Threadgill blinked again, and all was normal.

What was *that*? What was happening to him?

He sighed. Looked like the wreck at the Snow White would be a permanent part of him now. And a monkey bite. And Nadine and Johnnie. Everything.

Threadgill sat down to get his wits back on a cast-iron park bench, green and black, whorled metal leafwork cool against his back. A gray pigeon dropped down nearby on starchy wings.

Scratch, scratch, scratch.

The busy gardener with the rake wore dark sunglasses. He sported a brand-new pair of overalls – conspicuously short, so that a glimpse of white leg flashed over his socks as he collected his rising pile of dry magnolia leaves. A cigarette hung miraculously from huffing lips.

All at once, he didn't look to Threadgill like a man with a lot of experience raking. Too pink, for one thing. No stamina. He stopped every thirty seconds, elaborately unfolded a white handkerchief, swiped it across his forehead, his cheeks, wiped his eyes. He mumbled aloud to himself.

Some people ain't made to rake leaves, Threadgill thought.

Threadgill rose and struck off for the spot on Capitol Hill Johnnie had described. It didn't take long to find – a bronze star in the pavement at the coppergreen base of a hollow-eyed statue. A statue of Jefferson Davis.

The first president of the Confederacy – the *only* president of the Confederacy – seemed to proudly watch Threadgill approach. Threadgill made it a point to stand on the exact spot where Davis took his oath as the Lincoln of the South.

"Reporting for duty, sir," Threadgill nodded. He straightened and saluted.

Three people turned. One was the man with the rake. The others were a broad-shouldered man in a seersucker suit and his square-headed boy, ten or twelve years old, in a green-and-white striped shirt. Two fat peas from the same pod.

When the boy saw Threadgill, his eyes grew wide.

"Daddy!" he gushed. "Look! A Confederate soldier!"

The Daddy gave a laugh. "Looks like it, Bo Hog! For sure! Where'd you get that hat, mister? Sell that down at the State Archives?"

"I've had my yellowhammer hat about a hundred years," Threadgill answered, proudly.

"There you go!" the Daddy enthused.

"Daddy, he's got a real yellowhammer feather! Like Alabama Confederates wore!"

The father and son seemed awed. "Ain't this a picture, old timer? Right here, right on that star there, old Jeff Davis stood and took his oath of office. The one and only real president Alabama ever had. Might be the only one we'll *ever* have. Unless Governor Wallace keeps on like he's going."

The statue, weathered green, sported epaulets of pigeon poop. Jefferson Davis's eyes seemed surprised – astonished even, staring off into what had happened in history. And what hadn't.

"I seen a picture of Robert E. Lee!" exclaimed the chunk of boy. "He wore that same hat!"

"Well this hat's mine," Threadgill warned. "It don't belong to that no account. Some of us ain't never forgot he surrendered up yonder in Virginia. Offered to give his sword to a damn Yankee."

The Daddy roared.

"Bo Hog, you hear that?"

The boy's eyes were lit sparklers. "He's a real Confederate, ain't he, Daddy?"

"Reckon so. He shore talks like one."

"Can I wear his hat, Daddy? I'll take care of it."

"Well, son, you have to ask the man. Why don't you ask what this feller would take to let you just put it on for a minute?"

Well, there it was.

"Two dollars," the Daddy announced. "What you think, Bo? Would that be enough for five minutes?"

"FIVE dollars, Daddy!"

Bo Hog eyed Threadgill greedily. He was a stout child, about a hundred pounds, a young striped watermelon of a boy. Threadgill figured he didn't need a hat so much as a horse collar.

Scratch, scratch, scratch.

The creature with the rake swept into view, mouthing into his white handkerchief again. Leaves and magnolia cones flew all directions.

"Look, tell you what," the Daddy said. "I'll give you *five dollars* to let my boy wear your hat for five minutes. Five dollars. Hell, I'll give you *twenty* to buy it off you, here and now. I'll wear it in the Legislature next week – that is, if there's gonna still *be* any government left after this new nigger army gets to town."

Threadgill gave no answer to the man. His scarred scalp tingled under the headgear.

The child stared up at Threadgill's hat in a trance of greed.

"Daddy make him give it to me!"

Then it happened to Threadgill again. He blinked blood red. His head briefly housed a snarling noise, like an animal attacking out of a black hole.

It vanished with a quick squench of Threadgill's eyes, a shake of the head.

"Daddy!" squealed Bo Hog. "Make him!"

Threadgill tried a little distraction, his head faintly throbbing.

"Y'all live in Montgomery?"

"Andalusia! I'm in Big Gas!" the man announced, a booming voice. "Know them Fosher boys in the Legislature? Crump and Wheel? They work for me down yonder. Wells, gas pipelines, drilling equipment, even personnel. I brought Bo up to see the Capitol this weekend … while it's still standin'."

"I'm Threadgill Pickett," the old man said. "I'm on my way up north to kill the last Yankee soldier that's alive in this world. He lives in Bangor, Maine. Reckon I need my hat for that trip."

"Daddy, make him sell it," whined Bo Hog, unmoved.

"Boy, hush," his Daddy ordered. "You serious, mister?"

"I am."

Scratch, scratch, scratch.

Bo Hog pointed suddenly. "Hey!" he hollered. "That man's got a wire coming out of his handkerchief!"

They all looked. Sure enough, plainly visible in a bright ray of sunlight, a silver antenna gleamed above the yardman's handkerchief. Threadgill saw a tiny cord now, black as a snake. It squiggled down one arm into new overalls.

"I bet you that's a got-damn federal government agitator!" Big Gas whispered through his blocky teeth. "I bet you *anything* that sumbitch is one of Lyndon Johnson's government boys! Sent down here to try and interfere in our got-damn sovereign state business …"

The gardener jammed his telltale handkerchief in a bib pocket. Too late.

"Wait here, fellers," Big Gas ordered. "I'll get to the bottom of this."

He stepped toward the man with the rake. Then he broke into a run. He *had* to. The fake yardman threw down his garden tools and sprinted full out for a nearby white van. On the roof of the van, a very small dish of some sort stared at the sky.

"You! Stop!" yelled Big Gas, who moved fast for a blocky man in a seersucker suit. "You got some explainin,' buddy!"

The white van's back door broke open and the so-called gardener hurled himself inside. The vehicle jerked into motion, burned a blue twin slick of rubber, the open door slamming all by itself from the acceleration. Squawling tires echoed eerily off the alabaster walls of the Capitol building.

"Your daddy ain't never gonna catch that van," Threadgill remarked. "But whoo! Look at them legs moving!"

Big Gas, incredibly, *did* catch the rocketing van. He clawed briefly at its locked back door before it finally gunned away and left him, one shoe thrown, panting and disheveled in the middle of Dexter Avenue.

Bo Hog said nothing.

Threadgill should have been ready.

The boy's wild, flailing swipe knocked his hat sideways, almost off his head. Caught by surprise, Threadgill stumbled backwards and nearly fell over the bench. Bo Hog screeched like a mad wildcat.

"Give it! You *give* it to me!"

Bo Hog's eyes glittered. He looked like he would push Threadgill down and stomp a hole in him for that hat. So Threadgill did something he hadn't done in decades.

He took off running too.

Just like the gardener. Just like Big Gas. Just like a young man on a terrible hill in Georgia all those years ago.

His old legs rose to the occasion. The knee with the monkey bite hurt faintly as his gear banged against it. Even so, it was no contest. Bo Hog wasn't fast even for a fat child.

The youngster gave up at the edge of the Capitol square.

Threadgill still ran. Due north.

What a strange place the world had become.

It turned even stranger.

Many blocks after Threadgill stopped running, as he hassled like a hound with his head down over a filling station water fountain, every object in his field of vision changed color at every heartbeat.

Blink. Red. *Blink.* Normal. *Blink.* Red.

Something has happened. Something is the matter with me.

But Threadgill kept moving. The Alabama Capitol grew smaller and smaller at his back until finally he couldn't see even the Stars and Bars fluttering way up on top.

Chapter 19, The Crying Place

Outside Montgomery, Alabama – Summer 1964

The moon over Alabama that night rose white, imperious, a skull tossed out on a black highway.

Threadgill woke, and the furious lunar brightness hurt his eyes.

He raised his hand to fend the glare. He blinked into black cypresses. The trees so crowded a creek bottom off the two-lane that water barely had room to trickle through.

The empty road made its own lonely hum under the open sky.

A fire ant stung Threadgill's chest, under his shirt.

"Ouch!"

The old soldier sat up in his blanket and pinched desperately, two, three times, at the insect. By the time he drew the speck of crushed red pepper out on an index finger, a welt already rose by his left nipple.

"Wish to God I knew why creatures like you lived on this earth," he growled.

Threadgill scrambled to his bare feet, flapping his blanket, stamping the ground. If one fire ant stung, likely ten thousand lay in wait.

Troubles seemed to lurk everywhere on his quest.

Threadgill was well awake now, and he slipped off into the woods. His warm pee stream sprinkled creek water. As Threadgill shook himself dry, a solitary car passed on the highway with a long whisper.

"Shoot. That car might be headed clear to Maine," he gruffed aloud, mainly to hear his own voice. "Too bad, Threadgill. You missed a perfect ride."

The car and its loud radio station and secrets disappeared around a curve.

A new tiny firecracker exploded on his ankle. Two more stings quickly shot Threadgill a foot in the air.

He was covered.

Threadgill tore off his pants, and his underwear. He stood ankle-deep in the creek and shook his clothes a long time to make sure this time no fire ants lay in ambush.

The water around his ankles felt good, so Threadgill dipped his gnarled one-hundred-fourteen-year-old bare bottom in the tiny stream. It ran so narrow in Threadgill's bathing place that water pooled up behind him. He created Threadgill Dam, cool creek water pouring through sluices under his bare arms.

In the strong moonlight, Threadgill counted thirty-five welts on his shins and ankles. One truly painful sting inside his pale thigh, halfway to the groin, burned like a nettle.

I might be somewhere else tonight, if that Bo Hog boy hadn't tried to thief my hat, Threadgill thought, fanning creek water over the flames. *I might not be laying out here in the woods, anyway.*

Threadgill stopped, mid-splash.

He heard a sound.

Like a person crying.

Threadgill sat alert, perfectly still, in the creek.

He heard the noise again – something like short, staccato sobs. These tricked their way through the woods into the little clearing where Threadgill bathed.

Could it be an owl? Some kind of night bird?

The old man listened with a sense of uneasy curiosity. Yes – without question he heard hard, heartfelt sobs. Human sobs. No mistaking such a sound.

The noise was spooky. Haunting. Who in the world cried so sad out here in a swamp at midnight?

The old man stood up, dripping. He limped from the little brook. He felt terrifically stiff in the joints after his sprint at the Capitol. His old penis swung forlornly in the white fur of his groin.

The broken-hearted lullaby rose again. Threadgill rubbed his scabbed knee, holding for balance to the rough branch of a tree. He tried not to scratch his fire ant bites even as he scratched them. He cocked his head, a sentinel now.

Pickett the picket.

The noises rose in volume, so loud suddenly that they seemed to evoke faint, weepy echoes from the surrounding woods.

What the hell is *that?*

Threadgill felt spooked. He squinted uneasily down the creek, to where it disappeared into the black swamp trees, water running so slow it made no sound.

His curiosity proved too much. Threadgill picked his way down the bank, following the stream bed.

A cloud passed over the moon. The woods turned too black to see for a moment. But the cloud blew past, and all at once Threadgill could make out a dim figure. It resolved into view in the full moonlight.

Threadgill held his breath. He eased into a shadow to conceal himself. His naked body trembled, but not from cold.

The sobbing figure looked like a man, without question. A dark silhouette of a man.

The stranger sat huddled under a small willow tree, his back against its thin trunk, not thirty feet away across the little creek.

Threadgill could now see it was a Negro, a big hulking figure dressed in field clothes. The weeping willow limbs fell tent-like around him, green as candy, long wands with hard white summer catkins on the tips.

The sobbing man's work clothes appeared ripped and rumpled, his shirt torn open at the collar as if he had been trying desperately to get a breath.

Threadgill started when a new terrible burst of sadness wailed out of the shape.

He gave wild, gasping cries. The Negro's grief rose and fell, fluttered up and plunged down hard, a thing trying hopelessly to fly with broken wings. All at once, the man's gaping mouth opened hugely, issued a loud unearthly calf-like bawling. That lasted a few terrible seconds, then gave way finally to inconsolable sobbing again.

Threadgill gaped in amazement as the gigantic Negro's wracked body pitched headlong without warning, asprawl in its sorrow. The man's hands clenched black earth, unclenched again, and his black face pressed into the mud as if trying to bury itself.

Oh no no no no! Oh, dear sweet Jesus, no! Ah me, please no!

Threadgill took a cautious step back farther into the cypress shadows, thinking he would politely slip away from such a personal, painful moment. What in the world had happened to this poor man?

The cries guttered, a dying candle.

Threadgill furtively took a step or two back up the creek bank the way he'd come.

A good Samaritan could bathe and bandage and bed a sick man. A good nurse could offer a body food to heal, and water, cool water, to quench fever and thirst. Kindness and time might start life all over again. Didn't Threadgill know this as well as anyone? Wounds of the flesh could heal in time.

But this was some other kind of wound. Threadgill knew it without looking. A wound not so different from his own.

He dared a last glance. Threadgill could clearly see the Negro's broad bowed head, shaking, tossing side to side, *No, no*. The crying man once lifted his face in agony from the earth, and soil and leaves clung to his wool hair. The toes of his bare feet dug dark furrows. Sorrow ran shining down his wracked face.

A foolish mockingbird woke in a tree somewhere. From its perch, it answered the crier's song of grief. But after a few trills, it shut up, showed respect.

Threadgill slipped quietly away.

He returned to his campsite as quickly and silently as he could. With great stealth, he pulled on his pants and shirt. He put on his shoes. He wiped his blanket clean of trash, rolled it skillfully – he was practiced now – and stiffly turned for one last look at this odd event in the woods.

In a freak ray of moonlight, the crying Negro lay clearly visible now even at this distance. He now hunched forward on his knees, his pale palms clasped to his face. A glissando of sobs gave way every few moments to a new gigantic noisy yawp for breath. The huge mouth gasped, a black whirlpool that opened and shut under a caul of mucus and tears. The man's jerking, unstoppable, convulsive anguish had not slackened by a single teardrop.

Threadgill felt his own emotions surge.

A dead child? An unfaithful lover? A mother or father gone forever? A brother? This is a drowning grief, Threadgill thought. *This is grief that kills a man.*

He stood one more moment to watch this broken swimmer. Threadgill felt a cry from his own conscience: Would he let another human being sink this way? Hadn't good Miz Johnnie just scraped Threadgill up off the road and nursed him back to life?

Threadgill surprised himself. He took a leap, shirt still unbuttoned, tail flying behind him. He left one rounded bank of the creek and awkwardly launched to the other, arms windmilling.

The aches and pains of his body howled in chorus. So much for his attempt to be quiet too – his boots sank noisily to their tops in a gooze of wet mud.

Suck. Suck. Suck.

Out Threadgill struggled, a clumsy ruttling stumble over bony cypress roots.

He needn't have worried. A human being bereft as this crying man wouldn't notice the arrival of an elephant hauling church bells. The beast could clank up, rip out a tree by the roots, blare its trumpet loud enough to strip leaves off the branches.

This grief could not be interruped.

Threadgill drew close enough now to see, by moonlight, silver hairs shot through the Negro's shuddering head. Something about those old hairs made Threadgill even more miserable. He felt compelled to muster some word of comfort.

He formed sympathetic words in his mouth, a comfort ready.

"Ah …"

Threadgill's own head lifted sharply. Here came a new commotion, off in the dark just over there.

Another Negro.

Crying.

Threadgill could make out a woman, sobbing in gales, the noise of a strong wind blowing through the charred timbers of a burned house.

The sound at the end of the world.

She sprawled on her belly underneath another gentle willow. Her head scarf snarled in the tree limbs, ripped free. Her two delicate brown arms clung fast to the willow trunk, holding it like a dead lover. Her cheek pressed the bark, and the trunk of the tree gleamed in the moonlight with her tears, as if snails crawled there.

Unbroken sadness spilled from this Negro too. Her sobs blended with the sorrows of the crying man. It sounded weirdly like a sad slow song they sang together.

Now Threadgill realized, with a kind of dawning horror, that even more

Negroes – many, more – surrounded him in this moonlit swamp. He could suddenly make out dozens, scores, maybe hundreds, even thousands of Negro mourners, howling out some unimaginable woes. They filled every moon-ghosted clearing as far as Threadgill could see.

They heaped the earth under every tree like strange fallen fruit. Some lay flat on their bellies. Some lay on their backs with their arms raised to the sky. Some wept on their knees with their arms stretched up toward heaven. Some embraced. Some wailed alone and tore at their thick hair and clothes.

A Crying Place.

A black man with nasty scars on his back held fast to a gaunt woman. Grief shook them like a child's golliwogs. The black man's battered old hat fell to the ground, rolled away.

A pickaninny child, frowsy hair in dozens of bows, spun crazily out of the mothering shadows past the couple. After a moment, the little girl whirled like a top back into the dark again, arms spread, tears streaking her tiny face.

The fear of God struck Threadgill Pickett.

He bolted, for the second time this day. He fled loudly – heedlessly – across the little stream. He splashed loud as a horse in water.

He climbed the creek bank, stumbled, flailed branches back from his face, raced to his bedroll and haversack. Threadgill snatched up his gear, then sprinted with all his might straight through the woods, toward the lost highway.

Crying, behind him, drowned out all other sound in the world.

Threadgill kept his eyes locked on a clear place far ahead, where the kudzu-covered shoulder rose to meet the road.

"Just that far ..." he pleaded to his old bones. "Just to there."

The lamentations grew faint.

Threadgill finally dared open his eyes.

The trees and the stream and the bushes and purple air glowed with first sunlight.

The crying ended.

He lay in a field. The highway shone in the morning a hundred yards ahead.

For reasons he did not completely understand, Threadgill snatched off his clothes. Again? The first time this night?

He summoned his courage, walked a short way along the stream back into the woods, and he lay down again, completely naked, in the flowing water.

A pale Brahma bull wandered out of the woods to stare at him in curiosity.

The creek spoke once again around Threadgill's old body in little tongues, explaining, soothing. The water was cold as novacaine. The scab on his knee went numb, and the fire ant bites quieted.

Threadgill lay in the stream until he felt clean. Clean to the bone.

He took a sip of the water in his cupped hand.

It tasted faintly of salt.

Chapter 20, Here Comes a Man

January 1862 – Barbour County, Alabama

Threadgill woke on a frosty morning snuggled deep in Aunt Annie's feather quilts. Corn shucks rustled when he shifted on the mattress.

The tip of his nose told him that bed was the warmest place in the house. He could breathe out smoke into the cold. Aunt Annie's sniffles potion sat frozen on his nightstand. It made a little purple eye of ice on the spoon.

No matter. A warm surprise waited.

"Happy birthday, Gill!"

Aunt Annie's lined face glowed like a girl's. She held up a round yellow cake dusted in white sugar. Twelve candles danced in her big brown eyes. Her thumbs and fingers sported a mixed coat – black soot from teasing hearth fires back to life and white powdered sugar from her baking.

She looks like daddy, Threadgill thought. *How I remember him, anyway.*

Threadgill shouldered up, and the quilts fell off his growing frame. Brrr. Goose bumps shivered up and down lanky arms, over his chest and nipples, where red-blonde hairs had sprouted in the past few months.

The house smelled wonderful, pound cake mixed with fried bacon and fresh coffee and wood smoke.

"You get an even better surprise," Annie smiled. "But that comes later. How about you get dressed warm now."

Threadgill felt a rush of tenderness. How could he love anyone – even his mother or father – more than he loved his wonderful aunt? Where … and who … would he be if Aunt Annie hadn't taken him under her roof and raised him?

Happy birthday to you, Threadgill. Twelve candles … and twelve years of happy life … to you.

***

The frozen sun finally made it up over the river. It showed how far into the woods and fields the night's pale fog reached.

Threadgill smiled with pleasure. Annie gave him coffee with condensed milk on his birthday every year. Coffee was so hard to buy now, with the war going. Condensed milk seemed rare as golden eggs.

Threadgill opened a big gift wrapped in buckskin, a rawhide cord knotted into an intricate bow on one side. He lifted from this heavy package a fine new coat, a dark green oilskin quilted inside with soft wool. A long rider's cloak.

"I swear!" Threadgill whooped, throwing it on. "This is so warm, Aunt Annie. It's about as heavy as me!"

"A gentleman needs a coat," she clucked. "This winter's colder than most, and you're always out and about in just that old soldier thing of your daddy's. It's about worn through."

Aunt Annie, with a smile, produced a second gift, a round cardboard box, bright red. It looked expensive – Threadgill knew she hadn't made this gift with her own two hands, even as skilled as they were.

The box contained a broad-brimmed hat. Gray canvas. High crowned. Handsome. It was the finest thing Threadgill ever held in his own two hands in his whole life.

"It ought to fit," Annie prodded. "I measured your head one night while you were asleep. It came straight out of the hardware catalogue."

"Aunt Annie …"

"Pooh. Don't say one thing, Gill. Now why don't you step out on the porch real quick to try it on?"

It was bad luck in Annie's house to wear a hat indoors. Even in January. Even on your birthday.

The broad hat fit just fine. The jealous wind whipped at Threadgill's new coat and millinery. It seemed to Threadgill that with the hat on he suddenly felt taller – the height of a grown man – and that he could see a lot farther down the road in front of Annie's house.

He spotted a wild turkey out where the corn field ended. The big bird bathed, rustling up cold sand with its dark feathers, cautiously blinking around now and then on guard against wildcat or fox.

Threadgill stepped back through the door. He caught his aunt coughing into a handkerchief. The youngster turned his back respectfully, reaching up with frozen fingers to practice doffing his new handsome hat, grasping its full crown in his fingers. He proudly hung it on the rack by the doorway, by Aunt Annie's bonnet and the wide straw hat she wore when she worked out in the fields.

Threadgill turned again to the kitchen and watched his aunt furtively pocket a white lace handkerchief. She didn't put it away quite fast enough. Threadgill saw a spot of scarlet on the cloth, a blotch like a kiss.

A nosebleed, Threadgill thought. *She gets nosebleeds a lot.*

Annie looked so tiny, so frail, suddenly. Like a doll. Small enough to put in a pocket or a box for a long journey.

***

Amos, the slave, brought up Aunt Annie's horse from the barn. Dinah pranced in the chill with deliberate short, stabbing steps. Threadgill could hear a distinct *crunch, crunch* as the animal's hooves crushed earth spumed up a full inch by the hard freeze. Threadgill noticed how thin their horse looked. How thin Amos looked. Everything in the world seemed to be shrinking before Threadgill's eyes.

Everything, that is, except the view. How far he could see from Dinah's saddle now, with a grown man's coat on his back and a new hat atop his head!

Amos approached, tiny, birdlike. Very black. Quick-eyed. He handed Threadgill the reins, flashed a row of sharply filed teeth in an easy smile. The slave's cheeks bore rows of scars, little black lumps the size of engorged ticks that marched in three distinct rows from his hairline to each corner of his mouth. Threadgill heard some African tribes scarred young men's faces in heathen rituals when they reached manhood.

Amos's face would terrify almost anyone who didn't grow up seeing it every day. But his fierce countenance announced absolutely everything you would ever hear out of Amos. The slave had a most singular characteristic.

Silence.

Amos was either mute or able to produce only whistles and clicks, trills and birdcalls. Threadgill had grown up listening to these strange woodland utterances. They seemed normal to him by now, part of his world. Amos could guide a mule with his clicks as surely as any other slave could with singing gees and haws. Amos could carry on a clacking conversation about splitting wood or packing hay into the barn or hunting with a snare. Aunt Annie had even grown to understand him somehow and, for her part, she simply spoke to her tiny slave in English, slowly and clearly, and Amos seemed to have no confusion at all about her orders. Still, a diminutive mute scarred Negro slave would have a very hard life on another farm.

Threadgill patted the warm neck of his horse and waited for his aunt to step out on the porch to say goodbye. But Amos surprised him.

The tiny man reached into his breeches pocket and fished for something. He held it up to Threadgill in a closed fist the size of a child's.

Threadgill opened his own hand. Amos dropped a thing into it.

Two things. Two small carved wooden birds.

Woodpeckers. Yellowhammers. What better birthday present for a red-haired boy?

Click, *glock*, *click*, Amos said. He spread his diminutive arms to either side and moved his tiny black hands up and down, the way a woodpecker flirts its wings to spook insects for a meal. Amos smiled, even with cold lips, then issued a perfect woodpecker call – *chirrrr*! *chirrrr*!

"Thank you, Amos! Thank you!"

A cloud of smoke rose with Threadgill's happy words. He gripped the totems in his fist and held them high. "I'll bring some licorice back from town, okay?"

The cheek scars bunched with Amos's spiky grin. Somehow, that smile always left Threadgill feeling disturbed and delighted at the same time.

***

Annie dispatched Threadgill to Eufaula to pick up yet another birthday present – this one, his "big surprise." It would arrive, a special order, on the 12:35 p.m. locomotive from Montgomery. He was not to be late.

For the first time in his young life, Threadgill would ride to town alone – a whole day of travel down and back the sixteen-mile dirt road to Eufaula. He would be on his own.

Threadgill beamed. His birthday coat held back the cold. The fine new hat warmed his head. Little thoughts hatched like eggs under the crown of his grown-up top. Adventure thoughts.

He would follow Annie's instructions precisely – get to town and find Mr. Tom Carr at the train depot. Mr. Tom Carr would have Threadgill sign for his "big surprise," whatever it was, and pick it up. Yes, Annie assured him, he'd be able to fit the surprise on Dinah's back. It could fit comfortably behind him right on the saddle, no trouble.

But Annie did have an admonition. After Threadgill picked up the gift, he must return home as soon as possible. This was critical. A gray tide of clouds out there meant harder weather on the way tonight. All Annie's joints throbbed. Those hinges predicted weather like a crystal ball. Annie did not want Threadgill on the road after dark on a night so cold it might freeze a man.

A man. Annie referred to Threadgill that way for the very first time.

***

Now the front door creaked, and Annie stepped onto the porch. She wore a quilt. She seemed lost inside it. So thin.

Do I look that skinny to people too? Threadgill wondered.

"Be safe and come home quick with your surprise, Gill. Give Dinah plenty of water, and get back by dark. Don't make me worry, now. Not on your birthday."

Annie lifted her arm from the folds of the heavy quilt.

A silver dollar shone in the morning light.

"This is to use when you need it, Gill."

Threadgill took the coin with his own silvery smile. He gave a sharp whistle and slapped Dinah's flank with his new hat. Amos mimicked the whistle, his shrill like a warbler, and Dinah bounded off, past the gate in the white-washed picket fence and the winter-bare wild roses growing over it in waves. Threadgill galloped a little too fast, but he loved the speed – the cold wind on his face, the big sail of a hat on his head, the tails of his new coat flying behind.

Today he turned twelve.

Here I come. Here I come, Eufaula. Here comes a man.

Chapter 21, Cahaba Crossing

Summer 1964 – Shelby County, Alabama

Threadgill abandoned the road. He feared Bo Hog and his daddy rounding a curve when he least expected. Threadgill traveled north, always north.

He walked through woods and fields for three days, slept through another, a whole day without waking or even turning over in his blanket on the ground.

Threadgill followed running water. He finished the food from Jerry's Café. He ate berries from wild bushes. He ate mushrooms off logs and red plums off trees. He rested when he grew tired and whistled when he felt happy.

More days. He lost count of the mornings, but on one of them, Threadgill arrived at a V where his guiding stream joined a fast river.

Morning charmed wisps, graceful as young girls, from the surface of the river.

Threadgill stood and stretched in the strong sunlight. He tested his legs, his arms, his neck, his back. What a pleasure – the old wayfarer loved that his body was holding up just fine. He gingerly rubbed old muscles, now grown firm. Even the bite on his knee wore a hard scab, a brown blotch of sealing wax for his long-legged journey.

Threadgill knifed open a can of cold pork and beans he'd found abandoned at a Boy Scout campsight in the woods and shook them from the tin straight into his mouth. He chewed happily, fanning mosquitoes as he studied the river.

It rushed past at speed. Threadgill could see a swirlagig of channels and falls, a sunshot maelstrom of watery fits and starts, big bare rocks, shivering gravel beds, sudden gulping holes. White blooming lilies trembled in thick clumps on some of the shoals. Threadgill thought of how the magnolia blossoms on a tree shivered when a freight train thundered by a few days and many miles in the past.

Another thought darted in on Threadgill unexpectedly. This whitewater cascade between two green humps of mountain seemed immense, ancient, eternal. The old man fought back a brief, stinging insignificance.

What if I never make it to Bangor? Who in the world will ever care?

Up close, the river hissed with danger. The water ran high and fast.

Threadgill studied its shoals and spills. Crossing would be stone-to-stone, island-to-island, keep your beard dry. The leapfrog game would end some feet from the distant bank. Beyond there – no other choice – Threadgill would be forced to wade.

The water blew past his boots, gargling like strangled men.

Threadgill took a breath. His apprehension wasn't relieved by the sight of a child's plastic doll, naked pink, hair like brown seaweed, that tore past on the current.

Threadgill crouched and measured the water's depth with a pine branch. He didn't find a single spot deeper along here than his hips. But every fierce jerk of the branch showed how swiftly this current could knock a man down and sweep him away.

One hundred and fourteen years means nothing to a river.

Threadgill steeled himself, then hollered the only thing he could think to holler.

"CHARGE!"

He plunged. Water surged up scarily high, past his waist. Threadgill's gear soaked through, heavy at once. The river turned out to be very cold.

The icy shock, in fact, briefly took Threadgill's breath. He felt his testicles draw up in alarm, clinging tight to him like two terrified jockeys underneath a runaway horse.

How scary would this be … if I couldn't swim? Threadgill panted with cold, carefully balanced, as the shoals scrunched and shifted under his heavy boots. *When WAS my first river? I've been crossing rivers all my life.*

His legs trembled with cold.

"Hell! Don't get your hopes up, Billy Yank!" he yelled to build bravado. "It'll take more than one little river to stop Threadgill Pickett!"

He slogged a step forward, gear gripped in strong hands, held as high as he could manage. He fought the current out to an ankle-deep gravel bar with a floating platform of those white lilies. He stopped to warm, to catch his breath.

Threadgill now beheld a second river – a river of white lilies – that grew on the gravel shallows, stretching out of sight in both directions.

Blooms the size of morning glories rose on green stalks into the misty sunlight. The bulbs and roots of these plants somehow found crannies in the rock shoals, held fast, sprouted, blossomed. Threadgill's keen old nose tingled. A honey-sweet perfume filled the air, mist and a million lilies.

Threadgill drew a deep, intoxicating breath. He wanted to remember the smell for later, when he walked among the Yankees in their factory-fouled, stinking world.

Pay attention.

Threadgill leaped heavily to a new river rock. Despite the pine limb he used for balance, his left foot slipped on a slick surface, and his leg plunged into the current. He hauled himself up, distractedly rubbed a scraped shin.

The river applauded.

On Threadgill went in this way. He reached a gravel island. He made it to a natural stone dam – Threadgill saw an enormous catfish as big as a pony grin up at him from its sheltered pool. He climbed a limestone boulder pocked with old seashells and fossils.

Threadgill took one spill.

Straddled between two rocks as big and smooth as hippopotami, Threadgill's left foot turned traitor. He plunged down the slick rocks and splashed clumsily into an eddy, spooking up birds with his wild whoops. He scrabbled to his feet in chest-deep water, fuming and dripping, his sour embarrassed reflection blinking up at him.

Oh well. Oh hell.

After this, Threadgill simply sloshed along through the river toward the far bank, heedless of the cold.

I'll dry out over yonder. In the sun.

The river shot silver bubbles up his trousers.

Brrrr! N-n-nearly there n-n-now.

Threadgill hugged himself for warmth, his floppy gray hat dripping.

Just a few more f-f-fish to wade through ...

He reached his final crossing. Water dripped off his proud nose. He gauged the distance from this last rock to the solid bank yonder at twenty feet – not a country mile, but mighty far in water this fast.

He surveyed alternate paths. Upriver a bit, he could maybe try a short hobble across those rapids … or maybe he could find a shallow ford downriver in the dark shadows past the last bed of lilies.

Threadgill then felt something happen in his head.

Before his very eyes, the river seemed to gain velocity. It turned red, like blood. Then the old man saw a herd of foam horses gallop past, thundering, a lightning storm of froth manes and tails, mad eyes flashing blood red too.

A brilliant morning sun boiled in red water.

A kingfisher, patrolling tree to tree, sank and rose in its flight above the old man's head. Threadgill squinted painfully into the dazzling sky to follow it.

A blood red spy? Threadgill felt his head swim. *When were kingfishers red?*

An entire tree now shot past, glistening like a dugout canoe, the exposed wood soaked syrup-dark. Crimson bark crusted its trunk. Atop one single pitiful limb clung a turtle, still as a red helmet, holding on for dear life.

The weird howling in his ears faded as quickly as it had begun, and the river ran green and white again. Spray floated over the water, and an indistinct rainbow tinted the air.

Threadgill mustered his courage.

Twenty more feet, Threadgill. It ain't so far.

He took a deep wonderful breath, put one hand down, and stepped with faith off his slippery slab of limestone.

To his immense relief, he found a bottom, thigh-deep.

He took a sounding a few feet farther out with his pine branch – still shallow. But the fast water now nearly snatched the branch from his hand.

Nothing to do but plunge ahead.

A shock of rising, icy water once again took away Threadgill's breath.

Up to his armpits now. His old teeth sang like radio crystals. A painful pulse of cold throbbed in back of his brain.

Threadgill's boots slid ominously. The shoal bottom turned to tumbling dice, rolling bones.

Hang on, feet! Lord have mercy!

He took another labored step. The bank inched closer – just yards away shone wet limbs, the snake-black roots of riverside hardwoods.

Another Herculean step … and Threadgill's duffel and bedroll bubbled completely under, soaked and overheavy, the sodden load bumping underwater around his knees.

Still, Threadgill held steady. He leaned recklessly on the pine limb, teetering. The weight of the whole river broke around his shoulders. Tons of water, sheeting past.

Now he stood one strong lunge away. A long green spine from a gigantic blackberry bush dragged the water, playing the river like a phonograph needle.

Grab that sticker vine, Threadgill told himself, panting. *Grab it, Threadgill, and hold on for dear life.*

Something bright sped past his chin, spinning.

Threadgill saw a round red-and-white world, a small plastic fishing bobber. Then a bright yellow plastic antifreeze can swept past too, in a hurry, grazing the brim of his hat. A red lid from a beer cooler chased it. A passing slick of motor oil burned his nose. A life preserver banged against his shoulder.

Panic flew down on Threadgill. Something bad could happen right here. Something did.

An underwater object, big and heavy, struck both his legs at once. It moved at tremendous speed, and it hurt him.

Threadgill went gurgling under.

The world is green glass under a river. It swarms with silver bubbles, small black specks.

A dead man was under there with Threadgill.

The poor drowned devil waved his arms in slow motion, clasping and unclasping them around Threadgill's legs. The corpse wore a blue industrial uniform, one boot on, his face white as the lily clumps in the shoals. A lank grass of black hair swayed nonchalantly over the dead man's head, and the face had a sleepy, resigned look – *Oh forget them! Forget them all!*

The corpse nudged Threadgill with rubbery arms and legs, the two bodies sliding downriver along the loose bottom. Threadgill's back took a blow from something sharp. And now a loose snarl of fishing line netted the bodies, a tangle in terror.

Threadgill kicked mightily and shoved the corpse away in a jumble of loose gear and limbs. Silver bubbles swarmed like gnats. The drowned man's flesh felt soft and unpleasant, like biscuit dough.

The wicked currents and monofilament line snared them together a second time. Threadgill, desperate for breath now, yanked savagely at the corpse's arm to free himself.

The drowned man's shoulder came out of joint.

Threadgill's scream swept away, a new flurry of bubbles. He knew in some vague sinkhole of his mind that the river had begun to drown him now too, tying his fate to the dead man in the blue uniform, the two of them a bloated octopus of writhing limbs rolling along a jagged river bottom.

Panicked, Threadgill let go of his gear and the drowned man, and wildly kicked off with all his strength from a miracle of solid stone he found under his boots.

He felt freedom instantly, and shot toward green light above him, reaching with desperate fingers.

Threadgill broke the surface.

He sucked in all the air in the world. He inhaled the leaves on the trees, the white lilies and blue rocks, the brooding pines and high clouds. A red-tailed hawk. A cumulus sky. He breathed in the pure hot fire of the sun.

The drowned man bobbed to the surface farther downstream. A pale dislocated arm waved to Threadgill – *Come on! Come on! Time to go!*

Then the corpse turned slowly face up, floating away.

Come on!

A sun flared in Threadgill's memory.

He faced it again. The choice.

Threadgill could live. Or he could drown.

He could give up. He could give in.

Then he remembered Ben face down on a Georgia road.

Ben. His brother.

Murdered.

Threadgill threw himself at thick overhanging blackberry spines on the bank. He caught them in his hand, piercing thorns and all. He hung heavily as a huge fish on a line, water loudly rushing over and around him.

Then Threadgill pulled himself, willfully, up onto the safe bank of the Cahaba River.

***

Threadgill lost track of time. He couldn't lift his head from the gritty stone and black sand. He couldn't wake up.

The red thing happened again – wheeling thoughts, ugly piles, fire all around. Threadgill smelled sulfur, and he marveled as bent creatures on four legs hobbled from one heap of memories to another, sniffing, laughing like hyenas, hiking gnarled legs to pee.

He dreamed, in bright red, of an old man trying to cross a river.

That man sank slowly through a scarlet flood. He gulped fishy water. He walked in slow motion on a river bottom, one jerky colossal step after another.

He wanted air. He breeched, came clear out of the river to his waist. A waterfall poured off his battered gray hat.

Down again. Red fire glowed around him, the river bottom molten, flowing.

It would be so easy, he thought, *to let go now. To be done.*

The idea beckoned. It wrapped tender little arms around his neck, kissed him, caressed him. A sweet peace settled over Threadgill. The surface of the river now burned overhead, a new sky, and Threadgill watched the wave patterns, the red scarves and curtains like the pictures of aurora borealis on the TV at Mobile Sunset Home.

The old man felt something bump his leg.

The monstrous catfish rose from its deep cavern. The fish also kissed the old man's face – he winced at the sting from its fleshy barbel – and then the fish opened its mouth, and a silver bubble with a fish word in it wobbled up toward the open heaven.

The old man's yellowhammer hat let go.

His disfigured scalp took the shock of coldness, and the river suddenly snapped back to reality, loud and furious, green as glass.

The hat shot away in the current, quick as a stingray. It snagged once along the rough bottom, jumped to life again, sped off.

The old man lunged. Hand stretched, Threadgill grazed the feather in his hatband. *So close*! But the hat receded from view in swarms of bubbles. It rolled over and over, faster and farther.

It disappeared downriver.

***

Something tickled Threadgill's head.

He opened his eyes.

With his nose buried in the river bank, the lovely glinting mica flakes and chips of weathered granite seemed as huge as mountain ranges. Drowned pink earthworms loomed, the size of pythons. An ant crawled over a mound of rubble, an angry dragon with red antlers, vengefully hurling boulders to either side as it passed.

The old man struggled to his all fours, head hanging down. He blinked stupidly at the spot where he lay, crawled a few feet more up into the brush, collapsed again in arrowhead ginger. He lurched like a sick dog and barked up a quart of water. It drowned out the noise of the river for a few seconds.

With his insides gushed out, Threadgill covered his bare scarred head with both hands. He felt the exposed, ulcerated crown pulse in sunlight. The shame of disfigurement poured through his blood, scalding, acid. Even here, lonesome by a lonesome river, no living thing but a trio of wood ducks overhead, he felt … exposed. Humiliated.

Threadgill lay still a long time. The sun hoisted its old humped back higher above the tree line to the east, and the river gradually calmed itself under the growing August heat.

Threadgill's heartbeat tamed. His breathing slowed to normal.

Something tickled his head again.

Threadgill wearily flapped a go-away hand. A flying thing loudly clack-buzzed off his scalp and flew to his thumbnail.

He confronted a dragonfly, its goblin eyes staring, iridescent wings poised in an X.

The creature's two front legs crooked under its chin. It looked to Threadgill like a thing asking grace before it devoured him.

I ain't a bug. I'm a man.

Threadgill twitched his thumb. The dragonfly helicoptered away, a vulgar buzz.

In a moment, it returned. It lit once more on Threadgill's head, a grotesque hood ornament.

His faithful gray hat was really gone.

Threadgill imagined his headgear, upside down like a little gray lifeboat, bobbing over rapids. All his family and friends – nearly every memory he ever had – huddled inside the band. Frightened, they clutched the brim tightly, staring at the wild river with scared eyes, open mouths. Inside the band's empty gray hole, Aunt Annie and all Threadgill remembered of her world clung to life. Poor Ben held on for dear life. Folks at the Sunset Home – the Shangri-La. Bruce the orderly. Miz Lantern.

Threadgill Pickett had not wept a single tear in all the years since Ben died. A dry century.

Now, painfully, the dam of hard, jutting sobs gave way and forced Threadgill to lie on his back on the riverbank and cover his gasping face with the dirty wet back of a sleeve.

The dragonfly lifted from his scarred scalp, settled again on his muddy boot, wings shining in the sun.

Some time later, two boys found him this way.

***

He heard them approach, feet thumping the bank.

Threadgill raised, eyes puffed, head groggy. His scalp burned. In fact, The Unmentionable hurt like hell. Why had he passed out here in the blazing sunlight? Thin skin that hadn't seen a ray of sun in a century cooked pretty damned fast in Alabama summer.

The kingfisher, or another like the first one, passed over on a new patrol. The bird dipped white-and-blue through oak-leaf hydrangeas along the banks. A vapor of gnats steamed above a dead gar. Just downstream, a black thread of water snake sewed itself in and out of river lilies.

The barefoot boys clacked free of the bushes. Both wore cut-off jeans, the edges frayed, no shirts. Their chest bones stood out under coffee-colored skin. Each toted a bamboo fishing pole, and one rattled a rusty metal bait bucket. Threadgill could see, in their happy faces, big catfish already frying in hot grease.

"Hank Aaron! He from Alabama!" The first boy was proud, his face bright, teeth white.

The second, equally excited, chimed in. "Willie Mays too …"

The boy in front suddenly took root, eyes wide. His companion accidentally collided with him, tangling their fishing poles in the weeds.

Here's what stopped them: An old wet man with a turkey-buzzard head. He squinted at the boys with one open eye. He licked his lips.

"Boo," Threadgill finally said.

"AAAAAAAAAAAAAAA!!!"

The boys ran for their lives. One cane pole snagged the ground and bent double like a vaulter's pole and sproinged away far out into the river. Their metal bait bucket – an old aluminum cooking pot with broken handles – rattled down the bank almost to the river. It slewed wiggle worms and wet black dirt to every point of the compass.

Threadgill heard the boys hollering bloody murder clean to the top of the steep river bank.

The old man closed his eyes wearily. Another stampede. Another set of panicky feet thumping to escape him in this world.

The story of his life.

He reached up, out of habit, to snug down his hat. Instead, his hands found molten flesh, bubbled epidermis.

Oh. Right. His hat. Gone. Washed away.

Threadgill felt a moment's foolishness. Here sat a grown man, mourning a floppy scrap of old cloth and a tattered yellowhammer feather.

But children ran from Threadgill. Grown men would jibber like monkeys and throw stones. Women … well, never mind.

He would always need something to hide him. Forever, he would.

He would get even with those who did this to him.

Threadgill's eye fell on the boys' abandoned aluminum bait bucket. A little dirt and a cautious worm or two clung to its bottom.

Threadgill surprised even himself.

He threw back his head and howled with laughter.

The noise exploded blue Mr. Kingfisher off a limb in alarm. The bird made a blurred blue escape.

Threadgill doubled over, palms clamped to his aching ribs. Huge clear pebbles of tear fell down the wrinkled riverbed of his face.

The laughing turned to real crying again. The same old haunting.

The pounding brown shoe of the river faded.

After a long time, the jag passed. Threadgill felt better. The oxygen of laughter and weeping made the sun brighter.

The river sparkled.

Threadgill heaved to his weary feet, ready to move on.

His brand new aluminum bucket hat rattled a little each step.

He limped along the river bank for a good hour, picking his way among the trees and stones. Threadgill now served as aching host to a new colony of bruises and scratches, abrasions and pokes. A river crossing took its toll.

The new aluminum headgear grew metal-hot in the sun, but Threadgill left it. He'd grow used to this discomfort, like all else.

The cook pot made a decent fit, actually, snug on his poor head except when he looked straight down. It would wobble forward slightly then, but not enough to block his view. It kept the sun off. It would keep the eyes off.

Not far downriver, Threadgill enjoyed one stroke of fortune. He found both his bedroll and haversack, hugely waterlogged, snagged in a fallen pine that combed the river. To retrieve the sodden gear, Threadgill impatiently whacked a moccasin off the pine trunk. The creature spiraled downstream like a strand of black spaghetti.

Threadgill dried the blanket and gear in the blazing summer afternoon. His spare pants and shirt dripped into the bushes where he spread them. Meanwhile, he dozed in the flattest, smoothest place he could find.

He woke refreshed. He immediately slipped the bait bucket back onto his head. Force of habit.

"Battle helmet," Threadgill said aloud. "Made for battle."

He tapped the pot sonorously with his tough old knuckles.

Chapter 22, The Beast of Bama

January 1862 – Barbour County, Alabama

Bright midmorning, Threadgill trotted Dinah past the Hazel House.

It might have been settling dusk for all the warmth the sun gave the overgrown ruin.

In fact, it seemed to Threadgill that he and Dinah transitioned abruptly from a bright January day, with ice crystals sparkling in tree branches, to a place where earth and sky turned to gray lead.

Stormy clouds, low and swollen in the distance, perfectly suited the lifeless scrub of the Hazel estate. Through time, the vast cane and cotton fields of the estate had turned wild. Not even a bird flew from the tangle.

Oh, yes, Threadgill knew the legend of the house. A mighty and wealthy family, all found slain by some beast that left footprints no one could identify. Footprints no one had ever seen. The terrible creature, whatever it was, came to be known as The Beast of Bama. It destroyed utterly. Hazel family slaughtered, but only that family, not one other soul. All the slaves disappeared into the woods and swamps, not one ever found or heard from again.

Aunt Annie fascinated young Threadgill with the tale on prior trips to Eufaula. Threadgill felt the eerie power of the place then, and he still felt a strange unsettling … what? Foreboding? Attraction?

He slowed Dinah. He craned his neck and stood high in the stirrups as the horse clopped past the wreck of the great chalet. The wind made a harsh moaning sound through the grounds.

Did something move there, in one of the windows?

Thwack!

A sudden hard blow to the temple knocked Threadgill backward. He saw a sparkling seltzer of stars. He tumbled through space, limbs and light flickering around him. He hit the iron-hard ground, and the breath left him in a sharp bark.

Threadgill imagined a fish flopping on the deep grass by a pond.

Come on, breath. Come on … breathe, chest. Breathe please …. Come on …

At some point, the young man became conscious of Dinah muzzling his bare head, her breath warm and nose wet.

How long had he been lying here?

What happened? Where was he?

It took another few minutes. Threadgill finally picked himself up off the frozen road. Gingerly and with no small measure of hurt pride, he tested each of his limbs with a series of grimaces. Bright bubbles popped in his eyes.

Holy sweet honey, he thought. *Did I really fall off my durned horse?*

The culprit was a big hickory limb with a low crook. It stretched right over the trail, too high for most heads … unless the rider stood high in the stirrups for a gawking look at Hazel House. The bare hickory branch still trembled, as if furious, vibrating to the very tip of every black twig.

Threadgill blinked at the limb through stinging eyes. The branch swept him from the saddle like a reaper's scythe. The blow struck just below his widow's peak on the right temple.

He realized how lucky he was that Dinah didn't spook and run off. Another horse might already be back at the stable.

Threadgill snatched up his new birthday hat off the cold ground – *ouch* sang his shoulder. He clapped the hat back onto his aching head. His fingers found a trickle of blood over one eye. He wiped it with the sleeve of his new coat.

Not too bad. A little blood. A goose egg. A lesson.

Twelve years old, and you got knocked off Dinah by a tree limb. Real good, Threadgill.

"It didn't HURT!"

He snarled these words out loud, angrily, though garbled. His face had become a cold mask as he lay on the ground, so cold his lips couldn't move naturally yet. Now he found blood on his collar too, run down his face. His new coat already stained.

Damn! It DID hurt! Who am I foolin'!?

A quick motion in reply – something, a flicker – drew Threadgill's eye toward the old house.

What moved?

He didn't see anything.

But now Threadgill felt very strange.

Watched.

Dinah flicked her big ears anxiously, a sound like untied canvas in a gust of wind. She snorted and tossed her head the way horses do.

Threadgill fit foot to stirrup, rose back to the saddle. He angrily spit at the tree limb – he had blood in his mouth. He swore to pay attention. *No more daydreams*.

Still, he couldn't deny a last suspicious glance at Hazel House.

For a hundred yards down its long lane, poke and dog fennel and scrub oak sprouted from faded carriage ruts. The ancient live oak trees the Hazels planted down the drive had mostly splintered. One or two slumped across the drive like dead elephants.

A skull eye, a black unblinking upstairs window, stared straight through the overgrowth at Threadgill.

He nervously dug his heels into Dinah's flanks. She took off, and ate up the road in long strides.

Threadgill wiped away a little more cold blood from his forehead. He moved a loose bottom tooth with his tongue – a whole new hurt, dammit.

He clutched Dinah's bridle and galloped fast toward the waiting town, mad as a wet hen at his foolishness.

***

Eufaula was a river town. Its respectable commercial section ran at a right angle up from the Chattahoochee. At the base of the river bluffs, wooden docks and roughhouses welcomed steamboats from Columbus upriver and from the salt-water bay at Apalachicola downriver. These paddlewheelers delivered travelers and goods to the West, as settlers called Alabama in early times.

The steamers sometimes carried hides and barrels of turpentine, but mostly they came empty, to load cotton. In late November and December, as the harvests came in, some steamboats packed on so many bales that a rogue wave from some other passing paddlewheeler could splash over the first deck and drench the cargo.

Serving the commerce of the river, Eufaula developed into a rich, in-dustrious town with a main boulevard of oaks and magnificent houses. The planters, at least the most social of them, built ostentatious homes side by side within sight of the river. Their fine mansions, columned and finely gardened, made the town feel larger than it appeared on any map.

Every house, even brick ones, wore whitewash. Widow's walks capped three or four. The architectural feature seemed a rueful joke – the Civil War now made new widows in Eufaula every month.

In the window of Daniel King's hardware store, in fact, Threadgill spotted a new posting of killed soldiers. He knew some of the families. Mr. Sugarman, from west of town. James Hawkins, mortally wounded at some place called Manassas. A boy not much older than Threadgill, James Martin. Bill Crow, a half-Indian who could cast iron. Danny Pollock. John Shaw and his half-brother, Thom McRae, killed the same day.

Threadgill looked up from the posting, surveyed the town.

Eufaula would change.

That store yonder with the blackened windows – Chuck Reece's land office – would never open again. Down there stood the cotton factor's. Shaw and McRae, dead now, owned that, one of the two buildings in town with a telegraph. Since the war started and the two brothers shipped off, nobody could send or receive telegraphs except Mr. Tom Carr at the train depot, and sometimes that busy man worked repairs by himself on the train tracks and went away for days.

Threadgill paced his horse past Shaw and McRae's warehouse. He could hear the bright clacking sound of telegraph keys in the empty room. It sounded especially eerie in the darkening afternoon, the wind kicking up dust devils, speeding leaves past Dinah.

Threadgill could see that Eufaula was not doing well. The best mansion on the main street wore a shutter knocked crooked. Green moss stained one side of the Bibb House, where a governor used to live. More than one establishment displayed leaves packed hard in front of an entrance, or broken windows, or planks over doors. With its men gone to war the town felt meaner, poorer.

Threadgill pinched together the last crumbs from cookies Aunt Annie had slipped into his new coat pocket. He bobbed along on Dinah as far as the train depot.

This handsome brick building was newer than almost anything else in town, a very welcome introduction in the good times to a very welcoming little town. Today, the tall windows wore frost, and the wood stove in the passenger waiting area sat cold, unlit.

The sun hung low – always low this time of year – but Threadgill still did not think the hour so late. Where was everyone?

From every indication, the 12:35 from Montgomery had come and steamed away again, all passengers departed, Mr. Tom Carr closed up and gone home for the day.

What time *was* it?

Sure enough, Threadgill found in the depot window a message, hand-inked with a broad brush on a piece of pine plank.

BACK FRIDAY.

That was all. No envelope for Threadgill. No "big" surprise. No explanation.

The birthday boy cracked a skim of ice on a watering trough and left Dinah sloshing while he took a look around and figured out what to do.

At the corner of the depot, a gust of wind bulled into him, smarting his eyes. He felt thankful once again for his new hat and coat.

Threadgill didn't see even a stray dog. Last trip in, this past summer, mule-skinners hauling barrels and bags and hollering terrible curses at one another almost ran over him and Annie on their little buckboard.

Threadgill walked around the depot twice, checking entrances and window sills.

No package. No note. Not a soul.

The terminal, in fact, had the look it took on for a holiday, when the trains stopped running and the crews cleared out for big meals with their families or else hit the local boarding house … or the lively house above the bluff saloon, where brawlers occasionally flung one another over a banister into the river.

Unable to accept that he'd come all this way for nothing, Threadgill peered through the windows of the depot, one last look, fogging the glass with his breath. The cool window felt wonderful to the bruise on his forehead, so Threadgill pretended to stare in for several more moments.

"Son? You Annie Pickett's nephew? Ain't it Threadgill?"

Threadgill jumped.

Tim Black, the town undertaker, waited across the tracks on his buggy, his two mules black as tar, billowing steam in the cold like long-eared dragons. The wind howled so hard around the depot now that Threadgill didn't hear the buggy.

Plus, he'd been lost in his thoughts.

"Afternoon, Mr. Black. Aunt Annie sent me to town for some kind of package. It came in on the train. For my birthday."

Black stared at him for an uncomfortable length of time – that was his way, Threadgill recalled, those strange eyes like a fish. The man in the stiff dark suit spat snuff juice to his left, away from Threadgill. Some of it blew back onto the undertaker, speckling his pale face.

"Well, happy birthday, son."

Black wiped his cheek with a handkerchief before he spoke again.

"Mr. Tom Carr and most everybody else are just now leavin' a funeral over in the cemetery. Poor Shannon Hollowell. Train brought the body in today. Died from the pneumonia after he got shot. Mighty sad. That was a good Christian boy."

The eyes of the undertaker never blinked.

"I buried his mama too. Mrs. Hollowell, I mean. Last year. That Shannon was the last of that family in the whole world. Last Hollowell, I'm sayin.'"

Black worked his mouth.

"I reckon you could pick up some slaves pretty cheap for your birthday, son. The Hollowells had two, and now they got to be sold. Or give away, whichever. I heard Mr. Tom Carr say most folks these days can't hardly keep fed the ones they got …"

Threadgill, his hands deep in his pockets for warmth, found his fingers around the little carved wooden birds from Amos.

"Is there a way to open up the depot, Mr. Black? Could my birthday present be locked up for safekeepin' in there?"

Threadgill later realized it was absurd to suppose that the town undertaker had a key to every house and building. But who else could he ask?

Black spit again, this time directly onto the rumps of his mules.

"Here's what you do," the undertaker said, swabbing his chin. "Go up there to the hotel and take it up with Doyle. You know Mr. Kevin Doyle?"

"Yes sir."

"He'll be getting back to the hotel from the funeral directly. You tell him what you run into, and I know he'll do what he can to help."

"Ain't Mr. Tom Carr coming back?"

"I can't speak for the man. I do know the train's come and gone today. You missed that. And that feller we buried, Shan Hollowell, he was Mr. Tom

Carr's cousin. I reckon Mr. Tom Carr might not work any more today."

Threadgill stared at the depot platform, considering.

"What did you do to your noggin there, son?"

Threadgill's face flushed, and it caused a new throbbing.

"Took a bump. It's alright."

In the cold air, the word *bump* didn't come out right. *Mump*, Threadgill said it.

"I got some salve. It'll take the swelling out of a damn mule kick."

Threadgill felt an urge to run for his life. What kind of salve would an undertaker put on a person?

"It ain't hurtin.' Just a bruise."

"You gonna have yourself a couple of shiners. Salve would help …"

Two black eyes? More news to Threadgill.

Still, no salve on the fingertips of those white skeleton hands would ever touch Threadgill's face. Not while he lived, anyway.

"Thank you just the same, Mr. Black. I reckon I'll do without. And thanks for your advice. I'll step up the street and see Mr. Doyle."

"Say hey to your Aunt Annie for me? Tell her I will get out to see her one of these days."

"I'll do it."

"Oh, young Pickett. One more thing."

Black held the reins of the mule team in a pale hand. His sharp chin lifted, and the brim of his hat tipped.

"It was some snow out yonder in the graveyard. Fell to beat the band for a minute or two. We ain't had snow in this part of Alabama in many a year, but we might be due."

"Real snow?"

"Yessir. And I hate it. Truth to tell, this ain't the best time of year to bury folks. But that's neither here nor there – I'm just sayin' you oughten wait too late to start back. It could get rough on the road tonight."

Threadgill felt exhilaration.

Snow! On his birthday! Now THAT sure was a "big" surprise!

Threadgill hustled away to see Mr. Doyle at the Clark Hotel, leaving Dinah to wonder at the trough, her big black ears straight up, muzzle dripping.

Threadgill made a few hurried miles out of town before the snow started.

At first, he felt elation. Gorgeous crystals settled on Dinah's jet back, distinctly visible there, each a perfect little Christmas star of white that sparkled, softened, then vanished into a wet spot. As far as Threadgill could see in every direction, white snowflakes drifted. He thought of what fell from the sky after a bird took off, the little soft white feathers lost and floating on the wind.

Threadgill caught birthday snow on his tongue. As he tipped back his head, a little avalanche fell from his hat brim down his back. It settled on the saddle behind him – the place his surprise should have been tied, if he hadn't clouted his head on a limb, if he hadn't lain on the ground knocked cuckoo and missed the train, if Mr. Tom Carr hadn't abandoned the train station, if Shannon Hollowell hadn't been shot and then died of pneumonia.

If. If. If.

It was beautiful, though, this snow on his birthday. The cold kisses on his sore eyes and bruised forehead felt wonderful – maybe the best feeling all day if you didn't count his birthday cake this morning … and the hot water at Mr. Doyle's hotel. That good man let him wash the blood off his face with warm water from his tea-kettle.

Now Threadgill wished he could wash the inside of his head too, clean his throbbing brain under the goose egg the same way.

Here was the good news: Mr. Doyle, his wire-rimmed eyeglasses magnifying his eyes like an owl's, promised to watch the station for Threadgill's surprise. He'd sign for it with his own hand, he said, and keep it at the hotel until he had a day without guests – those days happened more and more now that the war had lasted longer than anyone expected, going nearly two full years already. Then, said Mr. Doyle, he would load the surprise on his own horse and deliver it to Annie's farm in person.

"I miss the little lady," Mr. Doyle said, and Threadgill thought he saw something cloud the older man's eyes. "It's been too long since I paid Miss Annie Pickett a proper call."

So away Threadgill rode, into blowing snow. In his pocket, he had licorice for Amos and a little Christmas bell made of silver for his aunt, both from Mr. Daniel King's hardware.

The small flakes began to clump and fall more heavily, wet and distinct now where they touched Threadgill's skin. Tufts hit limbs and broke apart into white pieces and spun crazily to the disappearing ground.

Dinah fretted. The old girl was soaking wet – her rump steamed, rivulets ran her neck and sides. The cold north wind turned to a constant ripping gale that threw the flakes past Threadgill and Dinah parallel to the ground sometimes. Threadgill knew his faithful horse needed to keep moving or she'd quickly stiffen up.

They did move, steadily, for miles. Then the weather grew even harder. Snow covered the road now. As long as he had daylight, Threadgill knew he could thread a path between roadside trees and bushes. Darkness would come early though, with this storm. Threadgill felt a little tingle of worry.

Even so, the once-in-a-decade sensation of an Alabama snowstorm fascinated Threadgill. (*On his birthday!*) He found the dance of particles hypnotizing, dreamy. Snow limned black branches overhead, and whitened the tops of a rail fence now and again, and collected in bare places and meadows like little cottage rugs. He remembered tales Aunt Annie read to him from her books, stories of children in England who walked through mountains of snow, fought with snowballs, ate snow with honey in it.

Aunt Annie. He thought warmly of her all at once.

His heels nudged Dinah softly. The horse was tiring. Threadgill knew not even a thoroughbred could run sixteen miles home. But this day, they had to hurry. Shadows already stretched long and deep around them, weird blue in places where snow lay.

Threadgill, for some reason, had a sudden vision of Mr. Black and the cemetery by the river. He thought of that dead boy, Shannon Hollowell, nailed in a pine box and stuffed under the black earth, like a worm. His young eyes open, but blind in the dark. Blind to the snow that settled over the beautiful grave markers and drifted down through the lustrous magnolia leaves, evergreens too glossy to hold the flakes so that they poured through the tree like white sugar.

Snow looked beautiful only to the living.

Happy birthday, Threadgill.

***

The dark became a serious worry two miles from Hazel House.

By then Threadgill had another concern.

He heard something.

Howling.

Off the road ahead.

The sound came to him faintly. Just the wind, maybe.

Just the wind howling.

But then Threadgill heard it a second time, a glassy sliver of sound, but clear and strange, like an animal with one foot caught in a metal trap.

Dinah nickered and tossed her head.

Not just the wind.

The steady clocktick of Dinah's hoofbeats muffled now in drifts. Snow flowed in a steady white river, so the road disappeared from place to place altogether.

Threadgill felt the fast beating of his heart. But he heard no more noise.

Just the wind, after all.

A powerful weariness poured from the back of Threadgill's brain all at once, down through his limbs and flesh. Had he ever in his life been so tired?

He had a mental flash of Eufaula, of white-haired Mr. Doyle in the warm sitting room of the hotel, a few lonely guests around his hearth fire, toasting the gift of snowfall that greeted January 1863.

May it lead to Southern independence, they would cry out. *Southern independence, by god! This year of our Lord!*

God bless Jefferson Davis! someone else chimed in. *They say that good man prays on his knees by his bed every night for our sovereign cause! God grant his prayers!*

Pay attention, Threadgill! You're daydreaming again!

He sat straight up in his saddle, windblown snow pelting his face. He shook his head side to side. He reached up his heavy, half-frozen hand to pat Dinah's neck, add a little encouragement.

And suddenly Threadgill wasn't tired in the least.

It wasn't possible in the snowfall to see what made the sound – a close spiraling murderous cry. It made every hair on his neck rise, and the bruise on his forehead beat like an Indian drum.

By gosh, either the wind passed through some knothole … or an animal has killed something in the snow right up ahead of me …

The terrible cry came again, louder, closer. Dinah shied, brought her front legs clean off the ground.

"Whoa! Whoa now, girl!"

Threadgill gentled his mount back to earth, scared numb himself.

He squinted into the blowing snow from under his heavy new hat, holding the wet brim with one hand. His heartbeat deafened him, a boom of fear that shook his whole body.

Now Threadgill spotted something.

It moved against the snow. Low and dark. A slouching thing, running close to the earth. It slipped into white bushes on the right side of the road and shook snow from them in its passing.

Threadgill realized now, with a horrible shock, that the black silhouette of Hazel House hulked in the darkness on that same side of the road. The house looked even blacker than the blackness. Cornices and uncollapsed gables held white accents of snow, like bones showing through skin.

Threadgill heard the noise again … a wavering wail.

Unmistakable. Just there. Ahead.

Holy god! What… in the … is it … calling my name?

Threadgill's heart thumped so loudly he couldn't be sure WHAT he heard.

But – *listen*! – it rose again.

Threeeeead … gillllllll!

Dinah sensed her rider's failing composure. Without warning, the frightened horse took off. Threadgill nearly pitched backwards off her, and when he recovered, the best he could manage was a tight hug to Dinah's neck for dear life. Big gouts of snow flew up from the horse's racing hooves, spattering the back of his new coat and hat.

Thread … gilllll!

No boy had ever been so frightened.

Ever.

Dinah flew through the narrowed shadows directly facing Hazel House.

Then something dropped heavily out of the dark and landed behind Threadgill on the saddle.

Muscular limbs latched fast around his chest. A grip of death – the thing squeezed brutally and screamed with laughter.

A demon had caught a boy alone on a cursed road on his twelfth birthday.

Thread … gilllll!

A panting, laughing mouth drew close to his ear, breath hot as fire.

Threadgill Pickett!

Oh holy god, oh holy god, oh holy god, moaned Threadgill, holding Dinah with all his might, eyes shut maybe forever. *Oh holy god, don't let this be the end of me …*

The thing behind Threadgill screamed and rocked him wildly side to side like a man lugging a heavy barrel.

THREAD … GILLLLL!!!!!

Dinah blindly galloped the road toward home. Her reins left black snake trails through the snow.

The horse would be his only chance, Threadgill knew. This terrible devil thing would kill him and take him to hell if he couldn't keep a grip on Dinah and ride on.

But he couldn't.

The pommel too wet and slick. Dinah's mane too slippery.

The monster in the saddle gave a tremendous pull and Threadgill rose from the saddle. He and the creature flew backwards off Dinah's rump, fell upside down, flopped into deadening snow.

The creature, laughing madly, still clasped Threadgill's back like an iron band, still squeezed so hard.

Arrrrrrrrgghhh! Threadgill screamed.

Desperate, senseless in terror, Threadgill somehow broke the thing's grip. He kicked and crawled away, managed to scramble to his feet. He found enough courage now to run for his life.

The thing made another grab at him. Threadgill kicked it as hard as he could.

Oh! Ouch!

That's what it said, plain as that. *Oh! Ouch!*

Then the thing shot out a rough snowy hand and grabbed Threadgill's boot and twisted it and threw Threadgill down in the slippery snow, and then it had him again. This time on top, staring down directly at his face.

Threadgill gazed into a strange mirror.

Another boy grinned down at him, wild in the eyes. He had the same face as Threadgill … only without a bruise on the forehead or two black eyes. His wide grin stretched across an identical face. The proud Pickett nose ruled his features.

Thread … gilllll! mocked his double. *Meet … Beeennnnnn … yer twiiinnnnnn …*

Threadgill learned that night of the bone-deep mischief and astonishing daring of his devil-may-care big brother.

Benjamin Randoll Pickett.

Ben had it in him to work out a big surprise with Aunt Annie. To arrive from Mobile on his own twelfth birthday. To step off a train alone at an empty station.

When Ben spied his identical twin ambling into town on a black horse to meet him for the first time, he schemed up a most monumental introduction. He impishly waited by an unfamiliar road in the snowy dark in front of a collapsed mansion for his baby brother to pass, call out his name with eerie voices, get him good and terrified, then drop from a low hickory limb onto his horse.

The kind of young man who just laughed when Threadgill swung to punch him in the nose and missed.

Threadgill's big surprise.

Chapter 23, Yellowhammer D.C.

Imagine a comfortable old gentleman, come courting. The suitor waits for his lady on a green cushiony couch of soft hills. He's not really handsome, but he has an interesting face – he has suffered. He has also mostly healed, doctored by a century of rising sap, rainstorms, warm afternoons, falling leaves, bandages of snow.

Yellowhammer beholds Richmond.

The bird's shadow passes fast, north by northeast, falling now on fresh-smelling countryside, now on crops. Peanut plants run long green rows, dark sentences across the fields. Farmers erase and rewrite the messages, year by year.

Yellowhammer sails past Fredericksburg. Spottsylvania. Chancellorsville. Cold Harbor. Manassas. Over Harper's Ferry. The air smells.

Cannons still guard these places, bronze barrels turned green. Trenches gape in moonlight, mouths hungry for the dead. Yellowhammer sees gray ghosts and blue ghosts still massed in shadows, moonlit bayonets fixed and ready, poised to rush over open fields as soon as the sun raises its bright arm and blows its golden bugle.

A wide river sniffs out a trail among house-sized boulders.

Yellowhammer dips to the surface of the Potomac.

Quick as that, Yellowhammer invades the north.

Anything seems possible now.

The river rolls away, low, luxurious, toward the distant shine of a sea. The sun crowns there, brightening sky over the Atlantic.

The top of a tall pale spire catches pink morning light. Other marble monuments huddle at its base – here's a city so heavy with marble it seems to sink slightly into the earth in tea-light morning.

Washington wears a halo of white doves, wheeling pigeons. The dome of the Yankee capitol pokes from the city, a child's newborn head brimming with ambition, hope, greed, mischief.

Avenues yawn, broad as airport runways. Dark lakes run along the mall under Yellowhammer.

Yellowhammer does not see its reflection.

Yellowhammer's eye looks only north.

Chapter 24, Brother Against Brother

January 1862 – Barbour County, Alabama

Aunt Annie settled a fresh hickory log onto the andirons. She heated an iron pot of turnip soup, then two buckets for baths. She worked hard to thaw out the bodies and souls of the twins, who stumbled in at almost midnight chattering with cold. Snow wept from Threadgill's ears. Ben's frozen hair hung a stiff flag down his collar.

The good aunt gave each twin a shot of whiskey, their first taste ever. The silver cup tasted cold, the whiskey breathtakingly hot. Threadgill screwed up his face, gasping. Ben's eyes opened wide in amazement. So did his mouth.

"Goddam!" he yelled. Shrinking under Annie's disapproving eye, he then croaked softly, "Goldurn!"

It took the boys a full slow hour to thaw. Then Aunt Annie surprised them. She floated from the kitchen bearing a simple one-layer birthday cake with twin candles – Threadgill's second cake of the day. The homecoming/birthday candles blazed. Tears sparkled on both of Annie's leathery cheeks.

"Happy birthday, Threadgill! Happy birthday, Ben! Welcome back together, boys!"

Hurrahs raised the roof. Ben exultantly told the story of his train ride and his ambush of Threadgill; Threadgill soberly described the emptiness of Eufaula, then *his* side of the ambush tale. The boys consumed the cake completely. Not a crumb remained, nor a lick of jam. After jubilation—Ben demonstrated quadrille steps he claimed to have learned in the social swirl of Mobile – Annie tied a bow around the birthday reunion.

She united the boys in their crib once again.

They would sleep in the same bed, in Threadgill's room.

The scuffle started just after 1 a.m.

Annie whisked in with a candle stand. One boy quivered at the foot of the bed and one boy at the head.

"He whammed me with his durned elbow! Did it on purpose!"

Threadgill dabbed a busted lip on his nightgown sleeve, his eyes amazed.

"No sir! Did not!" Ben vigorously shook his head, fists clenched. He looked so much like Threadgill that for a dizzying moment, Annie really couldn't tell the brothers apart.

"He DID SO, Aunt Annie! He told me to move over, then he whammed me! He busted my lip!"

"You was thrashin' in your sleep, little brother! You hit my elbow!"

"You're a liar!"

Ben narrowed his eyes. "Don't *nobody* call Ben Pickett a liar!"

The big twin lowered his head and charged. Ben windmilled his fists, pummeling a shocked Threadgill, who fell back on the bed and dove for cover under the heavy quilt.

WHANG-G-G-G-G!

Both boys jerked upright in alarm. Aunt Annie glared. Her heavy cast-iron stewpot lid rolled on the plank floor.

"That's enough!" she announced. "Stand up! Both of you!"

Aunt Annie might have not have understood a thing about the incompatibility of twin twelve-year-old boys in a single bed, but her fierce tone of voice snapped them to attention. They wore identical white nightgowns. Ben, fists still clenched, had an embarrassing swell in front of his, just below the waist.

"You two boys," Annie hissed, "are *brothers*! Picketts! And it's your birthday! And it's the first night you've been together since you were three months old! You ought to be ashamed of fighting! What are you thinking?"

A log shifted noisily on the fire. Utter silence otherwise. Finally, a tiny voice squeaked, "Sorry, Aunt Annie."

Of course it was Threadgill. Ben, out of breath and sweating through his gown even on such a cold night, continued to stare out the bedroom window with his fists balled up. He didn't speak.

Dear Lord, now he looks just like his father, Annie thought to herself. *That one is Randoll Pickett made over …*

It was a critical moment. Annie couldn't just let fighting go. Silently, unbeknownst to the brothers, she said a prayer, a little sparrow of hope.

"BEN?"

"Yes'm." Ben spoke in a voice suddenly deeper than a boy's. "I reckon I apologize, Threadgill. Brother."

The little sparrow sang.

Sweet heaven, Annie breathed, *he said the words.*

Still, Ben jutted out his lip defiantly. So did Threadgill. They looked to Annie like boys in a mirror, one with a bloody mouth.

Annie knew one thing Threadgill didn't know … and likely never would. Ben had been unhappy at his adopted home in Mobile. He'd somehow gotten irrevocably on the bad side of his uncle and aunt there.

Rose Nell and Dove wrote it all out in an October letter. Ben had started to "act up," they explained to Annie in careful language. Fights. Petty theft – a pocketknife, a live parrot from the docks, tobacco. More fights. Truancy. It got so bad that the aunt and uncle discussed serious and deliberate steps to hand Ben over to the Catholic home.

Ben traveled the road to ruin, they believed, the lost highway. The aging guardians confessed they could no longer meet the challenge of a fledgling rowdy.

So Annie stepped in.

She wrote a letter herself, sent to the Eufaula post office by a passing neighbor. She invited Ben to come live at a new home, begin a new life. He could start fresh on his twelfth birthday. He could have a home with her and Threadgill, his long-lost twin. He could live on soil where he came into the world, where his mother and father lay buried.

Where Annie would be buried too.

And?

Ben gave Threadgill a bloody lip – *Happy birthday!* – for a present.

It put Annie on full alert. So did the fact that Ben ate at one sitting almost all of a cake it would have taken her and Threadgill a week to finish.

What had she done?

Though physical affection did not much lay in her nature, Annie approached Ben and held out her arms. To her great surprise, the strapping youngster hugged her. The fireplace light, in fact, revealed a hot tear on his cheek.

"Ben," Annie whispered, "me and Threadgill want you here."

Ben glanced furtively at her then, and Annie caught, ever so briefly, a look. Oh, yes. He really was a wild one – wildness lived in there, crazy light behind the blue, blue eyes. But Annie also saw pain, a frightened boy. *They wanted to throw me away*, Ben's eyes told her. *They wanted to send me to the orphan home.*

"Why you huggin' that one, Aunt Annie?" Threadgill asked, dismayed. "I got the busted lip!"

***

Annie had never seen a human, or an animal of any kind for that matter, eat like Ben Pickett.

Times were hard, a war well along. You couldn't find salt or sugar on trips to Eufaula. And just last month the owner of the only baked goods store, Joe Weber, disappeared at war, missing at Malvern Hill. His family shuttered the business and moved away to Atlanta.

Annie knew the store would close, sooner or later. It didn't matter if Eufaula sat on a wide, deep river, but a Yankee blockade plugged its mouth, down at Apalachicola. No shipments of size came or went along the Chattahoochee these days. Where would a boat go … except to the bottom of the Gulf of Mexico?

Well, folks could live without much sugar and salt. They'd get by. Homemade jelly made a good enough birthday cake. And thanks to Amos and good old Dinah spring seeds still went into the ground and green leaves rose out of them. Food made it to the table.

But here, the dead of winter, Annie now cooked what she believed to be preposterous amounts for their meals – two skillets of cornbread, and on Sunday once a month a dozen spit-roasted doves Amos trapped, plus a half row – *a half row!* – of fresh-pulled turnip greens. And Ben, every meal, looked up hungrily from his sopped plate. *Is there more?*

What *was* Ben? A boy? A wolf?

Oh, Threadgill ate well enough – his appetite picked up substantially in the last year too. But the younger twin fed like a barn cat compared to Ben. Where did the boy put all that food? Did it leak out his heels and into his boots?

Annie began to seriously wonder if her provisions would get them through this winter. She felt guilty handing out a lighter-than-usual tin plate to Amos. But her own appetite had fallen off, so most of her own portion ended up feeding the diminutive African.

Annie no longer enjoyed meals. Nights, she felt a heaviness in her chest more and more. Food tasted … *peculiar* … after dark, like somebody sprinkled it with fireplace ashes.

Both boys shot up six inches from December to April.

Six inches! They went through two sizes of boots, and Amos had already measured out deer leather for third pairs, needed soon. Annie herself snipped and stitched new breeches for her twins, and new shirts, and then new breeches again, and by this time, the weather turned warm enough so they could go mostly without shirts, thank goodness.

Annie then saw the other changes – surprising tufts of spun-copper hair that appeared almost overnight under arms and over chests and legs. She noticed how the boys' muscles hardened with their chores, how their voices began to crack when they spoke. She thought of pullets turning into roosters.

***

Late afternoons when the warm day cooled, starting in late February and through the spring and into the hot months, the twins took off after chores and went to the woods. Annie watched them practically run the back acres, growing smaller and smaller and finally disappearing out past the rising rows of corn.

Sometimes, with their disappearance, her brave front gave way. She would cry and sit in her pine rocker, more tired every day than the day before. She coughed her sorrows quietly into strips of rag.

She would always throw the bloody thing into the fire and make sure it burned before the boys returned late in the night.

***

In those woods, in the fourteenth summer of their lives, Ben introduced his big idea to Threadgill.

"It ain't but a hundred and fifty or something miles up there, Threadgill. We could walk it in a week. A week or ten days. *Easy*."

"That sounds far," Threadgill admitted. "I don't know anybody who's ever been to Atlanta."

"People from Mobile go all the time. They say it's *great*. Like some Jerusalem or something."

"How do you even know the Confederate army's gonna be there?"

Ben sounded sure of this next part. "Atlanta is where all the train tracks meet," he said. "The army has got to guard a place like that."

"Well," reasoned Threadgill, "can't we just ride a train up there then?"

"Part of the way, we can. Maybe. But I heard from Mobile people that the Yankees capture the railroads first thing. They put their own train engines on 'em, big blue ones, and they got soldiers and rawboned bloodhounds to hunt down any Confederate folks they see walking the rails."

Threadgill considered this with some deliberation. The bloodhounds he'd known were big ugly brutes. He'd always been scared of dogs. (That Beast of Bama story always *really* scared him.) With bloodhounds involved, hiking overland to join the Confederate army suddenly seemed more sensible.

Something puzzled Ben.

"How come Aunt Annie don't keep a gun, Gill? We should bring a rifle, if we're gonna be soldiers. And a rifle would be handy if we run into Yankees before we hit Atlanta."

"Or bloodhounds."

"A rifle and some powder."

"And some shot!" Threadgill added. He knew very little about guns, even after a lifetime out here in the country, but Threadgill knew a gun needed a bullet.

No gun at Aunt Annie's. It *was* curious. Despite the fact that Annie lived alone, or almost, she kept no kind of weapon at all. The spear in the barn in wild Amos's hands would be the closest thing. Amos knew his work. He had brought a lot of meat to their table through the years.

All at once, it seemed a shocking revelation. *What kind of dreamy boy have I been?* Threadgill wondered. *Aunt Annie ain't safe without a gun! Daddy was right. What was I thinking?*

This thought nagged at him like a blowfly one late afternoon. At the time, the brothers followed a little trail through heavy hardwoods and tall longleaf pines at the far end of Aunt Annie's acres. Ben led the way, as always. The ancient trees towered over the boys – loggers and turpentine men never reached this part of the world.

The twins explored a whole distant new section of woodland earlier in the week, on the far side of Old Mercy Creek. That fast little course – it might be called a river some places – divided Pickett property from Oakley. A secretive man, Oakley owned thousands of acres, held scores of slaves. Folks considered him a hard case. You didn't go onto Oakley land without a reason … but what did two young boys know?

To cross Old Mercy, the brothers dropped from a low tupelo limb straight into the water. The creek banks, twelve-foot shelves of black limestone jaded with fern, proved a difficult climb; monkeying hand over hand out the tupelo branch and then letting go offered the course of least resistance.

The hanging summer garden on the banks looked lovely in the twilight. Threadgill's gawking almost made him lose sight of his big brother. Ben already slogged up the far bank.

"Whoa! Ben, wait!"

Threadgill scrambled. He splashed the stream, hustled along to a deer path running cleverly in and out of scrub oak and native bamboo. The trail led the twins away from a lowering Alabama sun, a ripe peach, and straight toward an early full moon. It rose from the heart of the forest. It looked like a ripe peach too.

"Listen!"

Ben drew up short, raised a hand.

Not again. Just about every adventure in the woods, Ben fooled Threadgill or scared him with some tomfoolery. Just last week, Ben threw down a black crooked stick in the path and screamed "Snake!" He laughed fit to bust when Threadgill leaped straight into a briar patch.

Snap! *Whoooo*! *Snapppp*!

Ben hadn't been fooling this time.

Unusual forest noises stopped Threadgill in his tracks.

What in the world made such a racket out in these deep places?

Ben seemed to falter at this point. He looked at Threadgill closely, seeking advice without words, his blue eyes very wide. Bluff and bluster disappeared.

"Don't ask me what it is," whispered Threadgill. "I never crossed Old Mercy Creek my whole life before today."

Snap! *Whooooo*!

The twins teetered with indecision. Did they dare go forward for a look? Turn around and run like hell? Come back by day when the sun shone bright overhead?

Mosquitoes played little fiddle tunes in their ears. Dark came fast.

Curiosity, of course, won out.

Ben's curiosity.

"Let's sneak up on it," he suggested. "Threadgill, we *got* to know what's making a noise like that one."

"You go. Then come back and tell me what you find … "

Ben sneered.

"You a chicken, Gill? You a poopy baby?"

"I ain't!" Threadgill felt color rise into his face. "Are you?"

Threadgill pushed right past his brother, who then noisily scuttled ahead again to claim the lead on the pathway.

"Hell," Ben insisted. "Hell, come on then."

Aunt Annie never allowed profanity, under any circumstances. But out on their rambles, Ben said *hell* all the time, like it was his favorite word.

"Hell, let's go then," Threadgill insisted.

"Hell, awright."

Ben moved well in the woods. For a kid who grew up in Mobile, a pretty big town from all folks said about it, he moved *very* well, Threadgill had to admit. Ben's quiet steps barely rustled the leaves, which lay so deep in places they almost buried the trail.

Still, no matter how quietly the two approached, it wasn't quiet enough. The noisemaker in the woods stopped the racket.

The Pickett brothers emerged from darkening thickets into a large cleared space. Part of the mystery now came clear. Some of the mysterious noises issued from a towering bonfire at the center of the clearing. It popped and shot up orange sparks that rose fast to turn into the night's first stars. Strange crackles and whooshes came from new brush, freshly tossed on the conflagration. The fuel popped loudly in the flames.

Nearly unseen, a small naked figure with a spear slipped like a puff of black smoke into the trees on the far side of the opening and disappeared. Both brothers caught a glimpse.

"Whoa!" Threadgill marveled. "Ben, what's Amos doing out here!"

"I been wonderin' where your little darky disappeared off to every night."

Revelation!

Threadgill lived his whole life with Aunt Annie and her tiny little slave. He never realized before this exact instant that Amos disappeared from the farm when the sun went down. When did Ben notice?

"Hell! Looka *that*, Gill!"

Towering old-growth sweetgums, tulip poplars and hickories ringed the circular space. It would take a man with legs as long as Ben's two hundred strides around the clearing to get back where he started.

Along the way, he would pass, every five steps or so, a chest-thick, chin-high log standing on end. From each of these, dozens of logs, carved faces – weird, beaked bears and laughing birds and gape-mouthed snakes – stared balefully at the twins.

The flickering fire light made the carved faces ghastly and powerful. Threadgill counted forty effigies before he got too boggled to keep up with the numbers.

"Whoa!" whistled Ben.

The totems waited like a night army of wooden warriors, bizarre masks where faces should have been. The carved army gave off a terrible feeling – the strangeness of hacked eyes and gaping mouths and flared nostrils made Threadgill continually glance over his shoulders into the dark woods.

The monsters considered Threadgill and Ben.

"It's a devil place," whispered Ben, standing very close to his brother for once.

Threadgill wouldn't argue. He felt too afraid to even open his mouth.

The twins moved back to back. The shifting firelight made the terrible carved army seem animated, alive.

"Let's go, Ben," Threadgill urged. "This ain't no good place."

But Ben now gasped upward, his mouth open in wonder. His goggling eyes seemed simply unable to comprehend.

"Godamighty *hell!* Gill ... look at *those*!"

In the trees over the terrible carved logs, some giant or magician had braided native wisteria and scuppernong vines into haunting faces and shapes. Painstakingly. On a gigantic scale.

Threadgill shrank from the fearsome woven shapes.

A gargoyle face thirty feet tall leered down, a black trellis of tongue wagging from its baleful lips. The vine face constantly changed expressions in the flickering bonfire light, scowling, winking, each aspect newly sinister, threatening.

"Look at *that* one!" Ben whispered.

Off past Forest Man, Threadgill beheld a massive animal figure, its head lowered, face studded with multiple fierce eyes. A single wooden horn the length of a railroad tie jutted off its brow. Beneath the beast sculpture, a vine-braided lightning bolt shot earthward in a sudden gust of wind, then tossed up again amid bonfire sparks.

Animals and masks and symbols of nature webbed the trees. In the blazing firelight, Threadgill and Ben could comprehend a complete tapestry, dozens of astonishing assemblages. Threadgill thought it looked like some gigantic spider had been at work, spinning out brown web arabesques – deities of the jungle and impossible creatures. What else on earth could create this kind of strange gallery?

"They're watching us, Threadgill."

Ben brandished a stout stick in hand now. His face fixed not on the arboreal sculptures but on shadows in the woods. Shadows, some of them moving, visible in the firelight.

"Who, Ben?"

Threadgill felt deeply, truly afraid now. He squinted to make sense of the secreted figures beyond the towering signal fire. He was ready to run on the instant … but he would not leave Ben alone, no sir.

"I don't know who they are," swallowed Ben. He didn't sound brave. "But people are out there. Darkies. I see 'em."

A gust of wind arrived, and the terrible beasts in the trees shifted, all together, like images on the billowing black sails of a ship. Did Threadgill hallucinate or did he really hear moans and hissess spatter down from the branches?

"Threadgill!"

Ben's voice made Threadgill jump. Big brother sounded a little panicked. "*Oh hell! Hell! Hell!* Look at THAT!"

An uncanny likeness of two brothers, carved from one piece of wood, stood to the right of them, in the ring of totems. The totem next to it resembled in astonishing detail a small woman wearing a straw hat.

Threadgill and Ben. Aunt Annie.

Ben jerked Threadgill's shoulder to turn him around. His face looked crazed.

"We got to burn this, brother!"

"What?"

"We got to … to *burn* it, Threadgill! This is a evil place!"

Threadgill's next words sounded even to him like a little boy's.

"Evil?"

"A devil place," Ben declared. "Them carved wood faces, them are *devils*. There's devils all around us, Threadgill! They'll put a curse on us."

Wind shifted the trees. A vine face wrinkled out of view, reappeared. Its eyes stared. Its mouth would open and speak any second. It would intone two boys' names, throw open its fanged jaws, shoot forth a thick green lizard tongue, *devour* them …

"Hurry, Threadgill. Hurry or they'll get us."

Even if he hadn't helped, Threadgill mused later, it would've happened. Ben already held in each hand a burning stick of fire, and he sprinted with the torches overhead all around the clearing.

Leaves began to snap and crackle and catch on the tree branches.

Fire took the trees.

One awful eye of the closest vine face flamed. A puff of wind whipped up a full head of fiery hair atop Forest Man.

That would kill a man, thought Threadgill, *getting burned like that.*

The beast with the horned nose writhed in agony. Up in red flames went dancing naked women, enormous turtles, lions and apes, huts and playing children and every other shape and figure the tree magus entwined onto the forest canopy.

The sculptures in the heights began to collapse and fall into the clearing, igniting the log totems. A hot rain of flaming leaves and debris threatened Threadgill and Ben with immolation.

The twins fled.

They splashed across Old Mercy Creek in the backglow of the inferno, embers hissing down around them. Their spooky fire-thrown shadows clawed at the steep fern bank before the boys reached it, clawing themselves up.

Threadgill could have sworn he heard distant screams.

Oh, how two Pickett brothers ran that night!

Hearts exploding, they finally burst out of the woods at Annie's corn field. They raced and stumbled down the furrows, knocked crooked many stalks of thigh-high green corn. Sweat burned Threadgill's eyes, but through the blear, back over his shoulder, he clearly made out a hot orange glow on the horizon.

He couldn't see stars in that part of the sky.

Aunt Annie will know.

Threadgill feared it with all his heart. *She will know what we did.*

Annie never would.

Threadgill and Ben, still out of breath and sopped with sweat and Old Mercy Creek, burst into the house. Annie sat in the rocker before her own very small fire.

Her eyes stayed closed when they entered. Her face seemed at peace, a blotch of bright blood on a handkerchief in her lap.

She'd gone to sleep.

Chapter 25, The Cobbs

Summer 1964 – Shelby County, Alabama

Threadgill walked a sun-charred, snaking mountain two-lane. The afternoon sun pounded the blacktop, a golden hammer on a scorched anvil.

Sweat drops dripped from the rim of the aluminum pot. Threadgill for some reason remembered the words of loony Larry LaRue – how long ago *was* that? – in the black Cadillac.

"We LIKE it hot, don't we Threadgill? We LOVE it hot!"

No sir. Threadgill didn't like it hot all that much.

He stopped in his tracks, amazed.

A wildcat sauntered onto the road ahead, a big, broad-shouldered brute in the broad light of day.

The cat padded up from a ditch. It was a male with no fear. The speckled pattern that made it magically disappear in woods stood out like a shooter's target against the black road.

A pink tongue covered in froth lolled from the wildcat's mouth. It hassled like a weary dog. It glanced neither left nor right, but padded – heedlessly, Threadgill thought – straight across the blacktop and onto the weedy shoulder.

Threadgill's knee tingled.

The wildcat worried him. Healthy animals don't act that way. Truth to tell, Threadgill had never once in all his life seen a wildcat in broad daylight.

Not 'til now.

Did it glance just once toward Threadgill with a sort of queer cat smile, black lips flecked in white? Did the snarl seem to say *Mad about you! You'll soon be one of us now, old man! Welcome!*

Threadgill studied the weeds where the animal disappeared. One thing was sure – if that cat had rabies, it wouldn't be happy when it hit Cahaba River.

People named it hydrophobia for a reason.

***

The heat was big.

Threadgill walked. On and on. Many minutes, many miles. The pot on his head tried its best to cook his brains.

After a long, long time, he rested in the shade of a sycamore.

No automobile of any kind had passed in hours.

A buzzard showed up overhead, joined clockwise circles with four friends, a black merry-go-round.

The hovering images took him back to Georgia.

Death angels, Threadgill grunted. *But they won't get this old piece of Alabama gristle ...*

"Shoo!" he yelled. "Shoo! Get on off from here!"

Threadgill flapped at the vultures, hands high. The steel pot clanged around his head. He felt dizzy for a minute. Then, to his great surprise, he couldn't stop the crazy dance. His jumping-jack motions got away from him.

Threadgill jerked and bounced around the road in a ragged, spinning tarantella that brought hot sweat flying from his fingertips. The highway turned a dull red where drops hit, and color slowly filled the road and overflowed into the ditches, then rose up fences. Crimson climbed the trunks of pine trees and spread out through fields and woods. It tinctured the sky, the high clouds, turned buzzards scarlet.

What the devil … is the matter with me?

Threadgill approached heatstroke. In moments he knew he would crumple onto the asphalt and melt like some kind of red tar between cracks.

Out of nowhere, a downgearing engine roared behind Threadgill.

The madness broke.

***

A black genie of exhaust belched from the stack of a six-axle Mack coal truck. It horsepowered up the long grade toward Threadgill, roaring its fury at the law of gravity.

The air horn blasted. Brakes hissed. The truck moaned to a stop in front of Threadgill, his clothes dark with sweat, the pot shiny on his head.

The powerful diesel engine shook the very earth as it idled, and shiny coal avalanched off the truck's sides.

A burly teamster in a filthy white long-john shirt and blue bib overalls manned the wheel. His hair looked like a run-over black cat. Blocky yellow teeth showed through a heavy beard, and the man's tiny eyes glittered like little pure shiny drops of oil.

The man lifted something off the truck seat. Bulky. It took both hands.

He hoisted the thing by the scruff of its neck with one brawny arm and swung it pendulously out the driver's side window. Blood drops spattered the road.

A male wildcat, freshly killed, dangled from one big hand.

The driver shook the limp creature to show Threadgill how utterly dead a thing could be.

"Durned cat run out the woods right back yonder, not a mile, and attacked my little Mack bulldog on the hood! Look! He clawed and gnawed the chrome slam off!"

The trucker's heavy beard made Threadgill think of a mass of mating black widow spiders. A broken-egg yellow grin oozed through.

"Git in the cab here, old timer. Too hot to be walkin'. We'll stop up yonder at Dawg's and git us a cold drank."

The hiker's head swam with relief.

"Obliged."

Threadgill scaled the cab like the face of a cliff. He took a toe hold, a hand grip, found another chink of truck for his boot. He reached at last a black seat sticky with sweat and coal dust and fresh wildcat blood. Adhesive tape held the seat's rotted black vinyl together.

"Stuff your stuff in the floor," the driver hollered. "It's cleaner'n it looks."

Maybe.

On the dash, used paper towels and an oily dipstick rolled around a bone yard of socket wrenches. Threadgill saw a bottle of baby aspirin, gummed-up honeybun wrappers, scattered playing cards with pictures of naked girls. In the floorboard sat a nasty-looking chain saw in a torn cardboard box, a strong smell of gasoline on it. The glove compartment door was lost to history. Inside it, a half bottle of whiskey sloshed happily as the truck geared forward. On either side of the back window, a rack of deer antlers hung onto a hunting rifle for dear life.

The slain wildcat stared wide-eyed at Threadgill from the seat.

"Goin' far as Hueytown," the driver hollered, coal-chunk eyes squinting. "You welcome to ride that far."

"Noisy!" Threadgill yelled.

"What's that?"

"It's NOISY!"

The trucker shrugged.

"Never been. But I know Chicago's there. I'm outta Bessemer myself. Them big steel mills. Keep you up all night when you're little, worrying about a blast furnace blowin' up your house 'n shit."

Threadgill reckoned the truck's engine made noise as loud as any blast furnace.

"That headgear cut down on noise?" The driver nodded at Threadgill's helmet. "Can't say I ever met a man wore a pot on his head."

Threadgill glanced in the truck's side mirror. The thing that blinked back wore a filthy gray goatee. Two exhausted whirlpools for eyes. He could have been an old turtle sucked from its shell and all boiled down to wrinkles in an aluminum pot. Upside down.

To hell with it.

"This here's my thinking cap," Threadgill yelled.

The driver snorted.

"Well, yeah! It DOES stink in here! This dead wildkitty don't help …"

Threadgill hollered back this time with such effort he felt something twang painfully in his throat. "Wildcat's got RABIES!"

The driver looked very surprised.

"Didn't SEE babies!" the mouth in the beard blasted back. "But I didn't think to see if she mighta had a litter in the weeds …"

Threadgill had to laugh at that. So the driver laughed too.

"Bull Cobb."

The driver offered a grimy handshake, big knuckled, calloused. Threadgill shook a hand of coal.

"Threadgill Pickett. Say, you mind if I eat one of them candies?"

A round pack of Rolaids rolled on the dash among all the clutter.

"Aw hell no! Put yer feet anywhere."

Threadgill tore off the paper and stuffed half the roll of mints in his mouth at once, chewing and smiling and nodding thanks to Bull Cobb with deep satisfaction.

"I reckon even a hitchhiker needs stomach acid relief," Cobb yelled.

"I ate fish bait for breakfast."

Cobb puzzled on this for a long moment.

"Well, I hate 'em too. I guess."

Threadgill happily crunched the disks. A starving dog would eat Rolaids.

The driver slowed all at once, and pointed.

"Now what mischief you reckon them two boys yonder been up to?" Cobb said.

Threadgill peered down the mountainous hood of the truck. The same barefoot riverboys he surprised that morning streaked along the roadside. They ran like their behinds burned with invisible fire.

"You reckon that wildcat spooked 'em, old timer?"

Bull Cobb looked at the seat. The dead animal leered up. Fleas now leaped from its cooling body, peppering the seats and both men. Millions of fleas. The moving insects looked like the spray over a freshly poured glass of Coke.

"Don't slow down!" Threadgill warned, the weight of the stolen pot on his head suddenly heavy. "Yellow jackets are all over them boys! I can see 'em from here!"

The truck blew past the kids, who wailed like sirens. Cobb gave a blast from his truck horn. Threadgill remembered the big freighter ships when they passed Goat Island, back on Mobile Bay, that lifetime ago.

"Thanks, buddy. I'm bad allergic to wasts. I swell up and turn pink like Spam."

Bull Cobb HAD heard Threadgill.

"I don't like a wasp," Threadgill yelled. "Nor a bee. Nor a hornet. Nor a durned fire ant. Nor a cowkiller ant. Nothing with a little hot nail in its tail."

They rocked along, back at speed now.

"It does get stale," Bull Cobb yelled over. "You right."

Well.

All back to normal.

***

They reached Dawg's, one ugly store.

What a better world, Threadgill thought, *since them Yankees took over after the war*.

Cobb killed his engine in the unpaved parking lot. He patted the dashboard of his truck.

"Named her Tammy," he shouted. "Fer Tammy Wynette."

Threadgill yelled back. "Who?"

"I did."

"Did *what?*"

"Named her her name."

"*Who?*"

"Tammy Wynette."

"She named your truck?"

"Tammy Wynette IS my truck!"

"Tammy *Wynette*? Who's she?"

Cobb stared in disbelief, as if Threadgill had all at once confessed he was a vegetarian. "You ain't never heard of Tammy Wynette?"

"Some kind of a medicine?"

Cobb's little black eyes shrank and hardened.

"Don't joke about Tammy Wynette."

Threadgill raised both palms. "Look Mr. Cobb, I wouldn't know a Tammy Wynette if one got up in the cab and put a leg in both pants pockets. Who is she?"

The driver brightened.

"Tell you what. Yer gonna meet Miz Tammy. Right now. Do this – punch in that eight-track."

Threadgill sat.

"That! Poke that little white Tammy tape in that little hole there. It won't bite."

Threadgill tried it. He jammed a plastic square of some kind into a notch on the dashboard. Wires hung all down under the notch, the way the guts hung out of the wildcat on the seat.

Threadgill pushed in the tape. Nothing happened.

"Upside down," Bull Cobb hollered. He himself ejected the tape and flipped it in his big dirty paw.

"You got a treat in store," Cobb announced, his face joyful. "I got this tape thang in 19 and 72."

Music boomed, so loud Threadgill felt his liver flip when the bass drum popped.

Threadgill flashed his broadest smile. "Sounds like a cat mating with a porcupine!"

Cobb nodded. His face glowed like the face of John the Baptist in a picture Threadgill saw in Mobile Sunset Home, the bearded wild man with black little locust legs stuck all in his teeth and honey blobs in his beard.

Now Threadgill's insides twanged. Tammy sang a song about D-I-V-O-R-C-E.

Bull Cobb bellowed "AWWW!" at the end of each verse, like a preacher in the ecstasy of his greatest sermon.

The song played to the end.

"Sounds like a good way to learn your spelling words at school," Threadgill volunteered.

"Ain't she great? Ain't Tammy sweet?"

Threadgill thought he could see little wet places under Cobb's eyes now. It could have been shining specks of coal dust.

"C'mon now, old timer. Let's get us a Dawg Dog And guess what?"

Threadgill's door already yawned.

"They got a righteous jukebox … three Tammys for a quarter. I put 'em in there my own self."

***

Dawg, a wrinkled old white woman, owned Dawg's Lucky Spot. She also owned Dawg's Kuntry Store and Dawg's Delicious Donuts, down the road. She was a Dawg queen.

She spit snuff while she spooned chili onto the eight hot dogs Bull and Threadgill ordered. Her chili pot had never been washed. The old woman said a word about every ten minutes, but Threadgill caught her sneaking a look. At him, Threadgill Pickett. Twice.

Bull noticed. "Believe old Dawg might be sweet on you, Mr. Pickett," he suggested, gobbling half a hot dog in one bite so ferocious every finger was at risk.

Six Tammy songs, three dogs and a big orange soda later, Threadgill's belly ached.

They finally reclimbed the face of Mt. Coaltruck.

Threadgill couldn't resist a look in the side mirror as they pulled away.

Sure enough, Dawg stood out by the road, a thin woman with a bump of snuff in her bottom lip. A cute little hump in her back. An old green dress blew around her legs in the truck afterwash.

What is it like? Threadgill wondered. *A man and a woman?*

The dead wildcat on the seat grinned up at him like it knew the answer to that question now … and all the others.

***

Tammy sang for forty miles, her mountain twang echoing from coal-seamed road cuts. This part of Alabama seemed truly forlorn, a strip-mined moonscape in places, just scraggly pines here and there on piles of rubble. Threadgill knew Yankees had done this to his beautiful state too.

A flashing red light came up behind the coal rig.

Threadgill watched Bull Cobb turn ghostly white.

"Shit, shit, shit," he whispered. "Holy shit!"

A big paw ejected Tammy. The cab soberly hushed.

Bull Cobb ground down through the truck gears. He finally knocked the stick into neutral, razzed the emergency brake.

"You let me do the talkin'," Bull Cobb said, fast and low. "Just play along. You're a hobo, and you're retarded. Or something. Got it?"

Threadgill nodded. His pot clinked.

A crown of a Smokey-the-Bear hat appeared in Cobb's window. State Trooper sported black sunglasses. Silver fillings gleamed in his teeth.

"See your license."

Bull Cobb nervously thumbed over the document. Threadgill wondered at the black nails on those oversized fingers. Was Cobb slowly turning to coal?

State Trooper peered up from the license, eyes visible over the sunglasses.

"You one of them Montevallo Cobbs?"

"Yes sir."

"You know Whanger Cobb?"

" 'At's my daddy, officer."

State Trooper's sharp face changed.

"Why, you do favor Whanger," he said. "One ugly sumbitch."

Bull Cobb just grinned like he was having his picture made for the high-school yearbook. "How you know Daddy?"

"Went to school with 'im. After we quit in the ninth grade, I started arrestin' him. Whanger was one hell-raisin' country boy. I ain't seen a lot of that sumbitch since we run him in for bootleg that last time."

"Crazy as a shithouse rat," Bull said. "You shoulda growed up in the same trailer with 'im. I MEAN!"

State Trooper nodded sympathetically. "That 'un a Cobb too?" He motioned at Threadgill.

"Not that he'll claim," Bull Cobb quickly answered. "Picked him up hitchhikin' down yonder at Little Cahaba. I don't think he's got a good mind."

"What's this here on the seat, Mr. Cobb?"

Bull Cobb raised the wildcat's head and it gaped, open-mouthed, wide-eyed.

State Trooper gave a low whistle. "That appears to be a protected animal, son."

"Not any more. It attackted my truck. It committed suicide."

"Run over it?"

"Yes sir. Busted it wide open. It's deader'n hell."

The officer pulled out a white handkerchief and mopped his forehead.

"Mind holdin' it out the door over this way, Mr. Cobb?"

The beast hung stiffer now. Its stubby tail dripped a little blood.

"Big ass wildcat."

State Trooper, it now occurred to Threadgill, must have stood six-eight. He actually looked dead on into the cab of the coal truck without a foot on the running board.

"That's enough. Take the kitty back inside, Mr. Cobb."

State Trooper turned his attention to Threadgill.

"Where you from, old man?"

Threadgill had a plan. He cupped his hand to his mouth and shouted back.

"Sixty four dollars!"

State Trooper looked at Bull Cobb, who just shrugged. He put on a your-guess-is-as-good-as-mine expression.

"Boys," State Trooper frowned. "It's too hot to stand out here and put up with bullshit."

Threadgill leaned across the seat, his eyes bright. "Big as a skint mule!" he hollered. "Big old hiney too!"

"Need you two out of the cab just a minute," State Trooper ordered wearily. "Come on. Do it now."

Bull Cobb swallowed. "Is this a search, officer?"

"What if it is? I ought to strip and cavity search both of you, come to think of it, just out of disrespect for old Whanger. Come on out. Let's get this over with."

Threadgill saw Bull Cobb's hand shake on the door handle.

What's going on?

Threadgill and Bull Cobb both leaned against the truck cab on hand painted letters – TAMMY. Threadgill got a nose full of black coal dust and idle exhaust. He sneezed once. He felt dirty now inside and out.

State Trooper wiped soot off his own face before he climbed up to search the cab. He poked around the dash, ran his hand under both seats, rifled the glove compartment. He poured out the quart bottle of whiskey on the road. He sniffed the barrel of the gun on Bull Cobb's antler rack. He totally ignored the wildcat corpse.

"Critter loped up on the road about five miles back yonder." Bull Cobb spoke loudly. "Come slam up on the hood. I busted 'im wide open. Look on the grille, you'll see hair and blood."

The officer showed a keener interest in the deer antler gun rack. Sweat rolled down State Trooper's face like condensation on a cherry Kool-Aid pitcher. He reached up and tenderly jiggled one point on the antler rack, then another.

"Daddy give me that .22 back in junior high school," Bull piped up. "Don't keep nothing in it but ratshot. For all them rattlesnakes around Blue Diamond mine."

"Bull," State Trooper remarked, looking down for the first time, "would you just shut up? I ain't interested in your goddamn .22."

They waited, scorching in the hot sun, Threadgill and a chastened Bull Cobb. Threadgill actually started to hassle like a dog. He thought the top of his head under the metal helmet might boil.

"Let me tell you something, Mr. Cobb," State Trooper said, finally climbing down from the cab. "Here's an idea for you to take home and ponder."

The road roared with afternoon heat like a furnace.

"Me and Miz Holly Gillespie is startin' a fish camp," said the lawman, "and I'm on the lookout for some of Alabama's finer deer racks to decorate our place. We're gonna have big striped bass on the walls, and boar heads, and prize deer racks. Maybe a stuffed bear. And a big tank full of live catfish. Folks can pick out the lunker they want for supper."

Bull Cobb's beard split and that yellow smile oozed through again.

"I got some good buck racks," the officer said, "but I believe that one on the back of your cab might be the finest I've seen lately. It would look mighty fine over the front door of Catfish Shack."

Bull Cobb stepped sprightly toward the cab.

"Hell, Officer, I'll give you them horns right now. They's a green screwdriver on the dashboard ..."

"Naw, naw!" State Trooper waved off the favor. "Hell, not this red-hot minute. Wouldn't look too good for a lawman to show up at the station with prize deer antlers in the patrol car, if you know what I mean."

Bull nodded. He was Whanger Cobb's boy. He knew how things worked.

"How 'bout I bring 'em over to Warrior Road next time I'm out there? I haul out of Black Diamond a lot. That would be an easy stop."

"Just the ticket," the officer smiled. "Just the ticket."

"I'll even tie a big red bow on them antlers," Bull promised.

"Shit, boy," State Trooper laughed. "You a good bit smarter'n old Whanger! He never could tie a bow."

Even Threadgill laughed. The sound rang nicely under the pot.

The officer turned to him.

"What you laughing at, Dummy? You understood a gotdam word I said?"

"Chinese, Alabama!" Threadgill answered instantly, spitting out the words like they tasted bad.

State Trooper licked his lips and winked at Bull Cobb. He strutted like a rooster back toward his cruiser. The red police light twirled. The patrol car rolled away.

Almost.

State Trooper abruptly stopped. He unfolded his lanky body out the cruiser door again.

Bull Cobb cut a new anxious glance at Threadgill. *What now?*

State Trooper unholstered his pistol. He mounted the Mack's running board.

He reached past Bull Cobb for the dead wildcat and lifted the animal's blood-crusty muzzle with the barrel of his pistol.

"No bullet hole to see," he shouted. "Just checkin' out your story, Bull."

The cat's grinning head flopped back to the seat.

State Trooper stepped down, brushed black dust from his blouse, reholstered the gun.

"See you real soon, Mr. Cobb. Tell Whanger I said hey. You too, Simple Simon."

The officer touched the broad brim of his hat, flashed his silver smile.

Threadgill saluted, hand to his aluminum-pot forehead.

"Have a nice hat!" he blurted.

State Trooper laughed all the way back to his cruiser.

Bull Cobb looked at Threadgill. The police cruiser disappeared around the curve on the northbound road.

"Jesus," Bull Cobb finally whispered with a long exhaled breath. "That was a close one, Bucket Head."

Chapter 26, Yellowhammer NYC

The dawn lights of Washington dim.

Metropolis spreads on, twinkling, a vast net of trapped luminous creatures, a Gordian knot of road and light. Demoniac car beams sweep the streets. Flashing cherries top ambulances, police cars. Parking lots and stadiums fluoresce.

Yellowhammer hears Yankeeland tumult – a constant, vague grumble like a stomach in trouble. The noise thrums louder by the mile.

Off east, the sun flops heavily into view, an exhausted swimmer. Dark night around Yellowhammer pearls, softens.

Yellowhammer is a heartbeat with wings.

There's Baltimore.

The old city glows like a drunkard's nose. At Chesapeake Bay, fog blows in – ghost surf – and shrimp boats with lifted trawls bob up, down, like drowned grasshoppers. Men in yellow slickers stare over rails at hard weather. Drenched, drunken, pelicans settle rain-blackened docks.

Yellowhammer flies.

Philadelphia seems like an old lie. The city of brotherly love wears a pall of exhaust and grime. Homeless men shame sidewalks. Rows of decayed buildings, black as dominoes, pass for neighborhoods. Cars smolder, here and there, and wolves on two legs prowl the smoking hulks.

Things should have turned out better, Yellowhammer thinks. After all the trouble these people went through to beat the South, things should have turned out better than this.

Yellowhammer looks away. Overhead, the Pleaides huddle, alarmed prisoners in a fading, star-crumbed sky.

Freighters moan and grumble, the sad sounds that came out of the world at the beginning, and fill the world till its great flaming end.

The bay turns into countryside. Black antlers of blighted elm jut from fields. Rain needles down on black-green tapestry fields.

A deep noise grows louder, constant as a waterfall. Yellowhammer thinks of a million freight trains rolling into stations. A sentinel pine scraggles from grass wetlands. A stinging, paper-mill smell rises off fogbound marsh.

Now it comes.

A great city, like a gaseous bubble, erupts from reed. Buildings baffle the view, crash the sunlight, rioting light and masonry.

New York City.

The great city prickles like a hedgehog, a cheval-de-frix of stone spire, antenna, guy wire, metal tower. The dizzy vast concrete sprawl takes Yellowhammer aback. Topography changes where two gray rivers meet a nervous harbor. A swatch of park green bandages this corrugated world, midway up a clustered island.

Yellow sharks, schools of them, burst forward as traffic lights change. The taxis race for their lives a quarter mile, stop cold for a new red light, strain with blowing horns a short second, lunge away again, leave signatures of rubber on the asphalt.

A man in a white jumpsuit tosses bundled newspapers from an enormous panel truck. Another man stands guard with a shotgun. A female, dress short, eyes daubed shadow blue, whistles from beneath a light across the street.

A Jewish man with a comical black hat, a beard of curlicues, flounces past. He holds holding something torn with his teeth. He trails crumbs.

East, a ten-story tenement burns merrily. Tiny, shiny toy firetrucks hose it down to orange shimmer.

The morning gathers strength. The great city smokes like a hot cup of coffee, swirling with commerce, the factories northward unfurling gray flags from chimneys and smokestacks. Yellowhammer's black eyes smolder, water. Gray feathers soon reek of gasoline fumes, burning tires.

The city stretches on, a steel sheet riveted with concrete bolts and lights and asphalt, civic centers, gas stations, clustered communities, glass-strewn basketball courts.

The spiky skyline gives way to Connecticut. It glows too, as if someone carelessly lit and then kicked the metropolis, scattering fiery ants.

Yellowhammer rises, moves along.

The odor of eight million human beings wafts away.

Yellowhammer smells the Atlantic's briny tang.

Chapter 27, Tammy II

Summer 1964 – Shelby County, Alabama

Threadgill nodded as Tammy chuckled to a stop in front of a tired mobile home on a weedy lot dotted with stripped and rusted carcasses of cars, refrigerators, stoves, stereos, radios, old TV sets. Some hulks wore faded decals on their sides, stock car numbers barely visible through honeysuckle vines.

The silence woke Threadgill with a start. Quietness could be as deafening as an engine.

A second burly man in a black beard appeared in the doublewide mobile home door. He wore flowered bermuda shorts, a Bama T-shirt. Otherwise, in every aspect of size and physiognomy, the man looked identical to Bull Cobb.

"Burvell Cobb," Bull pointed. "He's my cousin and my brother."

"How!" Burvell Cobb's hand rose, palm forward, an Indian greeting.

"Got the goods, bro!" Bull Cobb yelled.

"Was hopin'! Bring 'em on back to the shed!"

Bull Cobb, with a grunt, dragged the stiffened wildcat off the seat and wrestled its awkward body to one broad shoulder. It looked like a housecat there.

Bull turned half round under his load.

"C'mon, old man! Something you'll want to see back here! Guaranteed."

Bull and his wildcat stepped lively again, around the corner of the mobile home and out of sight. Bull followed his cousin and brother, who clapped his big hands and grinned.

Threadgill got a weird feeling.

Still, he followed. The brawny boys passed a new sprawl of stripped-down automobiles. Thistles sprouted everywhere, tall as pagodas, and a catalpa tree sagged under long green pods – Threadgill heard Eufaula folk in olden days call those "Indian cigars." A retired John Deere tractor with pieces missing barely showed under a quilt of morning glory vines.

They reached a Quonset hut, corrugated tin, not very skillfully made. Sheets of tin curled from the building's frame, the rivets sprung. A huge air conditioner spit sparks of blue fire from a hole eaten or beaten through one side.

Threadgill neared, passed through a garage door.

Thwoomp! The door lowered automatically. All the air left the hut.

Threadgill felt a little frightened, locked in. Someone had completely blacked out a lone porthole window with strips of black adhesive tape. It was impossible to see in or out. A smaller door stood ajar at the hut's far end. Threadgill eyed this lone opening and calculated how many steps, in a pinch, it might take to reach it.

But behold! One splendid object dominated the room.

A dazzling red machine – a thing Threadgill had never seen, something between car and helicopter – sat on a hydraulic lift. Immaculately construct-ed, low to the road, sleek as a scarlet snake. Its new and perfect tires gleamed through the gloom. Spotless black-leather seats.

Fluorescent tubes on snaky coils of wire dangled from the Quonset hut roof, illuminating the strange vehicle. Down both sides of the hut, metal shelves held countless tiny baby food jars and unlabeled shiny tin cans filled with screws and springs and widgets and tiny stoppers and god-knows-what all. Long shelves sagged with science magazines and old books, and Threadg-ill noted that many of the volumes bore the same word on the spine – *Physics*. Physics this, Physics that.

The machine's perfect red hood leaned against a wall. Meanwhile, the engine, glistening like a newly dressed buck, hung aloft on a cable over a work table. The cement floor beneath the engine block held a litter of oily pink rags, pans filled with bolts and screws, and green-and-white cans oozing honey-col-ored Quaker State.

"Ain't she a beaut?" beamed Burvell Cobb. He instantly talked in a famil-iar way to Threadgill, even though Bull hadn't introduced them. "And look here! This thang back here – that's its magic! Come see!"

Burvell Cobb caressed the machine as he walked past, the big fingers light-ly brushing a hand-painted number on the door – number 8, but a digit laid on its side like a peanut. An unwashed paintbrush lay by a bright yellow can of paint. The room reeked with fresh paint and rubber, and Threadgill could make out more automobile tires – at least a dozen – stacked like tumorous doughnuts against a far wall.

Burvell Cobb stopped in front of a lumpy object. A tarpaulin covered it. Threadgill thought he could hear ticking under the heavy cover.

"This is the shit," crowed Burvell Cobb, his voice rising with excitement like a girl's, absurd from his giant frame. "This goes right on top. It's the whole

Pickett's Charge

shebang, really. The racer there, it's just the chassis … and all that hanging up yonder, that's just the engine … but this here's the godblessed *soul*."

Bull Cobb scuffled up. Threadgill felt suddenly like a man standing between fur hills.

"All made from scratch," explained Bull. "We got spare parts from them old cars, plus TVs and radio crystals and wires pulled out of abandoned houses. Burvell got some really good stuff from the army surplus. He learned to do all this shit in Vietnam."

Burvell Cobb, all three hundred pounds or so, proudly nodded.

"This thang will mount right up on top of Tammy."

"On Tammy Wynette?" Threadgill was confused. "Your coal truck?"

Bull laughed.

"No, no, Burvell's tellin' you about Tammy 2! That's what we're calling this new machine. Tammy 2 – in double honor of Tammy You-Know-Who."

Burvell Cobb grasped the tarpaulin, prepared to lift, a waiter unveiling a fancy new dish. Threadgill saw pride light his eyes.

"Ta-da!" he announced, with a flourish.

Threadgill goggled.

It appeared to be a miniature city of tiny crystal tubes and dials and whirring gadgets and springs. Little lights shone all inside, bright here, dim there. Bubbles moved up and down glass cylinders. Intricate valves flapped, waited, closed. Needles spun round on gauges, and something like a silver puff of steam left a tiny vent every few seconds.

The machine whistled a note. It reminded Threadgill uncomfortably of the sound his ears made deep under the Cahaba this very morning – *tweee-weeeeeeeeeeee*!

"Tammy 2!" Bull proudly announced. "She's the world's first and only genuine, bonafide, hand-made … time machine."

Threadgill stared at both men.

They leaned in reverence over their curious device, thumbs identically tucked into leather belts.

"Time machine?"

"Yep. A time machine." The Cobbs answered simultaneously.

Threadgill felt baffled.

"You mean … like a grandfather clock?"

The brothers looked at one another oddly. They started to laugh.

"A grandfather clock?" hooted Burvell Cobb, bent over. "Hey, that's funny. A grandfather clock for sure *is* a time machine!"

Bull couldn't catch his breath to answer. His gargling laugh filled the little cheap metal hut.

The Cobbs sounded insane.

"But really – I'm confused!" interrupted Threadgill. "What do you mean, a time machine? What does it do?"

"Why, Bucket Head, it's a machine to travel through time!"

Bull was one of those men who cries when he laughs hard, and his cheeks glistened. "Tammy 2 can go back to the past – we done sent a pit bull back to The Alamo, we think. And she goes frontward to the future too. Once she's ready, mister, you can git in and go back to the day you was born, if you want. Eat yourself a picnic and watch the baby doctor spank your pink ass."

Burvell Cobb pointed to the chassis.

"Like I say, that'll mount right up on top of Tammy there, and we designed her to have good clearance for low limbs and overpasses and whatnot. Not much taller than the cab on your standard pick-up truck, really. She'll go wherever, even tight spots."

Threadgill wondered if the two men came into the world crazy or just took a short cut drinking too much. He stole another furtive look at the back door. Something small and furry – an opossum? – slipped out the opening.

"You don't see too many time machines!" Threadgill offered weakly

"If I'm lying, I'm dying."

Burvell Cobb drew up, hugely happy, his arms spread like an evangelist yelling hallelujahs.

"It ain't *about to be* a time machine, Pops – it IS a time machine. Me and Bull been working five years on it. Came right out of them fixit books yonder." He pointed grimy fingers at the Physics texts. "We're takin' a test drive tonight. Soon as we load it with fuel."

The beaming cousin now passed a meaningful glance at Bull.

"You *did* bring the fuel, didn't you, Bull?"

"Oh yeah. I got the fuel!" Bull crowed. "Yes sirree bobtail! Get it, Pops? *Bobtail?*"

Bull pointed to the wildcat carcass. Stiff on the floor, the dead cat stared, twinkling. Its open eyes reflected gizmo lights.

The brothers hooted and shuffled in a little bear dance.

"Up for a test drive, Bucket Head?"

"We'll go fast as a raped ape!" Burvell declared.

"Vaseline lightning!" answered Bull.

"Bitch greyhound with 'er tail on fire!"

"Shit through a racin' goose!"

"Tell him one more time what we gonna name 'er!" yelled Bull Cobb. "Tell 'im, Burvell!"

"Ready?" Burvell Cobb said. "In two-part harmony?"

Threadgill flinched. Sweat dripped off his bucket.

"Tammy 2!"

"Aww!" Bull Cobb shouted. "SWEET!"

The twin brothers that were also cousins slammed their hard palms together in the air.

Bull grabbed the wildcat by its nape and flumped it onto plywood laid over rickety sawhorses.

"How far can Tammy go?" Threadgill asked. "Will she make it all the way up to Maine?"

The two men looked seriously at one another.

"She goes a hell of a lot faster with Bull there drivin,' " Burvell grinned. "I got this pussel-gut, an' all."

"We don't really know quite yet," Bull confessed. "She's still bein' road tested."

"Shee-it!" went Burvell Cobb, so tickled.

The fluorescent light buzzed weirdly. Both men suddenly looked purple and yellow beneath it, bruised.

"Can we test it right now? To see if we get to Maine?" Threadgill dripped more sweat. "I got an appointment."

The two men swapped glances again.

"Well, that's up to this here wildcat," Bull said. "You see, this critter is the key."

Threadgill felt weird again, something unsaid in the air.

Burvell motioned. "Over here, Pops."

Threadgill moved uneasily.

Bull Cobb turned the wildcat supine on the plywood, stiff legs up. For the first time, Threadgill could see how badly the animal had been injured – busted wide open, sure enough, the length of its belly. The long open wound still oozed, entrails dangling. The rupture down the belly looked neat … and then it occurred to Threadgill. Neat as if a chainsaw opened it.

Threadgill saw a few late fleas hop free of the cold feline body.

"Pops," Bull said, pushing his arm up to the wrist into the animal's belly with a sucking sound. "What you're about to see's why I got so danged nervy when Mr. State Trooper pulled us over."

"Smokey stopped y'all?" marveled Burvell Cobb. "You didn't tell me that."

Burvell's big stomach pressed the plywood, and it accidentally slid a little.

"Oh yessir. At Limestone Point. State Trooper wants my twelve-point gun rack to decorate his durned juke joint. Whole time he searched the cab, he was looking through my back window at the load of coal. Trying to see if I was runnin' something. Dumb sumbitch didn't know he was near 'bout sitting on it."

Bull popped a fat bloody finger out of a small hole below the wildcat's shoulder.

"See that kittycat hole, Pops? I lied about that rifle. I shot this cat from the cab. A good shot too – I was moving and it was moving, just like cowboys and Indians."

Bull Cobb then jerked wide the stiff legs of the wildcat on the makeshift operating table – the moist tearing noise made Threadgill think of a leg pulled off a roasted turkey. The cat's white underbelly yawned, ghastly red inside, and the smell of its body cavity once more went straight up Threadgill's fine nose.

"Johnny Law didn't see a bullet hole 'cause I got out the chain saw and opened Mr. Wildcat up and made it look like a road kill. Smeared gristle up on the front of the truck. Swuft, huh?"

Bull turned with a sneer to brother Burvell.

"Officer Asshole even made a big prissy show of taking out his pistol and waving it. Like I ain't never seen a pistol. Shee-it!"

Suddenly, violently, Bull Cobb rammed his right hand up to the elbow into the gaping belly slit of the wildcat. The animal trembled.

Threadgill jumped back in shock.

"But we're still gonna have to figure out some new way to get the fuel up here soon," Burvell Cobb said. He stood thoughtfully for a moment, watching Bull grope the cat corpse. "They catchin' on, Cousin."

Bull Cobb's arm emerged suddenly with a loud sucking sound. His skin turned red way past the wrist. The wildcat's belly spilled its secret contents onto the plank.

Plastic bags. Two dozen of them. Filled fat with round gray soft objects roughly the size and shape of human ears.

One blood-slick bag slid off the plywood and landed on Threadgill's foot.

Burvell and Bull burst into giggles.

"Pick 'er up, Bucket Head. Open wide and say aaah. Time travel to Maine right now!"

Threadgill lifted the smeared plastic bag by a tiny corner, squinting at it in the fluorescent light.

The soft objects inside appeared to be … mushrooms.

"Bull, you'd sure as hell be on your way to Kilby Prison right now if that trooper was smart as he thought!" Burvell said.

"Got enough fuel here for ten trips back to the past," Bull Cobb crowed. "And ten more to the future!"

Burvell Cobb held up a bag, tore it open with eager fingers. He picked out four of the mushrooms, big ones, stuffed them all into his mouth at once and chewed blissfully.

"Gentlemen ... *chomp, chomp* … start yore engines!"

"God bless America," Burvell shouted. "And God bless Alabama even more!"

The two men danced a little brotherly jig in the purple light. When the dance ended, they searched the shop with black eyes shining.

"Hey!" yelled Bull Cobb. "Bucket Head! Where you go, Bucket?"

The cousins, comically searched the hut, the seats of the red time machine, the shelf of tools and paints, the pages of their physics books.

The little machine on the floor whistled and clicked, whistled and clicked. Beyond it, the back door of the hut hung wide open.

Someone had passed through, going very fast.

Chapter 28, Eva

Barbour County, Alabama – Summer 1866

Once a month, on the same day at the same hour, Colonel Able Sutton and his driver, Washington, boiled into Eufaula in a cloud of red dust.

All bushy beard and weary shoulders, the Colonel stumped on his peg into Mr. Daniel King's general store, sniffing at barrels. A man of frowns and low grunts, Colonel Sutton silently stabbed a finger at meager items – a small piece of pork, bottle of pain elixir – and Washington collected them with white-gloved hands as if handling delicate glass. Col. Sutton loudly bargained payment with the store owner while Washington loaded the prizes into a tattered buggy.

It was a surrey, in fact, and not long ago a perfectly elegant vehicle, its cloth canopy green as March buds. The velour seats once smelled sweet, and the vehicle sported silver fastenings and whispery springs under its axles.

Now, a year after Lee's white flag, the silver trim had been stripped and sold, and the carriage creaked and rattled like a farmer's wooden buckboard.

Washington, an elegant, thin man with the enormous brown eyes of a rabbit, was one of a handful of Eufaula slaves who remained in household service after the war. The aging Negro rarely spoke or drew attention to himself. If a white lady passed the buggy, Washington's bowler hat rose from his head an inch or so, showing close-cropped gray wool with an immaculate part, razored straight as a line laid by Mason and Dixon. If other Negroes happened to pass, Washington disdained them.

Before the war, Colonel Sutton's town visits gained a reputation as joyous moments for Eufaula merchants. Sutton made big money in cotton, and the Colonel routinely ordered big-money goods for his plantation – one wagon loaded solely with meats and game, another with strong drink, a third with flour and spices, and so forth. Mr. Daniel King famously closed the general store and sent his whole staff home, each with a fifty-cent bonus, after one spree.

Mr. King's muleskinners would race these mercantile goods out to the Colonel's estate, nine hundred acres of field and mansion and slave cabin and forest. Once, a King wagon splintered a wheel under one of the loads, and four kegs of cane syrup broke open in the hard red road. The ruptured barrels left a huge amber pool.

In two days, the lake of sweet syrup had collected so many honeybees and yellow flies and black ants that folks rode in from miles around to see the "natural wonder."

One moonless night, some unknown folk sculptor stole to the spill and fashioned a waist-high human figure of red clay and cane syrup. The artist perched it by the roadside on a gum stump, dressed in the clothes and straw hat of a tiny man. It sported a small corncob pipe in a pebbly smile.

The quaint figure sat by the road for months. The sentinel never spoke, simply waved travelers past, one red hand raised high. Some passersby believed it said hello. Others felt sure it waved goodbye.

The syrup man melted in winter rain.

***

Now and again, a green-eyed collection of freckles and red curls rode to town alongside Colonel Sutton.

Eva, at fifteen, wore her famously gorgeous hair long down her back. She held her white hands folded in her lap, but the green eyes flickered here and there, lively as hummingbirds, and took in everything. Her skin smelled of apple.

Home from the war, sixteen himself now and tall as any man in town, Threadgill rode old Dinah to Eufaula and Daniel King's store once a month too. He procured a quarter's worth of dry beans and corn meal, his staff of life these times.

Threadgill's sick and wounded and weak months lay behind him, a long, terrible dream. He'd even healed enough from the war to work at Slocum's Mill, where he spent days far from public view moving hundred-pound bags of grain in and out of lonely, dusty storage.

At night, he watched the fire in Aunt Annie's empty house.

Aunt Annie gone. Ben gone.

One Saturday visit, Threadgill clumped along the plank walk between apothecary and general store. He unexpectedly felt surviving hair rise on the back of his neck.

As always, his hat covered The Unmentionable.

Threadgill first thought a stinkbug crawled his collar. The youngster swiped there with a clumsy hand, knocked his gray hat slightly askew.

Eva watched.

This sunny day, she sat in cool green shadow beneath the canopy of the Colonel's surrey.

Alone.

Eva Sutton held her back very straight. Threadgill could see a little arch where a man's hand could go. The beautiful face seemed just on the verge of something, cheeks flushed, eyes bright. That famous hair shone in the sun like polished copper.

A strand blew across her cheek.

Threadgill couldn't see or hear the world for a moment.

Her astonishing eyes flicked away from Threadgill. But he could look nowhere else. He watched delicate red lips open, close. And now he could hear again.

A song!

> *Strike for our mothers now*
> *For daughters, sisters, wives,*
> *Freely would each bestow,*
> *Were it ten thousand lives.*

Little arrows, note by note, pierced Threadgill's heart.

He staggered out of the sizzling afternoon and into the general store. He moved stupidly, agog, right into the middle of the Colonel's latest shouting match with Mr. Daniel King over a penny discount wanted on a pound bag of salt.

Threadgill quietly slipped aside to the window, off balance, bewildered. The impeccable Washington stood there too, close at hand. Washington did not blink or move or acknowledge Threadgill in any way.

The youngster swallowed hard, a lump of honey and salt.

His heart felt flooded. He was sure every customer in the store, including the venerable Colonel Sutton and his Negro, could hear the damned thing beat.

EvaEvaEvaEvaEva.

Breathing was hard. Standing still impossible.

Threadgill wandered off among the back shelves of the general store, to find his wits. The Colonel blustered and railed, but Threadgill heard only singing, saw only a girl's perfect face. Did Eva have a little Milky Way of freckles under those eyes?

Angry voices trailed off. A door closed, hard. Threadgill decided to step back outside into the world for one more look.

Red-faced, Mr. Daniel King stood on the boardwalk and twisted his apron. He glared angrily down the street into a hot sun.

A plop of horse droppings marked the spot where the Colonel's surrey had stood.

***

Threadgill had gotten it in his mind somehow that he and Ben would be gone from his Aunt Annie's farm just a few short months. They would leave in summer, put the Yankees to flight, be home by Christmas.

Instead, Ben got killed. Threadgill spent four months in a flyblown Newnan dance hall-turned-hospital, convalescing from burn and bullet. Threadgill learned of Lee's surrender as he stared, fevered, at a cockroach ominously approaching his face on stained bed sheets. When another wounded soldier sobbed out the Appamattox news, a nurse ran toward him. The roach flew after her, landed on her back.

Months later, Threadgill planned the long walk home. Stage by weary stage, he would retrace the route he and Ben took through Georgia.

Threadgill departed the hospital on a hot August day. He carried a gift of wild red persimmons from the local ladies aid society. He wore his wide hat and his new scars and a donated suit of clothes, riddled with moth holes. Not bullet holes, at least. His pockets held crackers and pork rind.

His terrible wounds and his youth earned Threadgill sympathetic hand-outs along his route – most often pones of cornbread, sometimes an ear of corn, one time even a blessed scrap of ham. Still, for the last fifty miles of that long trek back to Eufaula, Threadgill ate next to nothing. He survived on dock roots foraged in the fields and tough mushrooms clawed off the sides of trees.

He reached home in October.

Annie's farm had weathered badly. Weeds choked the garden, overtopped fences, covered outbuildings. The barn? Burned and gone, a square of smut and a few charred posts that stank in rain. Threadgill found Dinah, the old horse, out in the woods with a herd of deer, nearly wild. Ben insisted Dinah, at her age, would break down on the quest to Atlanta. Dumb wrong, Ben. About that and a lot more.

Threadgill visited Aunt Annie's sad grave back in the field. The twins had laid her out under the biggest tree on the place, a soaring poplar thick as a wagon wheel. The tree rained down orange-green-white blossoms in spring. The twins carved crude initials on a stone – "AP."

Annie would not have made a show of her monument.

Some stranger had placed another memento – a rude cross – on the earth mound. Amos? The visitor garlanded the cross with a strangely woven vine wreath. Threadgill found the skeleton of a tiny bird in it.

And what of Amos?

Gone and away. The people in Eufaula weren't sure, but a story made the rounds that Annie's faithful servant set off for South Carolina determined to find a wife and child sold long ago in the Charleston slave market. Others had a notion he'd gone west, searching the Trail of Tears.

*****

Threadgill had grown into a man while no one was looking. He bore deep scars and a deep voice. He knew some things about the world.

At night, he sprawled on the rough plank floor of Annie's parlor. He preferred it to the empty feather beds for a reason he couldn't understand himself.

He kept a fire in the front fireplace, and he stretched his long-boned body, skinny as a winter tree, across the hearth when he took his meals. Threadgill stirred beans around on his tin plate, sopping with crumbled cornbread. He stared out the cobwebbed windows and pondered Ben and the war, the weedy fields, his aunt's house, the little cattle pond in the green valley – cows gone now.

He could see his father's gravestone on top of the hill, out past the pond.

Threadgill's skin and bone completely healed, in time. The other wounds, he kept well hidden under a broad hat.

*****

Even with the hardscrabble life and meager meals, Threadgill's frame gradually grew stronger again. The job at Slocum's Mill required him, day after day, to dump croker sacks of corn onto a crushing millstone. Threadgill would shovel-scatter the grain, dodge the rumbling wheel, shovel the crushed corn meal back into bags. He hauled the soft, clumsy sacks to waiting wagons.

Sometimes if a hard-eyed, sunburned farmer owned neither mule nor wagon, Threadgill would simply heave the sack from his own back onto the customer's. Once or twice a month, a man limped down the road for home stooped under a hundred pounds of corn meal.

Threadgill rarely spoke, a most agreeable trait in the view of the mill owner, Mr. Thomas Slocum. The doughty Irishman weighed his own words as carefully as he did bags of meal.

Threadgill never socialized. His habits and secrets stayed private.

He burned, though, as young men do.

***

Threadgill had seen beautiful Eva even before her siren song at Mr. Daniel King's store.

She happened to be a Pickett cousin someway, and once or twice in his life Threadgill's relations in the family converged with Eva's. It happened once at a wedding, another time at a dinner on the grounds for the washed-in-the-blood congregation of a country church. Threadgill noticed the redhaired girl both occasions, and felt – what? Something like gravity, only pulling him softly toward her face and hands and body, not toward the hard earth.

Aunt Annie rarely spoke of Sutton relations. Threadgill passed it off as an issue of haves and have-nots – the Picketts mostly stuck fast in the second camp. He wondered, too, if some old unforgiven wrong lay imbedded like a black arrow in the heart of the kinship.

One late-winter night, as the youngster stirred yet another smoking pot of beans in the black pot over his hearth, Threadgill considered the ways of his people.

Picketts. Flanneries. Suttons. Seales. Who could understand families? A civil war raged in most every one he knew, brother against brother, sister against sister, state against state, country against country. Even fathers against sons, mothers against daughters. Families used the same terrible weapons as war – explosions and slashes and sieges. Some battles lasted only a frightening few moments, but proved as bloody and mangling to the soul as a charge against massed cannon. Other family battles would only end when Armageddon blew out the light of the world.

Threadgill wondered if God gave humankind fire-and-steel wars as a blessing.

War let families kill people they weren't kin to.

***

Like Threadgill, Col. Able Sutton returned from the war with a grievous wound. Unlike Threadgill, the Colonel came home a hero.

Col. Sutton made it through three whole years without a scratch, fighting through Tennessee and Mississippi and north Alabama. He led Alabama boys with yellowhammer feathers in their hats against Grant and Rosecrans and, at the bitter end, Thomas. He was fifty years of age by one week when he lost his right leg to a bounding cannonball at Nashville. By then, the Colonel had earned immortal glory – and a battlefield promotion from Nathan Bedford Forrest himself – for an action on a lonesome hilltop in Alabama. For eight hours, Col. Sutton and ten tough rebels with only guile and squirrel guns held back a hundred bluebellies. In the end, out of ammunition and fighting like cave men, the Confederates rolled boulders down steep slopes onto the Yankees.

Threadgill thought a great deal about Col. Sutton during the healing winter of 1866.

He wondered if his distant cousin had seen action in north Georgia. Anywhere close to Pine Mountain. Threadgill craved a connection – *any* connection – that could bring him close to the Colonel's beautiful daughter.

***

Threadgill made sure he passed the Sutton place on his five-mile ride to the mill each morning.

The Sutton mansion, like all those still unburned, knew better days. It stood at the end of a long lane of splintered red-limbed cedar trees. A magnolia shaded the back of the big house; the tree's glossy branches brushed against second-story windows every time a good wind gusted. Mornings, a skinny wild guinea fowl, doomed for a stewpot sooner or later, skulked from one low copse of shrubs to the next, often trailed by the drabbest peacock Threadgill had ever seen.

An eyeblink ago, eighty slaves worked the fields and smithies and barns and kitchens of the Sutton lands. Now, empty overgrown fields flanked the back and west sides of the house. A measly, ten-acre planting of corn staked down the earth of the southern prospect. Even that crop appeared too tired to grow.

Threadgill could make out a pink marble headstone in the back yard, the monument fenced off by rusting wrought iron. Mrs. Dahlia Sutton rested there, herself a victim of war. While the Colonel fought to defend her health and honor on some distant field, she choked to death on a tough piece of mule meat the third year of the war.

Colonel Sutton smoked a pipe on the porch most mornings. As Threadgill passed atop Dinah, he would raise a finger hello. The Colonel leaned against a peeling column, his wooden leg stabbed solidly into the porch planking, and he narrowed a set of white-browed eyes. Threadgill even offered a smart salute once; he got back a deeper scowl and an angry puff of pipe smoke. After that, the younger man dispensed with greetings and cantered past the house with his hat pulled low, each time in a hurry.

Still, Threadgill's eyes always searched – beseeched – the windows and grounds.

Every night, he prayed he would catch a glimpse of Eva the next morning.

Threadgill clung to a faint hope – that the Colonel would tender his respect one day, his acknowledgement. Why wouldn't he? They shared wounds in common, family blood in common, the joined experiences of war and defeat. They shared a dark grief, a lost cause.

Threadgill may have become a man in body, but he actually remained far too young to understand a clear truth.

Able Sutton respected no one who looked the way Threadgill did at his little girl.

The maimed Colonel, as a widower, would now and always need family at the house to care for him. He didn't aim to let his only daughter run off with some shot-up shirttail farm boy.

Especially a Pickett.

On a hot April night in 1866, Uncle Cherry Pickett, age 65, passed away. He was Aunt Annie's last brother, and the last Pickett of his generation. Four other brothers died at Shiloh.

Cherry's family and well-wishers gathered at Providence Chapel for the goodbye. Forty or so mourners crowded a one-room plank church, white and pink wild dogwoods flush at the windows.

Eva Sutton and her famous daddy sat in an unvarnished pine pew up front, just one row behind the red-eyed but stoic widow and her multitude of children, grandchildren, great-grandchildren and even one red and wrinkled great-great-grandchild, still at its mamma's chapped teat. The Colonel sat a row behind the bereaved, as he usually did at funerals. It was natural here in Clio – most every Scots family in town claimed kinship some way.

During the preacher's eulogy, a honeybee flew through a window and tangled itself in the Colonel's beard. Eva swatted the insect with her bare hand. The preacher interrupted his fine words, and the grief-stricken front row rustled and fluttered in their black crepe and solemn suits to attend to the old hero.

Threadgill sat on the back row, hat firmly on his head, church or no church. He studied how Eva's flawless white hand brushed the insect, now in golden pieces, from her father's starched shirt. Her fingers looked cool and sensitive to Threadgill.

When the congregation sang an old tune about Jesus tenderly calling, Threadgill listened carefully and picked out Eva's lovely rising voice.

The preacher ended with a prayer. Then family and mourners shuffled solemnly out of the church to stand by yet another yawning Pickett grave in Alabama's red clay.

Threadgill waited back, perspiring, the spring day uncomfortable and sticky. The scissory whisper of black-suited legs and skirts, most smelling slightly of must, passed him in the sunshine. Hushed whispers, consolations, and dogwood petals fell.

At graveside, the preacher murmured a few additional words, led prayer, shared a confidential moment of sympathy with the family. The deceased had "joined the army of angels," he quietly declared.

Red clods spattered the top of Cherry Pickett's coffin.

His life was done.

***

Clumps of mourners in black clothes began to drift away from the grave-side, burned flower petals on slow-moving water. The preacher shook hands and smiled and swam the crowd.

Eva and Colonel Sutton made a beeline for the surrey, old Washington trailing with a small black parasol over the girl. Mourners stood aside respect-fully for the war hero, who at one point tottered awkwardly on his hickory leg in soft dirt.

The Colonel wore his full dress Confederate uniform. The sight of it struck some even harder than Cherry's death. Onlookers wept anew into their handkerchiefs as the Colonel clumsily rocked past, pretty Eva to steady his arm.

She stole a glance at Threadgill.

Through her black veil, daring eyes found him. She didn't blink or look away.

Threadgill suddenly felt as if he'd been shot again, this time clean through the heart.

The church bell tolled in his head.

Threadgill pulled together the straws of his courage.

He slipped awkwardly through war widows and sad-eyed Pickett relatives. No one in the crowd stood deferentially aside for Threadgill. Some of the gaunt old farmers, weary and red-necked, looked doomed to join their own army of angels soon enough.

Threadgill jostled past mourners clumped at the rusted churchyard gate. He stopped by Able Sutton's surrey.

Eva's black veil had a small hole. Threadgill could see her lips part in surprise as she saw him.

Colonel Sutton manned the reins of the surrey, Washington on a mule beside the vehicle. The surrey horse pranced impatiently, nervous among the wagons and carriages that crowded Cemetery Road.

Threadgill's heart pumped.

"Afternoon, Miss Eva."

Threadgill used his most respectful tone of voice, patting the flank of the restive surrey horse.

"I'm very sorry about Mr. Cherry, Colonel Sutton, sir. He lived a good life."

Colonel Able Sutton turned a sour eye to him.

"What in the hell did you know about Cherry Pickett, boy? I'd be surprised if he ever spoke a word to the likes of you."

Threadgill felt the breath fly out of him.

Eva's eyes dropped to her white hands.

"And who gave you leave to lay your hand on my horse, boy?" Colonel Sutton actually yelled this. Bereaved heads snapped to attention now, sadness disspelled. "Didn't folks teach you to keep your Pickett hands off what ain't yours?"

Threadgill couldn't find a single word.

The Colonel glared another moment. Then a canny look came into his eyes.

"Anyway, where your manners, son?" A crooked smile split the Colonel's face. "Didn't Annie Pickett teach you to take your hat off in the presence of a lady?"

So. There it was.

Public humiliation.

Blood boiled in Threadgill's veins. He almost lunged at the leering old bastard.

Sutton struck his horse a violent whip blow – *Gitup*!

The surrey lurched. Threadgill leaped aside. Eva frantically clutched both her hat and the side of her seat. A nearby mule team spooked, the animals banging heavily against one another. A rearing horse nearly tipped a buckboard with a Confederate widow and three children.

"Yahh! Yahh!" yelled the Colonel. "Move aside! Yaahh!"

For a dizzy, dust-choked moment, Threadgill fantasized giving chase on foot, hauling the old man down from his high seat, kicking him silly, running the surrey – *bump bump* – over his sorry carcass. Beating him over the head with his hickory leg.

But Threadgill sobered. How would it be when people whispered: "Yonder goes Threadgill Pickett! He beat up a crippled old Confederate with a wooden leg. Got mad cause the old man asked him to take off his hat to his daughter! At a FUNERAL!"

Threadgill breathed as hard as if he really *had* been in a fight. He watched the surrey rattle away toward Eufaula.

Threadgill decided, then and there.

He would take away Able Sutton's daughter.

Didn't she ask him to, with those eyes?

Chapter 29, Mad As Fire

Summer 1964 – North Alabama

"Well, Skeeter. It wouldn't hurt if I had wings too."

Threadgill held up a little flying squirrel, its lithe paws leashing his wrist. Cold grease glistened on the squirrel's tiny black mouth, the residue of day-old French fries found shriveled in a striped bag beside the blacktop. Giddy now, drunk on food and fire ants, the squirrel played on Threadgill like a carefree child.

"Yes sir, wings would be nice. Alabama don't never seem to end …"

The scab on his knee gave a twinge. It did not want to heal. It felt … strange.

Sun-up. Threadgill Pickett weighed his options. Yet another country crossroads lay before him. In all four directions, pine trees shrugged limbs hopelessly in a hot wind. On a single overhead power line, mourning doves drooped their tails. Some animal barked once, half-heartedly, out in the undergrowth.

Threadgill jerked in the direction of that bark, suddenly fearful. He blinked red for a moment – he saw a red panorama that resolved to normal green after a rattling shake of his head. Both temples pounded – Threadgill felt as if some brute carpenter drove a nail into his forehead and wrenched it free again, over and over. He wondered absurdly if the dog or fox or coyote out in those trees had rabies … and then, spookily, how the fur and meat might taste if he could sink his teeth into it.

What is the matter with me?

"Go north."

Threadgill looked around. He heard a voice, plain and clear.

No one there.

Great. Now he was seeing red *and* hearing things.

North would be right, of course, the right direction. But the mountaintop country road leading northward yawned with huge open potholes, deep and craggy. The paved surface looked crackly, like a burned man's skin.

Like his skin once looked.

But see here – the road east looked newer, smoother. More inviting. It would be so much easier to walk east for a spell.

"North."

Threadgill looked down now in surprise.

Who spoke? Who said *north*? Had the little flying squirrel uttered words? Was that possible?

In the past few days, something had happened inside Threadgill. After leaving the Cobb brothers and their mushrooms, he found a culvert somewhere off the main road and climbed inside its mouth. He hurt. He slept for a day and a night. He slept for another day and a night. When he came out of the pipe, his head throbbed and his knee felt on fire.

Sometime during that sleep, Skeeter sailed out of nowhere and latched to Threadgill's shirt like a torn shred of dream. The animal's soft impact woke Threadgill, who had been dreaming of vampire bats, those little bloodsuckers he once watched in morbid fascination on a TV show in the Sunset home. When vampires fed on cattle, they stood upright, on hind legs with their heads held high like horrible tiny men in bat costumes. Body-builders. Ugly bat heads. Satiny black wings.

Threadgill flailed mightily when Skeeter woke him from this nightmare, and his thrashings injured the poor little animal. Skeeter didn't seem able to fly any more now. Its little leg hung to one side and trembled in a way that made Threadgill feel a stab of guilt with every glance.

"North."

The Voice. Again.

No talking squirrel. No phantom Ben, like in the nursing home.

A commanding Voice in his aching head.

Ah, Threadgill thought. It's Revenge.

Threadgill slumped to cradle his throbbing skull. Another nail split his fingers, squawked loudly as the phantom yanked it free. The traveler lay down. The ground looked soft – an abandoned railroad bed grown over by blackberry and honeysuckle and Virginia creeper and smilax and – *who gives a damn?* – poison ivy.

Threadgill saw scarlet again suddenly. The vines writhed in a breeze, red as arteries in a human chest.

Threadgill took the red hat off his head, mopped his red brow with a wet red shirttail. The ruby red morning sun made his brain feel charred, something like biscuit blackened in a glowing stove.

He rested a moment. A wheel of fire like a giant eye rolled behind his lids. Revenge.

Thankfully, as he opened his eyes, the red mostly cleared. It left green – a nauseating watery green – stretching before Threadgill in every direction. His sore knee, with the monkey bite, ached badly.

The flying squirrel looked up hopefully at Threadgill's old face, its noble little eyes shining, soft and wet. A thought struck the tired traveler: The tiny creature was not just hurt, but sad too.

Threadgill hobbled farther off the road, into the shade of a pine, and put his back against its rough bark. He sat on his bedroll, found a lump inside. His stash. He smelled the hot leather of the pouch as he opened it and took out money. He cooled himself fanning with a handful of tens and fives and ones, sixty-four dollars in all.

Skeeter shrunk fearfully from the riffling paper.

Threadgill counted the money twice.

"Skeeter … I been saving this, just to use if I couldn't get to Maine no other way. Now this money might buy us a bus ride." Threadgill stroked the soft head of the little animal with his thumb. "We just need to find a driver what don't charge extra for squirrels."

How many days and nights on the march had it been? Threadgill hadn't even crossed the Alabama state line yet, and the moon was filling up again.

He blinked red. Blinked hard again – green.

Time to buy a ticket. Steal a car. Find the right train. Do whatever it took.

He wasn't getting more spry. He wasn't getting younger. Maine wasn't getting too much closer.

He wasn't getting saner either.

Threadgill fought off a strong impulse to bite his own arm, bite the squirrel on it. His knee shot sparks.

What is happening?

Am I going mad?

***

"North."

Mr. Revenge spoke clearly again. Threadgill pinched his eyes, but this time objects stayed red, red from the inside looking out.

A red crow flapped over, and the red needles of pine trees glittered in the sun like bloody quills.

A flicker of light caught Threadgill's attention.

Skeeter ceased purring and blinked attentively.

After a moment, Threadgill heard what Skeeter heard, a far-off puttering like a cheap lawn mower.

"Well, look a yonder."

Around the red curve, headed north at a crawl, chugged a little red turtle shell of automobile.

Hitchhiker's fear swam over Threadgill. No matter how welcome the ride now, even after days on the open road, the pit of Threadgill's stomach melted like hot cheese at the moment a new ride approached. Fate placed down fresh new cards on the table, a new hand every car, train and truck – and every round Threadgill wondered the same question.

Would this ride be his last?

He remembered a story once about a man who got a weird feeling and stayed inside the restroom at an airport and let his plane take off without him. It crashed into the side of a mountain and left every person on board in charred pieces no bigger than pig knuckles.

So many other horror stories on the road! So far, Threadgill's traveling companions had whispered worriedly to him of hogtied hitchhikers found strangled in a boxcar in Sylacauga, of a headless family found sitting with napkins still in their laps at a picnic table in Florence.

Threadgill blinked. *Red road. Red sky.*

Here came the little Volkswagen.

Threadgill could turn and run. He could lose nerve this instant and flee! He could roll away into roadside jemson weed and pokeberry, tunnel down through the reeking stalks, pop up somehow in Aunt Annie's back yard, right behind the stacked firewood. He could sprint through the weedy corn rows and crash into Annie's soft skirts and hold on with all his strength, forever and ever, and never leave home again.

Why had he ever left? Why? How in the world did he end up standing here in the blazing sun, his red thumb out and a hurt squirrel latched to his arm?

Ben. Ben was why.

The Unmentionable. Some things can't be forgiven. Can't be forgotten. Revenge.

"Wouldn't hurt to have wings, Skeeter."

The car sputtered to a stop.

"We could just fly on to Maine from here."

***

The Volkswagen Beetle somehow transformed from red to lemon-yellow before Threadgill's very eyes. Now it made a friendly whirring noise like an extra large sewing machine.

"Oh Jehovah," Threadgill muttered to himself. "It's a ride with a … what *is* it?"

The driver flung open his door.

"Hurry!" a voice cried. Threadgill winced at the man's high, needling soprano. "I'm – *ohhh*! – I'm passing a goddamn kidney stone! *Owww*!"

Threadgill hustled out to the absurd vehicle. The bedroll beat his ankles as he ran. Skeeter bounced like a yoyo on his wrist. Through a mephitic exhaust cloud, Threadgill made out a bumper sticker – *Kiss Me. I'm Irish.*

"Oh holy Christ! It's *killin'* me!"

The childish voice sirened into a wail that scared Skeeter clear up onto Threadgill's shoulder.

Threadgill stared into the car in jawslapped amazement. A little man in a vest and green bowler hat groaned at the wheel of the VW.

"Dear Sweet Jesus! Please! Old man, you got to drive! Get me to Mama! I'm dyin'!"

Threadgill had thumbed down a ride with a garden gnome – the genuine article, alive and squirming. Red beard. Red face. Red nose. Red pain-gnarled mouth. Little glittery red eyes that shot red teardrops into the air.

Threadgill blinked the red away.

Now he found the gnome decked out in a loud green jacket with flashy orange piping like cake icing along the seams. From the waist down, green flannel Robin Hood-tights disappeared into tiny sequined green slippers with pointed toes curled up slightly at the tips. The diminutive driver's shirt glowed white, a whipped-cream squirt of ruffles at the neck.

"Holy Mary!" the little man screamed suddenly, arching up, clutching the small of his back as if he wanted to dig out his kidneys with a spoon. He flopped awkwardly across the stick shift of the VW and wiggled into the passenger seat.

"Please, mister. Please, get in quick and DRIVE …"

And, thought Threadgill, *away we go*.

***

Little Green Man became Little Red Man the instant Threadgill took the wheel.

North. Mr. Revenge sounded emphatic.

Threadgill wondered if the little man's kidney stones could possibly hurt any worse than his head. Inside the car, the nail-driver went at it with a wedge-and-maul. Bang, bang, every beat of Threadgill's heart.

"Why are you waiting, mister! Drive! I'm going to die right here!"

Threadgill actually looked over at the red-clad passenger and thought of biting him – hard on the face – to shut him up.

Threadgill's knee screamed loud as a firehouse alarm bell.

I'm losing my mind. Something bad is wrong.

"Mama runs that tourist trap up on Sand Mountain! *Owww!*" The passenger flailed his tiny hands. "*Oh holy Jesus and Mary*! Take me there. She's got my medicine."

Little Green Man's misery grew very big. In his agony, he kicked off the pointy green platform shoes. They looked like doll shoes. In fact, the man himself looked like a doll. Threadgill figured he could not possibly be more than three feet high – maybe taller wearing the green hat in the back seat. Its jaunty orange feather trembled as the engine idled.

The gnome's closely shaved head wore a down of light brown fur. Had he been letting himself go?

Threadgill spotted a patch on Little Green Man's jacket breast pocket:

This land is EIRE LAND!
MORE ROCK THAN ROCK CITY

Threadgill would come to know that EIRE LAND sat like a gnome lord's palace atop the mighty bulwark of Sand Mountain, as high above Alabama as Valhalla over ancient Norway.

The fairy tale theme park and its amusements drew visitors from all over the state to gawk at almost Biblical believe-it-or-not splendors – a 40,000-ton rock balanced on a pebble shaped like a Chihuahua head; a Big Mama Squeeze, where morbidly obese tourists sometimes wedged so tight only bacon grease and jeep winches could free them; Humper's Hurl, where a mural showed the way a hundred Indian maidens once leaped to their deaths to escape the frolic of horny old Dan'l Boone. Fabulous caverns, "measureless to man or woman," riddled the mountain, these twinkling places made splendid with incense and colored crystals and hanging automobile license plates and rainbow-hued lights … and gnomes.

Gnomes! The Volkswagen-puttering, kidney stone-suffering gnome in the car sat caved in against the passenger door, sobbing into tiny hands – that poor fellow worked among an unlucky cast of twelve brothers and sisters who dressed their parts and pushed little wheelbarrows and toted pick-axes and filled lumpy sacks with gnome knick-knacks for as many as three thousand curious tourists a year.

Threadgill blinked a new sheet of red for a moment, and it occurred to him he could simply open the gnome's door and the little man would tumble off down the hillside. He'd be done with his suffering. Threadgill could steer this car straight on to Bangor. He had wheels.

If he could figure out how to drive a car.

He remembered his dream on the wild ride with Larry LaRue. He drove in a dream. He would drive now.

"North."

Threadgill blinked darker red.

He twisted a car key in an ignition for the first time in his life. Skeeter turned upside down.

The VW nosed forward. Threadgill used great caution. And why wouldn't he?

The world now burned in wild crimson flames around the puttering car. Threadgill could hear roaring inferno, trees exploding in fire, howling wind. Tongues of flame shot up from overgrown road shoulders, and shimmering lava sheeted the road.

Threadgill heard a tiny, faraway voice.

Pickett's Charge

"*Owww*! Drive it like Donnie Allison, old man! I'm pissin' gravel …"

***

Sand Mountain lost all its courage at Oogoochee. At the first sight of that community, the mountain abruptly ended. The tail of it was completely dissolved by the black acids and oils of the town's creosote factory.

Threadgill watched Oogoochee from above, at the first downward turn of road that would take him through that eyesore, then north up Sand Mountain. The Volkswagen rested here, thank goodness, against a deeply dented guard rail. Its yellow hood, buckled crazily, held the car fast to the guard rail.

"Oh holy God!" moaned the gnome. "You've killed me with my own damn car!"

Reverse finally worked. Threadgill felt the car jerk loose, suddenly zip backwards. It beetled back onto the road, crossed both lanes in reverse, whammed into the far guard rail.

"Stop! Stop! Oh God and Christ!" screamed Little Green Man.

"You stop!" Threadgill yelled back. "Hush that carrying on! I can't think with you makin' such a ruckus!"

Little Green Man clutched his back, arms behind him like chicken wings. Drool unspooled from his mouth as the car, still in reverse, careened free of the guard rail and out into the woods. The VW climbed some distance up a sheer rock promontory, bucking and roaring, before it stalled out with a great sputtery gush of blue smoke and a horrible grinding noise.

"Ohhhhh! Aaaaargh!" the gnome howled. The splintered limb of a scrub oak jabbed through the front windshield and into his ribs.

"You ain't close to dying," Threadgill explained, "if you can still holler like that."

"I'm PRAYING to die, old man! Just kill me, would you, and let's get it – *owww!* – over with!"

Threadgill cranked the car a third time. He turned the key too hard and long, so that the engine made a loud grinding noise even after the Beetle lurched off again. Threadgill dragged parts of the forest onto the highway, along with a big cardboard box.

Threadgill felt like he was getting the hang of it.

The gnome raised abruptly, wide-eyed. A teensie, trembling finger passed under his driver's nose.

"Is that a monkey? I *hate* monkeys!"

Skeeter hissed from Threadgill's shoulder, scared out of its mind, latched on there with all its tiny squirrel strength.

The gnome shrank, palms up.

"Oh God! Please, mister! Don't sic it on me!!"

Threadgill frowned. The VW dropped three feet off a rock outcrop back onto the highway. It even hurt *his* kidneys.

"Owwww! Owwwww!"

"You ain't got to be afraid of Skeeter, long as you quieten down. He panics when folks scream."

"Don't turn that monkey loose!" screamed the gnome more loudly. "I don't have as much blood as you big folks!"

The gnome slid at once into the shoebox of a floorboard, knees bent, elbows resting on the seat. He assumed a posture of prayer. The pained eyes of a small saint pierced with arrows stared at Threadgill, imploring.

"Just shoot me!" he begged. "Throw me out on the goddamn pavement. Lord God!"

Threadgill felt a stab of his own intense pain again, the nail in the forehead. He aimed the VW down the mountain. The road suddenly flowed blood red again. Threadgill straddled bright red stripes.

He had the overwhelming urge again to bite Little Green Man.

"Holy Mary!" the gnome screeched. "I'm having one goddamn drink! I don't care what Doctor Konner says!"

Tiny hands dragged out a sloshing fifth of Old Crow from under the seat. The bird on the side of the bottle stared knowingly at Threadgill, like a patient buzzard waiting on a low limb for the inevitable.

Little Green Man tilted the bottle. He raised three, four, enormous bubbles.

The gnome gasped for air, breath scorching hot. Tears flowed his face.

"All I ever wanted," he wailed, "in the whole wide world was Hollywood! I can do anything those damn Munchkins did! I can sing! I can dance! Well, tap dance a little, anyway. But what happens to me? I get drafted and go to Vietnam and blow up slopeheads in tunnels and get sick with kidney stones and get sent home to Squidfart, Alabama, to a fat old lady and eleven snot-nosed brats from her first five marriages and then I die with a kidney stone attack in a car wreck with an old monster at the wheel after I'm sucked blood-dry by a weird freaking monkey! Oh, holy shit!"

Skeeter hissed violently at this outburst. The gnome cowered again in the floorboard, his red nose glistening.

"*Ohhh*! Don't let it get on me!"

Threadgill, deeply moved, put his hand on top of the gnome's bald head. It felt like a hot fuzzy peach.

"I'm gettin' you to your mama, little feller. Just hold on."

But Threadgill felt again the rising, unbearable urge to sink his teeth into soft gnome head.

Is this … ? Threadgill's heart sank in horror. *Do I have the rabies?*

***

Little Green Man made it to Ogeechee Hospital.

An ambulance rushed him there, siren screaming.

The ambulance came not long after the green Volkswagen crashed through the glass store front of the Ogeechee Stuckey's. It was the first road-side attraction along the highway as you came down – or went up – Sand Mountain.

Like all accidents, this one needn't have happened. Threadgill let his attention lapse.

The onset of furious rabies will do that to a man.

The VW bug traveled as it chose for a mile or so. Threadgill, fascinated, watched the red wheel twist this way, then that. Abruptly it turned hard right and hurtled straight as a kamikaze into the colorful pecan-roll and gooey candy franchise.

The VW crashed the plate glass front and slammed to a hard stop against a big walk-in freezer in back. Little round vanilla and chocolate ice creams rained over the roof and hood, along with small wooden spoons and ice cream sandwiches and drumsticks and those broken brown ice cream cones that reminded Threadgill of wasp nests. The storefront vomited broken glass and splintered wood and a thousand gewgaws – snow domes and stuffed pigs and cigarette lighters and pecan brittle and Roll Tide pennants and hats and fishing poles and eight-track tapes and still more kinds of candy.

A dog barked furiously somewhere.

Accordion-folded in a hissing Volkswagen, Threadgill's noble nose smelled pecans and sugar.

Skeeter? The little squirrel went away.

Threadgill never found his overnight companion. He wondered for the rest of his days if the sad little flying squirrel made an escape into the happy attic of Stuckey's, a paradise of nougat and cheap felt and the kind of shiny small collectibles a flying squirrel could swap to mice and crows.

Luck finally struck Little Green Man.

At the impact of the crash, a wicked staghorn kidney stone passed right out through Little Green Man's tiny penis, like a porcupine charging out a garden hose. So the car wreck improved Little Green Man's lot in life – except for a nasty cut on the crown of his head that required eight stitches and overnight observation.

Threadgill? Threadgill wrenched open his groaning car door. He kicked it brutally to widen the opening extra inches. Squeezing through, he skated along on engine fluids and melting popsicles to a check-out counter.

The Volkswagen engine still gargled and coughed. It never occurred to Threadgill, who knew nothing of engines, that a simple turn of the key to the off position would have prevented the fire.

"Runs good."

Threadgill looked around for the voice. Mr. Revenge? Must be – he saw red again now, and his head shrieked with pain.

A huge dog, an Alaskan husky with eyes so red they thrilled Threadgill, flared its tail beside the front door.

"Whoa, dog! Easy now!"

Threadgill looked the animal in the eye. Long ago, he learned this trick for handling dogs.

He reached down a hand, and the animal licked it and beat its tail on the glass-strewn floor.

"Good feller," Threadgill whispered. The dog made a plaintive noise in its throat. Then it spoke to Threadgill in a clear deep human voice.

"Don't leave me here. You have no idea how bad this place is. No idea, mister. It's R-E-A-L bad."

Threadgill stared down in astonishment. The dog's bright eyes gleamed with intelligence, deep and intuitive. Sharp ears stood alert.

A bayonet pierced Threadgill's brain with a bright red blade of pain.

"Am I thinking," he wondered, eyes squenched, "that a dog can talk to me?"

At this very instant, the dog dropped its head dejectedly and resumed hassling. It appeared to abandon hope.

Threadgill's red field of vision deepened. His sensitive nose smelled smoke.

Far away, as if from some other dimension, he heard the piping voice of Little Green Man. Threadgill spotted him, Little Red Man again now, waving arms, rushing around the parking lot, blood on his noggin. And see! Two men in red uniforms tackled him, flopped him onto an ambulance stretcher. How he squealed, protested!

"I want Mama!" he bleated. "Mama!"

Threadgill tottered through the ruins of Stuckey's. As he passed a display case, the magazines let go and slid into the aisle, tumbling with them potted meats and sardines.

"North!"

Threadgill grabbed his throbbing head in both hands. Red sky. He slumped into a display of stuffed animals … and after only a short moment of hesitation, he finally let go.

Threadgill began snapping viciously at the stuffed creatures, quick nasty bites. He latched his jaws on a stuffed plush Santa, sinking furious teeth into the red fur, ripping out cotton mouthfuls.

A siren drowned out other noises.

Colors returned.

Threadgill realized, to his great surprise, that he sat flat on his ass among broken bottles and spilled Coca-Cola. The rack of stuffed elephants and eagles and bunnies and the mortally wounded Santa lay heaped over him as if dumped from a laundry basket.

Where on earth *was* he?

He woke from a kind of dream. Threadgill had never seen so many things on shelves – little candies in sticky wrappers and wrist-thick logs of candy in plastic paper and bags of flavored pecans in different sizes and souvenir pencils and T-shirts and Hank Williams key chains and shot glasses and Elvis bobble-heads and circus peanuts and girls bathing suits.

Over him, baseball caps sagged a rope clothesline. Smoke filled the air, much smoke.

One cap carried the strange picture of a man in a houndstooth hat, a football under one arm. He appeared to be walking on water.

Metal rectangles bore similar strange pictures: a mule passing gas – LBJ HAS SPOKEN; two pigs humping happily under the words – MAKIN' BA-CON. On still another, an old battle-scarred Confederate soldier waved the Stars and Bars and growled "FORGET HELL!"

" 'At's a license p-plate," rose an odd voice. " 'At goes on yore c-car."

Threadgill found himself facing a strange teenage boy. The youngster's head ballooned out just above the ears, swelling to the size of a lampshade.

A bright red lampshade.

Two intensely glittery red eyes beamed from a point low on the boy's gourd-shaped cranium. The eyes seemed nowhere near as smart as the husky dog's.

"Yes sir. I'm a wa-waterhead. Go right ahead and say it. Everbody d-does."

Threadgill suddenly wanted to bite him savagely. On the head. Like the stuffed creatures …

But now the boy's eyes switched, like traffic lights, from red to piercing green.

"I seen a waterhead before." Threadgill stammered. "Just not so close up."

"You give me a quarter, you c-can touch my head. It's s-soft."

An alarmed female voice fluted up from behind wrecked racks of disheveled record albums.

"Dicky!" she scolded. "Dicky, what did I tell you? Your head is private!"

A woman appeared in the smoke. Stump-round, a 60-something-year-old bag of biscuits in a flower-print dress. Her hairdo made a soaring tower. Her head looked as strange as the boy's. The ceiling fan threatened to lop off irregular knots and black curd toppings of her beehive.

"Mama, I'm j-jis trying to git us s-some money!"

Dicky's complaint widened her red eyes.

Threadgill crouched, prepared now to spring and attack. He felt a rushing of the blood. Slobber fell from his chin. He imagined his legs covered with shoat bristles, his arms sprouting painful patches of animal fur, his fangs lengthening.

Threadgill's own scalp, bare as the waterhead's, tingled under his hat. He would tear two freaks apart on his way out of this shattered South to get that last Yankee …

"There! That's him!"

Threadgill wheeled. A man in Yankee blue had a gun raised. He wore a badge. At his elbow stood Little Green Man, pointing a shaky finger.

"Whoo! Whoo!"

Dicky's mother flapped short little arms all around her son now. She stepped protectively in front of him.

"Dicky ain't stole nothing, Officer! He's been with me ever blessed minute since y'all put him in last time …"

Boom!

The policeman fired a warning bullet, splintered a ceiling fan. The fan flopped its way around one time or two more, then flew apart in pieces, flinging itself with a wrathful rattle at the policeman and garden gnome.

"Goddammit Maudie, I ain't here for Dicky! Get out of the way!"

He rushed forward, and Maudie and Dicky fell before the blue wrecking ball of the law like old columns on a porch.

Too late.

Threadgill, with a snarl, leaped a counter and raced fast *on all-fours* for the single back window, high above a deep freeze. The glass shattered in a million pieces as Threadgill dove headlong. He didn't even graze the window frame.

Threadgill Pickett streaked away, as fast as any wolf ever ran, into the dense woods behind Stuckey's.

He howled. He fled down a red path under the blood red trees. He snapped at red rays of sunlight.

Chapter 30, A Fete Worse Than Death

Barbour County, Alabama – Summer 1866

Dinah was a blessing.

Slocum's Mill operated on Hatchechubbee Creek, and Dinah could cover that five miles effortlessly, despite her years. Threadgill's boots lasted twice as long. More chores got done around Annie's house, shingles patched and wood chopped and fences resurrected.

Threadgill found Dinah deep in the woods, skinny as a stick horse, living with wild deer. Old, neglected, she still held her lustrous blue-black color, and the white stockings on both front feet made her look nimble at age twelve. The poor creature's teeth troubled her. Threadgill gave Dinah plenty of extra grazing time in the thick tangle that had taken over parts of the fields. The horse now had a stray eye too, milky white. It seemed to stare off supernaturally into some other world.

Yes, Dinah traveled well. She was durable. She didn't spook.

On the sleepy trip to the mill one morning, a green snake lost its sinuous grip in an oak tree and plummeted onto the middle of the red dirt road. It hit with a flop, a writhing knot, dead in front of Dinah.

This snake from the sky drew a mere flutter of Dinah's right ear and a whicker of disgust. She stepped squarely onto the writhing thing. She continued her patient progress.

***

Dinah freed Threadgill to roam.

Summer nights of 1866, he took to trotting down the Eufaula road, cutting through untended fields, maneuvering in and out of black woodlands, sometimes following old Creek Indian trails.

Night after night, every path somehow reached the same destination – a hilltop view of Colonel Sutton's mansion.

Eva's house.

This summer, Eufaula suffered drought. Days felt hot as a stove. The spell was so brutal that every midnight moon looked like a melting thing.

At the end of a sweaty gallop, Threadgill would slide from the saddle to let Dinah catch her breath. His own breathing changed too. He studied the big white house in the distance and dreamed – of what? Living there? Eva? What, beyond? Respect? A little baby Threadgill or Eva?

Colonel Sutton's corn field spread from Threadgill's pine-topped hill to the back grounds of the mansion. Most summers, with abundant rain, the corn plants towered high over a man. Now the parched tassels at the very tip reached only as high as Threadgill's eyes.

The mansion seemed shriveled too. The view was partly blocked by a soaring pecan tree, fanned out like a peacock tail against the stars. Threadgill could nevertheless make out a broken gap in the wooden rail of the wrap-around porch, conspicuous as a knocked-out tooth. The smokehouse leaned like a drunk.

Threadgill counted five brick chimneys on the back side of Sutton House. He never saw smoke rise from a single one, any night that summer. Only one or two of the windows shone with light. Threadgill, of course, studied every pane. Now and then, something thrilled him, a female-shaped shadow that blocked the light of a candle.

Rare signs of human activity came and went quickly, leaving the house even more lonesome and dilapidated.

***

One night in August, Threadgill caught a full glimpse of Eva.

A candle flared in an upstairs room, one of the back ones partly masked by the magnolia tree near the house. The room filled with pale light. Its window raised, and white lace curtains lapped the fresh air. Eva all at once appeared in the panes, her silhouette perfect, a wingless angel.

In another twinkling, she vanished.

The empty place in the window haunted Threadgill.

Every night of he summer after that, he gave Dinah her saddle early, just at dusk. Then Threadgill rode to the weedy hillock to hope for a single glimpse of the girl he loved.

Always, even by moonlight, Threadgill wore his hat. Eva might look out, by some miracle. She might see.

***

The next week, Threadgill was amazed.

Riding Dinah out of the low pines atop the hill, the youngster reined in. His heart hung on a barb. For a shocking instant, he believed the mansion to be on fire, ablaze from end to end, the greatest inferno ever seen in this part of Alabama.

He stood in the stirrups, simply and wholly afraid, his clenched hand in Dinah's mane.

The Sutton mansion *was* ablaze – with joyous, transforming light. Every room shimmered, chimerically alive in the glow of candles, cressets, tapers, flambeaux, every manner of lamp and lantern. Light leaped from every window, on every side of the house, flooding yard and garden, gilding the trunks of pecan and magnolia. The corn field glowed luminous yellow.

And people! Had Threadgill ever seen so many men and women in one house? The dozen rooms of the Sutton mansion swarmed with merrymakers, a happy confection of ball gowns and military uniforms. From this hilltop, Threadgill could hear a low constant babble, a huzzah of bees in a giant hive. Waves of lively music, crested by a laugh or a whoop of joy, rippled away from the happy revel.

What in the world? What occasion prompted this feast for the ages?

Sutton House, as in old times, bustled with black servants in white jackets, whisking in and out of the teeming downstairs rooms, straining under silver platters of corn, baked apples, sliced pears, watermelon, roast birds, beef. Threadgill could make out enormous serving bowls of rice and roasted potatoes, peas and okra and beans fresh from summer fields.

Ladies gossiped in upstairs rooms, their finery frothing the glass of the tall windows. Downstairs, in rooms with wood-paneled walls, men in handsome gray uniforms, yellow sashes, and yellow gloves threw their heads back and roared with raised shining glasses. A fair share of toasts no doubt bubbled upward to the ladies.

Threadgill pinched himself. One spooky moment, fear gripped him – he must surely be looking down at a house of ghosts, a changeling mansion, an enchantment that twinkled ephemerally before his eyes. He did not quite believe it real; a pageant of gaiety under those tall backyard trees, in a place so neglected and austere every summer night before.

The caterwauling of a fiddle rose. Dinah's ears perked.

Well … if ghosts played songs and clapped hands, then Threadgill's horse could hear ghosts too.

"Tarnation," Threadgill whistled. "The Colonel is throwing the biggest party since the start of the Civil War …"

A chiding voice spoke up inside him. *Why aren't you invited, Threadgill? Why aren't you in that house like other soldiers from Barbour County?*

Threadgill swung down from the saddle. He tethered Dinah to a scrub pine, sleeved sweat from his forehead.

I'll go a little closer … Surely tonight I'll surely catch a glimpse of Eva. I'll see her.

Threadgill crabbed sideways down the hill and noisily crashed into the corn field. He felt exhilaration, undaunted even as the corn stalks closed off the views of the mansion ahead, the hill behind, the stars overhead. The celebration seemed to hush too, as Threadgill walked the corn rows through frog racket and field crickets and whippoorwill mourning.

He found it impossible to see more than a few feet in any direction. Tangles of cocklebur and beggar lice clotted the path. The parched corn stalks rattled like snakes, a truly unnerving sound in a part of the world where snakes crawled every acre.

Corn blades slashed at Threadgill's face. He ducked, weaved, moved on. He fixed his attention on a plow furrow and tried not to lose sight. Fending stalk and leaf with his forearms. He shouldered through spider webs and tangles of pigweed. Sticky black silks from the corn covered his clothes; corn tassels and confused caterpillars spilled off his hat when he glanced down. He sweated so fiercely now that perspiration dripped from his chin.

On the row, Threadgill. Walk the row …

The air cooled unexpectedly. A breeze shifted dry blades, and the corn parted like a stage curtain. Threadgill could see and hear again.

Sutton House loomed, a great galleon. It blazed most gloriously, as bright as any house Threadgill ever saw. Music thumped and rollicked. He could imagine the entire roof hopping up and down, flapping with joy.

Excitement swept Threadgill, a green wind.

***

In the big parlor, servants bustled about a long oak table with a sumptuous spread of food and drink. Threadgill's mouth watered at the sight of whole hams and sections of beef, the very rarest of foods nowadays. Forty feet across the room, colored musicians thumped righteously along on a half-dozen instruments, the uniformed band directed by a tiny red-coated conductor with white hair and a white baton. In the parlor space between music and food, couples in perfect clothes flirted and bowed and curtsied under a high silver chandelier with a hundred blazing candles.

The conductor raised his scarlet arm, and a lively new fiddle tune brought resplendent soldiers rushing to the floor and a flurry of gorgeous gowns sweeping down the stairs. Crickets in the cornfield stopped courting to listen. A second fiddle leaped to life. A new instrument for the evening – a banjo – invited clapping hands, whistles and stomps, a giddy house-shaking.

Threadgill, spellbound, edged his way close. He glanced nervously from time to time around the yard, on guard. For … what, exactly? He simply did not feel welcome here. But the party absorbed him. He felt its pull, and he let himself go a little, vicariously reveling in the high spirits of the affair.

How had this party come to be? Threadgill had watched Sutton House every night for a month, and he'd picked up no sign – nothing – of such an event in the works. Somehow, a magician waved a wand over the mansion, made it new. Threadgill marveled at the work: Fresh greenery decked the windows; cedar garlands draped the porch, the broken section of banister stood miraculously repaired, newly whitewashed.

Threadgill felt hot lightning strike.

Eva! There! Eva!

She floated into the parlor on her father's arm, her face radiant, innocent beauty in those eyes. Her turquoise evening dress glowed like foxfire. Eva unsnapped a tiny ivory fan; her hands opened and closed it absently. Threadgill felt a stab of envy as she gifted an older gentleman in a Confederate uniform with a smile. The veteran, clearly a favorite of her father, kissed Eva's hand. Laughing, she shook back her red tresses, and Threadgill thought his jealous heart might fly out of him.

Colonel Sutton chatted with his old colleague, one hand on his daughter's arm, the other on the soldier's yellow-braided uniform sleeve. Eva's quick eyes darted here and there over the room.

Threadgill felt a surge of triumph, of hope. Eva rolled her eyes privately behind the fan. Though inconspicuous – and unseen by the Colonel – the signal was unmistakable. After a moment, the older soldier bowed, moved on.

Colonel Sutton announced his lovely daughter to the next young buck in uniform, clustered with his admiring fellows before an oil painting of a fox-hunt. Distress swamped Threadgill again. This young man had a fine face, a fine figure, blonde locks, a proud head held high.

A new miracle now. A jealous-eyed girl in a very green dress flitted up and coiled herself onto the blushing soldier's arm. She tugged him quickly away to a safe corner, her eyes narrow as she cut them back at Eva.

Colonel Sutton's daughter moved in elegant light all her own. Her red hair rippled thrillingly at the slightest motion of her head, a gesture bestowed every splendid gentleman conjured to her path by the Colonel's beckoning hand. Threadgill wanted to spit on the ground with each new introduction.

The Colonel summoned yet another soldier, straight as a rifle, and Threadgill plainly saw Eva stifle a small yawn behind her fan. Hoorah! He felt like a leap in the moonlight, throwing a fist and a hoot and a rebel yell.

Eva proceeded through the throng on her father's arm. To keep her in sight, Threadgill scrabbled sideways through scratching rows of corn to the next tall window, then the next.

After a time, Col. Sutton halted at the dinner table piled with the good roast and ham, the venison and baked chickens and heaps of fruit and vegetables, sweet potatoes, the ears of corn stacked like yellow firewood. Older Confederates, laughing and red-faced, helped themselves here to good whiskey, poured by old Washington himself from cut-glass decanters. Eva waved off her portion of food, but the Colonel stole a rib and ate it on the spot, his eyes closed in satisfaction as he chewed.

Threadgill's stomach growled. In his pocket, for supper, he carried one stick of cold cornbread.

Threadgill forced his eye from Eva. One by one, he studied the gay revelers. Now he noticed something. The jolt made him consciously pull down the brim of his hat.

A man in spotless Confederate gray held out his china plate for another slice of roast. The gesture seemed unremarkable … except that the other sleeve of the soldier's uniform hung empty.

Another veteran sat at the end of the dinner table, the back of his starched gray uniform to the open window. He sat, Threadgill saw, because he had no legs.

Someone led a newly arrived young man with long golden hair and a splendid, perfectly tailored gray cape to the whiskey service. Washington poured a drink, then steered it carefully to the soldier's hand. The man's eyes stared ahead, cloudy as December sky. A guide again took the blind man's arm – and Threadgill saw the guide's hand lacked fingers.

Threadgill felt horror well up. He began a silent roll call of veteran after veteran who paraded by the windows.

One soldier stumped past, his damaged leg straight and hard as a wagon tongue. Another wore his withered arm in a gray sling, held close to the breast like a nursing infant. Another soldier's bottom jaw had been shot away, and he wore a yellow scarf tied round his face to conceal his disfigurement.

A few soldiers bore no scars at all. Here they seemed not lucky, but simply godlike – like a separate species of whole, perfect immortals on a charity visit to inspire the ruined and halt and maimed of the world.

Eva belongs with one of them, doesn't she? She is perfect like that.

Threadgill found her again. Like a little girl, she playfully swung round a stair post and whisked to the second-story powder room, lifting her hem off the steps with both hands. Slim ankles flashed under a surf of petticoats. As if signaled, en masse, the other girls and women flocked upstairs too.

Threadgill imagined a mysterious boudoir, where women combed one another's hair and laughed hysterically at the men below. Not that the gentlemen cared a fig. As the last female vanished upstairs, the musicians struck a brighter tune. The old rebels – those able, at least – hove to their feet, glasses raised high. They roared out words to "The Bonnie Blue Flag" at the top of their lungs and shook every window.

Threadgill could see shining tears on faces.

With the last note, the boys – those who could – threw their hats into the air, and one or two stabbed drawn swords toward the fifteen-foot ceilings. Whiskey glasses glittered; brothers pounded the backs of brothers. Hip-hip-hoorays flew for the Colonel.

The band struck up "Dixie" now, and Colonel Sutton's revelers issued such a wave of newly energized roars and stomps that they drowned out the tune.

"Hurrah!" they shouted. "Away down South ... in Dixie!"

The door of the ladies social room upstairs suddenly burst wide, and the

flock of newly refreshed, colorfully bedecked females, young and old, fluttered down the stairs with most unladylike speed.

"Dixie! Look away!"

It was exceedingly cruel, Threadgill's memory. He saw no pretty dancing
ladies, no celebration. His mind filled with a solitary scarecrow, a dancing,
gangling boy with bloody feet. A pool of Ben's blood in a road. A stony,
sun-dazzled hilltop. Angry hornets. A fierce sting. Fire. The Unmentionable.

*A lost cause. I wear a scar that comes in one side of me and out the other, and my head
scares wild animals. For … what? I'm not invited tonight. I can't even be a guest in Eva's
house like these lucky devils. Why? Not man enough to suit Able Sutton?*

As if mystically summoned, the Colonel appeared in the window. His
great thatch of whiskers, combed and pampered, gave him a lionlike air. He
smiled, and every yellow tooth in his head showed. He basked in this grand
dose of glory from yesteryear. His majestic cranium nodded – *yes! yes! splendid!
yes!* His peg leg stabbed the floor; nailed him to the swirling, twirling world
for one more night of life.

I hope his leg catches in a knothole and breaks off.

Threadgill slapped a mosquito sucking his hand. He looked up to see the
Colonel, bright-eyed, stump to the center of the parlor.

Time for a speech.

He delivered with grand oratorical flourishes, some words about the quadrille and the gavotte and the fair distaff and other things Threadgill did not
understand. Glasses rose again, and a rousing new cheer.

The forlorn guinea fowl ran from under the magnolia tree and fled into
the night to flee the uproar.

Now the room rearranged itself.

The men in uniform divided into two groups, each to one side of the long
room. Threadgill imagined two colorful files of soldiers at inspection.

The ladies, floating swans, their lovely long white necks and arms fresh
and cool, their faces newly powdered and refreshed, took positions before
the soldiers, some obviously jostling to pair with the most handsome … and
undamaged … candidates.

The band played again, this time a waltz – slow, stately, gorgeous.

One by one, couples swept down the long parlor, one end to the other,
a twirling, spinning blown-leaf dance. Even the Colonel, beaming, limped

noisily but with no obvious embarrassment alongside his laughing daughter. Threadgill could see the eyes of nearly every man furtively or most obviously on Eva, her remarkable hair, that foxfire gown.

At the end of the promenade, dancers parted, and presented a breathless bow and curtsy to one another. The line reformed, shifting each partner forward a place. In moments, the original dancers rotated again to the front and launched away with new partners on a gay second swing down the magical parlor. This fresh pairing of couples happened a third time, then a fourth, fifth, and sixth, until Threadgill lost count. The splendid dancers reflected in twinkling glass mirrors, beveled house windows, shining eyes of admirers.

Eva soared past. This time, the sight spiked Threadgill's heart.

She hung daintily on the arm of a splendid cavalier, a lean and tall young man with cavalry boots shined so perfectly they reflected the candles like black mirrors. His fringed yellow sash flew recklessly. He wore a patch over his right eye, a dark and dangerous-looking badge of honor. Threadgill watched miserably as Eva romped the length of the room on the man's arm. At the end of their brisk promenade, her breast heaving, she leaned for a moment against the soldier to catch her breath. Roses bloomed in both cheeks.

Against all decorum, the tall soldier suddenly leaned and kissed Eva – full on the lips. It happened before she could react. A gasp rose from those who witnessed this boldness. Threadgill rose clean to his feet in a fury. Colonel Sutton set down his whiskey glass, his mouth a hard line.

And Eva? With every wondering eye on her, she spread her fan mysteriously before her face … and gave a little laugh. Then she slipped away like a deer into spring woods. The audacious soldier watched her swirl away, wordlessly gone, to the next lucky partner.

Animal rage burned in Threadgill. He gripped dirt in both hands – he had squeezed two clods of Alabama earth into trickles of red sand.

If it was hard granite, he swore, flinging the dirt, *I'd squeeze that to grit too.*

The patch-eyed soldier now made a second mistake. A blonde-haired, red-faced fellow with an empty sleeve approached, his drunk face bright as a lighthouse. He guided the cavalier toward the door for cooler air.

The gallant young one-eyed Romeo turned and bowed to the ladies – an obvious nod only to Eva. Threadgill fumed, eyes slitted, as the rascal and his drunken sidekick stumbled through a slatted door onto the broad Sutton porch, clomping and braying.

They stood only forty feet from Threadgill.

"Preston! You gonna get your ass shot!" laughed the blonde drunk, tottering. "Old Man Sutton keeps his dueling pistols well oiled!"

Threadgill could hear the flat sneer reply. "Let him. I kissed her, didn't I? So you owe me five silver dollars, Galloway. Five shiny ones …"

"Was that an official kiss, Preston? It looked to my eye more as you kissing, and her only watching."

The blonde drunk, Galloway, leaned his one arm on the newly repaired section of whitewashed porch banister … and it gave way with a shocking crack. Galloway and four feet of the rail tumbled off into space.

Oh, what hilarity! The drunk hit heavily, but blustered to his feet, swearing, smeared with dirt and peacock guano. The peacock itself stormed out of its hiding place. It sent up ear-splitting cries of alarm and fled across the back grounds with its wings spread and shaking showily.

"God blast it!" cried Galloway. "The ship has capsized, Captain! I'm a drowned man!"

"Sodden, I'd say," answered his eye-patched friend. "But drowned or not, you owe me five silver dollars."

"Yes, yes. Five silver dollars. Now haul me back on board, Cyclops!" The drunk tried to slap himself clean, with peacock shit all over his hand.

"Galloway, quit your yelling," hushed the soldier on the porch. "Else you'll be paying that dreary Sutton five more silver dollars for wrecking the woodwork from his house."

With his dashing friend's help, the drunk clambered back onto the porch. He heaved to his feet with only a slight sway.

"Gentlemen."

Colonel Able Sutton stepped from the shadows. Every pace across the porch sounded loud as a pistol shot.

This will be righteous, Threadgill thought, smoldering still. For the first time ever, he pulled for the Colonel.

But the soldier, the one who had kissed Eva, reacted to Sutton in most bizarre fashion. All at once, he appeared to suffer a seizure of some sort. Weird sucking sounds came from his open mouth. He reached immediately for his collar button with both hands, tearing at it, gasping for breath.

"Preston!" cried the drunk. "What's the matter? What in god's name?"

The strangling soldier ripped away the collar button – Threadgill heard it bounce like a pea across the porch. He fell against the porch wall, gasping for another few moments, an undisguised panic in his features. Still breathless, he appealed soundlessly to the drunk and the Colonel with something like terror in his face. All at once, he pulled from his pocket a white handkerchief. He leaned forward crookedly and coughed – a great tearing sound – and his one-armed friend pounded his thin back.

Threadgill heard a high sucking in of air, at last, from the one-eyed soldier.

"Jesus!" Galloway slurred at Able Sutton, trying to bring some levity. "That's some whiskey you serve, ain't it, Colonel?"

Preston bent with hands on his knees. The black patch made him look like an insect to Threadgill, a mantis twisting its head side to side. The soldier abruptly experienced another racking fit of coughs – this one so violent it buckled his knees and sent him onto the floor. Colonel Sutton kept his wary distance, and his grim silence. The drunk pounded his friend again.

"Preston? Holy Jesus!"

Light spilled through the house window. Some of the male guests now looked on in bewilderment, and the ladies jockeyed to see over their shoulders.

"Preston? Please! What the devil IS it?"

Threadgill saw the one-eyed soldier nod okay to his drunken friend. The stricken man then pulled his white handkerchief down from his mouth. He stared at it in utter surprise.

A perfect little devil's face of bright red blood stained the white cloth. A foaming death's head.

Threadgill knew consumption. He'd seen Aunt Annie's. He knew too where it led – to a stony place where no wind ever blew and no light shone.

Now the two guests clopped urgently in their fine boots past Colonel Sutton and down the porch steps. Into the yard. With the one-eyed man trembling against him, Galloway waved frantically for their horses.

A colored stabler raced away into the night, shouting commands to grooms. More boot heels rushed onto the porch with a noise like overturned baskets of sweet potatoes. The space quickly filled with young and old men, women and girls too, a seething Colonel Able Sutton in their midst.

"Colonel!" gallantly shouted one of the guests. "Shall I bring the scoundrels back at swordpoint?"

Enough. Too many people watching. Threadgill eased deep into the corn rows. But he could not resist one last glance.

Colonel Sutton had stumped out into the yard and stood jaw to jaw with the cringing young soldiers. The Colonel cursed aloud at them until the horses arrived. He even shook a fist under the nose of the one-eyed rogue.

The two visitors mounted quickly, one still coughing, and they galloped into the night.

Threadgill stumbled back through the long corn rows to his own lonely hill.

Dinah greeted him, trailing her tether. She had slipped the knot and found her way to a wild cherry tree with low branches full of sour fruit.

"Hey, Dinah! Found your supper, old girl?"

The horse tossed her head.

"Good girl," Threadgill said, emotion choking his voice. "Good faithful old Dinah."

He swung to her saddle, his eyes burning with unexpected tears. He looked back across the corn.

The Sutton house was already half dark. The party over, just like that.

Colonel Able Sutton, a lamp in his hand, stood at the missing rail on the porch. He looked like the captain of a ship.

A last guest rattled away in a buckboard, wheels churning a great darkness.

Upstairs, in Eva's bedroom, a perfect shadow appeared behind a white shroud of curtain.

A soldier with consumption kissed her tonight.

The lamp in Eva's room went out.

Chapter 31, Rabies!

Summer 1964 – North Alabama

Threadgill raged.

Rattling clouds of insects burst from his path.

A rampaging giant, he ripped through brakes of poke, sumac, fennel with his bare hands. He left a trampled, wounded stink in the bright red air. Rabbits streaked ahead of him, outracing snakes and mice and skunks and coyotes and armadillos and raccoons and opossums, also scarlet shotgun bursts of cardinal, mourning dove, quail.

Threadgill roared, red mouth agape, and his roar amplified the splintering of limbs, the crushing tread of boots, the panicked squeal of small beasts fleeing.

Rabies!

Threadgill's eyes blazed, and everywhere he turned those brimstones he saw spattered, discolored earth and nature and sky washed blood red. He hated that color, hated what it covered, hated all that lay in front of him, the land and the things that grew on the land, the days and the nights. The sun. The moon.

He hated the Yankee.

Threadgill gnawed loose drops of blood from his own wrists, screaming in fury. He rose from his all-fours and bounded away, gloves of red blood melting off his weathered hands.

He struck a beeline through the woods – due north – attacking everything that dared stand in his way.

Nothing, anywhere, no work of man or god, would be safe from his Revenge.

Waves of wondrous fury surged up Threadgill's spine, rushing his brain in bursts so powerful he sometimes simply collapsed, twitching on the ground.

In these moments, eerie red devils tongued great brass trumpets in a leering circle around him, and gongs and drums crashed along in time. Threadgill snapped at the devils, attacked the very earth, tore at clumps of grass, ripped the bark from trees. He left furrows in the world under bleeding fingernails, even in hard cherty places.

Savage, at the bottom of an ocean of sweet red rage, Threadgill attacked the face of the world.

He burst from a thicket onto a moonshiner's still, the stench of sour corn high in the air, the liquid bubbling merrily, shimmers of red heat rising from a red fire under a red pot. A trembling old moonshiner and a young grandson, terrified, aimed their shotguns over a stump straight at him.

"Git on! Leave us be, mister!"

Threadgill heard thin pleading, a faint mosquito whine of voice amid crashing cymbals and thundering devil drums.

"Go on from here! You got no bidness!"

Threadgill simply lowered his head, eyes glowing, and charged the whis-key-makers. He slavered, the delicious red apples of the boy's cheeks and the chewy throat flesh of the old man bright in his sights.

"Arrrrgh! Bite you! Make you like ME!"

The moonshiners fired all four barrels. Threadgill watched the buckshot slowly melt into bloody drops in mid-air as the blasts approached. The blasts merely spattered him with harmless color. He screamed and shivered and thrust his arms high into the sky in exquisite pain.

"Arrrrgh!"

Threadgill wiped fresh blood out of his eyes. The old moonshiner and his helper skeedaddled through the woods. They ran so fast that leaves swirled in small tornadoes behind them.

Threadgill ripped into the moonshine still. Instantly, steaming whiskey and stinking mash gushed from gaping, paw-sized rents in the metal. The distressed squawk of wrenched sheets of tin and pot metal filled the forest, along with Threadgill's baying rage.

A full-grown red bear bolted in terror ahead of Threadgill up the next hill-side, loudly grunting with the efforts it made to gallop to safety. Threadgill gave chase. The bear slipped over a rise and away down the thickets of a red slope.

Threadgill heard a splash over that red hill.

The old man stopped dead at the top of the rise, the stench of bear over-powering.

A pond shimmered before Threadgill's eyes.

Water.

The bear thrashed into the pool, a foggy red wake of mud showing the path it churned for a far bank. Dozens of turtles slipped desperately into the bloody broth, so frightened by Threadgill they didn't even pop their periscope heads back up.

Threadgill smelled it now, and his stomach and bowels clenched with pain.

Water.

Horrible water.

Threadgill's red eyes widened, and his mouth gagged in horror.

Run … water! Hate … water!

Backward and away he blundered now, tripping on a stump, settling again in the pumping red arteries and veins of a honeysuckle mass. The stench of the vines' watery crushed liquids nauseating him, fogged his thoughts.

Oh, Threadgill wanted to *kill* something.

A Yankee.

Oh, he would.

He tore a path toward dark red hills ahead.

North.

Big red pines jumped from his marauder path, and red clouds fled the sky, towed away by flapping crows.

He would find that last damned Yankee. He would find. He would.

That violent pleasure suddenly flowered in his mind, florid as a summer rose.

"Stop."

A tall stranger, the knob-ends of his bones bulging under his skin, blocked Threadgill's path. The woods hung low around the ominous figure like the mouth of a red cave.

"Mr. Pickett." The man nodded, smiling. "We meet at last."

The tall stranger wore a baseball cap stained with some dark substance. A dirty mud flap of unwashed hair hung down from the cap in back, long enough to trail grease onto the stranger's T-Shirt.

The shirt sported a jaunty red skull-and-crossbones.

"Mister, you best move aside. I got the rabies," Threadgill hassled. Red drops of sweat fell from the rim of his aluminum pot. "I got a Yankee soldier to kill."

The stranger lowered his head, studied Threadgill. The figure had one stray eye, this with a snake's pupil. Threadgill couldn't decide which orb to watch.

"I know all about you," the stranger drawled. "But I've come to collect you now. There's no way forward, Mr. Pickett. You've been a tough son of a bitch. But no man is tough enough and no man has will enough to live after contracting rabies. No matter how much he hates. No matter how much he loves."

Threadgill bared his teeth and spat.

Unimpressed, the stranger rolled his eyes.

"You tried mighty hard, Mr. Pickett, to fight a potent *Lyssavirus*. But we were bound to meet from the day my Missionary Monkey took a bite of your knee. I have to hand it to you, though – you have a remarkable focus. I have long admired your will to stick with this cruel world, even if revenge kept you going.

"We ought to have shaken hands a half-dozen times before today. I was in the woods near Pine Mountain with you. I rode in your hospital wagon. I made visits to Goat Island when you met the monster, fought the hurricane. But … well, that's all water over the dam now. Today I take you to your final rest, Mr. Pickett. This day. This hour."

Threadgill slobbered, the world blood red everywhere. Even his breath was red. It whipped in and out of his nose and mouth like dragon fire.

"So…" Threadgill narrowed his eyes. "Howdy do then, Mr. Death. You the sorry so-and-so took my twin brother. You remember coming to Georgia for a skinny kid named Ben, back in '64?"

"I come to get you ALL, Mr. Pickett." The stranger spat. Something bright and sticky and red landed on a bush. "Your Aunt Annie. Your old man at the mill pond. I was busy back in them Civil War times. Y'all like to wore me out rounding up boys and pieces of boys on all those battlefields."

Threadgill felt the world grow redder, hotter. Gongs and drums blared.

"That plantation girl you were sweet on back in the day – that Eva. Her old man – he come with me, not long after you run off. Then I collected that pretty girl too. She wasted to skin and bones from tuberculosis. I come to get all, Mr. Pickett, in due course. And today … well today. Lucky you."

Threadgill felt fury in his breast.

"Well, fiddle dee dee."

The stranger raised an eyebrow quizzically.

"That means you wasted a trip, you dumbass. *I'm tougher than the rabies.* I'm tougher than you. I've still got one piece of business. A score to settle."

Another scoff. Another red hocker.

"Ain't a soul on this earth ever lived through an attack of the furious rabies, Mr. Pickett. Nary the first one. A 114-year-old man ain't likely to start a new trend in this area of health care."

Threadgill spat his own red hocker. It glopped down close to the stranger's odd bare foot. Threadgill saw toes bunched in two knots, a slight split visible between them.

To Threadgill's enormous satisfaction, the stranger edged his foot back.

"The goddamned rabies won't kill *me*. If you think they will, you don't know Threadgill Pickett. It *ain't* my time to go. I got a thing to do still."

"They all say that, Mr. Pickett. Every knock-kneed so-and-so tells me that same sadsack story. It gits pretty tiresome to hear …"

Threadgill sneered, his teeth bright red.

"You know I got shot once?"

"Yes indeed. I do know."

"Did a bullet through the chest kill me?"

"I was amazed." The stranger scratched his arm, rolled his eyes.

"I got burned up."

"You did."

"And?"

"Fire didn't kill you. That was close to a miracle."

"Got chewed up by that ugly thing in the swamp."

"True."

"And?"

"Here you stand."

"Brain fever? Hurricane? Bad fish a dozen times?"

"Check. Check. Check. Survived."

"Car wreck with that little man, just a few minutes ago?"

"Uh-huh."

Threadgill felt vindicated. His bottom lip jutted out. An ant could walk a long way on that lip.

"Impressive. I give you your due. You have unusual focus. Unusual will.

But like I said, Mr. Pickett, this is the furious rabies. This is … the end."

The tall, sallow stranger in the skull-and-crossbones T-shirt did a cricket thing with one elbow and reached into a back pocket. He produced a wrinkled red scroll of paper and a red pen.

"Let's get 'er done. Make your mark right here, Mr. Pickett," Death pointed. "And come along with me. It's your time now. Your twin brother and mama and aunt and that Eva and all your family wait for you. Think of it as a family reunion."

Threadgill's head suddenly flashed with pain. For an instant he wondered, dazed, if lightning had struck him.

He reached a hand up and tipped his aluminum pot and found, to his amazement, that the paper-thin skull and thin burned skin of The Unmentionable had ballooned out like the weak place in an overly inflated tire. Threadgill cut his eyes up and could see his own stretched flesh, so thin it had grown transparent. The inflated sphere sloshed with nasty fever and virus and infection.

"See what I mean?" Death said. "You're a goner."

The stranger spoke as if anybody could see that this was Threadgill's last hurrah. The final hour. The end of the line. Last call.

Threadgill reached with both hands – his head felt gigantic! Like the one on the waterhead boy. Preposterously huge, alarmingly hot to the touch. He could barely reach his aluminum pot now, it rode so high atop the ballooned cranium.

Threadgill licked his lips, though his tongue felt dry as sandpaper.

It's the rabies, coming to a head.

The tall stranger tapped the paper impatiently. His pen left little dots of blood.

"Let's get a move on Mr. Pickett," Death said, "Sign right here. I'm a busy man. There's much to do these days too."

Threadgill didn't care if his head got big as a hot air balloon. He didn't care if the stranger in the baseball cap stood there with his precious paper and pen till the poison ivy grew and covered him and the woodpeckers hammered holes through his skull to let the light in.

"I ain't ready to sign a DAMN thing."

Threadgill lowered his head – he felt gravity pull him slightly off balance.

"You ain't gettin' Threadgill Pickett. Not today. I still got a damn Yankee to choke to death."

The stranger drummed pen against page, spoke in a flat voice.

"Threadgill, I hoped we wouldn't have to do this the hard way …"

On the spot, the stranger transformed. He stretched and widened into a huge red grim reaper, tall as an elephant, bulging with muscles under his ragged red robes.

Threadgill lowered his head like a bull and closed his eyes.

With his mind, his sheer will, he forced the rabies bubble to shrink. The fierce hot powerful glow of vengeance and fever and living rabies germs rushed from his dwindled cranium back into his body. Energy exploded him, swelling muscles of his arms, chest and legs.

"Ahhhhhh!"

Threadgill inhaled, looked up. The world danced in red cerements.

Old Death, idly swinging his scythe, had weathered his share of terrible fights. Nothing new. He wore a toothy fixed grin of confidence. Who could beat Death?

Threadgill Pickett.

Death never knew what hit him.

The old man sprang onto Death the way a wildcat dives onto the back of a wild hog, the way a hawk lightningbolts onto a still, timid rabbit.

In an instant, Threadgill's hands and feet and teeth clasped torn-out gobs of flesh. A long strip of ripped meat with a nose attached swung from Threadgill's slobbering jaws.

Death stumbled backward and fell clumsily into the bushes with a terrific splintering noise. He raised the kind of billowing dust and leaf cloud a great falling tree raises.

Threadgill, merciless, dove into the bushes after him. Threadgill savaged Death. And he savaged the earth and plants and trunks and stones and everything else close to Death.

Oh, but Death fought back! He fought with all his mighty might. Somehow, the enormous robed assassin managed to swing his scythe and dislodge Threadgill from a gaping hole at Death's hoary old throat.

But it was too little, too late. The stranger lay on his back in the weeds. A red liquid bubbled from the jugular, and only a pink froth came from Death's lips when he attempted to speak.

Threadgill kicked dirt in the froth.

"What you gonna do about THAT, you sorry so and so? Huh? What you gonna do NOW?"

Then Threadgill screamed with all his soul and hurled himself atop his gigantic enemy once more, rending and tearing with all the vengeful fury of all the rabid animals ever gone mad in the long mad history of a mad world.

Threadgill suddenly woke beside a two-lane highway in the shade of a pink-blossomed mimosa tree.

He felt cool for the first time in days.

A beautiful woman with black hair and a beaded Navajo headband blinked down at him. She lifted a streaming yellow sponge – *yellow*! – and squeezed a gorgeous trickle of water onto his hot face.

Sweet lovely cool water.

Suck this sponge, the young woman seemed to tell him, though Threadgill did not see her lips move or hear any words. The voice he heard in his head felt like a kiss. *A fever has you … dehydrated, I think.*

For one last instant, Threadgill's spirit left his body again for a little while and went on a walk into the woods to visit the stiff, badly beaten body of Death. Black flies buzzed all over it.

Satisfied, Threadgill returned to a scarred body with an aluminum pot on its head.

"Ahh," he managed to croak, settling in. "Water."

Chapter 32, Homegoing

Spring 1867 – South Alabama

The spring after Colonel Sutton's Confederate veterans' party, five months after that consumptive rogue's stolen kiss, Threadgill watched Eva Sutton cough into a white handkerchief. He hid in the new corn, lying on his belly to hide, early in the season this time. He heard the creaking ropes that suspended the wooden porch swing. Her saw how Eva's breath left a blood-red mark in the lace.

Threadgill knew everything it meant. Eva's soul was writing her last chapter. The words would appear in red ink on white handkerchief pages, one after another. At the end, her young sweet body would gasp for a last breath, lie perfectly still, green eyes wide.

At weary dawn, just hours after Eva's demon grinned back at her from that piece of lace, Threadgill lashed a light bundle to Dinah's back and swung into the saddle. He kicked off, headed steadily over flushed fields into the late spring woods.

He left the door of Annie's house unlocked and standing wide. Amos could have it now, if he ever returned. Or wild animals. He placed red wild columbine flowers on Annie's grave, and he stared in silence at Randoll Pickett's headstone. Then he whispered *goodbye*.

Goodbye to Eva. Goodbye to all that.

***

Watery blue shadows washed the trail ahead of Threadgill and his mount.

Yet again, Threadgill grieved for a lost loved one – poor beautiful doomed Eva. The only girl he ever loved would lie down with Death instead of Threadgill.

It broke his heart.

Eva Sutton would join Ben. And Annie. All of them.

A half hour along, Dinah picked a path down a little bank, splashed a creek, picked a way through a stand of huge longleaf pines. She trudged onto a westbound road. A stone's throw away stood Tom Slocum's mill.

The sight of the little enterprise filled Threadgill's eyes with tears for a third or fourth time this morning.

He had tried so hard to be one of them. The normal. The unscarred.
The living.

He tried so hard. He worked hard all day, and prayed on Sunday in the
church and showed himself conspicuously in town. He tried so hard.

Well, goodbye to all that too.

Threadgill touched his heels to Dinah's flank, trotted past the mill. Dinah
showed some dismay when Threadgill didn't stop this time at that familiar
wooden water trough by the chinaberry tree. Instead, Threadgill gave the
mill a sharp salute – goodbye – and he resolutely rode past. Through the
open door, Mr. Slocum worked by a glowing lantern in the early blue gloom.
Threadgill could hear the miller mumbling to his dogs … or maybe to the big
sacks of corn meal too dumb to breathe or answer back.

Threadgill felt a new and plangent twist of sadness for this good man,
who had put two dollars in his hand at the end of every month for a whole
year. And Mr. Slocum, alone of all the people in Eufaula, talked to Threadgill about the war. The miller had fought at Franklin and Nashville, at the
very end, with the Alabama 57th. He miraculously survived those slaugh-
terhouses. It was a miracle beyond a miracle that he came home untouched
and whole – at least in body. Still, whenever Mr. Slocum mentioned those last
days of the war to Threadgill, his eyes looked, for just a blink, like painted
wooden eyes.

***

So began the second great journey of Threadgill's life.

That first afternoon, very late, Dinah clopped through Clio. Threadgill
bedded down a few miles past that slow little village, under the open stars.

Young man and horse moved on. They passed through Clayton, then the
crossroads at Ariton. Soon, Threadgill left the native soil of Barbour County
for only the second time in his life. Threadgill felt a rabbit run over his grave.

The tingle of scalp and a stab of phantom pain jolted him momentarily.
Even so, the young man did not look back, not a single time. He felt sorely
tempted. Once, someone – a voice he couldn't quite place or remember –
called him frantically.

"Come back! Come back, Threadgill!"

That's just a mockingbird, he told himself. *That's just a little gray bird in a tree.*

***

Dawns and noons and twilights.

He journeyed westward, a little south thrown in each time the road forked.

Between Eufaula and Troy, Threadgill traversed a huge dogwood forest – a solid mass, unbroken for thirty miles, of pebbled trunks and white-and-pink flower petals, freakishly abloom late in the season. The trees held Threadgill spellbound. He rode and rode for days through broken pink light, no sensation of time passing. Morning came the same as afternoon, each pink dusk the same as each pink dawn. Threadgill's hat brim spilled pink-and-white blossoms when he nodded, asleep in the saddle. He felt enchantment, a sense of dream. He wasn't sure if he saw or simply imagined white deer around him, stags and hinds bounding fantastically, in and out of rose-colored shadows.

Some days later, south of Montgomery, he connected to the old Creek Indian trace. It led him through the blackest fields and thickest woods Threadgill had ever seen.

One night a week along in the journey, Threadgill bedded down at dusk close enough to a marsh to hear red-winged blackbirds creak like old hinges from countless nests in the cattails.

Black hungry mosquitoes boiled out of the night. Threadgill realized too late that it would be better to be caught out at dusk almost anywhere else in the world. Threadgill even gave half a thought to hurrying Dinah on through the night with moonlight on his back. But it would be too easy to step into a bog, gurgle down out of this world and come up dripping in the next one.

So the mosquitoes made their mischief.

At dawn, fitfully asleep on moist ground, Threadgill felt the hot early prickle of a fever.

The illness slammed him fast and hard. By mid-morning, he boiled inside, and he endured spikes of temperature so severe they took him back to the flames of the war.

For days (how many? who would ever remember?), Threadgill could find neither the wits nor strength to simply get up off the ground and climb into Dinah's saddle.

He dreamed wildfires, the hot coals crackling, live flames searing his legs and hands.

It rained once, maybe more than once. He thought steam clouded the air over his roasted flesh. He dreamed or imagined that someone stole his rotting clothes and made a leering gray scarecrow and raised it over him, mocking, to frighten the buzzards.

At last, the fever broke. Threadgill woke drenched and hollowed. His fever waned … but something worse hung on.

Panting, eyes open, sucking in deep breaths of syrup-thick swamp air, Threadgill struggled to his knees. His head reeled.

Good old Dinah, chewing a mallow, impatiently nuzzled him, *come on*.

But Threadgill felt still asleep – he shook his head to clear things, to wake completely.

Something was wrong.

To his horror, Threadgill only saw a horse's vaguest shape in a luminous blue-green mist.

Was it even real? Threadgill could not make sure it was Dinah at all.

Threadgill lay very still in the swamp.

Perfectly still.

He willed his eyes to come back to working order. He waited expectantly for sunlight to stream again. The world would be crystal clear, every leaf on every tree visible, each a different story of green. A sky so blue.

He was blind.

Threadgill grew more and more frightened. He imagined large, looming shapes in the translucent mist. He guessed their identities: T*ree. Sky. Sun. Horse.*

"Dinah?" he croaked, his voice also damaged by fever. "Is it you?"

Threadgill fought panic as he reached to find his horse.

Nothing.

He fought back an urge to run in terror, just run. What good would it do him to panic or lose his mind? He might wade deep into the swamps and never come out again.

Sounds and smells suddenly meant more. Threadgill's sense of hearing sharpened, overnight, by degrees of magnitude. The youngster could distinctly place every note of every bird, every breeze in a tree. His nose, too, magnified every odor. Smells summoned vivid images – sparkling stretches of standing water, cypress trunks with their little strange knees like rained-soaked monks under cowls.

Maybe I'll live like a bear now, Threadgill thought. *Maybe I will smell and hear my way through life. I'll just stumble from meal to meal, den to den. I'll live and die in these forests and swamps.*

Whatever else had happened to Threadgill, the rank sweat smell of his own flesh, after days of hot fever, now loosened a wellhead high inside his forehead. Mucus poured into his pinching fingers all morning, all day.

Still, Threadgill could not see. He snuffled about, praying on his knees for his eyes to come back from the clouds.

They did not. He dug frustrated fists into soft earth, opened them, dug his fists deeper.

After uncounted hours, Threadgill made an effort to travel. If he could reach some doctor somewhere ...

He found a short stick to tap before him. He grasped at bushes to keep balance. Yet any stumbling steps he took, sooner or later, sent him tripping back to earth, scratched and bruised. He fell into deep ferns once, and scrambled out panting and terrified of snakes.

Threadgill, finally, could not stop himself. Rage and cursing overtook him. Who could blame a boy who had seen so much in this world ... but now had lost his eyes? Hot sweat poured from Threadgill. His body drained its sickness and sadness.

How thirsty he grew! Exhausted by staggering, tripping and falling, he finally flopped motionless to the ground. He listened to his heart cry, trying to think what on earth he would do. How could he live without his eyes?

He woke some time later. How does a blind man know how long he sleeps?

Threadgill felt the hot summer blow down his throat. He heard the rusty-hinge calls of the red-winged blackbirds.

He carefully crawled toward the sounds of the birds. Long days and a different Threadgill ago, he'd seen water near his campsite. Hadn't he drunk from the swamp pond the night before the fever?

Yes. Here. It is. Water.

Threadgill alligatored through marsh grass and cattails. He reached a place where he sank to his elbows in swamp ooze. Stone blind, he drank and drank and drank.

Then, not really understanding why, Threadgill pushed both hands deep in the cool slick mud of the marsh bottom and brought up, with a sucking sound, a foul-smelling mud ointment. He smeared the muck over his eyes. He felt leaf bits and snail shells mixed with the goo.

The heavy mud clung fast as he flopped back, face up, the green cattails crushed pungently beneath his back. Snakes be damned.

He fell asleep again at once.

Early evening, twilight owls burbled from the trees. Threadgill woke and clawed at the caked mud itching his face.

It first happened in Threadgill's left eye. Moments after came the right.

The blue veil over his vision split like a rotted curtain.

Soft light misted through, and Threadgill could see a spectacular orange baby head – a full rising moon – crested over the marsh. A wilderness of cattail came clearly into view. Immense cypress trees slowly appeared out of nothingness. A star or two gleamed.

"Dinah!" he croaked. "I can see! It's night time! I can see!"

He reflected, down through the years, on what he might have become without his eyes – a gaunt, starved, disfigured Alabama wild man feeding on pond crustaceans, leeches, roots, stripped leaves, grubs, the black leaves, swamp mud.

The Monster of Pickett Swamp.

He rode Dinah all that night away from the foul place, risking deadly sump holes and all else. Threadgill would have trampled the Devil himself to escape that place. He trotted Dinah when possible, but spent most of the night picking his way through fallen trees, cypress knees, bogs of quicksand.

Next morning, after a happy night on a knoll on firm ground, Threadgill worked before sunup with a long buck knife. He carved earnestly on a branch of magnolia thick as his waist, a limb knocked clean off a primeval giant by some terrific wind. Threadgill hacked with both hands at the white flesh beneath the bark, roughing out a figure.

It lay on its back, a dead soldier in ivory, eyes weeping milky sap.

Threadgill left the effigy at the edge of the terrible swamp – a warning to fellow travelers.

***

In another twelve days, he reached the eastern shore of Mobile Bay.

Young Threadgill never imagined so much water.

"Looka that, Dinah! I swannee!"

He gentled back on the reins of the weary, mud-spattered mare. From the bluffs at Spanish Fort, the two travelers blinked in wonder.

Mobile Bay was a blue forever of siren mouths, opening, closing.

A constant wind here tipped back the flap of Threadgill's hat, tossed the mane and tail of his aging mount. The panorama and the fresh air exhilarated both travelers, and Threadgill suddenly felt like singing for the first time in many years.

The only song he knew was "Dixie," so he bawled it out, thinking all at once of poor Ben. His brother grew up across this bay, back in the good years, safe under the roof of Uncle Dove and Aunt Rose Nell.

Threadgill could see a long sloping horizon like the back of a whale – the western shore. Smoke rose over the port of Mobile, a little brown-and-white bird nest at the edge of the water. Sailing ships with puffed swan-breasts stood guard.

Threadgill thought of Eva. Poor Eva. She might have loved this sight.

It was always dark where her eyes stared now.

And Threadgill thought of Aunt Annie, who once took him on a trip to Eufaula just to let him pee off high bluffs and throw rocks at the river. Threadgill heard his aunt marvel about the Chattahoochee, how it was forever alive, always on its way somewhere. The mighty river had been the finest sight he ever saw.

But that was a river, Threadgill thought.

Here was the sea.

Surely, after all this toilsome life, if heaven turned out to be nothing BUT one big bright forever, it couldn't be a more awesome sight than Mobile Bay this fine morning.

Every journey should end this way, Threadgill thought.

He leaned forward to pat Dinah's neck.

Every journey should come to something so beautiful in the end.

Chapter 33, The Greyhound Riders

Summer 1964 – Off a north Alabama four-lane

Threadgill sucked the yellow sponge dry. Three times.

The beautiful woman with the Navajo headband next guided a stream of red wine from a leather bota into his mouth. She supported the back of his head with one hand.

The aluminum pot rang softly when she lowered him.

She had blue eyes and black hair. A necklace of cowrie beads dangled between her breasts. She smelled of incense. Threadgill found a flaw, however – a metal brace of some kind, rigged with stiff cardboard, kept her neck straight.

Threadgill felt much improved. His battle to the death with Death nearly did him in. Now he no longer saw red at random. His fever had passed. Birds sang.

Threadgill lived! Really lived – he tasted wine for the first time in his life.

A battered Greyhound bus threw part of its shadow over Threadgill and his beautiful nurse. A little crowd of men and women busied themselves with the bus's front right tire – a sad flat.

It wasn't happy work. The crowd by the tire seemed confused and short-tempered. What an odd group, too. Nearly all wore improvised slings or leg braces or splints.

Old Johnnie could fix that flat in a jiffy, Threadgill thought.

"Shit!" yelled a voice from the bus. "Not again!"

"What, Steven? You okay?"

A smallish man in a priest's collar peered anxiously up at the bus window.

"Kevin threw up the broth again. Can't we get him to a hospital?"

"What damn hospital in Alabama is going to admit him, Steve? Use your head."

The priest's face sweated with exasperation.

A disgusted growl returned from the bus window, a sneer by a brawny long-haired man in his twenties. The face abruptly disappeared.

Threadgill felt uneasy. These voices sounded peculiar, like people trying to talk with mouthfuls of hot boiled potatoes.

Yankees.

"How many miles to the Mason-Dixon line?" a man working on the flat tire groused. "Can we take a jet from here?"

The priest pleaded. "Hey, people. If we made that march last spring from Selma to Montgomery, we can tough it out a few hundred more miles!"

"Let's take a bus!" another person yelled, and a groan went up, punctuated by bitter laughs.

Disorder persisted. Some bandaged folks stepped gingerly down the bus gangway. Other bandaged folks climbed carefully back up. Bus windows rose, bus windows closed. Threadgill thought he heard someone sob.

The beautiful black-haired woman wiped a red spill from his mouth with her loose sleeve. She helped Threadgill sit. No small accomplishment, he in his weakened state, she with a neck injury.

Threadgill almost preferred lying down, after what he saw.

A tattered cloth banner draped the side of the bus. Parts of it smoldered, scorched black.

LET FREEDOM RIDE!

Threadgill could read some history on that banner and all over the Greyhound – bullet holes, burn, stains from hurled vegetables and other unnamable substances, dents and dings. One of the passengers – a man with a red bandanna wrapping a head wound – loudly wrenched a steel-tipped hunting arrow from the aluminum hide of the bus. Makeshift cardboard-and-duct-tape patches replaced several windows. Ugly jags of fractured glass miraculously hung in place in others.

The top of the bus gave Threadgill the biggest surprise of all – a gaping rent stretched through the metal more than half the length of the vehicle. Threadgill thought of a can of sardines with the metal top peeled back. Summer sunshine blazed through the opening.

"Holy mackerel!" A man with just one shoe and a huge bloody white sock pointed down the road at a round chunk of metal. "That damn rim went further than my family did on vacation last year."

A line of cars stacked up behind the stalled bus now, and the Greyhound riders seemed extremely nervous about those vehicles. The feeling must have been mutual – drivers blew horns angrily, then accelerated recklessly to pass the Greyhound. The bus passengers flinched often and noticeably, it seemed to Threadgill. Bandaged faces stared anxiously at the traffic from bus windows.

The black-haired woman silently offered Threadgill the bota again, and he drank deep draughts with great pleasure. Wine tasted a little sour, he learned. But after surviving rabies, a few gulps of it did wonders for a fellow.

What is this beautiful woman's name? Threadgill wondered, smitten. *How did she injure her neck? Can she talk? I wonder if she would travel north with me?*

In a smashed bus window, Threadgill saw an injured leg in an improvised cast – two tomato stakes, rolled-up newspapers, and duct tape. Suitcases and duffel bags wore charred spots and had smoke damage. A female foot hung over a seat, a long stitched-up gash across its top. Her toenails were individual Yankee flags, stars and stripes perfectly painted.

"Will you help me up?"

The beautiful black-haired woman smiled, silently nodded, and rose with Threadgill.

A voice yelled. "Ray, is there a spare? We're looking for another tire rim back here!"

A short lady with two blackened eyes shuffled past, resembling a raccoon.

"Ya head!" she commented to Threadgill. He quickly jerked his aluminum headgear more firmly into place. The wine had made him a little careless.

"What's your name?" Threadgill quietly asked the black-haired woman, happily holding her for support.

The woman reached into a very tight pair of jeans – awkwardly, thanks to the brace on her neck – and produced a small flower-bordered card. Threadgill read:

HI. I'M CHRYSALIS. MY VOW OF SILENCE WILL GO ON UNTIL THE POOR AND OPPRESSED SHALL B FREE.

She gave Threadgill a dazzling smile … with a missing tooth.

***

Not since his long trip on the hospital wagon in the war had Threadgill laid eyes on a worse bunch of walking wounded.

Twenty people, most of them young, hobbled and milled about. That many more sat inside the bus, too hurt to hobble. A few more stretched out in the vehicle's floor. Under the bandages and gauze and splints, Threadgill saw patched blue jeans, T-shirts with rainbows, head scarves, and lots of sandals, bells, beads. The Yankee travelers had come South with an abundance of hair; Threadgill had never seen so many men and women with pony tails and long collie-dog curtains down backs.

Wherever this crew had been … they'd had a long, strange trip. And very ugly.

Chrysalis wore a long-sleeved cotton shirt, sheer. It revealed her breasts. Threadgill felt dismayed – and thrilled – to see her nipples through soft fabric. He gawked shamelessly, but Chrysalis never took her steadying hands from him.

Now a gentle male hand gripped Threadgill's biceps.

"You appear to be badly hurt," said the priest. "Please let us take you with us to the hospital in Bethesda."

For days, Threadgill hadn't spoken many more words than Chrysalis. The wine didn't help now.

"I'm thinking y'all need to be the ones in the hospital," Threadgill managed, thick-tongued.

Threadgill hadn't expected the sound of his voice to cause three men and two women to burst into weeping and collapse against the bus with hands over their faces. A half-dozen colleagues took them into a huge consoling group embrace.

"Shhh! Shhh!" they whispered. "It's just his accent, Leah. He can't help the way he talks. It doesn't mean he's bad. They're not *all* bad. We're headed north now. We'll be safe again soon…"

The priest, chagrined, turned back to Threadgill. "I'm sorry," he said. "It's been a difficult trip."

Tell me something new, thought Threadgill.

***

The flat tire and thrown rim could not be replaced with available tools.

One of the bus riders – a man of some courage – flagged down a passing car and paid the driver $20, on faith, to send for Triple-A, whatever that was.

Faith did the trick.

After about an hour, a wrecker appeared, and a flatbed trailer. A taciturn white driver with slit eyes winched the bus onto the trailer.

As this work went on, the riders opened up to Threadgill. They told a hair-raising story. The priest, Father Conroy, did most of the talking, but others volunteered detail and their personal embellishments. Several said nothing at all – teeth lost, busted lips. They had trouble speaking.

Chrysalis stood close to Threadgill. She hugged his arm to her breasts from time to time.

They were proud to be Freedom Riders, the priest said. All from Boston. This was their second ride. The first time South, they made history – they marched to Selma with Dr. Martin Luther King.

A second trip had not proved lucky.

"It's still worth the hardship, the sacrifice," the priest insisted, eyeing his flock for support. "It's worth some bruises to support the struggle."

"The struggle?" asked Threadgill.

"The struggle to end the white apartheid!" answered a brisk little man with a beard and a pipe and a bandage that held his forehead on.

"To finish a hundred years later what Father Abraham began!" another man cried, this one a sad-faced fellow with thinning hair and a badly discolored nose.

"We played guitars and sang songs from the day we started," commented the girl with the Yankee flag toenails. "We can change and rearrange the world."

Something got rearranged, alright. Somewhere along one of the main highways east of Birmingham, a caravan of local cars attacked the bus like a wolf pack.

The assailants forced the bus to the shoulder of the road. The Freedom Riders bravely stepped off the bus and immediately got knocked to the ground, bloodied by baseball bats and two-by-fours and fists and lengths of chain and tire tools. The hooligan mob beat and kicked and spat on the Yankee invaders until they purely wore themselves out. They drove away laughing with their radios turned up.

"The thons ob bitthes thet my clotheth on fire and then pithed on me!" cried a man with a plug of gauze in his jaw. His angry face formed a purple cloud.

The mob set the Greyhound afire too. People in tall buildings in distant Birmingham saw the black cloud before the riders managed to snuff the flames. State troopers showed up about an hour after the mob finished its work. Another healthy wait later, two doctors appeared from Anniston. By then, some riders had rigged their own casts, made bandages with strips torn from their clothes.

As the priest finished his story, a defiant younger man, a tough-looking kid with an earring and a billow of black hair exploding from his skull in all directions, pointed his finger at Threadgill and yelled.

"Next time we come down South, we'll bring our own tools of emancipation! We won't travel these roads again without a way to defend ourselves!"

"We will act with the love shown by our Lord," the priest prompted him gently.

"Fuck. That. Shit!"

The young man stalked away to the front of the wrecker, muttering hotly under his breath.

Father Conroy turned to Threadgill, his face worn to old age with his efforts of patience.

"The lust for vengeance is strong," he said. "But revenge is like taking poison and hoping some other person dies. Forgiveness heals."

He looked Threadgill straight in the eyes.

"Fuck that shit!"

Chrysalis blurted out those words. Silent Chrysalis no more.

Threadgill couldn't believe his ears. A *woman* using words like those …

Off she stalked too, her lovely behind wagging, conch shells rattling. She followed the hothead to the front of the wrecker.

Threadgill heard a final groan as the Greyhound settled onto its towing platform. The tow operator threw a set of metal steps against the side of the wrecker.

"All aboard!"

The priest invited Threadgill to ride with the travelers as far as he'd care to go. They planned to get medical attention in Bethesda, Maryland, at the first hospital north of the Mason-Dixon line. Father Conroy felt sure doctors could do something to help Threadgill too. The priest made a point of mentioning that his parish back home in Boston specialized in providing outreach to homeless men …

The red wine, the weary bones, the face of Chrysalis – Threadgill just said "Yes."

The bus would take him north.

He'd be riding a bus riding a tow truck, going north.

***

The stench in the Greyhound made Threadgill's stomach rebel.

The torn seats and charred luggage reeked. Threadgill's nose burned with melted rubber-and-smoke foulness, blended with smells of human travelers in close quarters, spilled medicine, ugly wounds.

His mind went straight back in time to hospital wagons in a hot Georgia summer. He could hear again the cries of misery, feel the same rocking motion. He smelled suffering.

Threadgill, an angry old man, sought out the angry young man. The wild head of hair and Chrysalis huddled close in back of the bus. Both spoke in sharp whispers, seething. The man stripped off his white T-shirt in the heat. Stitches ran across the backs of both hands, and huge floral bruises covered his ribs. Purple rectangles clearly showed in his skin where links of chain had struck him.

Threadgill discovered a surprise, too. The young man fondled a monkey – a cute little squirrel monkey with a red collar.

It possessed a perfect little human face, and when Threadgill stopped and stared at the creature with his mouth agape, the monkey stared back knowingly, its soulful brown eyes unblinking. Defiant.

"I named it Leadbelly," the young man said, momentarily distracted by Threadgill's incredulity. "For Huddie Ledbetter, the Delta blues musician."

"Where did you get that monkey?" Threadgill stammered.

"At a vegetable stand outside of Birmingham," he said. "Some man had a cage full. I paid eight dollars for mine. He sold two more, one to Candace Dee over there, one to Irene, and one to the bus driver. All their monkeys got stolen by rednecks."

Threadgill turned to the youngster.

"What'd them people do to you, son?"

The young man looked at Chrysalis. Clearly, he had trouble understanding Threadgill's dialect.

"Did you get beat up?"

"Oh. Yeah. But I'm better off than most. I heal fast. My insides are still messed up. In a few days, I'll be fine."

"They beat you up too, Miz Chrysalis?"

The beautiful woman bit her lip and nodded. She opened her mouth and wordlessly pointed out the void in the top row of her smile. She'd returned to her vowed silence again.

"Are you really going back down yonder?"

"What's that?"

"Are you really going back one day to revenge them folks that done this to you?"

"By my God of Moses, I am."

The young man's eyes flashed, even as he stroked the soft head of the little monkey in his lap. He seemed to bow up in the seat slightly before speaking again.

"Father Conroy says an eye for an eye makes the whole world blind. But after this trip I believe that's the thinking of a damn fool and a coward. An accommodationist. A Neville Chamberlain."

Chrysalis nodded her head bitterly.

Threadgill jostled to let one of the riders take a seat. The assembly boarded again now, preparing for the tow truck to pull them away.

"Father Conroy raised me like his own son," the young man said. "Even though I'm Jewish. I found that out a couple of years ago. My real mother and father live in Israel. It's a long story. I'm abandoned."

"That's a nice monkey," Threadgill said.

"Yeah. But I been thinking. Who's gonna take care of it, if I have to come back South and settle some business? Maybe I didn't really need a damned monkey, with the new work I've got to do now."

The young man turned fiercely to Chrysalis.

"I shouldn't have listened to you. We don't need a fuckin' monkey. Now I've got to take care of my payback while I'm all the time packing around a fuckin' monkey? Shit if that makes sense."

Chrysalis's head snapped back in surprise. The neck brace squeaked.

She winced.

Threadgill left them to argue, him with snarls, her with cold silences. The old man made his way up the aisle quietly to the front of the bus.

He watched the final Freedom Riders load up.

Topping the bus steps came another young long-haired, beaded woman, pretty enough for a picture, only now her picture would have a black catgut stitch an inch long on the forehead. A strand of her hair caught in the stitches.

A meek-looking fellow climbed on, pale and shaky, his jaw tied shut and fat bandages on his burned hands.

Another man breathed hard and fast, clearly something extremely painful under the hand held to his ribs.

Father Conroy boarded last, his Irish face redder than a face should be. He yanked furiously on the mechanical lever that closed the bus door.

***

While Threadgill napped, the tractor-trailer towed the wrecked Greyhound effortlessly up and down Alabama hills toward a little unnamed town. The stony land rose and fell. It finally transformed itself into buildings and houses and chimneys.

They stopped in a busy little mountain community.

Threadgill woke when the tow truck turned off its loud engine.

Buildings jammed these streetfronts. Threadgill saw a butcher in one store bring down a cleaver on pink meat. He saw a woman adjust a hat on a mannequin. He saw a pet shop, and shook his head.

Who would have believed it? One of Larry LaRue's monkeys traveled north too, just like Threadgill. On the same bus even.

It doesn't get much stranger, Threadgill thought.

The folk singing on board had grown lusty now. A song told of young maidens bringing flowers to a cemetery and asking where all the young men had gone. The music moved Threadgill. He remembered Ben.

Many of the voices were practiced and excellent. Threadgill heard harmony, energy, an echo of happiness.

Father Conroy stood to make an announcement.

"We'll be spending the night in this little town." He held to the pole by the bus door. "And I think before we exit the bus for our hotel this evening, we should join in prayer."

In a beam of twilight that fell through the gaping roof, Threadgill could see a small insect of some kind crawl across Father Conroy's shoulder. The bug halted, took a new direction, halted again.

A roach.

"The war for the souls of men goes on, my friends. We sent our prayers of forgiveness … and our love … to those brothers and sisters of God's world – to God's children – in the South …"

Threadgill heard one or two boos – sour notes in the cheering – but Father Conroy soldiered on, hand raised.

"Like Christ, who forgave seventy times seven … and asked that we forgive those who have trespassed against us … who reminded us to turn the other cheek when we've been wronged … we pray for the blessing of peace to those who have misunderstood and misused us. We pray that their hearts will open, and that the miracle of holy blessing … and the peace of charity and the love that passes all understanding … will clear their eyes and open their minds to the wisdom of love, to love *all* men and women that God made. No matter their color. Or gender. Or age. Or … "

The roach disappeared down the collar of the priest.

"Amen!"

A tattered amen followed.

Threadgill itched.

***

He sat patiently, invisibly. Everyone shuffled slowly off the bus, many aided by friends. It took a full half hour for Threadgill to find himself alone.

A reporter happened up the steps, a man with a camera, but he did not ask Threadgill why he remained on the bus.

The Freedom Riders checked into a Howard Johnson's. While Threadgill watched, a worker came out of the motel office and placed the word NO in front of the word VACANCY on the hotel sign out front.

Threadgill rummaged through some Freedom Rider things and found a can of sardines. He'd developed a taste for sardines on this trip. He glanced up at the ripped bus roof, then with a twist of a key peeled back a tin lid to expose ten little oily headless fish. Immediately, they drew visitors – gnats.

Threadgill picked the fish out by their tails, dangled, then dropped them into his mouth.

His first food in days tasted like ambrosia.

He slept too. The rabies and the wine and the lull of the bus ride finally overwhelmed him.

He fell fast and hard.

***

When he woke, his things were gone. Knapsack stolen. Pockets turned inside out. Even the blanket thrown over him ripped away and taken.

What has the world come to? Will people these times even steal blankets off a sleeping man?

Threadgill staggered groggily to his feet. He balanced against a seat. Losing his gear was misfortune indeed.

Nothing to do for it.

He trundled from the bus and struck out for a green park across the street. Past that, he could sense a river. He'd lived close enough to water for so many years he just knew a river ran right over there.

In the late evening, his metal headgear felt cool.

At the river, Threadgill found odds and ends of clothing washed up along the bank. Rivers always carried clothes.

He found a blanket, muddy but dry. Actually, he found three blankets, three different places. The cotton one with rainbow colors would do. He only needed one.

Threadgill found food too. More food than he dreamed a man would find in a park in such a little town. Bags of salty peanuts. A whole uneaten sandwich, long and tapered, like a torpedo. A boiled egg, along with two sister eggs smashed flat, with tread prints of shoes on them. He found a half loaf of bread, some sweet pastry things.

Maybe he was like that fellow Job, Threadgill decided, the Bible man they talked about in church. Job suffered and suffered for believing without doubt. In the end, his courage and his faithfulness brought him seven-fold riches. Seven times the camels. Seven times the wives. Seven times the land. Everything a man could want.

Out of nowhere came kindness.

A pretty young lady, high school age, approached him, all long legs, her chestnut hair blowing. She looked dressed for church. She held out a pie plate covered in tinfoil.

"You could have this too, sir," she offered. Her voice rang like a little bell. "It's apple. I know you're hungry."

"That's mighty kind, miss. Thank you."

Her fingers grazed his when he took the pie. Hers felt sticky. Threadgill watched as she walked away.

The world is terrible. But the world is beautiful too, it struck him.

After finishing the whole delicious pie and running his fingers through the juice to get every honey-sweet drop, he took the empty tin plate and foil to a trash can.

He stepped back from a rush of black flies.

A little squirrel monkey with a red collar lay in the trash, grotesquely twisted. Its little mouth gaped, like it died screaming.

Threadgill gazed down on it a moment, then placed the pie plate and the aluminum foil carefully, reverently, over the little body.

Chapter 34, Goat Island

1867 – Mobile Bay, Alabama

From the eastern bluffs, Threadgill could see seven rivers empty into Mobile Bay, pouring their endless land stories into the great blue history book of the sea.

Threadgill and Dinah gaped at the shocking expanse of water. His awakened eyes drank in the miles and miles of currents and light. Had anything, ever, anywhere, been so beautiful? Threadgill surely had never seen anything like this.

He directed his gaze toward Mobile. He'd wanted to see that old French- and Spanish-tinctured city on the western shore since Ben lived there. He considered a journey onward to the port. He could find Aunt Rose Nell and Uncle Dove and learn how Ben grew up. Or he might enlist as a hand on a seagoing ship and leave behind all that he ever knew, all familiar.

A ship might be best. He could leave everthing in the past that ever hurt him. Ben. His wounds. All.

Threadgill fantasized a journey under white sails, the sea birds cutting, the swells tossing and rolling under salty decks. Off the bow, Threadgill imagined a place far from land, far from thorns and stones. Beautiful, dazzling light. A crew and the sea.

He felt a little motion sickness, all at once.

Then Threadgill's eye fell on a little island in the bay, a sickle of green. Isolation spoke to him that instant as clearly as a siren.

Alone.

Millennia of bay currents had spindled the island into the shape of a curved gourd, fat on one end, with a long hooked neck that scythed constant waves. From Spanish Fort, the breakers looked like never-ending rows of cotton.

A faded beach, yellow as old petticoats, surrounded the island, tapering to an end a quarter mile to the south. Big trees, primeval, anchored the island, kept it from floating from place to place over the surface of the earth. Threadgill could see marine birds, blown black-and-white ashes from some old fire, rise up and settle down constantly among the live oaks and cypresses and black tupelos.

Threadgill now knew what to do.

He unsaddled Dinah.

He would never need a saddle or a horse again in this life.

***

The Creole man who ran the trading post offered for Dinah and the riding gear: a cast net, an ax to hew out a new life among soaring hardwoods, fishhooks and other tools, vegetable seeds, rope and some salt, a measure of coffee, some whiskey, a little keg of nails, a box of dry foodstuffs.

The Creole man lived at the foot of the bluffs with a huge family. They filled a papery house on stilts that leaned out from shore over green sawgrass.

Threadgill, after the horse-trading, surprised the Creole – he handed over, with a devilish grin, all the rest of his money. Three silver dollars and loose change. This gift bought Threadgill a six-mile pirogue ride to the island … one way.

The Creole had more gold teeth than real ones. He suspiciously bit down on Threadgill's silver dollar. He smiled, delighted.

"For this much money, I build you a *bateau, mon ami*? And come out once a month? Bring you stuffs?"

Threadgill eyed the wizened ferryman.

A feral creature with wild hair, fantastic wrinkles in his cheeks and a fine French nose (with a missing tip) stood at one end of the pirogue, pole ready, the business end muddy, dripping. He represented a single, final lifeline back to the world, back to Alabama, back to the comfortable affairs people called normal lives.

"No boat," Threadgill said flatly. "No visits."

A latch clicked shut in his mind.

The Creole, disbelieving, let the pirogue drift slightly.

"*Monsieur*? No boat?"

"No boat. Matter of fact," Threadgill called up his fiercest glare, "I'll shoot you until my revolver is empty, if you ever come close to my island. Boom. Boom. Boom. Boom. Boom. BOOM. Understand?"

The smile froze on the face of the shocked ferryman. He nodded, once.

"You or anybody," Threadgill threatened. "I never want to see another person in this world."

Threadgill didn't own a gun. *But the ferryman doesn't know that, does he?*

The Creole's sons and grandsons and great-grandsons had watched in curiosity from the teetery stick house above the reeds as the old guide poled the thin young man with the feathered gray hat out to the island.

The patriarch returned just at dark, maneuvering the little boat alone through oyster-colored shallows. His family waited around a tall bonfire built to guide him home. Two dog-sized animals, dripping shiny fat down bayonet spits, roasted over the blaze.

The Creole gnawed his supper and worriedly told his family of the strange young man, of his ugly threat, his gun.

"We could row out and kill him!" growled one of the grandsons, reflected fire burning in his eyes.

It's okay, the old man told them, his hand raised. Be patient.

The old man took a bite of meat and chewed thoughtfully.

He will not, the Creole promised, have a very long life.

"Sor lives in the lagoon."

Chapter 35, Truckin'

Summer 1964 – North Alabama

Threadgill sat under his rainbow blanket on the bank of the river.

He knew in his bones the Greyhound used by the Freedom Riders had already departed. It made him happy. Threadgill did not want to travel another inch with that angry young man.

He thought of the stiff little monkey in the garbage can.

He thought of Ben.

In a while, Threadgill stood and put his back to the river and began to walk the kinks out of his bones along a northbound two-lane.

The Tennessee line would be only miles away now. He'd cross over out of Alabama at last. He'd be one state closer to Maine.

Finally.

An old pick-up truck farted into view. It was rusty red, painted by brush, the color of a barn. A stringbean mountain man with bushy black sideburns peered over the wheel.

He offered Threadgill a lift "just up a ways."

Threadgill tried to sleep with his helmeted head propped against the passenger door, but the uneven road surface jostled him too much.

In a while, the driver made conversation.

"Right over there," he mumbled, over a chew. "That's a meteor crater."

Threadgill sighed. He felt too bone-tired to be interested. He rubbed rough hands over his face. His head ached a little in his aluminum pot. Something hurt in his chest too.

"There's animal bones and turtle shells all in the bottom of it. Some kind of Indian eatin' joint, maybe. Played in there when I was a young 'un. Found arrowheads 'n' all kind of good stuff."

The truck sputtered past the black hole in the ground. Thick trees grew from the bottom of the crater. The morning sun would shine directly into the deep hole soon.

"Got my first piece of lovin' right yonder."

The driver slowed, hunched over slightly to see the memorable spot. He pointed vaguely at the crater.

"Gal's name was Eva Sweet. I ain't makin' that up. Eva Sweet. Sweet little Eva. Only gal I ever knew wanted to join the army. I shore wonder sometimes what happened to her. That one was a firecracker."

The truck driver, a long narrow man, leaned a little toward the window to spit. Threadgill wondered if he might have grown longer on one side walking these steep hills as a young man to see his Eva. He had popped eyes and a tiny head. Massive sideburns made his face look tiny.

"I mighta married her. But Eva used to keep snakes. That was just one habit I couldn't tolerate. Ain't no normal woman keeps a snake."

They rolled along. Threadgill felt a sharp pain in his head. Unexpectedly, a confession popped free.

"I ain't never been with a woman."

The sentence hung in the air for an awfully long time.

"Uh-HUH!" the driver finally said. He spat chew messily out the window.

"Don't go all flibbity on me. I ain't funny. The top of my head is missing. Women like their men to be complete, I reckon."

The driver said nothing, not another word.

He slowed the pick-up at the bottom of the next hill. Then he stopped. He sat at the wheel an uncomfortably long moment, silently staring straight ahead out the front windshield.

Threadgill took the hint. He sighed heavily. He climbed out of the cab.

The truck accelerated, changed gears, rolled on.

Chapter 36, The Island Army

1867 – Goat Island

Threadgill, late afternoon, stepped from the old Creole's jonboat onto his very first beach. He held everything he wanted or needed for this new life in his own two hands.

He did not spare a backward glance at the ferryman, smoothly poling away east on the blue mirror of Mobile Bay.

Instead, the young man gasped at the sky, a wild mountain range of summer clouds, some a thickening anvil-black at their bases. Far away to the south, over the Gulf of Mexico, a pitchfork of lightning stabbed the ocean. Fresh wind stirred the green island. A summer afternoon thunderstorm, faithful as religion, came his way.

Threadgill lugged his supplies up from the beach. Doing so, he discovered the first of the island's great secrets.

He set down a heavy nail keg in the white sand. All around its base lay some sort of blueberry-sized droppings, round and hard, like rabbit pills. Sweat fell off Threadgill's nose into them and on the soft sand.

The pills spread everywhere, thick as fallen acorns in autumn. Threadgill could not take a step without putting his shoe onto the odd spheres. He kicked at them, and the orbs avalanched down the beach, some rolling all the way to the surf. Little white ghost crabs scuttled away with these prizes, ducking down mysterious small tunnels in the sand.

At first Threadgill believed, happily, that the abundant leavings *were* rabbit pills. He smiled, sure of his skills at constructing rabbit snares. He would find plenty to eat, forever and always. He hadn't even begun to tally the kinds of fruit and bay fish and shellfish and birds and crabs and little wild animals he might spin over a fire here.

Just that moment, a pale shape shot ahead of Threadgill and made a splintery crash into the thick woods. Whatever the thing was, it made an unnerving sound – something really big had careened away through little scrub beach oaks and palmetto.

To Threadgill's dismay, he now could see countless weird eyes watching him, yellow and black and brown. The stares fixed him from under every little tree and bush and pile of driftwood.

Threadgill's shock went to the bone.

Yes, scores of baleful eyes observed him, unblinking, their dark pupils slit sideways, not up and down like every other wordly creature's.

The cold fright of that instant almost sent Threadgill sprinting back into the bay, flapping his arms frantically, screaming to the distant Creole for rescue.

Wolves? Devils? What in the world *were* these things? Threadgill could make out long hairy faces. Chewing, split-lipped mouths. Gleaming yellow eyes.

Threadgill yelled *yaaaaaaaaaaaaaaaaaaaaah*!

He crouched and brandished a beach stick in front of him like a sword. The rotted branch broke in two in his hand, fell ridiculously to the sand. Threadgill, more spooked than ever now, flung away the butt end of the wood and raised clenched fists.

"C'mon!" he yelled. "C'mon and get some, durn ye!"

Nothing at all happened.

Threadgill felt his false bravado collapse, like the rotted stick.

This would surely be the end of him. Now he knew he'd come to some place with naked savages in the undergrowth, killers with blowguns and bone clubs and poisoned arrows. He'd end his life like the gold-crazy Spanish explorers in his Aunt Annie's history book. Like Magellan. Like foolish Ponce de Leon.

Up where the beach white gave way to green, Threadgill now could clearly make out inhuman heads and rough beards and …

They appeared to have *horns!*

***

The restive tribe gathered in the shadows. One or two of the leaders stepped forward, into the hard sunlight of the beach.

Threadgill recoiled.

A frightful brown mask peered at him. And a white mask. And several black-and-white masks. Finally, yellow masks and gray and red, some bearing stripes the color of dry blood.

And Threadgill began to laugh – so hard he fell forward onto his face like a toppled Indian totem pole.

He sucked sand up his nose.

He laughed so hard his hat shook free and flew in the wind down toward the bay. Threadgill bounded to his feet, raced after it, swiped the hat from the tumbling surf with a joyful dive, then collapsed on his back in the dazzled sunlight, still laughing madly, sand all over his fine nose and lips, in his eyebrows, on top of his bare ruined head.

A Nubian goat put its curious nose to the top of Threadgill's scalp and sniffed wetly.

Goats!

A fierce tribe lived here alright – a tribe of goats. Big healthy happy stinky goats now stepped out from the trees on sturdy legs and cautiously flocked down the beach to see what on earth Threadgill could be – this gray thing rolling on the sand, bleating that way, with the chin whiskers and the strange furless newborn-goat-pink head.

The goats questioned Threadgill loudly.

Bwaaah! Bwaaaaaaah!

Threadgill sat and wiped his eyes and simply took it all in.

As far as he could see, goats. They thronged the beach. They lifted heads and horns from every conceivable hiding place.

Threadgill owned a herd! A huge herd of goats! Big goats, too – most stood as high as Threadgill's waist, and some could have placed their front legs on his shoulders with ease and licked his salty face.

A few of the males boasted iron-black horns so stout they actually intimidated Threadgill. Many nannies wagged big pink bags beneath, and baby goats pestered them. Every goat's short furry tail rose and fell almost like a separate live animal, and an endless supply of small black orbs tumbled constantly from their backsides.

Threadgill shook out a few goat droppings and patted his hat back onto his head. When he stood to appraise his gathered army, he found himself amazed once more.

Goats even lined the branches of trees!

Live oaks grew bent and twisted at beachside, mangled by wind, starved to preposterous dwarfish sizes by the poor sand. Yet just a few yards farther into the island, the oaks swelled to great heights, with branches that sagged to the ground. Nimble goats could easily scramble onto the limbs.

The arboreal goats were terrifically acrobatic. Threadgill watched a young one leap like one of its Rocky Mountain cousins, ascending higher and higher nearly to the top of one huge live oak. Threadgill could make out other dozens of the shaggy creatures staring down at him like sharpshooters, completely at ease in the sunshine-green dizzy heights.

Beyond the live oaks, Threadgill could make out a distant range of even taller trees – black tupelo and cypress and magnolia rose to preposterous heights out there. Threadgill could see creatures in these trees too, white egrets and tall blue herons and black anhingas and green herons, along with darting splashes of colorful birds he had never seen nor even imagined existed.

Threadgill brushed more sand and more clinging goat pills off himself. He cleared his throat.

"Y'all sure make a mess!"

He delivered his arrival speech, his first official words to a new island family.

***

The goat army parted like a red sea.

Threadgill stepped through, wrestling aside the more stubborn heads by smooth hard horns. Threadgill didn't laugh now – the weird goat eyes, no matter how hilarious, unnerved him slightly.

It was like being watched by the dead.

Nothing else in the cosmos had eyes like a goat – at least nothing Threadgill knew of. He always heard that Old Nick had such eyes.

Old Nick on Goat Island, thought Threadgill. *Me and my fuzzy little devils.*

Threadgill took notice of all the goat kids among the tribe, tottering to keep up with their nannies, butting one another in play, ducking beneath the mothers' fringed bellies to tug drops of milk from pink bags.

Milk! Another luxury! Goat Island might turn out to the best place Threadgill ever lived.

Threadgill surely looked like an Old Testament prophet as he led his complaining tribe down the worn paths that mazed the wilderness of Goat Island.

Threadgill wondered what century these animals had come to Goat Island. He knew goats could swim. These tough survivors might have washed down on spring floodwaters a hundred years ago from upriver plantations. Or they could have survived a French or Spanish shipwreck. They seemed tough as driftwood, able to find a way to live no matter what.

Like Threadgill, maybe.

He marveled at their sheer numbers. No question, a man here on Goat Island could find meat. He could find greens to supplement his goat diet too. Threadgill would eat what goats ate; what didn't kill a goat probably wouldn't kill him. He now shed any worries about predators too. There couldn't possibly be so many goats if dangerous predators – wildcats, wolves or bears – prowled here.

Threadgill pondered this last fact for a moment, a slow dawning in his mind.

Was goat meat tasty?

He remembered that Negroes roasted goats on huge open-pit fires from time to time. The newly freed slaves around Eufaula, in fact, delighted in these events. But most white people disdained goat as questionable food.

Maybe it was those eyes …

Threadgill knew one thing for sure – life just changed for all these capricious little fellows.

***

The goat army blithely tailed Threadgill, bawling and calling, as he explored. Sometimes they spooked mob-style, stampeding in starts and fits. Then they milled about as if embarrassed by their hysteria.

He came to a monumental tree, a cypress heaving up from a lovely standing black pond of fresh water. It took Threadgill's long legs thirty splashing paces to circle the trunk of the behemoth. He could not remember a bigger tree. Spanish moss dragged the water from its low limbs. Honeybees sparked in and out of a knothole.

He realized all at once that a curious silence hung over this spot. Threadgill looked back at the bank of the pond, a little uneasy.

Every goat had vanished from sight. Not one *baaa*! came from the thick woods.

How very odd, Threadgill thought, as he slogged back out of thigh-deep water onto dry ground.

When did goats get to be afraid of bees?

***

Threadgill tromped back to the beach, rejoining his crowd of shaggy admirers.

The goats spent the rest of that first darkening afternoon loudly and fussily advising their new master on how to construct a lean-to.

Goats scattering from his path, Threadgill first dragged together a clattery pile of dry driftwood poles. He buried the smooth ends of the poles in sand to form a standing row, leaned at a sharp angle away from the constant sea wind.

Between these anchor uprights, he laid smaller branches and still-smaller reeds, tying them in place with some of his Creole rope, then using hardy vine that railroaded out of the woods and down over the beaches. Threadgill used his knife to hack down a few incredibly tough saw palmetto fronds, which he wove in to block the wind. Those would keep the rain off. Threadgill had often used palmetto just like this to waterproof the boy forts he built in the woods back home.

Those woods in Eufaula taught him as much as any human ever had. In his boyhood, Threadgill raised and tore down a dozen hide-outs. After brother Ben showed up, of course, the forts got bigger, with rooms two boys could stand in and once even a secret tunnel under the floor. In their last fort, the twins wrestled together a rock fireplace with a limestone-and-mud chimney. When a fire burned, Threadgill loved to see the old seashell prints and fossils flicker in the shadow and light.

Dark stole over Goat Island. Threadgill's first night arrived. The wind shifted, rattling the lean-to. Threadgill stood back and proudly admired his temporary island shelter. The goats passed freely in and out of it, clearly impressed … and maybe a little suspicious of a thing so new.

Threadgill should have paid attention.

That night, a summer thunder storm swept in from the Gulf of Mexico, a howling electrical terror like no storm Threadgill had ever seen before. He surfaced in a panic from bottomless sleep to find the smell of lightning thick in the air. Convinced for a moment he'd somehow gone back in time to Pine Mountain in battle, Threadgill reared straight up. He clouted his soft bare head on the side of the lean-to.

All at once, as if signaled, the rain flew at Threadgill from every direction, lean-to or no, and it kept on attacking him that same way for three hours. Threadgill literally soaked until his bones felt soft.

Finally, the lean-to flopped down entirely. Threadgill admitted defeat and limped soggily away deeper into the wet woods. He crawled under the first wide fallen tree trunk he found, a stick in hand to whack any cottonmouth or small fierce animal with a prior claim to the precious dry ground.

Threadgill found a row of goats happily dozing here, piled in mounds, dry as camels in a desert.

Threadgill swallowed his pride and snuggled in among them, warmed and more than a little grateful.

Gale winds snapped limbs off big cypresses and oaks all night. The woods around Threadgill lit in ghastly panoramas as barbed green chains of lightning phosphored and hissed overhead. From time to time, a broken limb plummeted and Threadgill could see goats out in the woods scramble in ghostly waves to new hiding places.

And, Lord, the thunder! It shocked drops off gleaming leaves every time it boomed, and then the howling gusts turned the leaves inside out on black branches.

Waves slammed into the island, once or twice so hard that Threadgill felt the very ground beneath him shake, soft as pudding. The canopies of the trees roared like shaggy green lions.

Threadgill's heart beat twice as fast. One beat, he was so afraid. The next beat, he thrilled with the pure adventure. One beat, he cringed. New beat, he wanted to leap up and run out into the storm naked and screaming with joy.

He never got another wink of sleep that first night.

***

He woke in a bird-brightened morning. Threadgill climbed soggily to his feet. One goat eagerly licked his hand, apparently enjoying the salt. Or was it trying to eat him?

Threadgill shooed the beast. He stretched out the kinks of the arduous night, brushing sand and bits of leaf from every part of himself.

Hunger spoke loudly, but Threadgill started out his first full day on the island by picking his way up and down the beach, surveying the impact of a real bay storm. The curious goats followed.

It turned out to be a good thing Threadgill had company.

New arrivals in the night covered the shores of Goat Island – entire trees, enormous ones, ripped free weeks or months or even years ago out of the iron hills of north Alabama and the limestone river banks of Tuscaloosa and the chalk cliffs of Selma and the sedge brush plains of Montgomery. Pine logs and muddy hardwood trunks rolled over and over in the slow waves like drowned sailors.

The entire island today wore this new belt, a beach barricade of planks and trunks and branches and ropes and tangled vines and boots and fence posts and clothes and seaweed and other odd chunks of civilized world. Threadgill saw a goat triumphantly lift a lady's riding glove out of the surf and trot haughtily toward the woods with his prize, chased by jealous peers. Threadgill spied a bent horseshoe, twisted tight round a scrawny uprooted pine. Over there lay the head off a child's stick horse.

One object amazed him.

At the center of a charred hole in the beach on the Mobile side of the island stood a still-smoking antler of fused silica, blackened and forked, like a primitive glass tree. It reminded Threadgill of one of those strange carved woodland figures left by old Amos at planting and harvest times behind Aunt Annie's field. Totems to his African gods.

After much pondering, Threadgill guessed this must be lightning – an actual lightning bolt. He reckoned one of the lightning strikes in the storm struck sand here and melted the beach into its own replica, a blast turning sand to glass.

The goats swarmed the lightning bolt, worriedly sniffing the air and loudly bleating, their split black lips quivering.

Threadgill took the natural glass into the woods. He found it still hot, heavy and awkward, so he carried it in front of him on two driftwood poles, one under each arm. He set the lightning bolt upright on the thick back of a fallen live oak trunk.

The morning sun twinkled along the bolt's black-and-silver surfaces like a chandelier. Threadgill saw the gamboling goats multiplied in the facets.

The lightning bolt would be a remembering place. A commemoration of

Threadgill's arrival on the island.

It would come to commemorate even more.

Threadgill stepped back, sweating, to fully admire his newly installed sculpture. His foot came down on something pulpy.

It squirmed.

Threadgill knew instantly. Every boy raised in the South knows.

He leaped without thinking, on pure instinct. But he already knew it would be too late.

It was not possible to save yourself after you put your foot down on a cottonmouth.

The moccasin writhed, doughy and black, like a live turd. It boggled the mind that something so ugly could move so fast. But the snake struck like lightning itself – black deadly lightning.

A shovel-shaped head hurtled toward Threadgill's leg, the poison-mushroom mouth gaped wide, screaming, almost laughing.

That would have been how Threadgill Pickett died.

Except for the goats.

The goats saved his life.

Somehow, with speed quicker than Threadgill imagined possible, a big black ram vaulted forward from nowhere and seized the snake in mid-air behind its gasping head. The reptile twisted, flailed and struck blindly at the air, but it didn't matter. In no time, a dozen other snorting goats charged in and ripped the snake into small red mouthfuls.

The cottonmouth's severed head thudded down right by Threadgill's foot. Its snake eyes stared.

The goats chewed thoughtfully, appraising the taste of their black-and-red snack. The herd also kept their own strange eyes riveted on Threadgill, clearly watching for his reaction.

Well I'll be damned, Threadgill whistled to himself. His legs suddenly felt like warm jelly. *Well, I never.*

He'd never, ever, eat a bite of goat meat, was what he meant to say.

***

The litter that washed onto the shores of Goat Island would forever fascinate Threadgill.

Below scavenging clouds of sea gull and brown pelican, he salvaged gifts of ship dock, barnacled timbers, twisted metal tools, thick hawsers, uprooted thickets of native bamboo, shrouds of sailcloth, globs of pitch, oakum and tar, dead fish and stingrays and birds and skeletons he could not even name.

Once, a huge flat fish thing noisily washed up into the surf, beating enormous broad wings like a bat and brandishing a sharp coachwhip tail. It took the birds and crabs and goats three whole days to eat its black corpse.

Through the coming decades, Threadgill would discover even stranger things – gaskets and bags and hot-water bottles and life preservers and ice chests and ship buoys and stiff fishing rods and coat hangers and Coke bottles and strollers and rubber balls in every color and size. He had no earthly idea what people did with most of the stuff. Some objects, as far as he could tell, arrived as simple riddles meant to bewilder him.

Whatever the item, not much Threadgill found went to waste. And the goats took what Threadgill didn't. They ate almost anything. Threadgill noticed they had a special fondness for little pink baby dolls.

Occasionally, a magazine or a page of newspaper washed in. Threadgill would discover the melting paper halfway buried under heavy bay sand. Or he'd pull up an entire hardcover book, its loose, sopping pages sloppily riffling in the waves.

He carefully dried these literary discoveries on sunny limbs too limber for goats to climb. Threadgill loved reading whatever he found in the pages.

At night, Threadgill stared up at the golden stars, newspaper or battered book on his chest, the fire crackling beside him on the beach. The music of goats played, always.

***

Survival on an island doesn't depend on news. You mostly need an ax. You need fire.

And it helps to know how to dig rich-yolked sea turtle eggs and how to pull up swarming silver alewives in a cast net, and how to knot a clever snare to capture the feet of birds when they land. It helps to patiently learn to tell the edible seaweeds from the awful ones, and how to identify which species of wood-ear and oyster mushroom to chop free of dead gum and tupelo trunks. More than a timepiece, you need tough vines for binding, and fishing lines scavenged from a beach, and wood piled high to dry, day after day after day.

It took years for Threadgill to build a proper dwelling, cool enough in the summer, warm enough in the cold bay winters.

The young man figured it out piece by piece, raising driftwood poles, topping these with layers and layers and layers of saw palmetto and sago palm fronds. Years later, he would replace the thatch with long, battered sheets of corrugated tin, ripped by wind off Alabama barns and sheds far inland and brought to him twisted like curtains by the surging rivers and unpredictable currents. Threadgill eventually took down the driftwood poles he used for walls and rafters too, upgrading them with real milled poles, flooded away from docks upstate, or spilled overboard off lumber barges.

Through the years, he built a perfect hut. Threadgill could now lie on his bed of moss-stuffed cloth in the most furious storms, and never feel a drop of rain or a puff of gale.

Threadgill set up the shelter not too far from the island's lone freshwater pond, a miracle that somehow percolated right out of the ground on Goat Island and kept every creature there alive.

The titi and Alabama cane brakes fought for space around the fresh water. These plants shot up in dense patches along the pond's one-acre girth. Red-eared turtles and ebony crawfish that looked like something hammered from a wicked blacksmith's forge, and bright little needles of freshwater fish swam right up to Threadgill's hand, absolutely tame, when he came to the pond to get a drink.

The goats, weirdly, never got near the place.

Goats were just like that, he reckoned. Maybe they drank salty water. Or rain.

One morning, Threadgill leaned forward on his hands and knees with his face kissing the beautiful sunlit surface. The water sponged into his beard like Spanish moss. It tasted sweet, faintly of tree leaves, like a tea.

Threadgill washed his face the way a raccoon does in fresh cool water. Something about the light and the blowing shade of the tall cypress trees made him think of Sunday. He admired his reflection in the bright water.

A few feet away, something huge rose from the water and opened its jaws.

Threadgill, his face down, at first thought night had suddenly fallen.

Chapter 37, Yellowhammer Boston

Massachusetts now. Yellowhammer draws closer.

The Bay State rises grimly from the ocean, barer than any other place Yellowhammer has seen so far. Huge bald stones, in jumbles, hold patches of forest. To the east, rocks ring timber fishing villages. White cottages cling in places to the coast like barnacles.

Yellowhammer sees stony hills that seemed scraped into place by some gigantic child only weeks ago, a simple-minded child with a dull-toothed rake. Pebbles scattered everywhere. Some, big as houses, gape with awesome cracks. Yellowhammer wonders if sheer cold broke them open.

Yellowhammer wonders what escaped from them.

Boston seems tired, the most unsummery town in the world, its steeple bells beating in the morning mist like dying hearts. People pass without speaking. The vendors of newspapers and food make change with no acknowledgements. A beggar coughs into a car window, shaking a cup for money.

Yellowhammer veers. Through a vast mist glint picture-book views of the wild Atlantic. Boats beat toward the great fishing banks. The waves leap up and down against the hulls, trying to pull themselves aboard.

Another wildness – this one land – comes to light.

Maine. At last.

Chapter 38, The Beast of Goat Island

A monstrous alligator rose from the Goat Island water pond – a black-ish-green mountain range.

The creature's swollen body was the girth of a Viking ship, and the pond poured off its back in a roaring waterfall. The reptile's pale mouth gaped wide, and chopped chunks of fish as big as puppies dangled from the bladed grin.

The alligator flicked its huge tail once. It lunged forward toward the sandy bank, and it clamped its great jaws right over Threadgill's head and shoulders. The gate-like jaws slammed shut so fast Threadgill felt hot air rush out in all directions, sand and leaves whooshed away by a giant leather bellows.

He never had time to rise off his knees.

All at once some part of Threadgill Pickett actually seemed to separate and stand apart from his body, a fascinated onlooker. Threadgill didn't even feel much pain at first. The whole business might have been happening to someone else. He heard crunches and bony popping noises and some sort of wet sounds. He thought of a big dog noisily feeding.

Blood welled from dozens of punctures in Threadgill. The lacerations of alligator teeth felt like tusk wounds from a wild hog. Threadgill could feel his chest and ribs smash like a bird egg.

Still, even halfway down the alligator's reeking gullet, his feet kicking from the snout, Threadgill discovered in his head one of the queerest emotions of his life.

Pity.

Even dying, eaten alive … Threadgill still felt an uncanny true sorrow for the thing killing him.

The beast was just so … ugly. Just so hideous. In its life, it would always be despised and deeply feared by every other living thing. This alligator would sleep in the gloom of its own lost world, rise out of the deep to kill when it must, sink back to nowhere with its black thoughts bubbling and oozing, only now and then, toward the light. It would hate and never hope, plot and never plan. A creature like this would live a hundred years or more with no calling on earth beyond a pure reptile appetite. It would live to kill, and killing would be life. Forever.

Am I different? A thin voice inside Threadgill whispered the question.

Pain finally crashed through his defenses, and his pity washed away in screams.

So came fear. Threadgill felt himself swallowed. A gulp of thrown-back alligator jaws took his shoulders most of the way down a throat aswirl with reeking turtle chunks and sour blinding burning juices. Threadgill's head now wedged in airless tight utter blackness, his sensitive scalp and eyes seared by gastric acid.

What a predicament! A perfect Sunday … you blink … and you slide down the maw of an alligator. You die, inside an alligator.

Gulp!

The creature turned back a long blackgreen happy head, slit eyes partly closed with pleasure now, and with a giant swallow it gobbled down another healthy section of Threadgill Pickett.

Threadgill's whole head now washed in a lagoon of corrosive digestive juices and scraps of bone and shell. These sloshed loudly around in the monster's belly like tides in a cave.

Only one of Threadgill's bare feet now remained outside the reptile snout. Had a stranger on Goat Island come upon the scene, he would have marveled at the spectacle: An enormous alligator lay grinning in the sun. A set of five white toes waggled from its toothy snout like a cuttlefish.

Swallowed alive by an alligator, Threadgill shuddered, over a howling hurricane of pains.

Who could imagine his life ending this way?

***

It truly might have been the end of Threadgill Pickett, his undocumented primitive last call. Maybe a merciful end.

But the cold cruel world proved crueler yet.

Threadgill distantly heard a great primal roar.

That noise startled him even inside an alligator, even over screaming nerves and the sizzle of digesting skin. The roar certainly startled the alligator, Threadgill realized. It stopped swallowing him.

That wasn't all.

Threadgill felt a sudden twist, a giddy whirl. He bounced along for thumping short strides as his alligator scampered a few panicky steps on stumpy legs.

What in the world? Threadgill had mind enough to think. *What stopped this final meal?*

Amazingly, he found himself airborne.

Some gargantuan force had lifted Threadgill clean off the earth, alligator and all. And whatever-it-was shook Threadgill violently, so hard and fast his head rattled inside his wrinkled reptile casement like a seed in a leather gourd.

He next heard a tremendous moist ripping noise … and Threadgill all at once saw sunlight around him.

Sunlight.

Threadgill blinked.

He couldn't believe it – here shone the same Sunday light that just a few minutes ago gilded a pond as he knelt on his prayer bones to wash his face, take a cool drink.

How long since he last breathed fresh air?

Threadgill sobbed oxygen, sucked it down, a drowning whaler dragged to safety at the last moment over the gunwales of a harpoon boat.

It took him a stunned moment to blink away the burning stomach acid and make sense of his surroundings.

Here was a miracle. Somehow, he lived, outside the monster.

What saved me? How am I still on this world?

Then came just the second moment of his life he felt too scared to move. And not even seeing his brother in the hands of the Yankee army had given him quite the same shock as this one.

A second alligator – the terrible mother of all alligators – had risen from the pond.

Threadgill had never seen *any* animal so big, of any kind. This monstrous alligator, this primeval creature, made the first one look like a garden lizard. Threadgill could have stretched out and taken a nap between her eyes. Her nostrils blasted out air like black cannons.

With one powerful close of her jaws, this new monster had bitten the first alligator right in half. *Snap*, like that.

In fact, she had swallowed in one bite an entire *half* of the first alligator.

Only a tail now waggled from the beast's snout, writhing and lashing, a great green hungry tongue.

Threadgill twisted his bleached face and gasped air again. He could make out his situation now – he remained encased in the severed head and jaws of the first alligator.

His memory flashed to life. He remembered more than once cleaning a mess of catfish caught in the Chattahoochee River, throwing the ugly heads into the slow water.

Now *he* was a catfish head. His face peered out the bloody stump neck of a throwaway, and one foot hung from the long snout.

Threadgill heard a goat bawl somewhere.

The monster alligator's enormous eye shone big and yellow as a lantern-lit tent, with the same up-and-down slit at the entrance.

The creature surveyed Threadgill.

The young captive could see nothing in that reptile eye he understood.

Threadgill stayed very still. He wished he looked less like a sausage in a biscuit. He wished a lot of things.

Nothing happened until Threadgill made an offer.

"I'll bring you … bring you fish!"

He hardly recognized his own words – his throat had been seared hoarse, garbled by harsh stomach juices, his lips scalded.

The great knotty head tipped back in the black water and gulped, and the last squirming slither of alligator tail disappeared down its gullet. The toothy mouth closed with a faint click.

The alligator eyes gave nothing away.

"I'll bring you the biggest fish I catch. I'll throw them in the pond for you!" Threadgill rasped, barely able to finish. He suddenly felt the woozy shock of blood loss and trauma. The truth hit him like a falling tree.

He understood, with complete clarity, that he must get free of the gullet now, free himself quickly … or else die.

This day was proving to be overstuffed with luck, bad and good. The bad would be most obvious. But on the good side, Threadgill now found that violent death had slightly loosened the straitjacket of the alligator's throat and jaws. The carcass had gone limp. He felt wiggle room.

In fact, Threadgill gave one little push on the ground with his extended wiggling toes … and his whole body gushed forward.

He slid straight out of the severed alligator head onto the good warm sand of Goat Island. Lubricated by his own slick blood and the juices of throat and stomach, Threadgill scooted free, wet and limp. He was a baby born a second time … from a mother like no other.

The mighty alligator, the one the Creoles called Sor, stared from the pond. Not a muscle flexed. A blue dragonfly shimmered out of the cypresses and lit in a patch of sunlight atop the knobbed black head.

Threadgill lifted his own injured head. Breathing weakly, he made a promise.

"I'll be good to you."

It must have been promise enough.

The great creature in the pond slowly sank, down and down, until only two yellow eyes remained.

Threadgill mustered the will to crawl … and somehow found the strength too. Feeble, he made it as far forward as the pond. He lowered his lips to the surface again, just where he'd been when this terror began.

He drank and drank. He was somehow no longer concerned that the new alligator would simply open its jaws and swallow him like a white minnow.

It would have happened already. I'd already be gone.

He weakly splashed fresh water over countless new wounds.

The serrations of the first alligator's teeth tattooed him – stitching clear around his middle, scoring his thighs and buttocks, patterning his upper arms, even crusting the back of his neck. The wounds, he knew, were deep and dirty.

Life. Again, he had to fight to live. Threadgill had a tough row to hoe. Everything hung in the balance again.

He faced infection and fever and thirst and hallucination and blowflies and … who in the world knew what else? He would be lucky to live through this mauling. If you called it luck.

He raised his head, chin dripping water.

Two inscrutable yellow eyes sank like twin round suns. Without a blink of pity or praise, they disappeared.

This is the world, Threadgill thought. *This is the world we live in.*

Chapter 39, The Waters

Goat Island

Flock by flock, the birds went away.

The great blue herons rose first. In Threadgill's view, these sentinels seemed always the most aware of the island's creatures.

Threadgill lay in the sand under bladed palmettos. Flies swarmed his wounds, but he could not muster the will to shoo them. A fever from the alligator lacerations flowed like snake poison through his body, looping round and round, a coiling cold. The sounds of snuffling beasts and crying wind outdid the drummy thrum of fever in his head. Threadgill saw visions, felt the touch of sun and moon and creatures and inhuman things.

What made him even notice the blue herons? Maybe their beauty – Threadgill sensed the shadows of the first dozen or so of the great birds as they left off their priestly rounds and flapped sloppily up from black-mirror wading pools. Despite their great fanning, somehow these enormous creatures with their four-foot wingspans never even stirred the Spanish moss that clouded high branches.

Threadgill squinted into bright air. The birds looked beautiful, long, elegant. He felt something in him stir, a will to join them, to just fly off.

The blowflies landed on his lips. He blurted them away, a noise like a sob, a curse.

Next, Goat Island gave up songbirds. These departed almost by musical sections – thrashers, jays, finches, warblers. Threadgill felt as if he lost parts of his hearing one layer at a time.

The island grew quiet. He managed to raise his torso on mangled elbows. Threadgill perceived small flocks of heavy-beaked crows and red-headed woodpeckers as they moved away in colorful clouds, one bush and branch to the next, headed in fits and starts for the mainland. All moving away from the gulf.

The gulls passed over, white as the blown-loose pages of books.

Now Threadgill felt a real unease. The flies left him too, one by one buzzing up from the scores of scabs and open wounds where his skin had once held him together. Like that, his wounds breathed clean air.

Without the weight of the insects, his body lightened, almost floated.

A constant wind from the southeast grew stronger and stronger. The trees wagged their fingers, scolding.

What in the world was happening?

Threadgill painfully turned his head to the gusts. His red beard fluttered – his chin whiskers had lengthened and flushed out now, after all these days on the island. Since the alligator mauling, a part of the beard had prematurely silvered, like Spanish moss in moonlight.

Threadgill could better see the mysterious bird departures now. He found to his dismay that color left the scrub all around him, bright flocks zinging like grasshoppers, winging away through hard sunlight and soft shadow, into and past the cool arcades of oak limbs, then over open water toward Mobile and the mainland. Now he wasn't only losing his hearing. Colors vanished too.

Overhead, in a deep white V that arrowed through the firmament, a flock of cattle ibis flapped inland. A reed marsh coughed up one last cloud of redwing blackbirds, and they went boiling away too, growing small as a gnat swarm before they disappeared altogether into the distant green sawgrass of the mainland.

Mallards whirred, wings beating hard, necks stretched. More birds chased them – a flock of coots, threes and fours of wood ducks, black cormorants. Terns flew extremely high over the other birds, a scatter in darkening sky. Pelicans passed too, long filades that made their own V, fifteen birds at a time, their wings so close to the water that Threadgill could swear only magic kept them off the roughening bay.

Sparrows swarmed off, an endless rocketry of them, soundless but for an eerie applause of beating wings. A red cloud of cardinals flushed from a camphor tree. Curlews and sandpipers skittered in and out of the dollar plants and railroad vines and sea oats, coming at last to the beach. Their feet wrote strange warning letters on the sand. They launched just in time to avoid a splash of ocean foam at its highest point up the hissing beach.

Finally, the ospreys sailed over Threadgill, their scimitar shadows cutting the clouded light fast as an eyeblink. These predators today ignored the gulls and skimmers and other birdlife that would normally have been easy meals, a sudden bomb-burst of feathers in the sky, a shrill scream drifting.

What in the world? Threadgill wondered – had he missed some signal? Were all the world's birds migrating this single day?

He had witnessed events of surpassing strangeness in his time on Goat Island. He once saw a wooden ship ablaze from stem to stern, passing the island in the deep night, and he marveled at how the metal parts of the ship glowed white-orange like hot iron in a blacksmith's forge. Little dark man-shapes fell, burning, off the sides into its fiery reflection in the bay.

Another night, Threadgill saw a shooting star that split into three smoking chimes, a trick from a genie's hand. These triple bombs exploded in wracking, spectacular whitebursts over the phosphorescent bay.

Threadgill even once saw some kind of sea creature, black as a hole, rise from the ocean nothingness into yellow moonlight on a summer evening. Amazed, he watched as lesser fish – were they dolphins? – circled in joy around the leviathan. Sea birds settled on the beast's back and walked its spine like old sightseers. Threadgill could make out that a great fishing net draped one end of the thing. He watched the dolphins pick at the net, tugging and fussing, until the rotted bonds finally fell away. At that instant, the dolphins vanished, the birds rose, and whatever the deep-sea thing was snorted and blew a plume of white steam from its head and sank into the sea.

A man remembered anything here on Goat Island that changed the rituals. Even while he struggled to stay alive, nursing wounds that needed more than hope, the sameness of night and day, tide and beach, animals on their rounds, gave Threadgill a way to measure the life left in a day … and inside himself.

Still, Threadgill had never seen anything like this morning – the birds of his island leaving so fast for Mobile and all points inland.

It *could* be migration. Threadgill fixed the sun and tried to measure how many days until Fall. The evenings came sooner now, and sometimes night had the ghost of a chill. Maybe this year the birds went away early. Maybe today marked the day they lifted up together and waved their wings goodbye.

Threadgill turned his injured head to one side. To his surprise, he now saw other island animals joined in the freakish behavior. Ghost crabs, pale, scuttled up the beach toward the bushes. Threadgill could see them climbing like spiders into the limbs, so many that they weighed the branches down, hung like little white apples.

A raccoon chattered past, then two more. A thing with a shell that he'd never seen before, a small round animal that looked like a sailor's concertina, snuffled past. Threadgill was amazed to spot an otter, galloping in a curvy run up from the surf and toward a hole high in the root ball of a toppled cypress.

Most surprising of all – most disturbing to Threadgill suddenly – was the boldness of a pair of wildcats. Those were the most reclusive animals on the island, and Threadgill gaped as two mates padded up the path towards him, approaching to a point only feet away before uneasily slipping off the trail. With a relieved exhalation, Threadgill watched the pair grapple up the trunk of a lonely lightning-blasted oak.

The big cats disappeared, slipping entirely from view into a hollow shaped like a man's screaming mouth. Threadgill then witnessed something utterly improbable – a gray squirrel scrambled up the same trunk and tucked into the same hole with the cats. In a few minutes, so did a sleek opossum, climbing slow and fat and steady.

Threadgill strained to hear furious sound as the cats mauled their natural prey. But he heard nothing. In fact, after a few moments, he was astonished to see the little gray squirrel peek out of the hollow, look at him straight in the eye, scold the heavy sky, *tut tut*, then pop back down the chute.

One of the wildcats poked up its head next. It stared balefully, eyes green as lanterns on a passing ship. After a long, steady appraisal, it disappeared back into the hole without a sound.

***

Fever. Delusion. Hallucination.

The poison of the alligator attack surely ravaged Threadgill's poor brain. What else would make a man see such impossible things?

Threadgill felt a cold knot of fear at the bottom of his windpipe … just where he once made words. He knew speech didn't matter now, words would prove useless to any purpose in the universe.

A wave raced all the way up the beach to where he lay and licked his torn foot, tasted his flesh and blood.

All at once, he understood. The rising wave finally taught him.

It all boiled down to will now. The will to do as all the animals did. The will to get up and move to higher ground, to heights. To live.

Something terrible would happen soon.

His wounds did not matter.

He would die if he did not get to high places away from the water.

A fear rose in Threadgill that actually lifted him to his feet – he felt the old emotion grasp the scruff of his neck and jerk him upright. Crusted gashes and lacerations popped and hollered, opened little yelling mouths of pain. But Threadgill also found a stick in his hand and staggered with it, swinging crazy around its maypole, down the island path to find a higher spot.

What place could a man go here?

He walked until a black cloud and stinging rain struck and then he crawled to find the way.

***

Threadgill rose fast from the bottom of a river of pained sleep.

He reached surface to find the wind blowing very hard, steady all over the world, leaves flattening, branches fending gusts like matadors.

How many hours had he been under water, under the exhausted dream, the fever? The sky looked completely black, and rain spattered his simple hut, squirting through the cracks in places.

A noise startled Threadgill. He jerked around painfully to see one of the island's foxes – the pretty, long-nosed vixen that lived in the reeds on the south end – hassling loudly in the doorway of his palmetto hut. She looked at him strangely. Did she mean to come inside the hut? Her little black eyes shone in the red fur, and her worried whiskers twitched drops of rain.

In a moment, she trotted away, looking back once to see if Threadgill followed.

At first, he did not. He lay flat, eyes glazed, and watched her sideways as she trotted nimbly down a path and into the troubled overgrowth.

Threadgill got her message now. The hut would not be safe enough. He could still find a way to live. He had to do what the other animals did.

He opened up his wounds again and heaved to his sandy bleeding feet and hobbled out into the cold rain. By now it had turned so dark Threadgill had trouble seeing the path the fox fled, and with certain gusts he felt the rain might take the little remaining hide right off him. Sand scoured him one gust, then raindrops, stinging hot then stinging cold in the same single whip lash of wind.

The vixen led Threadgill to an old shell mound, a mysterious rise in the flat landscape of his little barrier island. Thick grass flattened and hissed along its top. Here rose one of the few spots on the island where real grass grew, deep and luxuriant. And among the high blades, nestled like lambs in a summer field, lay a startling menagerie – foxes and opossums and tiny gray mice and a mother raccoon and her babies. Threadgill limped on his stick a few feet closer and saw a pair of wide-eyed marsh rabbits, a big gopher tortoise with a gaping beak, even a shivering green heron with a malformed wing. Against all odds of nature, some common survival instinct counter-manded the lusts and enmity and hungers of the tough little island animals. Their hostilities lay by the wayside. Some threat now loomed so terrible it changed all Goat Island into a peaceable kingdom.

The red vixen slipped up the side of the mound, curled herself snugly into a ball. She lay down to wait with her nose in the grass, her sides heaving nervously, and she closed her eyes. Threadgill noticed then for the first time that she had fox kits huddled in the circle her body formed.

Threadgill crawled onto the mound on trembling hands and knees and lay down with the little red vixen curved into the hollow of his own torn body.

He closed his eyes and imagined what the end of the world would be like. He thought yet again of poor Ben, that hot dry death in Georgia. This death, tonight's flavor, would be very different. When it came to destruction, the universe seemed to find no end of creativity.

The hills around Threadgill this night would differ from those of Geor-gia. Tonight's peaks would grow no trees, hold no rocks. They'd be gray and wild with foam. Wind-blown spray would blast them hard as buckshot and those mountains themselves lunge at the land with frightening speed.

Threadgill laughed out loud suddenly.

It was a sound so surprising it startled even him. Every one of the beasts on the mound raised a head and cringed in fear, some halfway to their feet, ready to skedaddle. Most of them had never heard Threadgill make any sound at all, other than the tramping shuffle of his bare feet and the unruly noises of his island work.

"Storm coming, y'all!" he whooped, crazy with something in the air. "God damn it!"

He felt drunk – at least he guessed this was how drunkenness felt. He flailed a long arm southward – the gesture brought every animal bolt to its feet.

"Think Threadgill Pickett don't see what's about to happen? I might of been born at night, friends … but not *last* night."

He howled with laughter and fell back, suffering, his bare back flat on the cool grass. The rain fell hard onto his face and eyes. Out in the woods, he heard something enormous splinter and tear away, a branch or trunk ripped down.

Threadgill felt the hysteria pass, and a calm settle over him. He tugged his hat down over his eyes, its brim dripping.

Here is what would happen. Here were his options.

He could sink. He could swim. He could live. He could die.

All around him, Threadgill could feel and hear the little animals gradually settle again. He looked at them. Their little heads seemed bowed in prayer.

For a crazy impossible moment, the sun burst out of nowhere and burned heroically overhead. Threadgill watched it just that long. He wondered if it would be the last time he ever saw sunlight.

He could easily cross the border and pass on into the gray mists now, like his brother. He could follow so many others. The grotesque soldier he found by the roadside in Georgia. Poor pretty Eva. His momma, and his father, and his lovely Aunt Annie.

Threadgill felt something sharp against his foot.

He looked down, frowning. Without realizing it, he had scraped with his bare foot down into the top of the mound. A big clump of cover grass had come away, and Threadgill's heel rattled a collection of old clamshells underneath. The insides of the mound poured out, in fact, as he idly worked the opening, the bleached shells spilling like pieces of eight from a ripped treasure bag. With a few nervous kicks, Threadgill undid the work of hundreds of years of Choctaws, the dumped baskets of clam shells that had formed this mound pouring away.

The wind screamed and leaves and bay foam whipped past. So what? Threadgill refused to make his foot stop. In the morning, the whole shell mound could be on the bottom of the sea fifty miles out. Threadgill pictured his scarecrow body rolling along on a sandy bottom somewhere, studded with hungry blue crabs like medals.

That moment, his foot felt a sharp sting. He jerked it back. Blood ran from a new cut along his instep, not deep but clean and painful. How about that? Threadgill marveled he even had any blood left after the alligator mauling. What a thing, a man's body …

The animals spooked slightly again as Threadgill struggled upright to see what had cut him. The wind pasted the brim of his gray hat flat against his forehead.

A metal edge glinted in a quick flash of lightning. Threadgill yanked, and the clam shells parted with a noise like spilling marbles. The youngster extracted something from the loose heap. He pulled, and it came out and out and *still* kept coming.

The wind gave a mad howl now, blustering, and the Spanish moss overhead stood straight out from frantic limbs before it tore away in gobbets and whipped off into the wet night.

Threadgill marveled. Brown with age and corrosion, an old Civil War sword lay across his lap. He raised it in the air and the blade cut a musical note in the wind. The sword curved slightly from point to handle, and its handle flared outward like a hoop skirt.

Just under the sword's quillon, the calcified bones of a hand still gripped the handle, brandishing it righteously even now, years after probable death in a sea battle and transport by wave and unlikely burial in this place.

The little collection of animals stared in bewilderment at Threadgill.

One of the raccoons even bolted from the mound. Threadgill watched the masked creature disappear into the tangles of sea oak, now flat and trembling under the wind. Regret brimmed in him.

He lay the sword down to keep from scaring the other creatures. Then he stretched out beside it, almost on top of it, his arm shielding it.

Now he had a weapon. Now he would wage war against wind. He vowed he would never die without a fight. He vowed he would live forever, if it took that, to pay back the pain that Ben felt, that he'd been forced to suffer. What did he ever do but be born? Why did he deserve the wounds, the hurt?

Threadgill may have dreamed it, but for hours and hours he stood on top of the mound, slashing at the wind and the water. He hacked the heads off countless waves, and severed one monstrous gust after another. The wind blew every stitch of his clothes off as he fought … all except the old yellow-hammer hat, which would not let go.

Finally wind and a great wave swept Threadgill away entirely, out into the night, over and over in the dark, bound for glory, the sword lost, everything lost.

Chapter 40, After the Storm

Goat Island

Threadgill held fast, blown bodily into the tossing top of the island's great cypress tree.

He clung there through the whole long night of his first hurricane.

His fingers knotted into the bark – deep, then deeper – while colossal waves battered Goat Island.

The towering cypress shuddered and convulsed. The air all night cracked with its destruction. Stripped leaves blew away by the bushel basket. Limbs flew, broken by the cord.

Threadgill sadly watched the screaming goats in the high branches of surrounding oaks lift clear off their slick perches and blow away in the dark, swirling crazily, white-eyed, their beards blowing, a terrible and certain knowledge of death in their unnatural eyes.

Threadgill's heart split. He opened his mouth to cry out to those good friends – *goodbye! goodbye!* – and tasted the bitter storm in the dark, wind flubbering his cheeks, rain needling tongue and lips.

A wooden church roof sailed over Threadgill like a giant bird arrived from some distant world, and then the clothes of a sailor hurtled by, trailed by a sail and mast and all its rope rigging, an octopus of hemp and flails. The nautical gear shot past Threadgill so fast he jerked his head down, shrinking from the deep *whrooom* of its passage.

Threadgill barnacled the great tree trunk all that night.

***

The next morning, a sun delivered a day like most any other September in Alabama, a dollop of sizzling butter in a blue skillet of sky.

The wind did not blow hard enough to make a wave, not even a ripple, and the air took on a crystalline clearness that allowed Threadgill to see from the cypress treetop with some kind of strange magnification. His vision encompassed the Gulf of Mexico for miles and miles.

Wooden and metal ships littered every shore of Mobile Bay. Houses lay among the wrecks in splinters; uprooted wooden docks spined the beaches.

Chunks and flinders of porch columns, banisters and rafters, all distinguished by white paint, bobbed in hopeless bay water confusion together with raw logs, ragged branches, fallen trunks. White and black and brown corpses, most completely naked, hung from stripped trees or sloshed in waves.

The island sand gleamed pure and white below Threadgill's feet. Not a sprig of green – no leaf or blade of grass, no vine, no tuft or tussock – now graced the island anywhere.

Neither did one animal move, furred nor feathered. The island was empty, lifeless, a new desert.

Sky over the painted-picture sea was a perfect blue.

Threadgill, a naked young man under a gray hat, still did not loosen his love-lock on the splintered top of Goat Island's surviving tree. Eighteen acres of clean white sand spread below him, white unwritten pages in a new chapter of the bay's history book. Sand white as the shafts of sunlight he saw on that long-ago Georgia morning when the bullet and fire found him.

He did not want to go to the brighter light that other morning. And today he did not want to walk where white sand had replaced his green world.

So Threadgill Pickett stayed put in the cypress tree, hugging the cragged top with the might of a bear. He held tight all that day, wobbling in and out of shock. He dreamed, or daydreamed, mountainous waves that roared like panthers, dozens and scores and hundreds of the terrible beasts, leaping for his bare legs with fierce, sharp claws.

Now and again, Threadgill opened his swollen eyes – the beating rain and wind had nearly blinded him.

Once, through his squint, he watched one of the naked human bodies in the current. A woman. She slowly turned face up before rolling over again, gleaming, white as a lily among floating logs and limbs.

It was the only naked woman Threadgill would ever see.

The young man squenched his eyes shut. He licked the salt from his sore lips. He held the cypress trunk ever tighter. This terrible headache would surely pass.

Some hours or days later, he blinked out at the island and hallucinated that a great white-winged bird shook the sand off from a grave in the wet earth and shivered its muddy wings and flew up and up and up until it became a star, many stars, all over the sky, some of them falling back to the world in the backwash of its magical wings.

He took it for a sign to hold steady.

And so season in and season out, Threadgill embraced the solid tree trunk. When it rained, he drank – he opened his mouth and lifted his face like a baby bird. When he grew hungry, he ate the hordes of mosquitoes that came to eat him, licking them froglike off his own lips or else snatching them wildly out of mid-air to gobble by the fistful.

As the days, then weeks, and finally months and years passed under his bare dangling bottom, Goat Island slowly uncoiled from its shock.

Threadgill wondered if it were significant that green life began with a gnarl of devil vine. It sprang like the twisting hair of a witch from the wet tide line. Days passed, and more and more thorny shoots corkscrewed out of that wet biscuity sand. Threadgill even saw the serpentine thorn in his dreams.

 Not long after the devil vines, miles of tough little railroad vines sprouted along the island's fringes.

After that, Threadgill witnessed a slow-motion green explosion.

Plants reclaimed Goat Island. From his treetop aerie, Threadgill witnessed the unwinding wisteria, the untangling wild grape tendrils, so many vines, like little green snakes hatching from sand. Acorns buried in the storm shot up their stub green leaves like little hands, hello. And soon enough, familiar sea grasses and tough island shrubs clumped here and there, trembling in every afternoon breeze with some terrible collective memory of wind.

On a fine morning one spring, Threadgill woke to find a brown pelican comically loping along the beach with its wings fanned. He'd spied his first land animal. It had been a long wait.

From his lonely cypress tower, Threadgill always had a fine view of sea creatures – leaping dolphins and patrolling sharks. In the mornings and late afternoons, the clownish mullet popcorned in and out of view, jumping and jumping. In the curling surf, blue crab and schools of fish snapped and flashed. But above water, not even sandpipers had returned.

It is a truly lonely world without animals.

The pelican moved with a stumpy caper that reminded Threadgill of a farm hand in an emergency search for an outhouse. Then Mr. Brown Pelican noisily launched into the air shedding feathers on the way, and – surprise! – it folded out like a paper bird and turned graceful, magnificent, gliding toward

Mobile, the mainland, never twitching a feather.

Mr. Brown Pelican must have carried the avian world a good report. The next day, a scurvy crew of seagulls crowded a wet spit at the island's south tip. The rowdy rascals quarreled and bickered over invisible treasures, raucous as pirates in their delight and greed. Dollops of excrement purpled the gathering place.

They swooped away near end of day. Threadgill watched blue crabs paddle sideways through the foam of a rising tide and scramble up onto the beach to feast on the droppings. They jousted over seagull waste in their suits of armor as maniacally as dueling knights in storybooks. As maniacally as the men who fought in Georgia all those years ago.

Life returned.

Threadgill held fast to the cypress tree, a wooden spike that went clean through the island to the center of the world. Miraculously, leaves flushed out again on broken branches around him. The gulf breezes blew gently, cool as alcohol on a fevered cheek, an apology for old destruction. The sands gathered like blown salt round the cypress tree's roots, and dunes began to form again behind beaches.

In the dead center of the island, a new pond bubbled into existence. When the wind rippled the water on certain afternoons, in a certain easy light, the beauty of that fresh water broke Threadgill's heart. The spring was so crystal clear that Threadgill could see perfectly the old Civil War sword he found on the night of the hurricane. It stood, red as a wound, stabbed halfway to the hilt into the pond bottom. Excalibur, home again.

Time passed. Minutes. Days. Years. Centuries. The sun came on and went off like a lantern, bright and night, bright and night again.

One afternoon, Threadgill spotted a jaunty bullfrog kicking joyfully through the limpid depths of the water hole. When did it arrive? How?

Not too many days later, Threadgill spied a flotilla of little green fish. Then he noted another school of different little fish, holiday green with red fins, and after that still more little fish, hot blue ones, all cautiously nosing their way through the sun-dappled pool. Threadgill could see no alligators, large or larger – and he strained his eagle eyes from the heights to spot any sign.

He could see no goats either.

The world took some things away forever.

The fish hawks swooped close over Threadgill sometimes, and their jet black claws now and again clasped writhing mullet that shivered diamonds of water and rubies of blood down onto him.

Threadgill's alligator-torn body mended. The sunlight and fresh air in his perch did the healing. He believed it all started with the hurricane surge's salt water cauterizing him, then the scouring of cold hurricane rain. Threadgill came to believe forever after that he'd been purified that night, given some gift of survival. A miracle of endurance. How else would a man live through a great hurricane after his body had been mauled and mangled so badly? How else would he live so many years as he did?

His nose grew sensitive in the windy heights. He could smell a fish that leaped from the bay. He could smell a ship before the tallest mast appeared at the horizon. Threadgill could smell a storm three days out at sea.

The island greened, browned, greened again. It flushed and lushed with verdant palmetto and scrub oak and wax myrtle and red-berried yaupon. A trillion tidal grasses shot back up from the brown shallows – pin grass and duck grass and black grass and towering cattails. Red-winged blackbirds resumed their ageless quarrels. Raccoons and opossums and tiny beach mice swaggered along bleached logs under new canopies of live oaks and magnolias. Skinny tough pines dropped prickly needles and cones. Blackberry bushes and dollar-grass flats and countless other spasms of flora burst into existence, and these conjured green lizards, turtles, knots of oysters, syrup-slow snakes.

The island again grew wonderfully green, and Threadgill clenched the tallest place on it for dear life, feeling his mind, his hope, come back bit by precious green bit too.

He existed in sweet solitude at the height, up where goats once climbed in the neighboring oaks. He lived on sunshine. He lived the way the leaves lived. In warm weather, he transpired, his sweat cool as dew. In cold weather, he became tree itself, a weather-grayed protuberance on the bark of the biggest cypress anywhere, the unbreakable stanchion at the center of the universe.

Then, one fine day, Threadgill climbed down from the tree.

It took almost half a day to peel his chest and arms free. He felt bark shale from his back and tumble away as he made the achingly slow descent.

Gray Spanish moss hung from under his hat, inseparable in color and texture from his long hair and beard, those moss-gray too. He moved at sloth speed, slower than slow motion. The descent took weeks, maybe months. Yet down he came, gingerly putting out a cautious foot one afternoon to feel the warm sand again with his long toes.

He stood upright.

And Threadgill Pickett threw back his head and howled.

Let the birds fly over him like a white crown. Let the plants bow low as he shuffled on his way to bathe in the perfect water of the little spring-fed pool. Let the sun light his eternal path.

Let Ben look down from Heaven and see him, still alive, and determined to even an old score.

Fergit, hell.

Chapter 41, Yellowhammer Maine

At first, Yellowhammer thinks of a sort of make-do Stone Age, a grand rubble of prehistoric rocks, a house here and there. Feeble pines cling desperately to stones. The air breathes so fresh, like no other lungs ever held it.

But humans live here, somehow. Phlegm-hawking, bearded creatures stand on two legs in doorways, pinching at their genitals, breathing black cigarette smoke. Their eyes blink slowly, the color of stagnant water. They have teeth the color of old seed corn.

Yellowhammer feels a hot rush of anticipation. The moment of truth lies over that forest, over that hill.

Glittery black eyes look down at Bangor.

Yellowhammer sings it – Bangor! Bangor! It sounds like the perfect name for a Yankee town.

Maybe the good citizens here take Sunday afternoon to go out in back yards among ripped rubber tires and thrown-away car bodies. Maybe they bring hammers and bang away on pieces of sheet metal to pass their time. It seemed to Yellowhammer industrial noise like that – the noise of a so-called progress – would sound sweet as church music to a murder of ungraced Yankees.

Forests stretch to the west of the town. Canada invades Maine out there, secreting the lynx and moose and bear. Maybe wolf.

There's green yonder – the woodland seems to purify Yellowhammer's mind after the industrial fester of the Northeast these last flights. The ocean of trees seems to go on forever under Yellowhammer's left wing, and the cold ocean goes on forever under the other. Both expanses sigh and sough. One is green and fragrant, alive with bright wings and warm blood. The other is gray and oyster-thick, a broth of seaweeds and fogs and great mysterious cold-blooded fish.

Yellowhammer spots, away out there in the green forests, burning lights and churning smokestacks. Paper mills, odd as the outposts of settlers in Indian times. They sentry the far reaches of civilization here. Around the glowing spots, mange eats at the woods, a mile here, a thousand acres there. Yankee sores show through the hide of the whole world.

Yellowhammer sings again – a loud, defiant song.

Vengeance will be served here.

And not even a single gnarled and bitter skunk cabbage will sprout over the shallow grave of Billy Yank.

Chapter 42, Under a Bridge

Summer 1964 – North Alabama

A summer rain.

Threadgill sheltered under an old wooden bridge. He slipped and slid down a bank to the dry spot just as the first fat drops began to spatter, big as silver dollars. His aluminum headgear rang musically in the shower.

Threadgill watched the rain fall on a little creek and over the summer trees. Drops dribbled at a different tempo from the edges of the creosote crosstie bed of the bridge. The bridge might once have been a train trestle. It now held a poor dirt road on its back.

Threadgill opened a tin of potted meat and dipped stale saltine crackers into the paste. He chewed thoughtfully, crouched on his haunches, gear dry up the bank. After a last swipe with a thumb to get all the greasy meat, he tossed the tin into the creek and watched it float away like a little flashy boat.

"Say hey to Mobile Bay when you get there."

The can sped away as the creek narrowed. Raindrops splashed off it with faint tinny notes. It rode a sheet of water over a rock, then bobbed away down the rapids.

The shower made Threadgill pensive. The rain fell harder, and finally became so loud that he did not hear an automobile until it actually rolled, popping gravel, onto the bridge directly over his head. Startled from reverie, Threadgill jumped for his gear and made to scramble up the steep bank to hitch a ride.

Tennessee was just over a few hills. One state closer to Maine.

He stopped when he heard the serious voices.

"Do it in a hurry, boys."

All four car doors opened in the downpour. Threadgill heard a trunk creak open.

He was still about to yell a hello when a hand casually tossed something from the bridge. It thumped, rain-spattered, to the ground just a few feet from Threadgill.

What was it? Threadgill thought of an old discolored turkey neck and two large prunes.

"Goddamn it, Kenny. Throw that shit in the creek."

Kenny laughed. "You hunt coons, don't you Clyde? Feed 'em now, and they fat when you bring 'em home later on ..."

Another voice haw-hawed. "You reckon coons eat coon?"

"Well, they eat ever damn thing else."

A deeper voice cut through the malarkey. "I told you boys let's get done here. I don't like playin' grab-ass in pourin' down rain."

"Awright then. Give me a hand, Deke."

Threadgill heard noises men make when they lift something heavy. The rain poured even harder now, but Threadgill could hear the shock absorbers of the automobile squeak with relief. The men grunted under a load, and through cracks in the trestle over his head Threadgill could see two figures in T-shirts and one with no shirt crab-walking some oversized, clumsy load.

They put the burden down heavily at the edge of the bridge.

The car engine idled.

"Whew! At's one heavy fucker."

"I mean!" This voice breathed heavily.

"God damn it. Rain put out my cigarette, Deke."

The deep voice growled again. "Get it done, dammit. Might be a car along."

Threadgill could see the soaked silhouettes above him bend, then hoist their heavy load again.

"Get 'im *in* the creek," ordered the man with the deep voice. "Not on the bank."

"On three," grunted someone.

"One. And two. And ... *unhhh!*"

Threadgill watched a naked Negro tumble from the sky, slowly turning once in the air before hitting the creek with a tremendous splash. The Negro's body was huge and bloody. He landed on his back in the water, eyes open. He stared up at the men on the bridge. Rain fell in the unblinking eyes.

Threadgill saw that the Negro's hands were bound behind his back, and his feet held together at the ankles with adhesive tape. A bloody mess was between his legs.

One of the men spit from the bridge at the body, which now spun and began to pick up speed in the creek.

"That's it for you, nigger," pronounced the deep voice. "One less agitatin' preacher in the world."

Threadgill saw a pair of white hands just over the edge of the bridge, washing off blood in the rain.

Chapter 43, Happy Valley

1964 – North Alabama

For hours, a gale bent the trees. Rain deafened the world. The little creek rose high up the bank and swept the dead Negro's bloody parts away and downstream, chasing the man they came from.

Threadgill managed to sleep beneath the bridge. Pitch black howling shocked him awake. It sounded for a few minutes like a freight train passing, a ghost locomotive on the old trestle a few feet above his head.

A man can be haunted by a hurricane, Threadgill told himself. He will hear it in his sleep like a war. He can be haunted by so many things.

On this very afternoon, he saw a man murdered.

Who do you tell *that* to? You're on the road to murder a man too.

Threadgill thought about it.

The first person he would tell – farmer, truck driver, policeman, hunter, gas station attendant – might look him dead in the eye and hold up both hands.

Blood all over them.

What then?

***

Threadgill finally slept, finally woke. Just as after the long-ago hurricane, sweet sunshine warmed the world.

He scuffled up the bridge embankment to the road, and resisted a look down again at the surging water of the creek. He did not want another glimpse of the dead Negro man if by chance he'd washed into the nearby bushes.

Threadgill looked north instead.

A few gray clouds snagged on mountain ridges and tore off in streaming pieces, but mostly the sky showed blue. Green leaves seemed greener, rinsed clean by the hard rain.

He set off up the road. A persimmon tree had split in the night's turbulence, but Threadgill knew better than to even taste that green fruit – it would turn a man's mouth inside out.

He'd find sustenance ahead.

Didn't he always?

Threadgill brushed windblown pine needles from his clothes. He adjusted the cooking pot on his head.

A mile along, he waded like a bear into a briar patch.

Threadgill ate a double-handful of late blackberries. He also found three thrasher eggs and sucked the little shells. They caved in with soft whistling noises.

The food made energy engines inside Threadgill rev and whir. He felt the old familiar compass needle swing to its purpose.

North.

Today would be the day he set foot on Tennessee, the next rung of the ladder to Maine. No more Alabama now.

He hoped his second out-of-state sally came to a better end than the first.

Full of breakfast, a newborn man, he huffed and puffed an incline of mountain road. He reached its crest before sunlight fully cleared the eastern ridge.

A green valley spread below, a swale wide enough to make the next mountain look like a blue tent pitched on the horizon. That mountain, Threadgill reckoned, would be Tennessee.

He heard civilization down below.

Roosters stood on their tiptoes and yelled at the sun. A dog barked, and another. The farm noises grew louder as Threadgill rolled down the mountain.

Oddly, his nose picked up a pervasive odor he couldn't place. A factory? A barn?

The highway swooped around a house-sized stone, leveled, then straightened out under a long row of old hackberry trees. These showed severe storm damage, some trunks split, one whole tree blown down.

Threadgill rounded the great stone and now could view the entire valley, green as paradise.

It stopped him dead in his tracks.

If this were Heaven, the angels needed better feathers.

Thousands – *tens* of thousands – of white chickens thronged an old farm house and barn. Even from where he stood, Threadgill saw the flock was bedraggled and beaten. Many chickens lacked plumage. Their pinkish-white flesh glowed in the morning.

Now and again, one of the leghorns fell over and flapped a wing in the air like a drunk. Threadgill could hear a general disoriented clucking, loud as bullfrogs in the bogs of Goat Island.

Still more thousands – more *tens* of thousands – of leghorns lay scattered and stone cold dead. Carcasses hung from trees. They draped rain-blackened branches like huge sodden blossoms. White corpses littered a pasture. Mounds of slain chickens covered the roofs of a farmhouse and barn.

A gust of wind brought a snowdrift of feathers down around Threadgill. Remarkable. He was still a mile away from the wrecked chicken houses.

Threadgill put his hand to his helmet. He'd never seen so many chickens. Living or dead. An uncountable number.

Tucking his rainbow blanket under his arm, Threadgill knelt for a closer look at one of the dead birds, hurled all the way out to the road. He touched the wet corpse with a finger. A single blue-bottle fly buzzed heavily up from it.

Threadgill puzzled. What on earth happened? He discovered a chicken Gettysburg.

In another two hundred yards, he knew.

Tornado.

The twister buzz-sawed a clear path through a pecan grove behind the white farmhouse – thankfully spared – then skipped drunkenly through several pastures. It knocked a hole a hundred yards wide through a plank fence and harvested corn in a hundred-acre field. Yesterday, Threadgill reckoned, a green crop proudly shrined toward the sun. Today torn stalks remained, bent and angled like dead grasshopper legs.

Threadgill faintly smelled whiskey – the odor of broken ears of sweet corn simmering in summer morning heat.

The worst damage lay past the corn field.

Those four chicken houses, long as football fields, had stood side-by-side. The twister sawed a hole completely through all four structures – in one side, out the other. Chicken bombs exploded. Dead leghorns and crumpled tin rippled away from this ground zero, a molted white radiation.

What still stood of the chicken houses now trickled living birds, dazed and blinking at the sunlight. Chickens had to tiptoe, tumble, and awkwardly fly over white mounds of their dead comrades to reach the freedom of green fields.

Threadgill watched a red fox, in broad daylight, trot across the highway ahead of him. It toted a white feather bundle in its mouth. The vixen smiled the way foxes do. She slipped into huckleberry bushes.

The sky spun with red-tailed hawks and, of course, a first buzzard.

Threadgill marveled at such destruction. The tornado had snarled half-way up the side of the nearest mountain before it spun to a halt in thick pines and hardwoods. The mangled white flinders of wood up the mountainside made Threadgill think of broken bones. Festoons of white feathers and dead birds decorated the summer woods.

The wind shifted, gentler now, a tired sigh.

The odor Threadgill smelled earlier, far up the mountain, tingled his keen nose again. This time, he made a sour face. He'd found the culprit.

The twister had also ripped the roof clean off the chicken processing house. A stewed and fermented ammonia miasma mixed in the air with the reek of scattered guts, rotting skin and mildewed feathers. The fowl funk tainted the morning. It literally brought tears to Threadgill's eyes.

He made his way up the road with his nose crinkled, breathing only through his mouth.

Threadgill reached a faded, sunbleached sign: Askew Chicken Farm. Miraculously, the sign survived the tornado. But holes the sizes of coconut cakes pocked the plywood, and Threadgill realized with some alarm that these were chicken punctures – holes where birds blew clear through the plywood. He could see twisted sheets of corrugated tin with similar white-rimmed punctures, these sheets caught in the hair of the big pecans behind the farmhouse.

As Threadgill eyed the carnage, a single pure white feather twirled down from the sky.

Threadgill caught it – a snowflake of down. He brought his palm up to his lips and softly blew. The feather trembled, leaped off his hand, flew away.

He remembered a yellowhammer feather.

Then another vivid image overtook his thoughts – the Negro corpse float-ing so lightly down the creek last night.

War was hell, Threadgill thought. *But was peace hell too?*

Well-tended blueberry bushes lined the drive to the farmhouse. These hung wet and heavy with fruit, sweet and fat as any blueberries Threadgill ever remembered. He stopped to pick fruit with both hands for a second time this morning, stuffing the juicy blue marbles into his mouth as fast as he could yank them off the stems.

I'll eat 'em. I don't care if they're blue, he thought. Some juice dribbled into his white beard.

His guard was down. He left himself unprepared for a surprise attack.

As he squatted, grubbing the blueberry bushes, Threadgill got a dose of what he carried north to Bangor.

Thanks goodness for the gravel lane.

He heard an approaching crunch! crunCH! crUNCH! CRUNCH!

Threadgill wheeled.

A crazed snow-white rooster dashed toward him.

It happened in slow motion, as all dreadful things seem to. The insane little bow-legged white flame creature flew at him in a mindless rage.

A strange thought pierced Threadgill. Until last night, this farm harbored a rooster's paradise – a hundred-thousand plump hens cozied flank-to-flank in warm places. Hens oh so soft and fertile. Hen heaven.

Today? All gone with the wind. Literally.

Wouldn't it drive any rooster crazy?

Threadgill thought back to Ben, to the battle on Pine Mountain, to Aunt Annie and Eva, to the ashes of a home on Mobile Bay, to Goat Island, to his father and mother.

Oh yes. Grief could drive a creature mad. Grief could drive a creature to any measure of revenge.

The rooster flapped starchily into the air, spurs aimed squarely at Threadgill's aluminum cooking pot.

Threadgill instinctively swatted the bird aside with blueberry-stained hands. He swung hard enough to let the fighting cock know he meant to be left alone. The rooster came down awkwardly, a fiery crash.

Heart pounding, Threadgill left off picking berries. It disconcerted him to be attacked, no matter the creature. Even a lone yellow jacket could send a man streaking for cover.

A twelve-pound rooster caused real heartburn.

The bird hopped up again, ready for battle, but damaged and wary now. It stalked Threadgill down the lane toward the farmhouse, wanting a mistake, waiting for Threadgill to turn his back, just once.

"Good Sunday morning to you, mister," a man on the porch of the farm house called. "Can I help you?"

Threadgill warily proceeded backward into the front yard, rubbing his arm – the rooster's spur had gotten through his sleeve and gouged him, dammit. He'd want to wash that. Chickens were nastier than rats. Nastier than monkeys.

"Call off your rooster?" Threadgill suggested over his shoulder. He continued to walk backward and hunched, arms on guard to ward off a second attack. "He blames me for that tornado, I reckon."

"Wait right there."

Threadgill heard the screep of a screen door.

When the farmer reappeared, he stepped quickly from the low porch, sunlight gleaming on his big bald head. He carried something long and black.

Threadgill just had time to stick his fingers under his helmet and in his ears before the shotgun blast.

BOOM!

The rooster erupted white and red.

A smoking shotgun shell ejected and bounced with musical notes down the porch steps.

"Sorry for your trouble," the farmer called to Threadgill. "One more dead chicken this morning don't matter a lot, I reckon."

"Obliged!" Threadgill waved a thank-you hand. "Thing tried to eat me up."

The shotgun brought people scampering. A dozen or more folk, black and white, streamed into the yard. They drew up short at the sight of Threadgill. Sticky white feathers matted the hands and forearms of every single person.

"Everything's alright, folks!" the farmer called. "This traveler's just here for Sunday dinner!"

Threadgill liked the sound of that.

"Shoo! Back to work!" the old farmer hooted, waving animatedly. "This hot sun's gonna cook them chickens if we don't cook 'em first!"

Threadgill saw the design of it now. A picket line worked out there in the pasture, a host of women and men and children, all ages and sizes, colored and white, skinny and fat. They hefted hamper baskets and grocery bags and croker sacks and even laundry baskets filled to the top with dead chickens.

A pick-up truck with tall wooden slats on the back chugged out to these collection crews. The truck trailed feathers from more hamper baskets over-heaped with dead leghorns. Two skinny white teenagers grinned from the truck bed, sunburned already on their noses and shoulders.

The truck squawked to a stop. The boys vaulted down and effortlessly hoisted the heavy baskets. Dead chickens bounced each time the baskets hit the flat bed.

"Clay! You and Robin drink you plenty of water," the farmer admonished the boys. He pronounced it *waw-ter*. "Working 'round that charcoal pit will get you sunstroked if you don't drink a lots."

"Durned good piece of thinking," Threadgill said to the farmer.

"What's that, buddy?"

The farmer hobbled back onto the shady porch. Threadgill hadn't noticed that he wore a huge bandage on his right foot.

The farmer eased himself down on a metal glider, leaned the shotgun against the house.

"I mean a good idea to dress and cook all them killed chickens real fast," Threadgill answered.

The farmer licked the paper on a hand-rolled cigarette. "Aw, shoot, we thought about pitchin' 'em in the river. But it didn't seem right. They'd rot all downstream. Might even make it to the lake and kill the bass."

"Them fish might taste like chicken."

The farmer laughed.

"That's a good 'un, old timer. That thinkin' cap help you come up with your jokes?"

Threadgill sized the farmer up for a second. He had a big old bald head too. He was one of the ugliest men Threadgill ever saw.

Threadgill liked this old boy.

Chapter 44, The Imposters

1964 – Goat Island

Threadgill made the discovery before dawn on the north beach.

He had resumed a pre-hurricane habit – a daily walk entirely around his little floating kingdom. One walk in the morning. One walk in the afternoon. Theadgill became a watch hand, forever circling a white dial.

He'd grown used to the familiar path and patterns. Except for crews he could see on the occasional passing ship or fishing boat, Threadgill might have been the only living human on earth. That thought never really rooted, though. If Threadgill needed evidence that civilization persisted, he glanced toward Mobile. That place wrote its smutty words in the sky with chimney smoke and factory spume all day, every day.

Time changed things, oh yes. Threadgill lost count of years. Not even a view from the top of a great cypress tree, season after season after season, could tell him how old he'd become.

His health? Remarkable, to be sure. Threadgill lived on fresh fish and pure water and honey and cattail root and sunshine. His body felt just the way it felt when he set out on his journey with Ben, young and energetic. Vendetta preserved him. Never mind the beard that dangled to his waist, or the fishing net of wrinkles on his face.

Threadgill hadn't prepared, though, for what he found one morning.

He accepted a great deal of strangeness that appeared all around him through the years. Some things simply baffled him. Machines left the ground nowadays and flew into the sky. They carried men, their goggled faces bright between stubby wings. Some had four wings like a damselfly, often bright yellow. Some had just two wings, bright metal. And passing ships roared these days with great monstrous voices, while even the tiniest boats screamed with mechanical energy like waterbugs and shot up smoke from some apparatus in back. More and more, small craft flew back and forth across the bay like thrown knives.

Threadgill watched these signs and wonders unfold as he circled Goat Island through the years. His footprints wrote the whole long story. Forever, he found the surveillance fascinating, variable, his island kaleidoscopically in flux. Always, the sand and waves and wind sermonized – they told Threadgill nothing in this world waited, lingered, stayed the same.

Nothing but Revenge.

Not for a single moment – not in the top of that tree or now on the beaches, not in his deepest sleep or his most alert waking hour – had Threadgill forgotten or forgiven the wounds that ruined his life, the bullet that killed his brother.

He remembered poor Ben with every glance at the blue of the sky or the gray of the sea.

***

Footprints.

What Threadgill discovered on the beach stunned him totally, confounded him. He had to simply sit down on his old weathered bottom to make his head understand it.

The sun burned his back red before he moved again.

Footprints.

Not his own.

In the sand. On his island.

Threadgill put his hand down in amazement. He touched the tips of his fingers to the tracks.

The deepest print, nearest the surf, still bubbled, filling with salt water. Little yellow and blue coquinas burrowed to hide themselves in it.

The invader bootprints led to the woods. The beach looked plowed. A freshly foaming urine blotch marked the trail near the surf line.

A wild mix of emotions shot through Threadgill. His scarred crown pulsed again, the way it once did when rage or other passion filled him.

Men walked Threadgill's world! Invaders tread Goat Island! Trespassers in boots! Trespassers with full bladders!

At once, it occurred to Threadgill he was buck naked. Was this how Adam felt, he wondered, after the jig was up with the forbidden fruit?

The eyeblink of modesty faded fast. A hot new emotion boiled in his blood. He could feel his burned skin tingling under his yellowhammer hat. A locomotive whistle filled his ears.

Fury!

A red demon suddenly stared through Threadgill's eyes.

Ahh! It's plain who made these tracks! Who else but the old Creole who first brought me here all those years ago? Rascal! Did that old yellow man imagine he would find me asleep? Didn't I warn him?

Threadgill stood so fast his knees popped like twin muskets firing.

He picked out a sturdy driftwood cudgel, a bludgeon of hickory made twice as heavy by salt water soaked into its every pore. A deeply satisfying heft. Threadgill loved the fat smooth thickness of the pole in his palms.

He took the club in both hands, broadax-style, and swung the weapon in a wicked arc. It produced a deep, dangerous *vroom*. Threadgill whipped it back the other direction; the *whoosh* hurt the humid morning air.

What will this war club do to a man's skull? Threadgill wondered. *Can it knock an old Creole's head completely off? Can it knock his head so far it bounces down the beach to the waves?*

"They got no right to be on my place."

Threadgill spoke to himself. His self answered.

"You promised to kill him, Threadgill. The Yankee."

Threadgill tasted the word. He tasted every syllable, savory like salt. He tasted his murderous intention.

He *liked* that taste.

"Turn him into crab bait, Threadgill!"

His ears howled. A stitch kicked up behind one eye.

A rogue wave unexpectedly foamed his sandy bare ass and ankles.

"Yaaaaaahhhhhh!"

Goaded, Threadgill sprinted up the beach and into the woods.

***

His bare feet squeaked sand as he ran. He held his weapon ready.

His bare footsteps thrummed faster and faster. He could hear the wind whistle past his old yellowhammer hat.

It didn't take long until he heard careless loud voices in a clearing. Threadgill smelled percolating coffee, an odor long lost to him yet instantly familiar.

To his alarm, he spotted dozens more footprints. They went helter-skelter, everywhere, in the soft sand.

Metal clinged against metal. A rattle of weapons.

The old Creole has friends. He brought family. He came prepared for a scrap.

Too late now to turn back. Threadgill would *never* turn back.

"YAAAAH! YAAAAAH!"

Threadgill burst from a titi thicket. Naked old Threadgill savagely attacked the invaders.

Naked old Threadgill looked like an enraged shaved bear with a cudgel.

The poor bastards never had a prayer.

Eight soldiers in Confederate uniforms and five soldiers in Yankee blue leaped to their feet and stampeded one another, gear and grits and hot coffee flying. One man tripped over a little gas camp stove and went down in a crash. Another flailed into a pup tent and fell, entangled.

The soldiers too scared to run simply collapsed in trembling terror on the sand.

What is going on here? Why are Yankees and Confederates sitting around together eating eggs?

Threadgill noted a little mountain of camping gear strewn around, a half-dozen tents, lots of canvas, several loops of rope. A tiny campfire snotted smoke, and an open half-gallon glass bottle of Jim Beam whiskey glugged onto the ground.

Weirdest of all, Threadgill confronted a small square box, bright metal with knobs on its front. This eerie kind of music came out of it – *chug, chugga, chugga, wah.*

"YAAAAAH!"

The cudgel's mighty stroke split the radio into twin pieces of twisted metal – instantly silent metal.

Threadgill stood over a cowering invader. A chubby man with black glasses. He protected his head with folded arms. He was the only person not in uniform. The back of the man's expensive white pullover sweater wore yellow grits.

"Please, man! Holy Jesus! I'm just skipper of the goddam boat! Please!"

"Don't hurt us!" begged a young Confederate on the ground nearby. He sported a fuzzy blonde mustache the color of a week-old baby chick. "Who are you? Leave us alone!"

These invaders neither sounded nor looked like the old Creole. They didn't really look convincingly like soldiers either.

Threadgill stood perplexed, naked as the day he was born, gruesome with scars, wagging his cudgel in the air.

"Who are y'all?" he hollered. "Why you on my island? YAAAAAH!"

"Mister, stop!" shrieked another dark-haired Confederate. "Please! We ain't here to steal nor do harm!"

"Yaaah!" uttered Threadgill, but without as much heat.

He lowered his fearsome weapon slightly. From the woods and from the dirt of the campsite, he felt beseeching, frightened eyes. Every single man, at least a dozen, had his full attention.

Threadgill threw a sly look off to his right, and spoke to a holly tree in a loud voice.

"Keep an eye on 'em, boys. If this 'un here moves …" he gave a vague glance down that might have singled out any soldier there, "… you know what to do."

One of the Confederate soldiers whimpered.

"Mama's gonna KILL us, Ray!" Threadgill saw that he glared balefully at another soldier – a twin. "She told us not to take up this Confederate crap!"

Threadgill felt a pang. He looked around, just an instant, for his own brother, Ben.

Snap out of it!

Threadgill whipped the pole viciously. Its terrible ripping swoosh set every lumpy figure on the sand to trembling again. Threadgill thought of gray and blue cocoons just before they split and let out butterflies.

The little fire crackled like it was laughing.

"You." Threadgill poked the shivering figure nearest him. "You named Ray. What is your … uh …"

Threadgill simply forgot the next words. It had been a long time since he needed to use words.

"That's Ray," whined the twin, blubbering now. He wore a moustache of yellow snot. "Always got the big durned ideas, that Ray. Talk your way out of this now, jackass."

"You boys quit your mouthing," somebody scowled from the back of the ranks. "It ain't manly."

Threadgill stepped over bodies back to that volunteer.

"You sound like a Yankee, mister. You got on Yankee blue. Do you know I *hate* a damn Yankee? Before I kill you with this stick, tell why y'all are on my island. Out here in uniforms. With guns! *Talk!*"

Threadgill brandished the cudgel.

"Now just wait, mister …"

Before the Yankee could finish, a bawling noise rose unexpectedly from the first Confederate twin. Threadgill thought of a colicky calf. The youngster vomited a rope of yellow liquid that nearly put out the campfire.

"Gugh! GUGH!"

Confederate Ray completed the plea for his brother.

"Please don't kill us, mister! We ain't here to do harm. We ain't real soldiers! Them guns ain't real! This ain't for real!"

Threadgill, vexed, clenched the stick tighter.

"Ain't real? Them looks like guns to me!"

The Yankee tried now. His words blew puffs in the sand beneath his frightened red face. Threadgill smelled whiskey on him.

"We're in Moblie History Club, mister. We wanted to come out here and do a battle."

The sea wind blew over Goat Island in a low moan.

"What's that mean?" Threadgill finally asked. "It ain't clear to me."

Someone out in the woods called to Threadgill. "Jesus! It's like a war game, feller! That's all. We came to act out the old Civil War battle that happened on Goat Island back in 1864. We thought this year it might be fun to dress up like Confederates and Yankees, and we'd have a scrap out here where the real one was. But it's *pretend*, mister. It ain't a real fight. We ain't real Confederates and Yankees."

"You fellers … just *act* like Confederates and Yankees?"

"That's all, for god's sake. It ain't real."

Threadgill felt like he'd fallen through some kind of rabbit hole and come out in the strangest place.

"You mean," he asked once more, just to make his mind accept it, "that some of you just dress up like Confederates? And some of you just dress up like Yankees? And you play out here in the woods?"

Somewhere, way off, a ship horn blew.

"Right! We live over in Mobile and get together at Wentzel's and study the battles. Mobile Bay. The one over at Blakeley. And there's this other one over at Spanish Fort …"

"You really a sure nuff Yankee, mister? You one, I mean. Out in the woods. You don't talk like these others."

The man rose up from the shadows into view, barely. But he kept both hands on the back of his head. He had surrendered.

"I'm from Chicago, Illinois. And I'll have to warn you that I'm a plaintiff lawyer, mister. If you injure or cause emotional suffering to any man in this group … "

Threadgill poked the chubby Confederate in front of him, who gave a hurt yelp. The Yankee lawyer hushed.

"So you mean to tell me," Threadgill asked yet again, "that you dress up like soldiers thisaway … and you come all the way out to Goat Island … just to *play* Civil War?"

Several men on the ground and out in the edges of the woods mumbled optimistically, yes, yes sir.

Threadgill felt a red surge.

"Any one of you men ever see a Civil War battle?"

Not a word.

Now a buzzing like a giant mosquito rose from nowhere. Threadgill dared a quick glance up. One of the big metal flying things passed over his island. He could see the Yankee flag on the side of it.

What in the world was going on? Reinforcements?

A scuffling noise came from behind him. Threadgill turned.

One of the Confederate twins made a bid to escape. He spun his wheels in the sand.

Thwack!

Threadgill saw two Xs pop into the reenactor's eyes. The boy's tongue dangled out on the sand when his head hit the ground.

Thwack! *Thwack*!

Two more of the soldiers, one Confederate and one Yankee, pitched headlong to the ground, heads cracked.

But now they kept coming.

Thwack! *Thwack*! *Th* —

Threadgill felt a blow and, shortly after, his senses twittered out of his head. They circled his old gray hat like carefree butterflies.

The sand and leaves rose toward his face very fast.

Far away, he heard voices, like men trapped in bottles, yelling and whooping.

"Godamighty, Kenny! QUICK! Tie up the crazy bastard!"

A hound howled, then dozens more, hundreds, thousands more. Threadgill heard hurricane winds again. He couldn't make his leg stop jerking.

Like Ben's that day.

"Damn, Kenny!" yelled a voice. "Where'd you learn to throw a canteen like that?"

"Mardi Gras float. Give me that damn stick. I'm gone beat the tar out of that nut."

"Me too!" somebody else hollered.

Threadgill chose to go to sleep.

***

On the north beach Ben waited. Young and handsome. Unscarred. Crazy wild in his eyes. A big bushy pair of white wings down his back. The wind blew loose some of the feathers.

"You look like you're a hundred years old, Threadgill. Or maybe a hundred and four."

Threadgill did not answer in that confused first moment. He didn't trust his mind. He wanted a hurricane to blow him into the sky again, back up into the sheltering cypress tree. This time, he would never climb down.

Ben squinted, ran his tongue out the corner of his mouth.

"You think it's like a big green pasture, right? Lambs and woolly pups. Folks with harps. That what you think, brother?"

Threadgill closed his eyes and took deep breaths. The air smelled like reality, like ocean.

"Well Heaven is woods, Threadgill. Just big old thick woods like those back home. Great big old trees with the sun streakin' down all through 'em. Angels flying everywhere like those giant woodpeckers we used to see. Like me."

Ben shook his fancy feathers, and they shone like carved ivory and made a wispy noise. Threadgill had never seen anything in the world so white. They made beach sand look filthy.

"Can't you talk nowadays, Gill? Cat got your tongue? It's really me, come to keep you company. Just like when we was twelve. Want to tell old Ben what's on your mind?"

"Urrr. Rrrr."

To Threadgill's surprise, he couldn't talk. His throat and tongue and lips couldn't remember the trick of it now.

"What say, brother? Come on out with it."

Leave. Me. Be.

The look on Ben's face was not one a twin should ever see.

"What?"

A wave washed up over Ben's feet and a feather shed into the hissing foam.

Go on back.

Threadgill pointed up. His skinny arm trembled, but the yellow-nailed finger at its end jabbed defiantly. *Go. Go.*

"I can't leave, Threadgill. I volunteered to come see you and help you keep straight."

Threadgill dropped to his knees and began digging a hole. He dug and he dug. He made a long white shallow that leaked sand from the sides nearly as fast as he could dog-dig it out.

Finally Threadgill lay down in the bottom of the new grave, face up.

After a time, his brother stepped near. He peered over the edge.

"Mmm. Mmm. Mmm. What would Picketts and Flanneries think of you, Gill?"

And Ben rose on his white wings like a spirit, straight up into the sky, so fast that he could have been a falling star, only streaking up instead of down.

Threadgill watched him go.

Then he wept.

The tears he cried filled up the little grave.

The walls caved in on him like dissolved sugar, and Threadgill cried harder, hard enough to float him up through the heavy collapsed blankets of sand and wash him farther on up the beach into a heap of driftwood.

He woke. Threadgill could not say how much time had passed. It might have been years, like before. How would a sleeping man know?

At first, Threadgill could not tell his arms and legs from the driftwood.

And then, before he could figure out again how to move his limbs, a little yellowhammer woodpecker flew down into his open palm and – *surprise!* – laid a tiny egg, white as a blinded eye.

A baby yellowhammer was already hatching from the egg. Its beak spiked through a tiny shell, and the naked goggle-eyed head needled out, gaping, blinking.

The thing had the tiniest wings Threadgill ever saw.

He watched the wings grow, magically fast. In only moments, the bird stood, then fledged. And finally it flew.

A yellowhammer. Just a damned gray puff of nothing. But so beautiful.

Bring Ben back, Threadgill wished after it. *Tell him I'm sorry. Tell him I didn't forget him. I didn't betray him. Tell my brother. I didn't abandon him.*

Tell Ben I'm going north. I'll need to know when …

Threadgill opened his eyes in a nursing home, staring up at a small brown stain on the ceiling, his old gray hat perched on a bedpost.

Chapter 45, Dinner on the Grounds

1964 – Happy Valley, Alabama

Gideon Askew's family settled Happy Valley 200 years before. Some of the pioneers married Cherokees. After that, folks said Askews would marry anything.

"We had tornadoes before," Gideon assured Threadgill. "We'll have 'em again."

It was a pure miracle this tornado killed no one … and only hurt one person – Gideon. He stepped on a rake in the stormy dark trying to close the barn after the wind blew it open.

This, too, would pass.

The two old men sat on Gideon's porch. One of Mr. Askew's pretty granddaughters brought out biscuits and gravy, fresh canteloupe, slices of cake. She wiped her hands on her apron before shaking Threadgill's hand. A polite young lady, pretty, brown hair and big eyes. She didn't mention Threadgill's bait-bucket helmet.

Threadgill ate every bite on the platter, of course. And the two men drained a quart of ice tea.

Threadgill felt deliciously happy for some reason. He found himself at a *home*, not a truck cab or a Greyhound or under a bridge.

He'd been invited to Sunday dinner too. Any traveling man would be happy at that prospect.

Dinner, in fact, cooked just over there. A 50-foot-long roasting pit sent up smoke on the shady side of the barn. Dozens of men and boys, blacks and whites together to Threadgill's slight surprise, swabbed an endless supply of fresh chicken with long-handled mops daubed in barbeque sauce.

All morning, one car and truck after another pulled down the Askew driveway. People got out blinking, unfolding sunglasses. They carried foil-covered bowls of potato salad or beans or slaw or rolls. Arrivals gradually parked farther and farther away. Before long, they'd be hoofing it in all the way from the county road.

It seemed every family in Happy Valley, black or white or red or whatever, showed up for the big feed. Word traveled fast in these parts. People came ready to work too. The men wore overalls and lugged cooking gear or cleaning stuff or tools. The women toted baskets and cooking oil and baking pans and lettuce keepers.

The children and dogs streaked for the fields. Their job would be preposterously fun – herding chickens. To make this possible, sweating teams of black and white men and boys worked together, stuck fence posts in fresh holes and unrolled chicken wire. Other men and boys with hats in hand shooed chickens down these gauntlets, and still more kids and dogs served as beaters, driving snowy fowl in from the fields in clucking masses.

Someone in the back yard, under the shade of the pecan trees, struck up a tune on a fiddle. A flat-top guitar joined in, beating a rhythm like a heart. Soon as the music started, Old Man Askew eased himself up, stumped across the porch, and gimped down the steps out to the yard. Soon, he and Threadgill sat in metal lawn chairs right by the music.

"So," Askew said, "this last Yankee lives in Maine."

Threadgill's head felt light as a bubble. He'd told a lot about his life to Askew, as they sat together on the porch. The man's great bald head gleamed.

"That's quite a hike, ain't it? To Maine, I mean?" Askew pulled up a blade of grass from beside the chair and put one end in his teeth. "I imagine one of my boys would give you a ride up yonder if you asked polite."

"A ride to Maine? All that way …"

Before Threadgill could finish, a lean gentleman stepped out the back door of the house. He carried a black bag, its leather shining. The fellow wore his silver hair combed straight back, and wore a string tie around his neck. He looked a lot like that colonel on the chicken boxes Threadgill sometimes found on roadsides.

"Mornin', Gid! Who's your buddy?"

"This here's Mr. Threadgill Pickett," Gideon answered. "He's a traveler. He'll be helpin' us eat this chicken the Lord has so plentifully provided."

"This here's my little brother," the old man told Threadgill. "Dr. Gaydi Askew. Here to look at my foot. And eat chicken."

Gideon looked amused. "If I still have my appetite. Those feet ain't purty, if I recall." The physician eyed the bustle of activity around the improvised fire pit. Hundreds of chickens roasted now, breasts up, drumsticks fat and sweating. The golden skins of the birds gleamed with dark barbeque sauce.

The sauce dripped, the glowing charcoal and hickory chips spit, sizzled, shot clouds into the air. If flames rose too high, hose men snaked over with spray nozzles and shot soft rainbows of water over the conflagration. Steam rose with a delicious, thunderous hiss.

The doctor shook Threadgill's hand. Gideon thrust iced tea in a Sterling cup at his brother.

"Whoo! At's good!" exclaimed the doctor, mopping his pink face with a handkerchief. He rattled his ice. "Hot day!"

Gideon grinned, a few good teeth still showing.

"Try standin' out by that pit, brother. Hell ain't no hotter."

"Speaking of Hell," the doctor asked, swallowing tea, "you heard if Billy is coming?"

"Soon as he's done preachin'," Gideon said. He turned to Threadgill. "Billy's our 'nother brother. Got a church over to Ider. He's over here most ever' Sunday, rain or shine. He won't miss a barbeque chicken party for sure."

"If you ask me, Billy ain't worth a shit." The doctor stirred his tea with one finger, squeezing in a wedge of lemon.

"He shore ain't," Gideon winked at Threadgill. "It does look to me like could be better connected to the man upstairs. Why you reckon Billy would let the Good Lord send a durned tornado through our chicken houses?"

"Sinful chickens," Threadgill said.

Dr. Gaydi spit out his tea. He hooted and slapped his knee.

A very big man in buckle-strap overalls with no shirt underneath ambled around the corner of the house. He lugged a huge red plastic cooler under each arm, like a bear with hives of honey. He flashed a big smile – minus front teeth – at the men on their metal chairs under the pecan trees.

"Thought some silver queen corn would go good with them chickens," he yelled.

"Chicken we got!" Gaydi grinned drunkenly.

"Always appreciate good corn on the cob, Booger," said Gideon. "Put them coolers in the barn – you'll see a spot." Gideon waved the direction without getting up. "Then come on back and get you a swig of this good tea."

Booger winked, pink sweat rolling down his forehead. Jolly dimples at the corner of his smile looked deep enough to swim in.

"Cut you some front teeth out of that watermelon rind, Booger," hollered

Gaydi. "It'll help you gnaw the corn."

Gideon snickered, then leaned over to Threadgill.

"If you think that big old boy Booger will eat the most in this whole bunch, you'll be wrong. Put your money on Aleph. That's another brother of ours. You ain't met Al yet. That 'un don't weigh more'n a good-size bird dog, but I swear he's got two hollow legs. Even Booger can't keep up with him."

A black, old-time pick-up truck chugged into view.

Hallooo! Here we go! The cry rose from the men working the fire pit. Threadgill saw why – in back of the truck lolled a mountain of watermelons, fat as pigs.

A colored man, high-yellow, red hair standing straight up on his head like frozen fire, climbed from the truck. He left the door open and the engine running. He made a beeline for the pecan grove.

"Yo Gideon! Gaydi! Where's Booger 'n' Billy?"

"Booger's here! In the barn! Preacher Billy's on the way after church, like ever' Sunday!"

Behind the colored man, men and boys swarmed over the watermelon truck. In no time, an impromptu brigade pitched melons one man to the next all the way back to the cattle cistern and plunk into cool water.

"Now you ain't hardly gonna believe this," Gideon whispered to Threadgill. "But that colored boy just drove up? That's Aleph. He's the brother I mentioned. The big eater."

Threadgill might as well have heard all Askews could fly.

"Course, we ain't but *half* brothers," Gideon explained. "But ever' damn drop of a man's blood is the same color, now ain't it? Askew blood is pretty much all red."

Gaydi leaned in.

"Preacher Billy? The other brother you been hearin' about? He's colored too. Half colored, anyway. Me an' Giddy and Booger, us three, and Aleph and Billy – all of us grew up close as the fingers on your hand here."

Gideon explained.

"Daddy had two families," he said. "He kept our mama, and he kept a Negro lady up the road. He loved mama, and he loved that colored woman. All us brothers and half-brothers grew up like one big family. It ain't your usual story."

"Aleph saved Booger's life one time," Gideon said. "They was in the woods and went creek swimmin' and Booger hit his head on a rock and sunk slam out of sight. Aleph couldn't even swim – still can't swim – but he dove in and someway got that big old boy out all by himself."

"Booger never did have good sense," Dr. Gaydi said, "before or after that knock on the head."

Gideon chuckled. "Close to the truth, brother. But I tell you what. Mr. Pickett, don't let old Booger ever hear you throw off on Aleph or brother Billy. About their color or all of Aleph's wives or young 'uns or nothin' else. You badmouth Aleph, you'll come away hurtin'."

"All Aleph's young 'uns?" Threadgill asked.

"Lord yes," grunted Gaydi in admiration. "Al's a busy man on Father's Day. Close to twenty children. Five or six different women. Even a white woman, and they had two mostly white children. Got eyes blue as yours, both of 'em."

"Colored children, and got blue eyes?"

"They all Askews to us," pronounced Gideon. "Ever' white and coffee-colored one. You'll see 'em all over the place here today. They're mostly chasin' chickens right now."

Gaydi chimed in. "He's a good old boy, Aleph."

The brothers all greeted the colored man as he returned. Gaydi even went to fetch a chair, after seating Aleph in his own. Aleph proved a wiry, alert man with a lethally handsome smile. He wore a tie loose at the top, and yellow slacks with no socks.

The newcomer brother looked a little suspiciously at Threadgill, embarrassed at all this slightly sugary affection. But he politely lifted a sweating tea glass in Threadgill's direction.

"Yo' health, Mr. Pickett!" he said. "And to yo' fancy hat."

Aleph nudged with his shoe the big bandaged foot on the ground in front of Gideon. "An' here's to old Hernando."

Gideon jerked his foot back. "Hernando?"

The lethal smile broke.

"Yeah, Hernando … de so' toe."

Gideon snorted. And brother Booger now puffed up, lugging a pair of cement blocks and a two-by-eight plank. He improvised a bench and took his seat, quickly dusting his hands off on his overalls. He gave Aleph a huge bear hug.

"Where's Preacher Billy?" Aleph asked Booger, peeling himself moistly from the grip. "I'd figure him to be here early, what with all these young girls and free barbeque, all you can eat, and cold watermelon and whatnot."

"He'll be here! Hit's Sunday, ain't it?" Booger said. He shook his head. "It ain't but half past noon. I imagine he'll still be preachin' another hour."

"At LEAST!" laughed Aleph.

A troubling thought came over Threadgill. *A preacher … a black preacher?*

Booger was ready to party. He drank half his glass of ice tea in one gulp. "Aleph," he smacked, "how 'bout I bring y'all a load of wood, when all this blowed-down pecan gets seasoned?"

"Got plenty, brother," the colored man grinned. "Same storm hit them woods back at our place. Thank you kindly though."

"How 'bout some barbeque chicken then, Al? We got a right smart," Gaydi clucked.

Aleph snorted, then turned to his host.

"Gid, how bad is it?"

The oldest Askew looked up at the sky before he answered.

"Buildings. Trees. Corn crop. Fences and some roofing. Killed about seven, eight thousand chickens, I reckon. Them boys is counting by the basket," he said. "See yonder."

The big vegetable truck bounced in from the field as Gideon spoke. The red wooden-slat sides clacked as the truck shuddered to a stop. A mob of folks spilled down, muscling hamper baskets heaped with hundreds more dead white chickens.

"I think in all we'll lose forty, forty-five thousand dollars. Could be a lot worse."

"Could be a lot worse," Aleph amened.

"This place runs like a little army," Threadgill offered, impressed by the system in place to field-dress thousands of slain birds.

Willing hands passed the hamper baskets to more willing hands, then more. Just past the fire pit ten or twelve cast-iron and aluminum cauldrons of water boiled, gas jets glowing blue underneath. A dozen more Happy Valley folk, black and white, young and old, worked yet another makeshift assembly line – or, in this case, dis-assembly line.

Threadgill focused on a big black woman, with a red scarf around her hair. She lifted two dead chickens from a peach basket and dunked them into a bubbling pot. She counted – one, two, three seconds – then lifted out the streaming birds. With two expert swipes, her strong hands violently stripped most every feather. She flung the balled wet mess onto her soggy blue tennis shoes – it looked to Threadgill like she stood in a burst bale of cotton.

The men and women at other cauldrons worked with the same frightening efficiency.

Threadgill felt glad he wasn't a dead chicken.

He really came to the edge of his seat, though, over the next stage of processing.

The woman in the red scarf wiped sweat from her face with a huge shiny forearm, avoiding the gummy mass stuck to her black fingers. She pitched the naked birds, pink and limp, onto hot corrugated tin sheets torn from the henhouses by the storm. The tin sheets lay across sawhorses and cement block stacks.

As birds banged down on the tin, a new wave of women and men went to work. Dressing knives flashed in the sunlight, quick as movie swordfighters, and Threadgill felt his heart throttle at the bright red blood – so much blood. It seemed strange to realize, this day and age, that chickens had blood. They usually just appeared on a rest home cafeteria tray.

These processors adroitly gutted, shook, scooped, jointed. Chopped-off chicken heads and feet flew over shoulders into spattered 55-gallon drums. A legion of barn cats stalked the barrels, tails lashing, and gawky hounds skulked up to steal mouthfuls.

Buckets heavy with plump dressed leghorns left this area, clanking at the sides of sweat-soaked black and white teenagers. Two colored men with heavy hoses knocked the final gore off the carcasses, dumped the birds, rinsed the buckets.

Other boys then toted sheets of plywood loaded down with dressed chickens to the fire pit. The old black men "accidentally" jetted off streams in the direction of giggling children, black and white, who danced naked in the frigid spray, shrieking with delight, looking something like plucked birds themselves. If the work seemed grim and hot, nobody let on. The laughter and hijinks made the enterprise feel like a huge picnic.

What's in the water here? Threadgill wondered. *Why is everybody in Happy Valley so damn happy?*

But everybody wasn't.

A sudden loud cry sailed from the barn.

Booger, the stout brother, had gone to the hayloft for some forgotten item. Now he danced through the barn door into view, his gap-toothed mouth open wide as a jack-o-lantern.

"Whooo! Lordy! Run everybody!"

"Uh-oh!" muttered Aleph. He screwed around in his chair so he could see over his shoulder. "Booger got in them yellow jackets!"

Sure enough, Booger thundered from the gabled shadow of the barn into the sun, arms flailing. A glowing halo of yellow particles whirled and darted around him like electrons, mostly too fast for the eye to see.

Aleph stood up quick. "Somebody get that fiddle started again!" he ordered, excited. "Booger's gonna buckdance!"

"Mama! Mama!" hollered the bedeviled brother, fleeing past. "They gittin' me!"

Scores of folks scattered, most of them laughing, leaving off work at the barbeque pit and processing lines for a moment. They ran as much to get out of Booger's way as from the stings.

"Where DID that fiddle player go?" Gaydi demanded, finally turning from Booger to pour another glass of iced tea.

The fiddle and the guitar lay on the ground behind two empty folding chairs.

"Them was Booger's twin boys playing our music," Gideon explained. "You remember them boys, Gaydi – you brung 'em into this world. They helpin' load down them hamper baskets right now. See them purty girls yonder? That's why they went down there.'"

Threadgill couldn't say when he had last enjoyed a day more. He laughed and laughed. So did they all, hooting and slapping their shanks. Gideon poured more sweet tea all around – a lot spilled during Booger's buckdance.

Aleph raised his silver cup in the air, sparkling in a beam of sun.

"I got one question," he asked, looking at Threadgill and winking. "How come nobody told that boy about them yellow jackets in there?"

Gideon waited for a long time, every eye on him.

"I be durned!" the old man finally said. "I thought them was June bugs!"

Aleph got strangled midway through his fit of laughter. Gaydi and Gideon lifted his arms over his head to help him catch his breath.

Threadgill luxuriated, deep in the golden glow of a close family.

All this, he thought. *And we haven't even eaten yet.*

***

Mama came out on the porch and chewed to paste most of a tin of Prince Albert, then stuck the spit-moistened tobacco on all seventeen of Booger's yellow jacket stings. She used band-aids to hold the tobacco in place.

In a while, Booger trundled warily back down to the pecan grove. He looked like the world's worst shaver. He even had tobacco poultice stuck in his short hair.

The big boy had brought his accordion out of the house. Booger's sons, blocky, broad-faced boys like their dad, walked out on either side of him. They looked like one whole side of the line on a college football team.

"Play!" Gideon, for all his mischief, was too kind now to tease his brother. "Play 'Soldiers Joy' for old Pickett here."

Booger set up the accordion in his lap and closed his eyes. His head resembled those close-up pictures of the moon on TV, big knots and craters.

Booger got this look when he played. You didn't much care how his face sweated, how long his ear hair, how lunky. That accordion sounded like sweet honey poured all over something good to eat.

Meanwhile, a group of men dragged a sheet of tin with smoking coals on it to the mouth of the barn. They choked all the yellow jackets back into their nest. Then they brought gasoline and finished the business.

The day passed. Threadgill could smell every aroma on the farm at different times – the ammonia persisted, but it was overwhelmed by one sensationally aromatic tin sheet of barbequed chicken after another coming off the fire. Men wore muleskinner gloves to drag the hot tin. Crews with pitchforks speared the chickens into cardboard boxes, then crinkled down heavy aluminum foil over the food to discourage bugs.

It was getting early afternoon when the big vegetable truck jounced in with the last chickens. Gideon did an inspection and judged the birds still fresh enough to cook.

Elsewhere, citizens and family and employees and neighbors of the Askews carried out a final clean-up. Boys with fishing poles knocked dead fowl out of trees. Nimble youngsters with ropes around their waists skidded bird corpses off rooftops. Children made a game of this: They stood with baskets under the eaves, guessing where the next dead chicken would slide off. Threadgill didn't see a single bird hit the ground.

Booger and his boys played old time songs for hours.

"Nice, real nice," the brothers nodded, Aleph most enthusiastically.

"You play pretty good for a knothead," Gideon Askew said, winking preposterously at them all.

Booger grinned. "I got yore knots for you, right here on my freckled butt," he drawled. He pointed at his massive behind.

"You meet Mr. Threadgill Pickett, Boog?"

"Not really." The big man threw out a hand the size of a skillet. "Seen you, but didn't get to talk. Booger Askew, and pleased to meet you."

Threadgill thought how hard Booger's grip felt. A working man.

"Already feel like we met," Booger allowed. "You seen and heard enough by now, I reckon, to be a blood brother with the family."

"He's on his way to Maine," Gaydi explained, motioning north with a pocket knife. He sliced a ripe peach he'd pulled off a tree somewhere, fighting to keep juice in his mouth as he talked.

"He gonna visit the last Yankee soldier," Aleph said, proudly. "Sucker lives way up yonder."

"Shoot," Booger said. "I want to go."

Gideon scowled. "You ain't goin' nowhere for at least a week, brother. You got a little piece of work to handle."

"Playin' music?" Threadgill guessed.

The flattery made Booger beam. "Naw, heck," he snorted happily. "I'm just an old insurance claims adjuster."

All three other brothers stood and simultaneously lifted their silver cups of sweet tea to honor this announcement.

"Thank God for Booger!" they cried. "Thank God for Happy Valley Insurance Company!"

They fell about, laughing like they were drunk. So did Booger.

Threadgill understood their nonchalant joy now. Life was good, even when tornadoes struck, in Happy Valley.

***

Far off across a field, a horn blew. Gideon tapped his brother, Booger.

"Yonder comes Billy an' them!" Gideon said. "Finally."

Threadgill felt a breeze of relief.

"He must have coolly laid a sermon on the lambs today," declared Aleph. "It's gettin' late!"

Booger squinted, then excitedly announced, "I be durned if he didn't *bring* the lambs, y'all!"

"Lord, would you look at that!" whistled Aleph.

Threadgill swiveled. A long procession eased down the driveway toward the house. The car out front, a big black Cadillac, burned headlights, and so did every other one of the sixteen cars that crawled behind.

Out by the highway, a courteous Sunday driver, on his way with his family somewhere up the valley, pulled to the shoulder out of respect for what must surely be a funeral cortege. When the cars turned unexpectedly into the Askew's drive, Threadgill could practically see the driver's confusion. After a minute, the car backed up in a cloud of angry dust, made a hasty U-turn in the bright Sunday afternoon, and streaked back in the direction it had come.

The church cars disgorged black men and boys in white stiff shirts that would be ruined with barbeque sauce and other stains before another half hour went by. Those crinoline Sunday dresses the black women girls wore – doomed too, Threadgill thought.

The mamas and daddies didn't seem to care at all. All laughs and smiles, they humped it down the drive with platters of cake, jars of pickled peaches, casseroles, glazed this-n-thats, and so much other stuff Threadgill couldn't take it all in.

The brothers watched for Billy to climb out of the front car.

"Well, where the devil is Big Brother?" Gideon griped. "I'm about to starve."

Deacons in black suits embraced the Askew brothers and shook hands energetically with Threadgill. Out of the house streamed Mrs. Askew, the family matriarch, and the wives and daughters and friends and helpers who'd been working in the farm house all this time.

Everybody hugged and mingled perfumes – "getting neck sugar," the Askews called it. Lipstick and eye shadow and pancake makeup smeared clean shirts, greased eyeglasses. Fresh flowers in hatbands got knocked cattywampus.

Happy Valley, thought Threadgill. *Seems like folks everywhere would want to live like this.*

An impressive man in black raised his hand and spoke to the Askews.

"Mr. Gideon, we waited a whole hour on your Billy to come preach. He must be sleeping in today. We just decided finally to come on without him."

Gideon frowned and looked at his wife.

"We ain't heard from him today either, Brother Ort. You mean Billy never came to the church?"

Threadgill felt his breathing stop.

The black deacon shrugged theatrically. "It happens, Mr. Gideon. He mighta been called down to Birmingham, all that mess going on."

A flock of white and black children flew past, playing chase.

"Well, shoot. You just go on and bless us then, Deacon. Folks here so hungry they're digesting their selves."

Deacon Ort, still all in black, stood in the middle of a huge colorful circle. And Deacon Ort asked a blessing on all of them – a big blessing, since two hundred or more stood bareheaded in the late hot sun of that place.

"Dear Heavenly Father," he prayed. "It's too hot to ask you for much right now. Just please let your blessings continue to fall on this family and all these good people. We play for Booger, in his time of insurance adjustment. And we give thanks for all this bounty you have, in mystery and incomprehensible wisdom, laid on our tables this fine Sunday. We got to say you work in strange ways, Lord. Your world and your works are good and decent. We are lucky to be here in this place, every one of us. Amen."

Staccato applause … then white and black people ran like white and black deer for the paper plates and cups of iced tea, the improvised tables with dinner on the grounds … and the Sunday windfall of good barbequed chicken for all.

Chapter 46, Billy Yank

The day dawns gray as diphtheria.

A house sits atop a hill.

It's a curious stovepipe hat of a structure, tall and crooked, an unkempt beard of shrub out front. The shutters wear a shade of blue that Yellowhammer intensely dislikes – the color of a Yankee uniform. Rain falls ceaselessly.

An American flag hangs, sobbing, over the porch.

An old face stares out an upstairs window.

The old man looks like he's been waiting one hundred years for some visitor to arrive. He's dressed in a blue robe, white chevrons on the sleeves. He reminds Yellowhammer of a blue jay.

The bird streaks down straight out of a dream.

The old man sees slashing feathers in pouring rain. Yellow accents, gray wingtips.

The old man sits without moving, as if blind. The fuming window obscures him. A face in a rainy mirror.

Billy Yank surprises Yellowhammer.

He moves very slowly, reaches underneath his chair. Gnarled fingers hoist up a pistol, black. The devil's right hand.

Billy Yank aims.

A loud thunderclap rolls over Bangor. A flash of big lightning. The window spits crumbs of glass.

Yellowhammer feels heat pass, loses feathers. Yellowhammer spins in a crazy spiral halfway to the lawn. Yellowhammer catches its balance on a drooping willow frond.

A wisp of gunsmoke unspools out the upstairs bedroom window. Tiny cracks radiate from the bullet hole.

Good, thinks Yellowhammer, after a steadying moment. The bird's head spins a bit.

Billy Yank is ready.

This way, it won't be murder.

Yellowhammer flits up from the willow, shaking loose a white rain of droplets. It hovers outside the window and beats its wings insolently against the glass.

The Yankee's face stretches, a rictus, lips brown at the corners. Age? Blood? Snuff? Who could tell?

A crazy blue light dances in crazy blue eyes.

"I hold the high ground, Reb! We'll see which one of us gets to spit in the hole when the box gets lowered down!"

A second bullet breaks glass, a hopeless miss this time that raises a muddy splash far down the hill. The top right windowpane lets go completely, splashes down into the yard.

Yellowhammer wheels like a cavalry horse.

Yellowhammer takes aim at a broken window, an open space.

Yellowhammer falls like a thunderbolt.

Chapter 47, Bounty

Threadgill put worry away. He ate like a soldier. The bounty of the land lay heaped before him.

First, he spooned onto his oversized paper plate the "green" things – carrot salad with little golden scuppernongs. Fresh tomato-cucumber-sweet onion salad. Poke sallet wilted in a skillet and dashed with vinegar. Three-bean salad. Fresh corn sliced off the cob, with red bell pepper slices. Cole slaw with purple and white cabbage. Three different kinds of lettuce and tomato salad. Six different deviled eggs – eggs with paprika, cracked black corn, chow-chow relish … and, and, and. Pickled peaches. Homemade dill and sweet pickles. Pickled okras, onions, beets, carrots. Fresh-sliced, salted-and-peppered tomatoes, ripened in the sun.

Threadgill next sampled the vegetables. He'd forgotten so many existed in the world.

He spooned on golden fried okra, fried green tomatoes, plump boiled potatoes in little red jackets like train ticket agents. Stewed okra and tomatoes. Cheese pie. Succotash in long baking dishes. Black-eyed peas, knuckle-hull peas, English peas, crowder peas, pink-eye peas. Butterbeans with ham hocks lurking under their green buttery surface like alligators. Fresh green pole beans scorched just so in a skillet. Corn on the cob, creamed corn, corn off the cob fried with cream and bits of pecan. Casseroles of all kinds. Bowls of fried fresh mushrooms. Fiddle-head fern baked in a deep dish. Beets chilled or beets spicy. Rutabagas mashed just like potatoes, pooling butter and speckled with black pepper. Greens, with ham and bacon. Onions baked in aluminum foil, buttered yellow.

Next came the breads – fresh biscuits, of course, piping hot. Corn bread too, in pones large as Threadgill's palm, flecked inside by fresh buttermilk. White homemade bread. Dark bread, too, already lathered with flavored butters from secret crocks. Spoonbread, fried perfectly. Breads with Spanish olives. Crackling bread. Bread with pepper and cheese and pimento tornadoed together.

Threadgill barely had room on his plate for the chicken.

The meat fell off the bones.

A grinning, blonde-haired country woman served the chicken portions. Pretty in the face. She looked to Threadgill like she might be having the best time of her life so far serving this barbequed chicken. Droplets of red sauce freckled her face – a second layer of freckles on that pleasant countenance. Flyaway bleached hair dropped into her eyes, and she brushed it away with the back of her wrist. She licked the corner of her mouth and forked out smoking portions of chicken.

"Betty, we love you," Gideon praised, as he took half a bird.

"Thank you, Mr. Askew," she answered, beaming, wiping her hand on an apron. "We're grateful to be helping out, and I'm speaking for every one of us that works for you. God bless you – you Askews is mighty good people."

She winked at Threadgill, next in line, as he received a generous breast. He felt color rise to his cheeks.

As Threadgill followed Gideon back to the grove – dessert would come last, naturally – he found himself a little short of breath.

He took a seat between Aleph and Booger, black and white, both men gnawing drumsticks so big they had to be held with both hands. The brothers looked like innocent children. They scooted chairs to the side to make a place for Threadgill.

He felt something in his chest. Not a bullet. Not a broken heart. Not guilt. Not a cold stone of vengeance.

For the first time in so long, he felt … something close to *peace*. Despite everything, one full moment.

He glanced back over his shoulder at Betty, and caught her watching him. She didn't look away.

Oh, dear, Threadgill thought.

I got everything right. But I got everything wrong.

And Threadgill toppled forward onto the ground. His plate spilled, his helmet banged the leg of a folding chair.

Chapter 48, Pickett's Charge

The rebels arrived, group by gray group. Threadgill recalled the flocks of birds leaving Goat Island before the great hurricane.

Ben's face was unshaven, a red scraggle, and a light burned in his eyes – blue as if perfect sky on a July afternoon shone down through the top of his head. Threadgill's twin glowed again with youth, hard muscles, sure moves. He dressed in gray.

So did Threadgill. Amazed, the steadfast traveler extended his arms, beheld a fine new Confederate uniform, perfectly cut, not a crease in the butternut fabric. Nor did line or wrinkle mar the skin of Threadgill Pickett. On his head he wore his fine gray hat. A yellowhammer feather jaunted from its crown.

His head felt strange, different. Threadgill uneasily edged back the hat brim. He tentatively moved his fingers.

Hair!

The thick stuff covered territory where The Unmentionable throbbed painfully for so many years. Threadgill could hardly believe it – he reached beneath his hat a second time, let his fingers stroke, tug.

Real hair. Yes. Real, red, soft.

Threadgill pulled the front of his uniform from his body. He peered down, his heart beating wildly.

His chest had no scar. And the deep, nasty serrated marks from alligator teeth were only memories, long-ago dreams.

"You all fixed back now good as new, Gill!" Ben whooped. A slap on the shoulder knocked Threadgill forward a step. "Got you a head of hair and all your scars patched and a whole new everything!"

Threadgill would marvel later.

Just now, the woods filled with new arrivals.

Colonel Able Sutton, for one. The dour, perfectly dressed, portrait-handsome officer appeared out of nowhere, with a noise like jingling spurs, directly in front of Threadgill. The Colonel looked youthful again, a picture of health and golden vitality, not the old disillusioned peg-legged bastard who fenced off his daughter from Threadgill … so she could die alone, mostly a skeleton, upstairs in a house haunted by dead Confederate ghosts.

"Threadgill Pickett, sir!" Colonel Sutton gave a sharp salute. Threadgill couldn't hear one note of irony in his voice. "Colonel Able Sutton. Ready for orders."

What in the world was going on here?

What *out* of the world?

Threadgill gaped. A geyser of smoke suddenly boiled out of the ground. Spurs jingled again – many spurs, many jingles. Bull and Burvell, the Cobb brothers, appeared from nowhere. The brothers sat grinning like coons atop their whirring time machine.

Tammy 2's gleaming doors popped wide. From the back seat poured a small congregation of Eufaula people from a century ago – Allen Baker and Samuel Solomon and Marcus Childress and Thom Junod. Tommy Stoddard and Jackson Pendarvis. William Hutto, the newspaper man. Billy Crow and Al Parker. Thom Franklin and Doug Monroe, from the seed store. Quinten Hudson and Jimbo Lipscomb. Joshua Jacks. Nicodemus Purdee.

They wore Confederate gray, a twilight-colored horde. Threadgill nodded to them, their smiles and congratulations raining down, a flurry of halloos, rebel yells.

Little Green Man showed up, full uniform. A waterhead boy. Lash LaRue.

This gray army seemed to be made of every person Threadgill ever met.

"Fasten bayonets!" Threadgill cried. His voice, ringing, surprised even himself.

Steel rattled, a colossal clicking that passed like a telegraph message through the woods. A panorama of soldiers, a gray mist from all the memories Threadgill knew in his whole life, stretched away into the trees. Streaming light collected in white pools on the floor of the forest, and in that light old acquaintances appeared and disappeared, waved and nodded, lifted their hats. Threadgill proudly lifted his own.

Horses thundered through, dragging a heavy wheeled thing, cannon or caisson.

Threadgill found himself standing over a map. Unrolled on a makeshift wooden table, the parchment weighted at the corners by Minie balls. Ben and Colonel Sutton stood close, watching intently over his shoulder. Men in perfect gray uniforms awaited their orders.

On the map, Threadgill traced with his long index finger the Confederate position, a mile-long formation masked under a great forest. The woodland gave way on this map just there – Threadgill's finger tapped – to a rising field, and across that field, a distance of a mile or so, a long stone wall that snaked the brow of a little ridge. A cemetery put up spires not far beyond the wall.

A mass of blue soldiers, like an ocean behind a dike, seethed in back of this stone wall and to its left and right for miles. Light sparkled on countless bayonets.

Threadgill nodded orders to a man with a heavy beard – who was he? Where had Threadgill seen him in a long life?

All at once Confederate artillery opened up, a deafening thunderous cacophony across the front of the whole army. The bombardment shook the very earth. Smoke from these batteries turned the afternoon in only a few moments from blue to gray. Threadgill watched his soldiers, poised in the woods in their units, bowed under the roar, humbled beneath terrible thunder.

He took a wonderful deep breath of the gunsmoke. Thank goodness for his nose now. Thank goodness for every smell he ever knew.

"General Pickett, sir, the men are ready."

That was Ben, a smirk on his face. Even here – Threadgill was sure of it – mischief ruled his twin. Even here.

"Stand by for orders," Threadgill said in a low voice. His eyes studied the stone wall atop the little ridge.

The dirty-cotton smoke cloud cleared momentarily, and the Yankee position came visible. Threadgill somehow, impossibly, could see an old Yankee soldier at the top of the ridge. The last Yankee. He stood behind the stone wall dead in the center of the Union line, and the vast Union army spread like blue wings on either side of him.

Now is the reckoning, Billy Yank.

In reply, Threadgill heard the old Yankee's words, as clear as a church bell tolling for the dead.

"Come and get me, Johnny Reb."

Threadgill wiped the back of his hand across his mouth. Black powder smudged his cheek. He felt terribly thirsty all at once.

Another massed salvo blast from Confederate artillery. The cannonade shied the horses of a group of mounted Confederate cavalry, these led by the miller, Tom Slocum, and the train station keeper, Mr. Tom Carr. Beyond them, on foot, Threadgill made out David Langness and J.C. Crowley, with more men from Eufaula. He saw Bradley Hutchinson, the printer. More figures from his life continued to arrive in the smoke. Alan Baker, the barrister. Franklin Crockett was there, chewing tobacco, raising a sword. Jim Martin and Glen Turner and David Thomson.

Where are you, Threadgill? What is happening to you?

No time to ask, no person to ask. The gray army waited, expectant, thousands and thousands of soldiers, all his relations and relationships, everyone he'd ever known in all his memories, all stretched out through the woods. They stood in perfect formation, ready on the moment to let bright cloth flutter loose in the breeze, the Stars and Bars, and let the flags lead Threadgill's mile-wide army in majestic attack.

Silence came like a finger snap.

Cannon ceased firing. In the stone quiet, Threadgill waited. Not a bird sang. Not a soldier coughed. The silence seemed even more violent than bombardment.

Threadgill squinted into the lifting gunsmoke haze. A riderless black horse careened across the field in front of the blue line, stirrups flying under the empty saddle. In a few places, the artillery assault had blasted smoking holes through the stone wall. The horse disappeared through a rubbled opening.

"Come on, Johnny Reb."

The last Yankee still stood, yonder on the distant hill, implacable. His blue army waited behind its stone wall, as silent as the rebels in the woods.

Threadgill raised his right arm high overhead.

Now! Now men!

A great shuffling noise arose, massed footsteps on leaves, hard stones and roots, the tread all at once of thousands and thousands of boots and bare feet. The earth itself seemed to stand up and move forward like a gray wave on Threadgill's right and left, and flow from the woods onto the green field and then on toward the distant wall.

Far away, a drum rattled, a fife tweedled like a lunatic.

Threadgill led an army – his gray avenging army – into bright afternoon light. The sun blazed. He flinched a bit in its sudden brightness. Or maybe he flinched from the sudden naked exposure, passing from the sheltering cover of chestnuts and elms into open view. Threadgill and his men now gave thousands of gray targets to the blue enemy on the hill.

Well … bluebellies be damned. Damn their rifles. Damn their cannon. Damn their bayonets. Damn their bodies and brains. Damn their Yankee ways.

The last damned one stood atop that hill, surrounded by the ugly cohort he summoned. Invaders. Meddlers. Hypocrites. Cruel murderers.

Just a single mile more now. Just one more mile, and Threadgill would fulfill the greatest mission of his whole life.

"Good order, men! Keep moving!"

The gray line stepped out. It was not the jerky, tattered advance you might expect when thousands of human beings moved simultaneously up a hill and across open ground. The Confederates marched with perfect precision, textbook fashion.

The tread of boots came as one – one man walking, one gray man advancing one yard at a stride across a green field. Threadgill closed his eyes for just a second, and he imagined a giant – a lone gray god – with a footstep you could hear for miles, all the way up the distant hill.

A lone puff of smoke rose from the ridge. An instant later, Threadgill heard the report of the first Yankee cannon.

A black steel ball arrived at unbelievable speed and plowed into Threadgill's soldiers. It ripped friends down like a blade. Arms and legs and heads flew with a sputtering wet noise.

A mist of fresh blood speckled Threadgill. The blood of people he knew and loved.

Artillery now opened up across the entire Union front.

Threadgill, amazed, glanced back from beneath his upraised sword.

Gray men flew into the sky. They showered down in parts and pieces over comrades. The grass turned red behind the holes in the ranks. Threadgill's soldiers advanced with their heads down as if against heavy rain.

"Steady! Dress the ranks! Close it up boys!"

Threadgill's voice somehow carried up and down the line, loud enough for all to hear, amplified by some trick of the afternoon. His men quickly dressed gaps in the ranks with perfect discipline.

A steel ball skipped past Threadgill, only yards to his left. He caught sight of familiar faces – Glenn Harady and poor Jim Hawkins – changed to red pulp, like smashed fruit, on the spot. The shot took their bodies, left their legs standing, briefly defiant, before they wobbled, crumpled.

Threadgill felt sickened, sad. Again, it happened.

He had seen the great Civil War.

He had seen all the wars.

Was this what he willed and wanted with every bone of hope in his old body, all those years?

Another row of brave soldiers fell away, gray corn to a blue scythe. Threadgill imagined that the smoke pouring from their open wounds let loose souls, spirits, hopes, dreams, hates.

The charge faltered. Still, the Confederate assault, tattered here and there, had now surged past the halfway point to the stone wall.

The deadly thump and scream of heavy shot increased now, if that was possible, and more men went down and flew apart and vaporized in crimson mist. The advancing line let the dead lie behind and pressed on, the way a gray ocean wave breaks around lone buoys, then continues. The Confederates left bodies, thrown equipment, broken flags, flung boots, canteens, powder flasks, swords, their red, white and blue flags.

Yankee rifles now found the range. A solid blue line of smoke rose from the repeaters. Threadgill heard a loud ominous thrum – a volley of bullets arriving together. Hornets buzzed in the air again.

A knot of lead whipped through the fabric of Threadgill's fine jacket just under his upraised arm. All around him flew horizontal hail, and bullets splatted into flesh and bone. The grunts and screams and little songs of instant death ruffled the gray ranks to either side of Threadgill Pickett.

He saw his brother Ben now, hit in the stomach, his breechloader dragging in back of him by a strap. Ben bent nearly double. He struggled, still moved forward, still stumbled up the goddamned ridge.

Lord. What have I done? Threadgill felt a flash of horror. *What bloody purpose have I held onto all my years?*

Another cloud of smoke and the clatter of rifle fire rose over the Union line and, with them, the cannon boomed, jerking back on wooden wheels. Threadgill and his men now marched close enough to see grime on the faces of the men in blue, to clearly see the swab men, bare-chested, plunge brushes into the great smoking barrels of their guns. They loaded grapeshot now, and the deadly balls scoured down gray ranks in twenty-foot swaths.

Threadgill heard such terrific noise now that he heard nothing at all. The clamor of Yankee weapons had drowned out the world, muffled out all … all except one sound that inexplicably, undauntedly, idiotically rose higher in the face of slaughtering fire.

The rebel yell.

The gray soldiers, bent in a hurricane, rushed against winds of killing steel. Threadgill led the army, sword arm still raised high.

Revenge! Revenge was invincible.

"Yeeeeee-yeeee-haaaaaaaa!"

Had there ever been such foolish bravery?

Threadgill thrilled to his marrow.

Then Ben, his wild brother, stopped in his tracks. Threadgill watched it happen. Ben's beautiful face looked surprised by the ball passing through his forehead. The back of his head opened like a violently red flower. All Ben ever knew and loved flew out the fatal wound into the sunny afternoon.

Threadgill couldn't stop now.

He didn't know why.

He wanted to stop all his life, in some deep place in his heart. But he could not. Not ever.

Threadgill looked back over his shoulder at the field. He now led an army of the dead. He could have walked all the way back across the field to the woods on the fallen bodies of his brother and friends and family, his good-natured carpenters, blacksmiths, grocers, farriers, farmers.

Threadgill moved alone now, walking at a steady pace straight up the hill toward the stone wall. The last Yankee stood just beyond it, behind his own blue men, his own conjured armies, his own never-ending damnation.

The expression on his face? Smug.

A bullet pinged the steel of Threadgill's upraised sword. The blade shrapneled violently into sharp flying pieces. Threadgill did not stop. The wall lay just fifty feet on now. He gripped the broken handle of his sword, and walked ahead.

Threadgill could see the whites of the eyes of the grim blue soldiers, the stony sad misery they took in the murderous work. They sighted at Threadgill down barrels so hot from firing that their fingers blistered.

A bullet whipped through Threadgill's leg at the knee. The wound raised a scream from the relentless old soldier. But how would one more small pain in a lifetime of pain stop him now?

Threadgill now knew that no gray soldier was left to follow him to the wall. He knew in his heart bone's soul – he knew all of them, his friends and family, the dying and the dead, the living and the lost, the sons and daughters to be born and all those already born and gone, the whole broken and beaten Confederacy, all of it was a thing of the past. Sad and done.

Revenge endured.

Threadgill leaped to the top of the stone wall. He struck to both sides of him with the toyish handle of the broken sword. Grown men went down in twisting agony, on every side.

Threadgill tossed blue dolls from his path. He overpowered man after man. He attacked the enemy, Achilles in gray. He would not be beaten.

A Yankee infantryman rushed forward with a bayonet, but then flew magically backward into the air and away from Threadgill.

A cavalryman charged on a black stallion. The trooper raised his sword. Threadgill grabbed the horse by its nostrils and jerked it snout-first into the earth, and the Yankee flew amazed over Threadgill's head, over the stone wall, and hit with a heavy thump far down in the smoldering battlefield.

The last Yankee stood unprotected now, shortly up the slope and under the shade of the great trees on the crown of the ridge. Billy Yank carried his own shining sword in one hand. He wore his hair long, swept back – long hair like a woman, Threadgill thought.

Yeeee-yeeee-hawww!

Threadgill swept down, a gray wolf on the fold. He threw aside his useless broken sword. He lunged for the Yankee, oblivious to the man's slashing blade. He took cut after cut on his attacking body.

Threadgill got his hands around Billy Yank's soft throat.

He looked straight into the man's red face, his blue eyes. He squeezed. He squeezed without mercy or forgiveness.

He felt the Yankee's legs weaken and leave the earth. He heard the moist fleshy sound of windpipe cracking, neck bones breaking. He felt life drain out of the last Yankee's body with his escaping piss and shit.

There.

At last.

Threadgill's work was done.

***

Weary.

Weary and deeply sad, unexpectedly.

Threadgill struggled to his feet.

He still felt the warmth of the dead man's throat in his hands. The dead Yankee's life, still pulsing there in his hands.

Threadgill seemed to come out of a spell, a dream. He looked around, took stock.

On the field behind him, stretching for a whole long mile across the bloodstained grass, lay gray corpses. Little fires burned on some of the bodies. The smell of human insides, the shock of blood and gut and bone and brain, clouded the afternoon.

So many dead.

In fact … all of them.

Everyone Threadgill ever knew. His brother and his father and his aunt and his friends and his townsmen and his Eva and all of them, every gray one of them, lumped and knotted there on the slaughtering field. Terrible and sad.

It would be even sadder.

It happened with his eyes wide open.

To his amazement, Threadgill stood in the summer woods again.

The rebels arrived, group by gray group. Threadgill remembered the flocks of birds leaving Goat Island before the great hurricane.

Ben's face was unshaven, a red scraggle, and a light burned in his eyes – blue as if perfect sky on a July afternoon shone down through the top of his head. Threadgill's twin glowed again with youth, hard muscles, sure moves. He wore gray.

So did Threadgill. Amazed, the steadfast traveler extended his arms, beheld a fine new Confederate uniform, perfectly cut, not a crease in the butternut fabric. No did line nor wrinkle marred the pale skin of Threadgill Pickett.

His face and hands glowed. On his head, he once more wore his old gray hat. A yellowhammer feather.

A deadly chill passed through Threadgill's old body.

He understood.

He would lead this gray army up the long green hill again.

And then again.

He would look back at its utter destruction, every man lost, every dream wasted. All that time and promise. Wasted.

He would crush the old Yankee's windpipe in his furious hands again.

Again and again.

Vengeance would give him all he ever wanted. Vengeance would cost him all he ever had.

THE END

Acknowledgements

I began serious work on this book in 1996, after leaving BellSouth Corporation and striking out on my own into the unknown, like Threadgill Pickett.

My journey, unlike Threadgill's, began by sitting still. This happened at a desk in the basement of the Olde New York Book Store on Piedmont Avenue in Atlanta. I worked in a free space in the basement, typing atop a desk that store owner Cliff Graubart told me Pat Conroy had used when writing *The Lords of Discipline*. Thanks to Cliff and Pat … and that desk.

From this starting point, my gratitude roams broadly. I cannot possibly include here every good person who encouraged me and every good writer who inspired me. A list would require more pages than this book. Thank you all.

I owe special thanks to the one and only agent of my life so far, the late Frederick Hill. I thank my first editor, Robert Wyatt, and current editor, Jay Schaefer. My publisher, Joe Taylor, stepped up when this book called; Joe is man of the hour for *Pickett's Charge*. I thank my publicist, Alison Law.

Let me note the role that Walt and Mike, two Delta Air Lines IT guys, played many years ago, rescuing first chapters of this novel from the hard drive of a derelict computer. I also owe thanks to a friend who long ago sent information on life in Union prisons during the Civil War.

For early readings and encouragement, I credit Sam Rainer, David Langness, Tom Mullen, Mel Konner. Thanks to Sarah Barnett for proofreading and typing.

I thank The Verbalists for fanning the flames of fiction. I thank Herb Perluck for a literary life that guides like Polaris.

I am grateful to my brothers and sisters and my beautiful mama and all my family, the wellspring of my storytelling.

I am thankful to Mark Childress. I'll never know a better writing friend.

Above all others, I thank my daughter, Bonnie. No words, written or spoken, would ever be enough to express what you mean in my life.

Charles McNair, a native of Alabama, brought out his first novel, *Land O'Goshen*, to critical acclaim and a Pulitzer Prize nomination in 1994. He currently lives in Atlanta and makes a living as a freelance writer and communication consultant to major corporations. He has served as Books Editor at Paste magazine since 2005, and he routinely publishes essays, reviews, and articles in national and international publications. He reviews regularly on Atlanta radio station WMLB 1690 AM, and he conducts *How to Tell a Better Story* workshops nationally for corporations, businesses, and universities. His third novel, *The Epicureans*, is in the works.